LOS ANGELES, 1966.

HAPPY RANCH TO WATTS

T. Lloyd Winetsky

T. Lloyd Winetsky

First Edition
Printed and bound in USA
ISBN: 978-1-940222-27-1
LCCN: 2014904426

Cover Design: Nicholas Shipley, Warhorse Studio
Interior formatting by Kimberly Pennell

Although this story only touches on the significance of their lives, the author humbly dedicates this work to the memory of four great twentieth century leaders in the order of the deranged violence that took them all:

Mohandas Gandhi
John F. Kennedy
Martin Luther King Jr.
Robert F. Kennedy.

9-13-14

Sarah -
  Thanks for being
a "three-time" supporter.
Look for Belaganna, my
book about our time on
the Navajo Res. Best,
          Torry W.

This world is white no longer,
and it will never be white again.

– James Baldwin

1

Monday came fast, and Allen was heading for Watts—not to pass by on the way to some ballgame, and not because he would take a wrong exit off the freeway. *Rolling on down there on purpose—like it was nothing.*

He had twenty-five minutes before his ten-thirty a.m. appointment with a teacher who was supposed to be his mentor. He drove his grey-primered '51 Volvo down the off-ramp from the Harbor Freeway; it was about eight blocks to the school, right through the heart of Watts. *You can still turn around.* Before Allen came down to a green light at the first surface street, he cranked his windows most of the way up, locked the doors, then made his turn.

The neighborhood looked similar to an area he'd once ridden by to play JV baseball in a different part of South-Central L.A. The houses had that same post-Depression stucco-or-frame-with-a-dash-of-Spain architecture as his neighborhood, Los Feliz. Some places were well cared for but seemed to be under siege from the surrounding ramshackle houses with dirt yards, scrounging dogs, and trash of all kinds around discarded appliances and vehicles.

The school district secretary had told him it was an "in-service day between semesters," so there were kids everywhere making the best of their day off, chasing around and having fun as if the whole neighborhood were just a run-down playground.

A few adults wandered past a guy with an Afro the size of a beach ball; he watched Allen's car from the stoop of a small shopworn market. A siren shrieked from the next block, but hardly anyone bothered to watch the cop car go by.

He made a turn and there were the Watts Towers, just ahead. Allen had only seen the seventeen spires on TV, but he grew up hearing about them from Los Feliz bullies . . . *gonna tie you kids to one of 'em and leave you down there for the boogies.*

Now the actual towers seemed less menacing, like a pointy skyline on some gaseous planet visited by Flash Gordon. He still drove by as fast as the law and traffic allowed. Allen had to stop for a red light, where a boy in his early teens, perched on a fire hydrant, blasted Motown from his portable stereo. A fair-skinned woman in heavy makeup and a thin dress—she could have been thirty or sixty—slouched in the remains of a phone booth. She was trembling, though it was warm for the beginning of February, even for L.A.

The DTs—Jesus. "Who were you expecting—Aretha?"

A black man in the next lane heard Allen speaking to his windshield. Behind the wheel of a brand-new white '68 Chevy, company logo on its door, he was in a suit and tie. The salesman looked down his nose at the old Volvo, then at Allen, who glared back. The man turned away.

Allen didn't have to stop again before his turn onto Harding Place; the school was just ahead, its front building almost a city block long and attached to eight-foot chain-link that surrounded the grounds. There were only two cars out front; he didn't see anyone walking around as he pulled to the curb.

The building was another of L.A.'s three-story, flat-roofed halls of learning, except it was more worn out than his schools, and the windows on the bottom two floors were covered with army-green steel grating. The chalky white-brick exterior was cracked in places; illegible black initials had been sprayed over two blotchy stains. Behind a yellowing lawn, half-dead arborvitae covered in spider webs stood tall along the front of the school like a line of dusty dark-green sentinels.

He turned the other way to another fence, this one drooping and only four feet tall around three sides of a paved but potholed city lot guarded by a large windowless security hut. Its crude Dutch door bolted and padlocked, the shack could have once been a mother-in-law cottage.

The parking lot was about two-thirds full of vehicles. Allen entered, took the first open spot and turned off the motor. Still with more than fifteen minutes, he looked at the school, shaking his head.

The interview panel he'd faced before the weekend consisted of five veteran teachers and a vice-principal named Godina, the only one who introduced himself; the others just read aloud the brief questions. The entire process took twenty minutes. They had three hours to hire eight emergency teachers for Thurgood Marshall Junior High, recently renamed from Warren G. Harding, Godina said, "to honor the first Negro Supreme Court Justice."

When the vice-principal asked Allen why he wanted to teach, his answer was, "Maybe I can help some kids with skills they need to make it through school." *Pretty good for BS I made up on the spot.* Only Godina and an elderly redheaded woman didn't seem to scowl at his answer. He was sure that an honest vote would have gone against him, including the only black teacher; she was glaring at Allen by the time it was finished. He began to doubt his decision as soon as he accepted the job.

Now he was gazing at the nearby cars—a rusty T-Bird, a renovated Chevy from the late '40s, a new '68 Bug—maybe they would tell him something about the people in the school. *Stalling—move it, chicken-shit.* He reached for his windbreaker, but it was getting very warm, so he left it and got out. With some difficulty, he tucked his new Pittsburgh Pirates T-shirt into the snug size-38 belled black jeans he'd bought the day before.

Allen locked the car, then entered the crosswalk at the end of the driveway, carrying a book he'd been reading. He crossed slowly, went up a few steps to the front door and peeked through a pane at a dozen or so kids and parents, all black, standing in line, likely to get something solved for the new semester.

He backed off from the door and turned around to the lot. His dilapidated car, familiar and comfortable, seemed to beckon him. Before Allen moved forward or back, a drowsy boy opened the door, looked around, and said, "It's open."

"Yeah, thanks." The kid didn't answer and got back in line as Allen entered.

The hallway, clean but scuffed, had a glass trophy case and a lot of old wooden trim. He looked up at a clock protected by thick wire, then read some of the chintzy trophies and photo captions from as far back as the '30s.

Allen sighed, then ambled toward the office. A woman in line grimaced at him as if he had just crawled out of the L.A. River. He nodded to her and said, "Morning." She turned away, and he entered the office. She was probably the first black person he had spoken to since he last chatted with the mailman.

A secretary, about five-four and in her mid-twenties, stood behind the far end of the counter, quietly preoccupied with two families. She had flawless café au lait skin, slightly pointed ears and nose, striking dark eyes and a short, neat, light-brown Afro. He couldn't help but notice how nicely she filled out her pastel-yellow pantsuit. Surreptitiously, he watched her answer the phone, listen to a parent in line, and shuffle papers—all at once. *Hell, she's the one who should be teaching.*

Seeing no one else in the office, he checked the time on a wooden clock that had Roman numerals and a pendulum. Hopefully his mentor would be that redheaded lady from the interview who seemed to be on his side.

The secretary hung up the phone and looked at him pleasantly. "May I help you?"

"Yes, I'm supposed to meet Mrs. Dorsey now."

"She's probably just leaving her meeting. I'm sure Miss Dorsey will be right down." She turned to the people in line.

"Thanks." *Man, that smile.* He leaned on the counter and opened his paperback covered with two glossy pages from a Dodger Stadium program. He found where he left off with Ray Bradbury, then tried to read, but his mind wandered—first to the cute secretary, then to the out-of-the-blue phone call from his friend, proposing that he apply for some teaching jobs.

"So what's the desperate emergency, Dan?"

"The openings are in ghetto schools—teachers quitting at midyear, or they already left."

"They're going to send an untrained white guy to East L.A.?" *To get the living crap beat out of him?*

"There, or South-Central."

Allen snapped out of his recollection as the same black teacher who'd glared during his interview walked toward him from an interior corridor.

4

She was about five-ten and stick-thin; he had maybe four inches on her and enough pounds to make another small adult. She wore a white top under a plain tan suit made of heavy twill, and her skirt, right out of the '50s, was below the knees. The lady came closer; an old-fashioned brooch was pinned to the lapel of her open coat, and a small gold cross hung in front of her high-buttoned blouse by a thin necklace.

"Mister Greene."

Mister. His tongue sticking to the roof of his dry mouth, Allen just nodded and attempted a smile.

"In case you do not recall, I am Miss Dorsey." Her words sounded intentionally formal, the *Miss* made very clear.

Moistening his lips, he reached out to her. "Miss Dorsey."

As if he were contagious, she barely grasped his fingers. She seemed to look askance at his spare tire, made worse by the tight jeans. She saw his paperback. "A baseball book?"

"No, science." *With Martians.*

"This way." Holding a folder and a small grey purse, she led him out a side door into the empty hallway. Her skin wasn't light or dark brown, but almost raven; she was the darkest black American he had ever seen in person. Before she'd read aloud in the interview, Allen half-expected her to have an accent like some of the African students at his college.

Dorsey was around fifty, with a countenance somewhere between plain and homely. She had straight black hair that stopped abruptly at mid-neck in a hint of a wave; her mouth, nose, eyes and cheeks seemed disproportionately compressed like a puppet with a partially flattened head. Maybe her face would fill out if she ever smiled.

She turned but looked past him. "Where is it that you live, Mister Greene?"

"Los Feliz, just before Glendale."

She made an even deeper scowl. "I have heard about Glendale." They entered a conference room. Dorsey stopped at a table and turned, sneering for a moment at his long curly black hair, full moustache, and mutton chops. "With so many applicants last Friday, I do not remember much about your college background other than your English degree."

"Valley College, my BA's from L.A. State."

"Yes, no education courses or student teaching, if I recall correctly."

"That's right."

"And how did you find out about our openings?"

"A friend of mine teaches math. He just finished student teaching in East L.A."

"Oh? We are still one teacher short, and it happens to be in mathematics. I assume he has a job."

"Yes, he does."

"And what was it that you have been doing since college?"

"Delivering flowers mostly."

"Flowers. Please have a seat while I get your materials." She practically marched to the far end of the long conference table, her medium heels clicking in cadence on the buffed linoleum floor.

Allen's last answer had him mulling over his omissions and fibs since Friday. For starters, he had been delivering flowers for only a month and still had the part-time job. On the district application, he obfuscated the fact that his degree took six years, and he didn't list a post-college two-month stint in the Peace Corps, quitting after "medical" problems. She started back to him with folders, a binder, and a textbook in her twig-like arms. *Did I mention, Miss Dorsey, that I hated school since sixth grade?*

She put the materials down and sat one chair away from him, priggishly stretching her long skirt over joined knees. "Is there something troubling you, Mister Greene?"

"No."

"You appear to be upset."

"Just a little nervous."

"Not surprising." Her face changed from serious to cross. "Before we begin, I need to clarify some things."

Allen just nodded again.

"I do not support the idea of placing untrained staff in our lowest track, but no one in the department would switch. To be direct about it, I agreed to mentor you and Mister Fife to get the extra planning time, and because I don't want our school to end up with more . . . pardon me, it is not my place to say that." She made a frustrated sigh, then continued.

"Anyway, I cannot teach you to be a teacher—one either finds a passion for it, or one does not. If a prospective teacher has indeed made a conscious decision to help students—I am sorry to say that some have not—I believe he or she can learn through experience. You see, without genuine expectations for students or new teachers to learn, we can be very sure they won't." After that rare contraction, Dorsey paused again.

He took paper from the back of his book and began to take notes.

"Now, if you are here just to draw a check, I will use my time with you to make sure you do what is required until June, if you last that long. Then you could go sell cars or join a commune. I don't care."

"Um—"

"Excuse me, but you do not need to respond to that, your actions will show your motives. My responsibilities will be to observe your instruction, review lesson plans and answer questions. Mister Godina will occasionally be with me for official evaluation. Do you have any questions so far?"

"Not yet."

She reached for the thick LANGUAGE ARTS book. "Seventh-grade instructional goals correspond to this text. For track-one students it is not necessary to use it all of the time, especially if there is an effort to teach them basic grammar and phonics. Most of our track-one students want to read. Some will even pretend to be reading when just looking at pictures . . . ."

Dorsey soon transitioned into a description of materials, equipment and a lack thereof, followed by several more minutes to explain some obvious recordkeeping. ". . . and teachers *must* turn in report cards on time." Handing him the three-ring binder, she frowned at the eye-patched Pirate logo on his shirt. "You will find the school rules in here and also posted in every room. This handbook is required reading, and I suggest close attention to the section on professional guidelines, including facial hair, dress . . . ."

He waited for her to pause. "This isn't what I would wear tomorrow, Miss Dorsey."

"I did not expect so, Mister Greene." Dorsey went on to the subject of discipline. "The key is to have clear consequences. When a teacher is firm but fair, a few students will complain, but most will respect it. Later on, the teacher can begin to ease off a little. A permissive approach," she raised a brow at Allen's clothes again, "or downright meanness—neither extreme *ever* works here. Most of our students will behave if given a chance."

She seemed to be reading his body language, staring coldly at Allen for a moment, as if daring him to differ.

"In twenty-two years, Mister Greene, I have never had one class in which I did not think most of my students were taking care of business, which I define as trying. Unfortunately, trying to learn does not always translate to academic success. Willing but low-achieving students deserve as much time as we can give them."

He jotted again. "And the ones who aren't trying?"

"Our apathetic students include a few individuals in special education, but many in that program are hard workers. Most students who don't try have normal IQs or higher and have been convinced over the years that they are dull—I believe it is the teacher's job to disabuse them of that notion."

Dorsey drew a breath and removed a hankie from her pocket for a quick and proper nose wiping. She turned to him, almost wistfully. "And we do have a small number of openly aggressive students who have mostly quit on themselves *and* everyone else. They can be both destructive and self-destructive—their attendance is usually poor, although their abilities also vary. We cannot give up on them either, but a teacher must be practical and not allow a student who is acting up to disrupt learning or abuse the other students or . . . the teacher."

"And how often, um, would you expect those kids to—"

"That also varies." She looked at him askance again. "It is not unusual to have two or three students in each class with records of aggression, plus one or two more who might cross that line with peer pressure. The procedure for emergency assistance is outlined in the handbook. The reality is that the more a teacher requests it, the less quickly they will respond."

"So if a teacher really needs help and calls, then nobody shows up, what does he do?"

"His best, Mister Greene. Prevention is our most effective tool. As I said, it is imperative to establish concrete consequences, and then be firm but fair. Keep saying that to yourself, and it will go well most of the time. You will need to be especially strict in homeroom—seventh-grade boys from all three tracks, some of whom do not see each other all day, except in there. Discipline is also supported by good time management—using more than a minute or two just to get started is a waste of time that invites chaos . . . ."

She explained some basic methods for starting class, and then said, "That's about it, except for your questions. See the secretary in the morning for keys and your attendance—"

"The one who's there today?"

She glowered at his eager question. "No, she's Miss Watson—Mrs. Venable is the head secretary. Miss Watson mostly handles reception, registration, supplies and orders. By the way, if you need something that is not already in the school, she probably will not be able get it for you. Other questions?"

"Can I see the room?"

"Not with Mrs. Venable out today, unless you care to run down someone who has a master key. The room is like any other. I have told you what to expect to find in there."

"Okay. What about the Creative Writing class?"

"Yes, I did forget to mention that."

"Are they all track-one kids too?"

A faint pallor materialized on her flat nose. "I am sure you are aware, Mister Greene, that a *kid* is a baby goat. The *students* in that class will be seventh graders from all three tracks, some of whom did not get the elective they requested. The handbook has broad goals for Creative Writing, but the teacher decides the activities."

"How *creative* can the writing be?"

Her glare endured. "As some of them won't be able to write a complete sentence, that might be a logical place to begin. So, do you still want the job?"

He stared at her.

"Well?"

"Yes."

"Fine." As they stood, she handed over everything with a scornful crease of a grin that did not fill out her squashed features. "Very well, then, Mister Greene, perhaps we will see you tomorrow."

Yeah, perhaps. "Thanks for your help."

2

After the meeting, Allen still wanted to see a classroom. He stopped at the first one and looked in through some thin wires embedded in the rectangular porthole's glass. With all the shades down in the unlit room, he could make out rows of desks and not much more. Allen walked to the foyer and saw Miss Watson typing in the office. He went right outside—it was useless to talk to her if he decided not to come back. *Good excuse.* The parking lot was still quiet; he got into his car. *Like Dan says, Ex-lax a minute.*

He leaned all the way back, closed his eyes, and focused on his breathing until his mind was clear. Then he listened to individual sounds, trying to think only about the next noise: *distant siren —chattering mockingbird—the city's hum.* He had been reading some Far-Eastern thought for months. Dan called him *Gunga Din* after Allen tried to explain that he was experimenting with his own take on "mindful breathing." *Car horn—slamming door—buzzing inse—*

A loud explosion jolted him straight up. He hunched right back down, peered through the steering wheel and carefully scanned the street and the parked cars. *Firecracker—freak out, why don't you?* He sat up slowly, checking the building. A uniformed guard calmly strolled along the sidewalk while a tall woman walked down the school's front steps with a small boy.

Allen put in the clutch but let it out. After another deep breath, he looked at the English book on the passenger seat. Maybe he could take the job and find his own apartment. *Get away from that bastard for good.*

He put the transmission into first, turned the key, then slowly left the lot, locking the doors. Allen passed right by the mother and son he'd just seen;

they were side-by-side, waiting on the curb and laughing about something. It was possible that the kid was in one of his classes and couldn't read a lick.

Driving cautiously but at the speed limit away from the school, his mind flashed to his own childhood, shopping with his mom downtown and staring at a pretty "Negro" woman who had a boy his age in tow. Allen was fascinated when the kid begged for snacks the way he always did. When they left the store, a white teen at a shoeshine stand had yelled at an old black man, *"Boy, hurry up with my shine."* Allen's mom wouldn't talk about something like that, but his dad liked to include him in light-hearted debates with Negro men at minor-league ball games in those pre-Dodger days.

So? You don't have a clue about any of this. Allen reached down for a cartridge from the shoebox on the floor. He inserted *The Ventures Play Telstar* into the eight-track player Dan had installed for him under the dash. Trying to suppress everything that was on his mind, he drummed on the steering wheel almost all the way to Los Feliz, rewinding the one tune with any words—three. He growled "Tequila" in an exaggerated deep voice each time it came around.

He stopped for gas in Atwater, then walked into Bill's Place and called, "Hey, Tommy, French fries and a shot of tequila." He took it with lime and ate the potatoes, nursing a cold draft that he ordered. Allen began to rehash his situation at home and everything from the morning. He had a second shot of tequila, ruminated some more, then got up.

What the hell. He walked to the pay phone and called the flower shop in West Hollywood. Although his boss knew about the interview, Allen apologized for not giving her more notice, but she congratulated him effusively. *For what?* Half drunk, he went to the barber next door and blithely asked to be trimmed "about halfway to respectable."

He arrived at home after one; his brother-in-law's new white pick-up was unexpectedly in the driveway, McMANUS FULL SERVICE and the phone number stenciled on the doors. Allen pulled the Volvo to the curb in front of the boxy little tan house and spotted Rick in the long narrow space between their place and the neighbor's tall thick oleander hedge.

Allen got out of the car with his things. Rick was in a T-shirt and swimming trunks, fooling around near the back of the house. Heat waves pulsed from the black screen at the top of the robot-shaped trash incinerator that hadn't been used for years.

He walked onto the small front lawn, glowering at Rick, who began to walk up the shaded lane. Allen's refuge as a kid, the space was just wide enough there for him and sometimes a friend to play catch or shoot cans, mess around with bugs, make forts in the hedge, or play with his legions of plastic cowboys and Indians.

Allen stopped beneath their tall old avocado tree as his brother-in-law approached, a long fiberglass surfboard under one arm. In his early thirties, Rick wasn't close to his professed height of five-nine, but he was both slim and muscular. Allen's pretty sister and her tan, rugged-looking husband still had the reputation as one of the handsomest couples from Adams High, although they weren't involved much in school social life—he was into cars and surfing, and Trudy volunteered at hospitals.

Rick's long and unruly bleached-blond hair lit up in the sunlight as he passed the corner of the house. Allen took some steps in his direction. "What're you burning back there?"

"None a' your damn business." Flip-flops slapping at his heels, he moved his bantam stocky frame toward the driveway.

"It's against the law."

Rick stopped and rested an end of the board on the grass, looking at Allen suspiciously. "What is?"

"Burning, what do you think?"

"Who gives a shit?" He picked up the surfboard. "You take that job? Maybe you can finally pay your way around here."

"How much money will you make in Malibu today?"

"Mel's got my shift. Answer my damn question."

"I start tomorrow."

"Where's the school?"

"Beverly Hills, what do you care?"

"Where the hell is it?"

"Watts."

"What? Are you nuts?" He made a horselaugh. "The niggers'll waste you without blinkin' an eye."

"Your concern is touching. You don't know what you're talking about."

"More 'n you do. They come by the station on the way to Griffith—it's spook city over there on weekends now."

"So? It's a public park." Allen started for the house.

Rick laughed again as he came to his pick-up. "Man, you better stick with bein' a flower boy." He secured his board in the truck bed. "You won't last one day, fat-ass." He got in and backed out of the driveway, still guffawing.

Allen walked up the driveway and under his mother's old rose arbor toward the back door. He and Trudy had lived by themselves for years in the family's small Los Feliz home after their parents' death when he was sixteen. The insurance paid off the house and debts, but the bills piled up, so he took more delivery hours. Everything changed after Trudy quit her Master's in Social Work and Rick moved in. Allen knew the McManus brothers and had attempted to warn her. After she married him, Allen tried to butt out, staying with them on and off. Now, after a miscarriage, she was seven months pregnant.

He went in but didn't feel like going down to the *cave*, Trudy's name for his primitive digs in the half-basement. He had given up his small bedroom recently for the baby and for Rick's barbells, but Allen hadn't really settled in downstairs, keeping most of his scant possessions in boxes.

After splashing cold water on his face in the kitchen, he sat at the oval cherry-wood dining-room table in front of his typewriter, reference books, and a file-box full of personal papers. He picked up the school handbook without opening it. A minute or two later, he caught himself staring at his mother's furniture, china and silverware.

Trudy can keep it all, except Pedro. Sleeping on his perch near the sunny dining-room window, Pedro was an old powder-blue and black parakeet with touches of white. He had been trained diligently by Allen and his mom to speak at least a dozen phrases; Trudy even helped sometimes. Rick constantly bellyached about the bird, but Allen refused to move him down to the musty basement.

Pedro woke up and danced a little jig, squawking his favorite refrain, "Geev Pedro beeg kees, beeg kees"—a line from a cartoon that Allen and Trudy liked as kids.

Allen walked over and put his face to the cage at the top of a five-foot stand. "Okay, boy." Pedro jumped, attaching his feet to the wire by Allen's lips. With the bird's rapt attention, Allen repeated, "I tot I taw a puddy tat" about ten times, then said, "Sorry, ol' bird, that's it." Pedro flitted to his favorite perch, where he began to chatter back to sleep.

He spent the afternoon trying to make sense of his teaching goals and meager resources, stopping only to stretch or talk to Pedro. After five o'clock snuck up on him, Allen sighed; he only had the crappy textbook plus a couple of ideas for Creative Writing, but Dan had offered to help him and was expecting a call.

Not wanting Trudy to worry about his dinner, he wrote her a note, then changed Pedro's water and seed. As if to thank him, the bird bowed over and over and began to cluck. Allen picked up his school materials and left the room; Pedro had stopped the noises and was saying, "I'm a chicken, I'm a chicken . . . ."

Allen was back at Bill's by six. After having a burger, onion rings and a beer, he bought his favorite chocolate-coated honeycomb candy bar from a vending machine and ate a third of it on his way to the pay phone. He dialed Dan's number, listening to the billiard balls slamming and clicking. The Beatles caterwauled "All you need is love" ad nauseam from the jukebox.

Dan's phone clicked. "*¡Bueno!*" he answered in anglicized Spanish.

"What's that about, O'Mara?"

"You're not the only one who speaks some *español*," he said, the "pan" as in *panda*.

"Sounds great. You guys eating?"

"We're finished, Jen's giving the baby a bath. Sounds like you're at Bill's again. Having another gut bomb?"

"Salad."

"Sure, Chubs. So, are you going through with the job?"

"I am for tomorrow."

"You sound thrilled. I warned you it wouldn't be easy."

"I know. C'mon, Master of Education, share some of your extensive knowledge."

"That's *expensive* knowledge, and just in math."

"Okay, listen . . . ." He told about the meeting with Dorsey, explaining first how she sneered at his clothes and hair. Dan had a good laugh, then Allen told him some details and finally finished with, "She's tough, but you can tell she cares about what she does."

"Yeah, maybe. She did give you a lot of good advice."

"I know, but I'm lost on the actual teaching."

"Just start out by seeing what they can and can't do. Then, hell, you're the damn writer, and the book should give you some broad ideas. Look, I'm probably as nervous as you are."

"How do you figure that?"

"The district moved me since I talked to you. I have eighth-graders tomorrow."

"Damn, just like that? Are you all bummed?"

"Nah. With all the turnover, I'll be back in high school by next year."

"Do you still have mostly Mexican kids?"

"Yeah, thank God they didn't send me to South-Central."

"Thanks, that makes me feel better."

"You might be okay down there, you've always been, uh—"

"Always been what?"

"You know what I mean, nobody could even say *coons* or *spades* without you having a friggin' cow."

"So what? How does that matter tomorrow?"

"Actually, it could be a problem for you."

"Now what are you talking about?" Allen had some pique in his voice.

"Ex-lax, will you? Let me think it through. By the way, it's *Latino* now, not . . . ."

Dan's brief lecture reminded Allen that Dorsey hadn't used any racial term at all—he would stick with *black*, what the younger leaders from South-Central were saying on TV.

". . . now there are families from Cuba, Puerto—"

"Okay, Dan, I get it."

"Hey, about what I said a minute ago—you remember when we were around twelve, shooting cans in the L.A. River, and we all got into that fight?"

"What does that have to do with anything?"

"Don't get pissed, hear me out."

"I'm not pissed."

"It all started because you shot Damon."

"In the shoe, with a BB."

"Yeah, from an air-rifle—because he wouldn't stop trying to kill birds."

"So? I'd probably do it again."

"Exactly. Look, your, uh, *sensitivity* for the underdog could get you in trouble down there tomorrow. What I'm saying is keep your eyes open and watch out for yourself first."

"Jesus, I know that. I was scared shitless half the morning. I don't have any delusions—it's good ol' one day at a time—hell, one hour at a time. I'll see if I can handle it."

"Good philosophy, Gunga Din."

"Thanks, smart-ass."

"Talking about Damon reminds me—I saw him with Gary at a Lakers game. They said to say hi."

Demon and his spawn.

"Allen?"

"What do you want me to say?"

"Man, you do carry a grudge. It's a wonder you're still friends with *me*."

"Bull, you know anybody else I let call me *Chubs*?"

"Your sister."

"Not anymore, she calls me *Bear*. You and I will be friends until you get sick of me, and you know it."

"Yeah, don't get mushy. Ha, I just got it—Trudy calls you *Bear* because you live down in the cave. Maybe *she's* the one who's getting sick of you."

"She's sick of me arguing with Rick the Prick."

"Find the right woman, and you'd be outta there in nothing flat."

"Don't hold your breath."

"Maybe it'd help if you didn't talk about 'Walden' and his pond when you go on a date. Look, I'm worried about something else for tomorrow—now maybe I'll really piss you off."

Allen chuckled.

"Good, laugh a little. All right, I'm wondering how you're going to deal with the school, the same things you called bullshit on at Adams after your mom and dad—sorry, man, I—"

"Forget it. That's what you think I'll do?"

"No, just the opposite—you'll have your face in a damn book all the time, and now you're into this Gunga Din crap. It's not just Damon and the rest—at college, people thought you were pissed whether you were or not."

"That's their problem."

"Okay, but only up to a point—you have to get along with those teachers tomorrow. I'm not saying kiss their asses, just make nice a little."

"Sounds like your handy hints on women."

"It's similar. Rub a few elbows, keep the teachers off your back and save your energy for the classroom—that's where you'll need it."

"Okay, so give me some good lines for the teachers."

"It isn't difficult—start by smiling like Howdy Doody, then just stick to sports or the weather."

"I think I can handle that."

"Never know, Chubs, there might be a fine young teacher there you can schmooze."

Or a certain secretary. "You're a broken record, O'Mara. I'm going to the library for a while to work on my plans. You've actually been some help, even the Dear Abby crap."

"You're welcome. Call me this weekend, sooner if you want. See ya, Bear."

"Say hi to Jen." Allen hung up and stared at the last hunk of candy in the wrapper. He tossed it into a trashcan.

On his way out of the tavern, "All you need is love" was moralizing again from the jukebox. *Geez, give it a rest.*

Up early the next day, Allen avoided his family and visited with Pedro. The morning was mild when he left, almost cool; he stopped for coffee and a donut. Just at seven, a half-hour before his starting time, he pulled into the staff parking lot. There were no kids around, only a few cars had arrived ahead of him, and the old shack in the lot was closed again.

He parked, then picked up his sturdy waxed fruit box, complete with lid and air holes, its sides printed with plump Golden Delicious apples and lush green leaves. He started for the street, the half-empty box and Bradbury under one arm.

The school's front door was locked, but a parent let him in; he walked past a line of kids and adults waiting for Miss Watson. She was deftly handling multiple tasks again, much too busy for him to barge in with a *good morning.*

Several feet behind the other end of the counter, a light-complected, dark-freckled, very heavy black woman in her fifties completely covered an office chair in her tent-like tan shift—not even the casters were visible. She was involved in a loud personal phone call. Allen moved closer and saw MRS.

VENABLE on her desk sign. He put his box on the counter; the offices behind the secretaries appeared to be empty.

Allen started to open his book but remembered Dan's advice. He stood there until the older secretary finally hung up and started typing. "Excuse me, I'm new here—Allen Greene."

She raised her head and peered at the box, then at him. He checked the "presentability" of his clothes, a light-blue dress shirt and half-belled navy chinos.

The secretary furrowed her dark brows. "Allen Greene?" He nodded back; she chortled without smiling and jotted on a pad. "Works for today."

What?

The woman pointed her pencil at the short door below his knees. "The lock is on this side—I'm Mrs. Venable."

"Yes, hi." He picked up the box, reached over to flick the lock, and walked in. Before Allen came close, Venable had one hand on her phone and the other in the air like a traffic cop.

"The mailboxes, Mister Greene, are in there." She pointed to a hallway between two small offices. "Your room is 329—upstairs. In your box, you'll find keys, the bulletin, student schedules, papers to fill out, roll book, and class lists. Read *all* of the bulletin before you come back with any questions, and nothing non-vital on the PA system. Mister Schultz wanted to meet with the eight of you before school, but he was called away—he'll arrange something soon. Do you have a mentor?"

"Yes, Miss Dorsey. I—"

"Good, she's at the south end of your floor, room 365. I suggest you see *her* with any questions." She turned to the telephone and began to dial. "Welcome to Thurgood Marshall."

He walked into the office corridor; a middle-aged white woman in a business suit glanced at him dismissively as she entered a door marked TEACHER'S LOUNGE. He found an entire wall of wooden cubbyholes, the name labels at eye level and below. Not finding his, he spotted eight boxes segregated at the very top—the second one, evidently a typo, said MISS GREENE. Allen reached up for his pile of papers and found an envelope with a regular key and a small one. Keeping the bulletin and keys, he put the rest in the fruit box and entered the hall, where the guard he'd seen before walked by, talking on a radio.

There was no sound but Allen's footfalls as he started up the middle stairway reading the bulletin, his hip sliding along the wooden banister to keep his balance. It was equally quiet on the third floor. Painted gunmetal grey, the long hallway smelled of wax and had six low-watt bulbs spaced evenly along the ceiling, each in a metal cage. Like a tunnel, dull light entered the dank corridor through a small window at each end.

He unlocked the third door on the right; his room was actually closer to the north stairs. Allen walked in, turned on the banks of fluorescent lights to see four off-yellow walls and standard classroom equipment. The long green chalkboard faced one-piece desks in five long rows. Made mostly of metal, each seat had a bin at the side with scratches and chips in the tan finish; the writing surfaces resembled scarred kitchen cutting boards with years of graffiti preserved in clear lacquer.

A solitary poster in the room listed the school rules on a bulletin board over the only long table. A black metal music stand near the teacher's desk apparently served as an ersatz podium. Above the chalkboard, rows of commercially made cards, faded from red to pink, presented the parts of speech: NOUN—THE NAME OF A PERSON, PLACE, THING, OR IDEA. VERB—ACTION . . . .

He quickly checked out his scant supplies in the desk and cabinet, including a lifetime hoard of white hole-reinforcement stickers, stacks of worn texts, and primary-school handwriting books. He opened one of about thirty threadbare, dark-blue Webster's to the copyright page—the dictionary was pre-Sputnik.

Allen went over to one of four tall windows. *No jail wire up here.* Beneath his view of dingy grey skyline, the nearest building was also white brick and three stories, but not as long as Main. Between its first-floor windows, iron rails ran up concrete ramps to three cafeteria portals. Like at his schools, they probably sold sweet rolls, juice, milk, and hot chocolate there in the mornings. A courtyard about the size of a college gymnasium floor separated Main from the cafeteria—at each end, a red brick archway connected the two buildings. The only indication of recent physical improvement was new black asphalt.

Sitting in a lopsided swivel chair at his desk, he checked the schedule. After a long homeroom, the seven periods would be shortened all day. His second hour was free; Dorsey had called it *prep.* Allen stood at the board and printed GREENE. *Damn, the chalk's trembling.*

He read his sketchy lesson plans before he checked the white-faced clock on the wall. Deciding to use his last minutes to take down the old grammar strips, he found a staple-puller, pushed a chair to the chalkboard and climbed up to begin working.

The bell rang as he ripped off the last of the brittle, dusty cards. Less than a minute later, some girls rushed into the room; they looked more like mid-teens than seventh-graders. "Can I help you?" He jumped down; they just sat and giggled as several more girls entered. Allen searched through the papers on his desk and found the homeroom list. *Thirty-one girls for Miss Greene—terrific.*

3

The tardy bell rang, followed by a buzz on the intercom. The girls stood and started to quiet down to face the flag and the black PA box next to it. While they waited, a few of them glared at Allen as if he were crashing a party.

He smiled sheepishly and pointed at the board. "My name's Greene. There was apparently a mix-up with the paperwork—they thought I was a woman." Most of the girls laughed right over the kids on the intercom who had started to recite the Pledge of Allegiance.

Every last girl was black, from one with pale skin and a short wheat-colored Afro, to another whose face was as lustrous and dark as obsidian. About a third of them wore trim natural hair; most of the rest had ponytails or permanent hairdos.

The laughter diminished as announcements began on the PA. Only a few girls looked like children; the rest were in makeup. Those with darker complexions wore light eye shadow while the fairer ones seemed to use black, blue, or purple. Most of the adolescent girls had on bright blouses; a few of them were in mini-skirts, and Allen told himself to keep his eyes up.

It took about fifteen minutes for attendance and to have them fill out school forms—the girls complied, just griping a little before he started to hand out their schedules. Denise, a tall girl with short natural brown hair and a dark pretty face, scowled at her card, and then paraphrased Maxwell Smart from TV. "Would y'all believe I got him *three* times?" Several others groaned about their classes, then most of the girls went on chatting or laughing.

Allen put his papers on the music stand, but it slid down to the bottom, causing more giggles. Denise pointed at him. "Name like that and bein' so white, you ain't no Mexican. You dye your hair black?"

He didn't answer for a moment, caught off guard by the blunt question. "Uh, no, I had two swarthy grandparents."

"They had what?"

"They were swarthy—dark."

"Don't be callin' *me* that."

"Okay, Denise."

She nodded to the box on his desk. "You sellin' apples, Mister Greene? Little *green* apples, like in that dumb song?" That started another bout of raucous laughter; Allen couldn't help but smile, and he was surprised she had called him *Mister*.

When the girls began to settle into quiet conversations, he took a step toward Denise and the others nearby. "All ready for the new semester, girls?" They raised their brows or frowned, turning away. Still with ten minutes, he opened *The Martian Chronicles* at his desk. *Perfect for Allen the alien.*

Denise pointed at him again. "You readin' a school book?"

"No, they're stories."

She turned to the nearest girl. "Must be dirty."

He waited for the laughter. "Why do you say that, Denise?"

"You hidin' it with that cover."

"Oh. The stories aren't dirty, I'm just private about what I read. If somebody asks, I usually tell them."

"I ain't askin'. But when I'm in your class period three, can I bring my own book from home an' keep it covered?"

"Sure."

"And do I gotta tell you what it is?"

"No, you don't."

"Okay then."

Allen watched Denise turn back to her friends. *So far so good.* He scoffed to himself—it wasn't girls who raised most of the hell in his junior high. The bell rang. "Okay, that's it, you'll probably have a female teacher tomorrow."

"No more Mister Little Green Apples?" Denise's remark prompted more laughter as most of them started to leave.

The handful of homeroom girls who stayed on spoke to those who entered and had them laughing about Allen right away. *Firm but fair* on his mind, he left his desk to use the music stand. He pulled it up from the floor, but it slid right back down halfway. Amidst the snickers, he retreated to the front of his desk and leaned back on the edge.

His mouth completely dry again, Allen peeked at the class while he skimmed the list; only a few of them looked resentful—most just talked as they waited for the bell. Although the room was starting to fill up, this would be his second smallest group, twenty-seven on the roll, nearly even by gender.

The kids were much closer to his age than the teachers he had seen. In general, the boys seemed younger; more than half of them were pre-adolescents, dressed similarly to a skinny little guy up front in a holey Flintstones T-shirt tucked into loose blue jeans. Two of him could fit into a desk; his pant legs were somehow too short, not reaching the tops of the red socks in his ragged grey sneakers.

Of the other boys, a few of the taller ones looked like they already shaved. Some were in dark pants and synthetic gold or black shirts, those in gold sitting near others in gold, and black with black. *Damn, nobody mentioned any gang crap.* Allen had been exposed to two types of gangs, the Mexican *pandillas* that usually left him alone, and the so-called high-school service clubs—future frat boys, all white, who had rumbles after dark.

Many of the adolescent males wore thick Afros, but one big kid had flat processed hair, a conk job—Allen knew the term from a Richard Wright novel. That boy had planted himself by the window in the last row, his head on the back rest as if it were a pillow; he extended his long torso beneath the desk, his feet touching the seat ahead of him. He had hickory-brown skin and a black shirt with long collar flaps like crow's wings, touching the squared shoulders of his thin black windbreaker.

A darker boy next to him, also in black but not quite as brawny or tall, had a long comb protruding from his helmet-like Afro. They sneered at Allen, who pretended to check the roll. His peripheral vision picked up a paper wad sailing across the room; he saved his ire for something that mattered.

After the tardy bell, the class calmed right away, apparently curious. A couple of stragglers came in. Allen's tongue peeled from the inside of his mouth like a piece of masking tape. "That's your one freebie—tomorrow I turn in a tardy." He made a quick count—twenty-five students.

"Are you going to call roll?" a very small girl asked from the front row in a cross tone; her English was more formal than the other kids he had heard. She was nearly as fair as a redhead, though she had dark eyes and brows, her auburn hair banded behind in a wiry ponytail. A puffy port-wine birthmark the diameter of a fifty-cent piece stood out on the light skin of her left cheek.

"A sign-in sheet is starting around. Print your name on it please, or you're absent." Most of the students turned to the first row.

The same small girl pointed at Allen. "How can you learn our names?" Her clothing was unique; she wore a long, prim, white dress, no ruffles, not quite as folksy as a prairie-schooner outfit.

"One at a time, I guess. What's yours?"

She made a haughty smile. "Charmane Muhammad."

A boy with a dark complexion and short natural hair jeered from near the back. An inch or two taller than the other pre-adolescents, he had some baby fat on his arms and neck. He wore a black T-shirt and jeans, probably to be like the two surly boys behind. "That ain't your name, Charmane." He tried to rhyme the last two words; several kids laughed.

She looked straight ahead. "Shut up, Marlon Brown."

"All right, that's enough. We have short periods today—let's get going." Allen directed their attention back to the board with his thumb. "My name is Greene with an *e*."

Marlon's face broke into a wide grin. "Green with a *e* looks like whitey to me." While most of the class chuckled, the two boys behind Marlon ignored the fun, still glowering.

"Okay, as you know, this is Language Arts—"

"Dumbbell English." Marlon raked his short Afro twice with a black comb.

"Boy, don't you ever shut up?" Charmane still didn't turn back to him.

Allen faced the middle of the class, between the two adversaries. "My answer for Marlon is that I don't care about your previous academic record. What I do—"

"I don't play no *ac-a-dem-ic* records, jus' my brother, James Brown." Marlon smugly slid the comb into his chest pocket. This time, the two tall boys smiled along with the general laughter.

Charmane faced the class. "The fool doesn't even know the teacher's talking about grades." Mostly girls laughed at that.

Marlon shrugged. "Least *I* know he's lyin' about it." The class stilled after the accusation, turning to Allen.

"Look, I was told your testing in sixth grade put you in this level. Well, that's old news as far as I'm concerned, and so are your grades from first semester—I haven't seen them, and I don't need to."

Marlon grinned again, poking himself in the chest. "I got a *D*, now you know one."

"A *D* for dummy." Charmane made a feisty grin.

"Yeah, you got a *C* for cracker."

Some boys laughed, then more joined in after the tall kid with the processed hair chortled to his buddy. Allen waited; he looked at Charmane, then Marlon. "All right, knock off the put-downs, both of you." Marlon scoffed; Charmane reddened in a slow burn. "My point is that today all of you start from scratch in here."

Allen turned from the mostly ambivalent faces; the list had stopped halfway down the first row at the desk of a boy with a shaved head. Besides his singular baldness, he was the only one of the smaller boys not dressed like a child. He wore dark pants, shiny shoes, and a shimmering gold shirt with its sleeves rolled up, showing prematurely developed muscles. A tall boy in a yellow shirt sat to one side of him, two more right behind.

"Would you pass on the sheet please?"

The boy looked up from staring at his desk. He had an oval sepia-brown face. "My pencil's busted."

The kid didn't seem to be playing around; Allen walked over to him. "Here, I forgot to put a pen with it." The boy printed his name and passed the pen and list back to his pal. "Your name please?"

"Ronnie Crawford, teach." He snuck a glimpse at Allen with lively but solemn dark eyes and thick brows.

"Okay, while the list is going around, I'll explain what you can expect to be doing in here."

Over some low griping, Marlon spoke right up. "You ever teach before?"

"No, Marlon, I'm new at it. Let's get—"

"Man, another one." Marlon rolled his eyes.

"Boy, why don't you shut the hell up and let the teacher talk?" Charmane fumed toward the ceiling.

"Muslims ain't supposed to swear—*you* shut up . . . ." He added a word partly under his breath; it sounded like *gimp*. Only a couple of boys laughed; Charmane cowered a little.

Allen stiffened his posture and pointed emphatically. "Okay, that's it for the put-downs, the swearing, *all* of it." That opened some eyes. "Now, when you come in the room tomorrow, you start writing, you don't wait for the bell."

A few hands shot up and there was some grousing; Allen acted as if he didn't hear a faint "bullshit" from the big boy with slick hair behind Marlon.

"Hold the questions just a minute. So what do you write every day? Whatever you want, and if that's too open, I suggest a journal—what you did or observed since you last wrote. It's up to you how personal it is. I'm the only one who will read it, unless you choose to share it." There were more groans. "This is called informal writing, and you—" A hand went up. "Yes, Charmane."

"Informal means not fancy, right?"

"Yes, exactly."

"Charmane the brain." Marlon waited for the laughter. "Muslims ain't supposed to kiss up to the man either."

"You don't know anything about Muslims," Charmane replied in a matter-of-fact tone, still looking straight ahead.

Marlon just grunted, so Allen used the lull in the bickering. "Okay, this informal writing time is when you *don't* worry about spelling, grammar, anything—you just write."

Next to Charmane, one of several girls who could pass for sixteen or older raised a hand. Like some others, she had made an effort to dress nicely for the first day of school. Burly but not obese, her hair was coiffed into a stiff pageboy; she wore eye shadow matching a ruffled powder-blue blouse that didn't completely veil her mature chest. Her mocha facial features, full but uniform, gave her an attractive mien, though she had mild acne problems.

Allen nodded. "And your name please?"

"Sandra Small. I want to ask—"

"They ain't small at all." Marlon's face was sly but his voice audible. A nearby girl warned him, and a few boys winced as if he had crossed some line.

"You say somethin', boy?" Brows raised and eyes ahead, Sandra was asking and daring him, but he didn't answer. "Well?"

Marlon looked around helplessly. "Nuh-uh."

"Didn't think so." She turned to Allen. "Don't let that little boy bother you." Extending her hand to Charmane, they casually slid open palms together, then Sandra faced him again. "Mister Greene, if you don't fix our English, how we supposed to get better at it?"

Attempting not to show too much appreciation for her question, he walked closer; she had silver fingernails, as long as small penknives. "We'll work hard on formal writing in here, Sandra, but to be fluent, you also need time to just write and not worry about rules."

"You mean like speakin' in French or Spanish?"

"Shit." The muffled expletive from the same boy in back sounded like *she-yit,* but the class didn't react.

"Yes, *fluent* can mean speaking another language well. If your writing is fluent, that means it can just flow, sort of like thinking." Making a fluid motion with his arm, he faced the whole class. "So during that time, all I care about is that you write. By the way, when I explain something that isn't clear, ask about it like Sandra did—it shows you're learning." He turned to be sure he didn't embarrass her; she was grinning.

"Okay, for fluency writing, the work stays here in folders until mid-semester. Tomorrow, your file box will be the first one, right there." He pointed to the long table under the bulletin board. "I also have some old pencils—so, no excuses—you start to work right away every day."

Nearby, the only adolescent boy not in black or gold grumbled, "Sounds like Dorsey."

Ronnie Crawford raised his hand tentatively.

"Yes, Ronnie?"

"How long do we get to write when we come in?" His voice was clear, and no scorn came from the class except for another jeer from the critic in the last row.

"Okay, another good question. You'll have ten minutes, more if you're early. Once you have a full paragraph, you can change to reading. Looking at pictures won't count."

"Haw! It's good you said *that,* Mister Greene." Sandra turned to Charmane. "These boys are *always* lookin' at pictures—the same kind—*allayall* know what I mean."

Most of the girls laughed. "They *all* nasty, even them little boys," a tall girl chimed in, starting the rest on a long laughing jag.

Allen waited, again trying not to smile; a few boys scowled or shook their heads. "Okay, let's go on. For reading, I'll have a shelf of books, and we'll be going to the lib—"

"Bullshit." The oath, loud this time, was followed by some *ooos* and mumbled comments from the kids. The boy behind Marlon stood; he was over six feet tall, his flattened wavy black hair reflected the lights overhead.

Allen clenched his jaw. "Your name?"

The boy ignored him and just moved slowly forward, his left hand holding something in the front pocket of his black pants. The class hushed; Ronnie and the other boys in gold glared at their rival, who stopped several feet from Allen, checking him out head to toe. "You ain't no teacher, jus' a fat hippie." A few boys chuckled, including his sidekick, who was also walking to the teacher's desk, his long comb handle sticking out of his Afro like an arrow in his head. He stopped to invite Marlon, who just kept looking down at his hands.

Allen pointed at the two boys. "I want you both to take your seats—now." His voice was uneven; his neck throbbed.

"You gonna make us?" The taller boy moved much closer, his hand still in the pocket.

The class silently turned to Allen, who made his tongue moisten the roof of his mouth, then his lips. "If you already decided to act this way, I can't *make* you do anything."

His minion laughing behind, the boy's fair handsome face formed a knowing grin. "*That* shit you got right." He pointed at Sandra. "You think these bitches are funny? I got somethin' funny for you, Greene." With a cold chuckle, he slid his hand very slowly from the pocket, cupping it on his hip to hide whatever was underneath.

Allen glanced at the intercom, his pulse pounding. The boy looked down and began to move his fingers, everyone watching him. Like a time-lapse film of a blooming flower, the boy's hand opened very slowly, revealing only the black fabric of his slacks. An exhale filled Allen's cheeks, escaping in a rush.

A mirthless grin crossed the boy's face before he shouted. "Hah! Scared a' somethin', teach?" He started to saunter away, touching a bulge below his windbreaker's left pocket.

The second boy snickered, walking past Allen. "You turnin' green, Charlie Greene." A three-inch white scar stood out on his dark chin. Not in any hurry, he followed his cohort toward the door.

The leader snarled at Sandra, then they both smirked with superiority toward the boys in gold. The two of them gradually strutted and cackled their way into the hallway, leaving the door wide open. Allen walked over to close it. *Okay, teach, a long quiet breath.*

4

Allen faced the class. Charmane and many of the others were just waiting—
a few kids, including Sandra and Ronnie, stared at their desks. "Somebody
want to tell me their names?"

Most turned away, but Sandra looked up at him. "It don't matter. They
came just to show how bad they think they are. They'll just run off or get
caught by the cops."

Allen walked to the chalkboard. "I still have to report them." He reached
up and pushed the PA button.

Sandra was looking down again. "You do that, Mister Greene, but we ain't
gonna rat on nobody, not even them."

He waited for Venable . . . nothing. There were a few chuckles for his
ineffectual effort; he turned to the class. "Look, I admit he scared me—you
guys got pretty quiet too. He had *something* in his jacket."

The PA crackled. "Yes, office." Regardless of the static, Venable's tone was
clear: *What the hell do you want?*

"Two boys just left—"

"They what? Can't hear you."

"Two boys left my room without permission!"

"I hear you now, Mister Greene." That brought some titters from the class.

"I don't have names—I didn't finish attendance yet."

"And the others won't tell you, right? You might try taking roll at the
beginning of the hour." More kids laughed.

"One of them might've had a knife or something—they're both wearing black."

~"That helps," Venable said aside as if Allen couldn't hear her. "All right, I'll tell security." The PA clicked.

The sign-in sheet had returned to the front; he picked it up from Sandra's desk. She was looking right at him. "Mister Greene, I'm gonna say somethin' the school already knows 'bout that fool. He's been in trouble with guns, an' I don't mean no zip guns." Sandra intrepidly squared her jaw. "I ain't scared a' him, jus' not gonna be stupid about no guns."

"Makes sense to me." He cleared his throat. "Okay, there's time for a short assignment." A few kids began carping, but *Just get on with it* was on most of their faces. "Who needs paper or pencil?" After more groans, several students crowded up to the pencil sharpener while Allen hurried up and down the aisles with materials for some kids who had raised a hand.

He waited for the last pencil to grind. "All right, tell me about *you*, whatever you want. If you can't think of anything, write it like an autobiography— you know, 'I'm Joe—I was born in Cucamonga. I have two sisters and a cat named Fido—blah, blah.' This writing is also private, unless you choose to share it. Okay, about eight minutes left." Most of the class started to work; Allen began to compare boys' names from the sign-in and class sheets, but some hands went up. He put the lists down and worked with the kids until the bell.

"Be sure your name's on your paper, and leave it on the first desk in your row with my pencil, if you borrowed one." Most of the kids were already on their feet. "See you tomorrow, be ready to write."

Two of the smaller girls walked up to him, their faces serious. "Remember, Mister Greene," one said, pointing to the papers at the front of her row, "nobody else gets to look at what we wrote in there."

"Yes, girls, that's right." Like most of the others, they walked away talking about class schedules, not the incident with the boys. Allen picked up the two lists again; Ronnie was hanging around the front door by himself. Charmane, moving with a decided limp, hobbled toward that same door with Sandra.

They stopped, turned, and Sandra said, "Mister Greene?" Ronnie was behind them, but he left when he realized they were waiting for the teacher.

He approached the girls; Sandra removed a wallet from her small purse.

After watching the last kid leave, Charmane turned to him. "I don't usually like English much, Mister Greene."

Allen was taking a peek at the lists in his hand; her statement didn't sink in right away. "Oh? What do you like to study, Charmane?"

"Math, and especially science, but sometimes they only let boys do the interesting stuff."

"That doesn't sound right."

Sandra handed him a snapshot. "See there, Mister Greene?" All the toughness was gone from her voice.

The trimmed Polaroid had to be a shot of her baby sister, all smiles in pink ruffles and ribbons. "Very cute, Sandra."

"That's my baby, Melissa." She beamed at the picture.

My God. "Uh, I can see why you're proud, she's a very pretty child. Right, Charmane?" He passed the photo to her.

"Yeah, I babysit her sometimes—she's the cutest." She gave the snapshot back to her friend.

"Ain't she?" Sandra carefully inserted it into a plastic sleeve. "I'll show you a better one of her tomorrow, Mister Greene." She put the wallet away; her affable demeanor morphed into a frown. "My mom usually has her when I'm at school. I ain't gonna quit, no matter what these fools say." She glared at the desks as if they were still occupied.

"Good for you, Sandra." He smiled. "I think you'll both do very well in this class. Don't be late now."

With big grins, the girls hurried away; Sandra turned to him. "We'll see you last period, Mister Greene."

Allen waved back, but seeing the lists in his hand broke his good mood. He hurried to his desk to reconcile the names, relieved that it was his free period. He finished, then got up and poked the PA button; Venable answered moments later.

"Mrs. Venable, the two boys who left, it's possible one of them had a gun."

"Names, Mister Greene?"

"Including those two, I marked three boys absent—Michael Bradley, Martin Lynch, and Rupert Washington."

"Michael and Rupert for sure—I'll tell security. Is that all of your absences? You didn't put your attendance out."

"Sorry, those three and Aisha Hall." Venable was gone. He checked his long third-period class list; he would have to work on a tougher introduction. Allen went over to lock the door, then came back to the windows. Two boys ran frantically into the courtyard below, a guard only seconds behind them. He sighed and sat down in a student desk.

With his heels up on the iron steam-heat registers that ran along the wall beneath the windows, he was listening again: *chairs scraping—somebody whistling—buzzing fly—trash can lid—slamming door—breeze in the eaves.*

He finally opened his eyes, making a long exhale. Allen had relaxed enough that it took a few seconds to place exactly where he was. He stood, then gazed out through the smog at the silhouettes of distant signage, TV aerials, and roof crowns. He looked past the far end of the cafeteria at an old spindly eucalyptus with about ten picnic benches below in two rows. Outside the fence and across the street, a solitary wide palm, not the tall kind, survived in a front yard, some of its fronds brown and desiccated. *A tree grows in Watts.*

Allen faced his desk; the music stand had slipped down again, as if set up for a performance by a small child. He smiled about Sandra and Charmane, but how many more Michaels and Ruperts would he have? And there might be more smart-asses like Marlon with all his pejoratives—*gimp, cracker,* and *whitey.* A childhood ritual came to mind, avoiding sidewalk squares with *WPA* or other letters stamped into the concrete—step on one, you'd be slugged and called a "nigger baby." He sighed, took out blank paper, and started a new introduction.

After a few minutes, he read his lecture. *What crap.* He stared beyond his desk and back into his high-school days. Adams High had a handful of black kids, one was a blind girl they treated like a mascot, and there was a guy who hung around with rich kids and ran for student council. Since Allen didn't know him or his opponent, he wrote in *Alfred E. Neumann.*

His friends argued about whether the black guy was cool or uppity—Allen stayed out of it; he had his own racial baggage. After his parents died, he told Dan that his father's people were Rom Gypsies from Vladivostok who had changed the family name to Greene after they fled to the United States. Dan laughed at him. "Big deal, mine were shanty Irish. You don't have to hide it, nobody gives a damn, everybody in their own little world . . . ."

Allen faced the desks as if they were occupied. "Okay, I'm the alien in charge of *this* world, and don't you guys forget it." He looked guiltily at the PA, then crumpled the introduction and tossed it. After he wrote a new lead-in, Allen added most of what he said before about the fluency writing, which made him curious about the assignment from first period. He took a few minutes to read their papers.

Four of them were blank, and about a third of the kids only scribbled a few choppy words. One boy didn't get Allen's joke or was being sarcastic. He wrote:

Im Joe born in kookamunga and got a dog name Fydo.

Several more had a lot of mistakes but in long sentences; Sandra's was one of those. She wrote about plans to take her baby to see Martin Luther King in L.A. Charmane wrote the most—factual, linear, and with nearly perfect grammar and punctuation. She was born in Chicago after four brothers; she didn't mention anything about her bad leg. Allen put Charmane's paper with Ronnie's on top of the pile. He quickly read Ronnie's again:

> **When I notice things, if I tell anyone except my uncle, they think I'm wierd. Like when I was walking to school today and saw this bird, a sparrow I think. It was flying real fast, but not like a plain that flys all steady. The bird was flying thru the air like a car moves.**
>
> **Fast and then rest, fast and then rest. When somebody says there in a plain and flying like a bird it doesnt make sense because**

Man, give him time to finish. He checked the clock, then revised his speech again. He practiced it once, then made a few more changes before he unlocked the door for period three. When the students began to come in, tall Denise from homeroom started them laughing right away about *little green apples.* He checked the list—thirty-six, only fourteen boys. If all the kids showed, they would be a desk short. Except for some homeroom girls, the faces were new, but their physical appearance was about the same as period one. "Okay, sit where you want, but sit."

When the tardy bell rang, there were a few empty seats in the room. To keep Venable off his back, he dispensed with the sign-in sheet to call the roll. Allen picked up his list and waited for them to quiet down; nobody came in late. It took almost five minutes for him to say the names, crossly ignoring or staring down a few wisecracks.

With five absentees on the slip, he headed for the clip outside the door, talking at the same time. "As you see on the board, my name is Greene. Here's the deal: wherever you sit tomorrow will be your assigned seat on my chart. If you decide to mess around there, you'll get one warning, then I move you."

Ignoring the gripes, he put out the slip and returned to his desk. He stood next to his outline, waiting until there was near silence. "Okay, when I'm teaching, I want and expect questions, but for the next few minutes—*no* questions." He toned down his harsh voice. "I have a little secret for you."

Most of them were listening; he glanced at his paper. "The best-paying job I ever had was for one-seventy-five an hour, delivering candy in L.A. Here's the secret." He tried to sound slightly incredulous. "They pay inexperienced people like me more than *four dollars an hour* for teaching you guys."

He expected some remarks, but there were only a few murmurs. "So why did they give me this job? Because I finished high school and my English degree. I worked part-time in college and wasn't the best student, but I made it. So this is the most money I ever made, and I intend to do my job." *For now, anyway.* He ignored more grumbling.

"There's *nobody* in here who can't learn if you're trying. I expect every one of you who wants to learn *will* learn. I think most of you want that—maybe a few don't, for whatever reason. One reason I *won't* accept is if you think you aren't smart enough."

Like a predictable response to a TV straight line, one boy blurted out that some other kid was stupid. Allen loured at the perpetrator, then turned to the poster. "I added a rule to this chart in marker—the first one." He pointed to I-A - GOLDEN. "The golden rule in here goes like this: nobody says someone is stupid, a dummy, or makes *any* other sort of put-down. You don't want to hear that about you, so you don't say it about anybody else—period."

Most of the kids were thinking; a few looked at him as if he were crazy—only two or three didn't seem to be listening. "Finally, I won't put up with anybody who disrupts your learning by breaking that rule or the other ones." The room was silent.

"So what happens if one of you is goofing around in class? If I decide it's harmless, and if you knock it off when I ask, then it counts as a freebie. If I think you're trying to be disruptive or mean, you get an actual warning—do it again, you get isolation here in the room. The last step before involving the school is me calling your parents. Any questions?"

There were sneers and a few low complaints; he was about to go on to fluency writing, but two hands went up. Allen called on a short boy up front in an oversized white T-shirt. The fairest and most overweight kid there, he seemed almost as round as he was tall. "What's your name again, please?"

"Darrel."

"The little white barrel," said a lanky pre-adolescent boy sitting three rows back.

A few boys laughed; one girl said, "Mister Greene, Raymond sound awful mean to me."

"Raymond, you heard what I just said about put-downs. That's your warning. Do it again, and you go to isolation."

The boy slouched, jeering unintelligibly; Allen marked his name and turned. "What was your question, Darrel?"

"You jus' said it again. Ice-a-something—what's that?"

Geez, he's serious. "Isolation—your desk goes in a corner, and you do your work alone so you don't bother anybody."

"Oh." His brows up, he looked impressed. "An' after that, you'd go to all that trouble to go down an' call my gramma?"

"I hope not, Darrel, but if you get a third warning, you can count on it."

Some kids groused, but Darrel nodded gravely, then looked at the board. "How come you don't put *Mister* with your name?"

"It doesn't bother me to be called *Greene*." He backed up and pointed to the rules. "It's all in how you say it."

Thick creases formed on Darrel's forehead. "We can't do that with other teachers."

"Yes, well, neither can I."

Denise, who hadn't commented as she did in homeroom, finally put her hand up from the back row.

"Yes, Denise."

"You said you wanted *us* to try. How long will *you* be trying—two days?"

Most of the class laughed; he waited. "I don't know. They have me signed up until June—you think I can make it?" He grinned; she bristled and turned away. "All right, I'm going to explain what you do every day when you come in. First . . . ."

Their questions on the fluency writing were about the same as in period one, but no serious problems seemed to be brewing. He began the assignment, and only a few kids didn't start to work, including Raymond, who sulked with his head down.

Static and then a voice came on the PA—nearly the whole class stopped writing. ". . . your attention. This is Mister Fogle—the following boys with schedule problems are to report to my office . . . ." The kids waited more patiently than Allen did for the list to end; none of his boys were called. He got the class back to work, then picked up the roll and walked around the room, taking questions and trying to learn names.

Allen turned in his lesson plans to Dorsey at noon; she actually chuckled at his explanation of the homeroom mix-up. He skipped lunch, refined his intro and read more of the papers.

Halfway through period six as the kids were writing, it seemed that his last three classes had almost gone too well, as if they were daring him to implement his rules. Almost on cue, a girl got up and started to leave; he asked her to please sit back down, but she just said *Fuck you* in a see-you-later tone and took off. The kids laughed as he reported her to Venable, then they went on as if nothing had happened.

The bell rang to end the period. "Okay, be ready to write when you get here tomorrow." He checked the list for his last class, Creative Writing—it would be his smallest group, only twenty-four, including Sandra, Charmane, Denise, Darrel, Ronnie, Michael and Rupert—the last two likely gone or kicked out.

He made a quiet sigh of relief; some girls came in and rushed immediately over to speak furtively to a few others who stayed on from period six. Charmane entered, limping quickly toward Allen's desk. She was breathing hard, her slight frame practically hopping inside the yards of loose, plain clothing. "Mister Greene." Brows furrowed, her voice was low but urgent; the red birthmark on her cheek seemed larger and darker than before.

"Charmane, what's wrong?"

"Sandra won't be here, she's in trouble."

"What happened?"

"In P.E., she, um, sort of pushed a teacher."

The tardy bell rang. "She did what?"

"It's worse than that." Her voice was even lower. "They had to take the teacher away in an ambulance."

"My God. All right, let me get class started."

5

As Charmane sat down, Allen took quick stock of his small class so he could get to Sandra's situation. Ronnie was there with one of his buddies in gold—just eighteen students in all, and many of them had already heard his new speech.

After he called roll and took the slip out to the hall, most of the kids sat sullenly through his shortened diatribe. "... and in this class, instead of fluency writing when you come in, you'll have a prompt for a short writing project." He turned toward the board. "Here's today's: 'You suddenly have all the power you need to change this school. What three things would you change and why?'"

He answered questions while handing out some paper and a few pencils. "Okay, get going—I'll be right at the door." He nodded to Charmane and followed her out, keeping the door ajar.

Once out of view from the class, Charmane was in tears. "It wasn't her fault, Mister Greene."

Allen pointed inside at a few talkers, then turned back to her. "Okay, tell me what happened."

"I can only tell you some of it. Sandra, she, um, all of us were mad." She paused to glare at a tall girl who walked by. As soon as the girl entered the next room, Charmane drew in a long sniffle. "That teacher, Hambone, she's crazy."

"Hambone?"

"That's what she said." Her tone had turned more defiant. "She's new and strict like you, but she's stupid—she didn't care that a lot of girls are in good clothes today, and she tried to make us do exercises!" Charmane was loud enough that some of the students looked up from their work.

"Okay, Charmane, try to take it easy."

"Yeah." She sighed. "So Sandra, it's her, uh, time—you know what I mean—and she's having a bad one. She tried to explain it to that bi—" Charmane composed herself with another sigh. "But she just told Sandra to get in with the rest of us." She paused again, angrily pursing her lips.

Two girls were talking in the room; Allen pointed at them. "Okay, go on."

"She told us to take off our shoes and line up for exercises. We complained but started to do it, except Sandra went back by the bleachers—the teacher yelled at her, but Sandra didn't move. So Hambone walks up to her and yells again, but this time Sandra cusses her back like she deserved. Then that teacher makes a big mistake—she grabs Sandra's collar real hard, and pulls it. Sandra turns and just pushes her off, and the teacher trips over some wires for the bars and falls right on her face. First, we're all laughing, but then—" Charmane looked at Allen with a determined frown.

"This part's real important, Mister Greene. That teacher, she was moving around, her face still on the floor—no blood or nothing, but Sandra shows us this big red scratch on her neck. Then somebody, not Sandra, and I won't tell who, goes to beating on the teacher until she stops moving." Charmane turned away. "We didn't want to all get in trouble, so we pushed the call button and yelled to the office that a teacher was hurt."

He sighed. "Go on."

"After that, we almost had a fight because some of us said we'd tell part of what happened so Sandra didn't get blamed for the beating." Charmane glared at the tardy girl's room. "We were still arguing about it when a guard and Mister Godina got there. The teacher was moving around by then."

"No one's going to tell who did it, not even Sandra?"

"Nobody. That teacher only knows who pushed her. We'll tell *why* she got pushed, but that's all." The pleats in her brow deepened. "Me and those other girls could still get beat up just for saying this much." She looked down at her feet. "That's all I can say, Mister Greene."

"Will you tell it to the principal?"

"Only what I already said. It won't matter—they'll kick Sandra out."

"I don't see why, not after what you told me."

"They'll believe whatever that teacher says."

"We'll see about that."

She faced him again. "What can *you* do?"

"I don't know—whatever I can." He opened the door. "You can go on in and start your assignment."

"Can I do *fluency* instead? I got a lot to write about."

"Okay, do that, Charmane."

They walked in; some whispering girls went back to work. He hit the PA button, then walked toward a boy who had raised a hand.

"Office."

Glad that it was Miss Watson, he asked her to please tell an administrator that he had information on the P.E. incident. Allen circulated around the room, helping the kids, until someone knocked on the door a few minutes later. "Okay, keep writing. I'll be standing right there again."

He opened the door; an Asian woman glanced at him from across the hall and down one room. She peeked in through that portal, then started toward Allen. She was over five-six in heels, her business suit meticulous and cream-colored, like her complexion.

Still at his door, he saw Charmane talking and gesturing to Denise. Allen mimed "writing" to them with his pen. The woman, in her late thirties or early forties with medium-long black hair and dark eyes, approached; she was pretty but not attractive, like a mannequin.

Allen had known several Japanese-American kids since fifth grade when the city closed a school on the L.A. side of the tracks from Glendale and moved those mostly Mexican or Asian students to his elementary. In high school, he and his knot of friends got along fine with Japanese-American boys but were of the general opinion that the "Jap girls were stuck-up snobs." He once told his friends it wasn't true for the Nakamura twins, but when Damon said to name another girl, Allen admitted that he couldn't.

The woman stopped nearby and seemed to grin and grimace at once. "I am Mrs. Ishimoto, vice-principal."

He attempted a friendly tone. "Hi, Allen Greene." He was about to lift his arm to shake hands, but she was already pointing at his door.

"Please close it all the way, Mister Greene."

Allen complied, then knocked on the glass portal so the kids knew he was still there. He watched them for a moment, then turned to the vice-principal.

"All right," she said, "tell me what you know about the incident in the gym with Miss Hamblin.

"Yes, Charmane Muhammad came to me. She told me that the teacher . . . ." He watched her reactions as he spoke. Even through the violent part, the vice-principal's grin endured. ". . . so Charmane and some others argued about . . . ." Allen checked the kids again. ". . . and then Mister Godina came in. That's it, Sandra was defending herself."

"And you really believe all that?"

What? "Charmane seems to be a very reliable kid. There's no reason to think she's lying."

"I'm sure she *is* lying, Mister Greene."

He made himself take a long breath. "I don't agree. I think it's admirable that she stands up so strongly for her friend."

"I see. You seem to have some influence with the girl—you are obligated to ask her for the truth."

"I already did. She made it very clear what she would and would not tell me."

The vice-principal stepped forward, glared into the room, then faced him again. "What is she writing?"

"She's working on a journal. Why?"

"I might get the information I need from there."

"I can't let you do that—it's private."

"Is that right?" She sounded scornful and sarcastic at once. "Well, I don't have time to make that an issue." Her grin became a smirk. "I'll find out soon enough who those girls were, and what Sandra did."

"I hope you do find them, but I'm sure you'll also find out that Sandra was defending herself."

"You're something, Mister Greene, an expert after one day."

"No, not at all, I just—"

"Please send Charmane out. I'll wait."

Shit. He walked in, came to Charmane's desk and whispered to her. "The vice-principal is waiting to talk to you."

"Mister Godina?"

"The other one, uh, Mrs. Isha—"

"Ishimoto." She practically spat the name. "I won't talk to her."

"But you said—"

She gritted her teeth. "Mister Godina or Mister Schultz, not that bitch."

Some nearby kids chortled. "Charmane, you can't—"

"I know. Sorry, I won't swear anymore." Her little nub of a chin lowered into a pout. "I hate her."

"Okay, take it easy. Just tell her you want to talk to someone else."

"I don't want any trouble, Mister Greene, but I won't talk to her at all."

"All right, I'll go out with you." Allen turned to the class. "Okay, everybody back to your writing." He walked into the hall with Charmane, who brought along her things.

Ishimoto no longer had the pseudo-smile pasted on her face. "I don't have all day, Mister Greene."

"Charmane would like to talk to Mister Schultz."

The vice-principal peered condescendingly down at the small girl's plain apparel. "Fine, come with me." Ishimoto resurrected the grin and walked off briskly, her high heels reporting on the slick floor like steady muffled gunshots. Charmane followed her and turned back to Allen, glumly circling her crown with a forefinger, then pointing at Ishimoto.

Yeah, but how much pull does she have? He hurried back into the room. "Good, it looks like most of you were writing—sorry I couldn't help more. We still have a few minutes. Keep going, or read what you've written."

He had difficulty concentrating on a few questions from the kids before the bell. "Okay, see you tomorrow." After their end-of-day mad dash, he exhaled deeply as the last student left. Static began on the PA, then Venable announced that new teachers were to meet with Schultz in the morning. He quickly collected all the papers, intending to go right downstairs to find the principal.

Venable came on again, shouting over some racket in the background. ". . . a change for tomorrow. The meeting for new teachers is postponed. Instead, the entire faculty will meet in the cafeteria before school about today's incident in girls' P.E. If you have any new information related to that, let me know, and I'll get you in to see Mister Schultz before you leave. Also, don't forget to turn in your . . . ."

Allen hit the intercom button as soon as Venable finished. She came on right away. "What is it, Mister Greene?"

"I have information on the P.E. incident."

"Stay there."

Yeah, boss. He waited for at least a minute, staring at the first day's accumulation of student writing.

"Mister Greene?"

"Yes, I'm here."

"Mrs. Ishimoto said they already have your information."

"Wait—" The PA clicked. Allen started to go down there anyway, but he stopped—they probably wouldn't talk to him after he pissed off Ishimoto. *At the meeting, then. Great.*

He walked to a window and watched three elbow-to-elbow middle-aged white female teachers quickly cross the courtyard, two in suits, one in a dress, looking around warily as they chatted. Allen tried to study their faces. Were Ishimoto, Venable and the interviewers an accurate sample of the staff, or were there more like Dorsey?

Back at his desk, he started on the first paper from Creative Writing. Denise wrote that she would change all the P.E. teachers into frogs. He finished all but two of the rest; their writing wasn't much better than his regular classes—from very good to nothing at all.

Allen had kept Charmane and Ronnie's papers for last. He read hers, a half-finished account of the P.E. incident in angry, precise detail—no new names, as expected. Ronnie gave plausible reasons why the school needed a vegetable garden, aquariums, and a bird pen on the roof to raise pigeons. Allen clipped on a cover sheet, then corrected papers for another hour and a half.

He got home at dusk. Unexpectedly, Trudy's '56 "Ladybug" was parked in the driveway. Rick had refurbished the VW before they were married, then he gave it a coat of red paint and added round black spots. Trudy didn't have the heart then to tell him that he overdid it.

Walking in the front door, Allen smelled chicken frying but didn't see Trudy. He put his holey box on the dining-room table, trying not to bother

Pedro's slumber. The toilet flushed, then his very round sister wobbled in from the hall in a plain white peasant blouse that served well as maternity wear.

Trudy was about five-seven like their mom but with the paternal black hair that she usually kept straight and in a ponytail. She had the same fair skin and black eyes as Allen, but not his bulbous nose or dimpled chin. Her pregnancy somehow didn't betray the good looks and slender symmetrical features she had inherited from their mother.

"You been here a while?" He nodded to the kitchen.

"I was sick again. I'm finished with that crappy job."

"Good, about time. Why don't you take it easy, I know how to fry a chicken."

"Thanks, but I need to keep moving as much as I can." She started for the kitchen. "Hang on, Allen, I want to hear everything about today. You look like you could use a beer."

"Sure could, thanks."

She turned the chicken, then came back with a bottle and sat across from him with an eager smile and a glass of water. She laughed at his fruit box. "Nice briefcase, Bear."

He grinned. "It's just right, Turd-ee."

"Haven't heard that one for a while. Are you going to tell me about your first day or not?"

"Sure, if you want." He took a slug of beer. "When did Rick say he's coming?"

"He's working a little late."

"Bull, his truck was at Bill's, or I would've stopped."

"I don't want to talk about him."

Allen started on a general rundown of his day, stopping for questions and for Trudy to turn the chicken. He told her some details about the homeroom mix-up, the first-period incident, the kids' writing, and especially the situation with Sandra.

She shook her head. "That's awful, what will you do?"

"Try to speak up for her, I guess."

"You damn well better." She smiled. "I thought you'd go back—if you make it to Friday, Rick has to fork over ten bucks."

"Good, I could use some extra incentive."

Trudy walked away, turned off the stove, then returned. "I know it's only one day, but how are you feeling about the whole idea of teaching?"

"It happened so fast—one minute scared of the kids, the next minute impressed by them, and then pissed off by that vice-principal." He scoffed a little. "It was pretty intense—seems like the sort of thing *you* always wanted to do."

Sitting down a chair closer to him, she sighed. "Yeah, let's not start on that. I've got to live with my decisions."

"Whatever you say, but he's lying to you again. God knows what else he's doing."

"He's making enough money to pay for the baby and for me not to work for a while."

"Three cheers, how long since he slugged you?"

"Don't exaggerate, Allen. He hasn't touched me since I started showing."

"Big deal, being a father won't change him."

"That's my problem."

"Okay, but I'm going to look for an apartment soon, whether I stick with this job or not."

"Maybe that is for the best, but this is still your house too. I have some money saved—I can help you."

"No thanks." He drained the rest of the beer, picked up his box, and turned to Pedro. "Still asleep."

"That little stinker has been good company."

"Yeah, I'll see you later. I'm going to the library."

"What about dinner?"

He headed for the back door. "Rick won't miss his meal, and I don't feel like listening to his BS tonight."

"Allen, if you do move, you'll still see me, won't you?"

"Of course, but not here if I can help it."

6

Not long after the dawn of what was to be his second day of teaching, Allen left home even earlier, again avoiding Rick. Some lights were on in back rooms of the tidy stuccos and frame ramblers in Los Feliz. In one yard, a man in a cardigan polished his antique Model-A Ford; bottles clanked from a block away—a milk-truck driver on rounds. Empty cloth saddlebags on his handlebars, a newspaper boy coasted up a driveway, hopped off, and let his bike fall. An old lady in overalls planted flowers in her small perfect yard. A Japanese gardener, the father of boys Allen knew in school, was edging the lawn of a large home that always looked out of place on the block.

Life in Happy Ranch. His nickname for Los Feliz reminded him of some local history he dug up for a social studies report in high school. The neighborhood's unofficial boundary was up in the Hollywood Hills, but most locals who lived below on what was once a Paleocene flood plain said Los Feliz began at the main entrance to Griffith Park, Allen's childhood stomping grounds. More like a small mountain range, the park was named for its benefactor, a land baron with the redundant name of Griffith Griffith, who was also known for serving only two years in San Quentin after shooting his wife in an alcoholic rage.

To Allen and his fellow urchins, the park was endless miles of sylvan playground and the setting for many of their favorite science-fiction movies. Los Feliz kids were fascinated when suction-cup-fingered aliens from *War of the Worlds* and atomic-mutated ants from *Them* died in the L.A. River near the park. Dan always said it was the smog that got them.

He rolled down his window, listening to the radio: "Yes, warmer today, *Angelinos*—again tomorrow, then a perfect weekend to be outside."

And forget all that crap in the air. His Volvo sputtered as he crossed into the next sleepy block, bringing to mind one of Trudy's wisecracks: *We live between Sodom and Jerusalem—Hollywood and Glendale—where the libertines meet the Daughters of the American Revolution.*

Trudy sometimes pronounced *Los Feliz* in Spanish to piss off locals, who always pronounced it *Loss-FEEL-us.* The original land grant owners named it *Rancho Los Feliz*—Ranch of the Feliz Family. More loosely derived, it could be *Ranch of the Happy Ones*, or *Happy Ranch*—an eternal taunt to the erratic life of Griffith Griffith.

Allen passed some small businesses on Los Feliz Boulevard and crossed over the same concrete sewers—the L.A. River—where the giant movie-ants nested. He approached the Golden State Freeway, where long-ago clandestine raids by Allen and Dan on survey markers in *their* park failed to sabotage the construction of Interstate 5.

In those days, Roy Rogers and Gene Autry were always nearby on their spangled saddles, crooning to the movie cameras not far from Griffith Park. The black celebrities were all buffoons—Buckwheat, Rochester, Amos and Andy. Until later, anyway, when Jackie Robinson and Willie Mays entered their lives.

Allen drove up the freeway ramp, releasing a deep breath that finished as a sigh. How many of his fellow *aliens* would be giving Sandra a fair shake that morning?

About twenty minutes later, he approached the same rundown grocery on the arterial to Marshall. A polished black '61 or '62 Olds with half-moon chrome hubcaps was parked by the building in the shade, the silhouettes of four guys inside, the driver's Afro touching the headliner. Their heads turned, following Allen like the man on the stoop did the day before.

It was 6:35, nearly an hour before his required starting time, when he looked through the school's front door at the empty foyer. About to pound on the door, he put his coffee down and accidentally dropped all the cardboard he was carrying.

"May I help?" someone asked from behind. He turned and recognized her right away, the tiny redheaded woman from the interview panel, the only one besides Godina who hadn't scowled at him. She handed him one of his fallen flat boxes.

"Thanks. Allen Greene, from the interviews." She was at least sixty, though her pale unwrinkled face seemed youthful enough to get away with the crimson lipstick she used. With a broad smile, she shook his hand, bending her head back as if he were seven feet tall, not six-two.

"*Oui, bonjour*, I'm Monique Morgan." She helped him gather the cardboard. "We're neighbors, and in the same department."

"Thanks for the help." After they finished, she hefted her huge straw purse, bulging with books and materials and covered with bright red and orange paper flowers.

As he fitted all the boxes under one arm again, she made a playful smile. "I saw you yesterday, Allen, but you didn't see *me*."

"Oh? Sorry, I had a pretty full day."

"Yes, I know." She slung the heavy purse with difficulty onto her shoulder, then gave him his cup, a wad of keys jangling in her hand. "You're lucky I'm early." She unlocked and pulled open the door, her brocaded silver-streaked orange hair a foot below him as he entered first. As they walked, she looked up and smiled. "So how are you doing after all your trials?"

"Okay, I guess." He glanced at the dark office. "Didn't get off to a very good start with Mrs. Venable—we also had a little mix-up." He explained about the girls' homeroom as they approached the middle stairway.

"They'll straighten it out in a day or two." She chuckled. "Mrs. Venable pretends to be a crosspatch, but our secretaries hold this place together. I tell new people to focus on what she does, not how she sounds." They started up the stairs at her casual pace. Between the lapels of her brown business suit, a stunning turquoise and silver necklace hung down over her well-supported heavy breasts.

Good God, don't look there again. "So you heard about the excitement we had in first period?"

"A little. Do you want to tell me about it?"

"Sure." He gave her a quick summation, finishing as they started up the third flight.

"I think you handled it well for your first time."

"Didn't seem like it. If you don't mind me asking, how often do you deal with something like that?"

She grinned. "Well, the ol' red widow has some tricks up her sleeve, but in a good month things don't get that difficult for me more than once or twice."

"How do you handle it?"

"It nearly always plays out like it did for you—they just leave. If not, and no help comes, I just do what I can to keep anyone from getting hurt, including myself."

They came to the third floor and started down the hall; he shifted the boxes to his other arm. "Have you ever been hurt?"

"Some of my students are quite protective of their doddering old teacher. I've been pushed down a couple of times over the years—no permanent damage."

"Glad to hear that." They stopped outside of Allen's room; he leaned all the cardboard against the wall. "What have you heard about the incident in P.E. yesterday?"

She let her purse down to the floor. "Charmane Muhammad is in my homeroom—she came to me after school with the whole dreadful story. You seem to be in the middle of it."

"Yeah, do you agree that Sandra was defending herself?"

"Absolutely, but she's in a rough spot. I don't know her very well, but it doesn't hurt that she's friends with Charmane, such a wonderful girl . . . ." Monique went on to say that she knew Charmane's brothers and thought very highly of the family. "Greg, uh, Mister Schultz, will try to be fair, but he'll get heat from all directions."

"I haven't even seen the man yet. I sure didn't think much of Mrs. Ishimoto's attitude."

She frowned, it seemed to age her face. "Did you know that some L.A. hysterics believed that the Japanese were using the Watts Towers to spy on the U.S. during the war?"

He chuckled at her strange question. "You're kidding."

"No, it was a similar mentality that sent Japanese-Americans to the internment camps, including Mrs. Ishimoto's family. Unlike many others who suffered that injustice, she developed a cold shoulder for those she considers to be beneath her—I once told her as much to her face. I think it would be best for you to avoid our charming vice-principal as much as possible."

"Yeah, I think you're right." He took out his keys.

She pointed at Allen's stack of cardboard. "So what are all the file boxes for?"

"One for each class—journals."

She strained to lift her purse again. "Good idea, let me know how it works out."

He nodded, watching her move toward the room across the hall. "You weren't kidding, you really *are* my neighbor."

She took out her keys again. "Yes, *amour.*"

Amour? Geez.

"Allen, would you mind if I tagged along with you to our meeting?"

"Not at all. I'll meet you out here—about when?"

"Seven-twenty?"

"Okay, see you then." Allen tossed the cardboard into his room, then ran back down to the car for his teaching box. He left the school's front door ajar so he was sure to get back in.

By seven fifteen, he finished assembling the six file boxes. Allen grabbed his lesson plans, hoping to review them during the meeting. There were a few teachers in the corridor, most walking toward the middle stairwell as Monique left her room. She carried what seemed to be a home-kilned white coffee cup, yellow wildflowers on the sides. He smiled at her.

"All set, *chéri?*" She headed him toward the north stairs, avoiding most of the teachers.

"Monique, do you expect anyone will speak up for Sandra?"

"Mrs. Berg, the girls' counselor, and maybe yours truly—perhaps a couple of others. Are you going to?"

"Probably, but why would anyone listen to me?"

"Some won't, some will."

As they started downstairs, he asked Monique about her teaching assignment. She had been an art teacher for years until reassigned to Harding for budget reasons. She was allowed one period of art but had to teach eighth-grade English and take over the only foreign-language class. "You see, the previous principal overheard me say *oui-oui* on the way to the restroom, and that qualified me to be the French teacher."

His face was blank momentarily before he laughed a bit.

"Sorry, I'm notorious for bad puns. The actual reasons weren't much better—they decided someone with my name and a college French class in 1931 was just who they needed."

They came down to the first floor and walked into the north archway by themselves, then started across the courtyard. She shaded her fair complexion with some papers she had in her other hand. Allen squinted at the opaque sun just above the third story of the cafeteria. He pointed at the building. "What else is in there?"

"You haven't been in Harding Hall? That's the official name, though hardly anyone uses it. It's mostly classrooms on the second and third floors—there are offices behind the kitchen for the cook, nurse, and security guards."

"How many guards?"

"Two, we share one with Grant. I suggest you get to know them soon."

"Right." They came across to the south archway, where several teachers were walking by. Allen moved ahead of Monique, pulled open the cafeteria door, and followed her in.

The walls inside had scars and pocks, poorly disguised by slathered layers of the same off-yellow paint as in his room. Tall windows protected by the ubiquitous green steel grating looked out both sides of the cafeteria to a red brick auditorium on the left, the courtyard and Main on the right. Three cooks in light-blue uniforms scurried around a crusty-looking paneled kitchen and serving line at the far end of the hall. The old cafeteria had one saving grace—warm molecules of pungent cinnamon wafted into Allen's nostrils from baking sweet rolls.

There were two dozen or so long folding tables on wheels, two of them placed between the three outside portals—milk crates, plastic utensils, and napkins on top. About ten tables were set up nearby, where at least thirty pattering teachers milled around a tall coffee pot and a huge tray of rolls.

More of the faculty streamed in from the stairs and doors. The majority of both sexes were in business attire, just a few men in casual work pants and print shirts. A handful of women sported slacks or short skirts; two wore "granny" dresses.

The teachers were almost all white and about evenly split by gender. Perhaps a dozen seemed to fit in Monique's almost-retired category; most of the rest were middle-aged. With the exception of a few individuals in their twenties and a like number of black teachers, the staff resembled the irritable, stodgy faculty at Allen's junior high.

Miss Dorsey sat at the far end of a table where Monique seemed to be leading him. Ishimoto was standing up front with Godina near some chairs set up behind a microphone. At the interview, Allen had pegged the chunky Godina as a middle-class descendant of Mexican immigrants. In his tight suit, the middle-aged vice-principal was about five-six with medium-brown skin, dark brows, short black hair, and a patch of moustache. Since Charmane seemed to be okay with Godina, maybe there was a chance he would support Sandra.

Monique tugged Allen's arm. "How about a sweet roll?"

Sure, Chubs could scarf a few. "No thanks."

She sipped from her cup and sighed. "Well, I guess you should officially meet our department chair." She led him to the near end of Dorsey's table and the pasty-skinned man who had read aloud one of Allen's interview questions as if he were disgusted.

The department chairman began to stand up. In his fifties and about five-nine with a steady cross mien to his round face, he had thin buff-brown hair—the end of a beige necktie stuck out from his tan suit because the slacks were cinched below his protruding paunch. He had a long, quarter-inch silver chain attached to his dark belt, fastened at its other end to a sturdy briefcase; his keys were snug to his gut on one of those retractable metal gizmos the size of a makeup compact.

The man gave Monique a patronizing smile after his eyes had lingered for a moment on her chest. "Good morning, Mrs. Morgan."

"Morning, Simon, uh, Mister Nash." She sounded cordial but distant. "Remember Allen Greene from the interviews?"

"Yes." Nash raised his arm doubtfully. "Mister Greene."

He shook the man's limp hand, making an effort not to be unfriendly. "Good morning." Allen sat on the other side of Monique, away from Nash. At the end of the table, Dorsey wore the same brooch on a different drab suit and chatted with a sober-faced black man in his mid thirties. About to sit down, he was an inch or two taller than Allen, just as heavy, but more muscular; he kept his neat Afro about an inch thick. Wearing slightly worn jeans and a blue denim shirt, he had the proletariat look down pat. Dorsey paused mid-sentence and turned Allen's way; he smiled at her. She just raised a brow to him, then went on talking.

"It shouldn't take long to expel this delinquent," Nash was saying to Monique, intentionally loud enough for anyone within ten feet to hear.

She sighed. "No, Simon, there are extenuating circumstances."

Nash took another furtive peek at her chest. "Not according to *my* information."

Acting as if he didn't hear Nash's snide remark, Allen opened his lesson plans and glowered at them, not able to read a word.

7

A stately, urbane-looking man in a grey suit joined the vice-principals at the head of the meeting. About six-four with a medium build, he was an impressive figure, but the principal was definitely showing his age. Below a full wave of white hair, his features, probably sharply Germanic at one time, drooped like a basset hound.

Schultz spoke to Ishimoto, her outwardly sanguine demeanor on display. Godina just listened, then the vice-principals sat together. She crossed her legs properly, the toe of one patent-leather high-heeled shoe arrogantly tapping the air. More of the faculty filed in, some leaning on the windowsills instead of sitting down. A grey-haired man with a sweet roll, math book and slide rule sat between Allen and Dorsey.

The principal came to the mike. "Okay, we don't have much time." Somber but patient, he waited for his garrulous audience. They finally took the clue; the jabber diminished. A middle-aged man and woman scurried together to Allen's table.

A few more late teachers entered; Schultz didn't even look at them. "Thank you, just the one topic today. If you have other items, please save them for our regular meeting tomorrow." He let that sink in for a moment.

"First, in case you didn't know, Miss Hamblin was released from the hospital with no permanent injuries." He waited for some low griping to peter out. "After I heard her side of the story, she was informed that her services are no longer required. I gave her the option of a hearing—she declined. I'll briefly share with you now what I believe are the facts of the incident. After the bell, Miss Hamblin . . . ."

Allen heard only minor deviations from Charmane's story.

". . . girls who assaulted her, May Jones and Idajean Whitley, are expelled and now in juvenile hall." A satisfied mumble rose from the audience, followed by some applause; Ishimoto gloated to Godina. A tall, blond middle-aged man in sweat clothes came over from a nearby table to shake Ishimoto's hand. The coach's exuberance caused his whistle to swing over and knock the side of her head; she chafed slightly through her pliable smile.

Monique whispered to Allen. "Van Burton, P.E. chair."

He nodded. *Got their pound of flesh—maybe that will help.*

Schultz glared at the mike, then looked up. "The punishment for those girls was pretty clear, but it's not so obvious for Sandra Small." He lowered his eyes. "She won't say she's sorry in so many words—only this: 'I should've just pulled her off my neck. My mistake was pushing her away.'"

He waited again for some grumbling from the audience. "Okay, I heard several strong opinions yesterday and this morning. Many of you believe Sandra's actions were very serious, others consider them mostly justified—I haven't heard much middle ground. He glanced at the two vice-principals. "We have a difference of opinion on whether she should be suspended for ten days or expelled."

Expelled?

The principal stopped talking when a man in a tweed sport coat, apparently a guard, entered holding a walkie-talkie. He went to Schultz and spoke, covering his mouth with a hand.

Monique whispered again. "Are you okay, Allen?"

"No." He watched Ishimoto join Schultz and the guard, who then walked away amidst loud gab from the teachers, their tone now more anxious than accusative.

Ishimoto sat again; Schultz faced the staff. "Nothing to be alarmed about, just a squabble outside."

The grandfatherly principal waited yet again for the grousing to die down. A male teacher at the table behind Allen said, "Means they didn't need an ambulance."

"Back to Sandra." Schultz sounded more forceful. "This is ultimately my decision and I'm leaning one direction, but I want to hear more of your input. I'll take a few more opinions, especially if I have yet to hear from you. I'm also open to any new information, if there is any."

On the other side of Monique, Nash stood up, the chain to his grey briefcase not quite taut. "I would like to respond."

Schultz glimpsed the yellow ceiling, keeping himself from rolling his eyes. "Mister Nash, your opinion on this is already very clear to me."

"As Alliance president, it is my duty to represent our membership."

"Please make it brief."

"From what I have heard, I believe my opinion reflects the overwhelming majority here. To put it plainly, we cannot give the impression that we have *any* tolerance for violence perpetrated against staff. If this child is allowed to return after only two weeks, it sends the message that she got away with striking a teacher. She must be permanently expelled by the school, and she will ultimately face God's judgment for her behavior."

Sitting down smugly, Nash nodded to loud applause and favorable remarks. Three tables away, a lanky older woman in slacks and a long-sleeve shirt raised her long arm. Monique smiled to Allen and said, "Sharon Berg."

Schultz nodded. "I've also heard from you, Mrs. Berg, but it's only fair for you to respond. Please go ahead."

"Thank you." She stayed seated, stroked her short boyish brown hair once, then turned to Nash. "This *child*, as you call her, gave birth to her own child last July, and if she is going to face judgment from God, Mister Nash, so will you." Ignoring a few gasps, Mrs. Berg turned to the principal. "I want it made very clear that against all odds, Sandra has managed admirably to take some control of her life. Since September, her behavior has been just fine, and she has formed new friendships here with positive role models like Charmane Muhammad and . . . ."

The guy who made the ambulance remark mumbled, "Muslim."

Berg was concluding her remarks. ". . . I hope you consider those facts when—"

"Your comments are irrelevant, Mrs. Berg." Nash was back on his feet. "Her personal situation is no excuse for striking a teacher. Most of us would never tolerate such behavior, and we cannot allow permissiveness and the resulting savagery to take over this school and undermine what we have accomplished."

Strong applause followed again. One lady shouted, "That's right!" The same smart aleck at the next table said something about *Simon's briefcase,* which brought gales of laughter from the teachers around him. Monique cringed to Allen.

Nash was still standing. "And I might add that—"

"You have had your say, Mister Nash." Schultz faced the counselor. "Mrs. Berg, did you finish?"

"Not quite. Mister Nash has now exaggerated twice. *Striking* someone is not the same as a push. That's all I have to say." A middle-aged man in a summer suit sitting across from Mrs. Berg made a show of reproachfully shaking his head toward her.

"Who's that guy, Monique?" Allen asked quietly.

"Fogle, boys' counselor."

His mouth close to the mike, Schultz sighed. "All right, are there any comments or opinions I have *not* heard before?"

The teachers looked around at each other. Monique nodded to Allen encouragingly. He stood slowly; many in the audience turned his way.

Schultz started to address him. "Mister, um . . . ." The principal leaned over to Godina.

Allen had a strange sensation that he was removed somehow, watching himself. Mrs. Berg's slender mouth was open in apparent surprise, but she looked at him hopefully.

Schultz turned, clearing his throat. "Mister Greene, my apologies to you and all eight of our new teachers." He sighed again. "Well, seven now—we will meet soon. Go on, please."

Allen had to release his dry tongue with some spit. "I, uh, don't agree with Mister Nash on at least two other points."

Nash chortled. "I only made one point." Titters from the faculty followed his comment.

"Actually, I think you made three or four." Some teachers by the windows had stopped chatting to face Allen. "You said there should be no tolerance for staff being assaulted, which I'm sure we all agree with, but you also assumed Sandra was part of the assault and had no right to defend herself."

"Ridiculous." Nash started to get up again.

Schultz glared at him. "Mister Greene has the floor."

Dorsey, expressionless, watched Allen; he turned to Schultz. "It seems to me those other girls are being justly punished, but Sandra's situation is much different. It was Sandra who was acting in self-defense—the P.E. teacher apparently manhandled her for disobeying an unreasonable order. The teacher incited this, which I assume is why you dismissed her." The crowd began grousing again; both Nash and Van Burton jumped to their feet.

"Quiet please." Schultz was louder than before. He faced Allen. "Did you finish, Mister Greene?"

"Almost. Mister Nash also said that Sandra's personal life and her progress were irrelevant—I think they *are* relevant. She seems to take her parental responsibilities very seriously, and she's already shown me that she cares about her education." Allen saw another smile from Mrs. Berg; Monique patted him on the arm. He sat to very scattered applause, then the long room was momentarily silent as two cooks hauled a large metal vat toward the portals—another worker followed with a tall cart of steaming sweet rolls.

"Mister Schultz." A thin woman of average height stood up just a table away.

"Librarian," Monique whispered. In a charcoal suit, the woman's brown hair was in a tight bun; she wore little or no makeup behind black-rimmed glasses on a thin chain. Not even middle-aged, she looked very pleased with her prematurely achieved matronly script.

"Mrs. Anders." Schultz sounded polite, but his blank face said that he'd rather pass on her comment.

"Our newer faculty," she paused as if *faculty* were an overstatement, "are not aware of prior anti-social behavior of students such as Sandra Small. It isn't appropriate for me to mention her previous offenses now. It is sufficient to say that before she came here, Sandra Small repeated sixth grade for *good* reason." Her emphatic finish brought supportive applause.

Schultz's face was somewhere between a stare and a glare. "Has she had any serious trouble with you, Mrs. Anders?"

The librarian was momentarily dumbstruck. "Um, well, nothing serious I can recall right now, but Sandra does not show proper respect. I am sure that other teachers have had—"

"Okay, I'm not aware of any major scrapes for Sandra this year. Anyone have conflicting information on that?" Schultz paused; Miss Dorsey's burly friend grinned to himself.

Nash stood so fast that his chain caught on the corner of the table, yanking his briefcase. "First, a novice teacher's bad judgment is not the issue, and it doesn't matter if the child's behavior has improved." He was practically shouting. "This latest incident, *pushing* a teacher to the floor," he snarled at Mrs. Berg, "supersedes everything. She must be expelled." He took his seat, again to loud support.

Monique stood up slowly. "Mister Schultz."

The principal's face seemed to relax a little. "Mrs. Morgan."

"Yes, I taught my two daughters to resist abuse, and I'm sure that those on our staff who have children did likewise. Why would we expect less from our students?" She paused. "Sandra defended herself from that woman, and then did not join the assault—she should not be suspended at *all*." Monique sat to groans and faint applause. Allen patted her on the back; Nash gave her a sour look.

"Thank you," Schultz said, "though I must tell you I am not considering the option of no punishment. Anyone else?" Two teachers stood just as the cooks unlocked the portals to some students in line. Both teachers sat back down, and many others watched the portals uneasily.

"All right, I think all viewpoints have had their say. We only have fifteen minutes before the first bell. I'm going to give you my deci—"

Van Burton was halfway to his feet. "We should vote."

"As I said, this decision is up to me, and I am no longer hearing anything new."

Nash stood again. "I agree with Mister Van Burton. We should have a vote so you can see how strongly we are united on this issue." This time, the support for Nash was not as loud.

Mrs. Anders got up again, nervously glancing at the kids. "We have time for a private written ballot." Her suggestion rejuvenated some strong applause.

Schultz squinted, looking almost cross. "No, this is not a democratic exercise, my decision is made. However, if you wish, you can have a show of hands." He paused for more grumbling. "Okay, Mister Nash, conduct your poll—make it quick."

Still standing, Nash pointed at the portals. "Perhaps you could have those windows closed, Mister Schultz."

"I'm not going to do that."

Nash scowled. "All right, those who agree with, um, my position show hands and keep them up." Maybe half raised an arm, including two black teachers—an older man nearby, and a young P.E. teacher with Van Burton. At Allen's table, the math teacher, the couple who came in late, and Nash voted.

Nash finished counting and scribbled on some paper. "I make out thirty-seven votes, well over fifty percent." He sounded miffed by his own exaggeration. "Those who agree with Mrs. Berg." Nash counted a scattering of voters, including Allen, Miss Dorsey, and Monique, who raised her arm reluctantly.

"Thirteen, which means about twenty did not vote." Nash sneered at Dorsey's friend. "That still leaves us with a very strong statement of how most of us feel on this issue."

"Okay, Mister Nash, you had your vote." The principal barely paused. "My decision is suspension for ten school days."

Complaints erupted; Nash pointed at Schultz. "At the very least, you should double the suspension."

"Have a seat, Mister Nash." Schultz glared at him until he sat down. "Quiet please." He waited again, then spoke over the remaining noise. "Mrs. Berg, please arrange for Sandra's schoolwork." He faced the whole audience. "Teachers are expected to cooperate with Mrs. Berg's requests. Okay, that's it—everyone try to have a good day."

Most of the faculty started to leave, but Nash and a couple of others immediately cornered Schultz to bicker. Allen got up from the bench and heard a lot of teachers complaining as they herded themselves to the exits. Monique went over to Mrs. Berg.

The imposing man who was sitting with Dorsey walked right for Allen. As he approached, his eyes seemed aggravated and droopy at the same time; his complexion had the sheen of a pecan shell. "I'm Frank Williamson, Social Studies—I need to talk to you for a second outside."

Allen nodded, then they walked together to the south exit. Williamson took a pen from his denim shirt pocket, where he wore a picture button of a familiar-looking middle-aged black woman. "I'm helping Mrs. Berg." Eyes forward, he spoke in a full but very deep voice, unconcerned that nearby faculty might overhear.

They entered the archway; Williamson jotted something in his three-ring cloth binder, its orange cover with U.S. GRANT HIGH SCHOOL in black script. "Besides your two classes, Sandra has me in *sosh* and a sub in P.E.—her Math, Science and Home Ec. teachers will stall with her homework."

Allen answered quietly. "But Schultz said they had to cooperate."

He was still looking in his notebook. "Yeah, can you have her work to me tomorrow?"

"Yes."

They walked out of the archway into the courtyard; the non-uniformed guard was on patrol near long lines of students at the portals. Most of the teachers had scattered, but two women glared at Allen. He turned to Williamson. "Do you know what Sandra's troubles were in elementary school?"

He was writing again. "I guess she was a brawler—even beat up some boys. Missed a lot of school."

"Can I ask why you didn't speak up for her?"

He raised his thick brows but still didn't face him. "It wouldn't have helped—I sat this one out."

"I noticed you didn't vote."

His eyes narrowing critically, Williamson finally looked at Allen again. "I knew the suspension was coming. Besides, my vote was with Mrs. Morgan."

"Yeah, that should've been an option."

They stopped in the middle of the courtyard at a brick kiva, about ten feet across, probably a garden at one time. Williamson put his foot on the short wall, flipping to a different page. Three kids, eating nearby, walked slowly away.

Allen stared at a thin cypress in the middle of the kiva—beneath it, wads of old chewing gum pebbled the hard dirt. A galvanized trash can nearby smelled of sour milk. "Don't you think Schultz did all he could?"

"It helps that he's a short-timer." Williamson kept studying the notebook.

"What do you mean?"

"Schultz is retiring—he's actually stood up to them three or four times this year."

"Oh. What's the story with the vice-principals? Godina seems okay."

He faced Allen again. "Ricky *Guh-dye-nuh*—that's what he calls himself— Ricardo usually goes along with the status quo."

"I already had a run-in with Mrs. Ishimoto over Sandra."

Williamson's solemn face momentarily shadowed a smile. "Well, that's to your credit." He put his leg down. "That woman is a menace, a cop in a bad crime movie—Mrs. Moto, like the detective."

What detective?

The social studies teacher frowned again, closing his notebook. "Here's another news flash for you—Moto, Ricardo, and some guy from Verdugo Hills are the three finalists to be the new principal." Williamson walked away without another word.

8

Allen continued with *firm but fair* that Wednesday, starting with what was still a girls' homeroom. Plenty of juvenile antics counteracted his rigidity during the day, as well as a couple of minor confrontations. The worst incident was a fight between two small boys over, of all things, a toy car. They landed some glancing blows before he stopped it, eventually taking them to Godina, but it was such a generic kids' tussle that Allen laughed about it to himself.

He worked on some papers after school, then went downstairs to ask Venable for an outside key. She said there weren't any extra keys and told him that after he got into "the swing of things," he wouldn't need one. On the way back to his room, he stopped in to see Monique. Allen knocked and entered, finding her stirring some yellow tempera paint at a sink near the end of the long counter beneath her windows.

"Another day under your belt, *mon ami*. How did it go?"

"Better than yesterday, as far as discipline. I do have some good writers—Charmane is one of them."

"I hear the inevitable *but* coming."

"Yeah, from what I've seen so far, their abilities run the gamut from illiterate to poetic."

She kept stirring. "Yes, very true."

"I had fewer kids today—only two of my classes were about the same between the two days. Is it always like that?"

"We have some stable times, but attendance is always a problem."

He tried to disguise a sigh. "I just have a couple of ideas about what to

64

teach. Once I have a better grip on what they can do, I was hoping for some help from you."

"Of course, whenever you're ready." She began pouring the paint into jars.

He told her what Venable said about the key. "What does she mean by the *swing of things*?"

"It means here at seven-thirty when they open the front door and gone at three-fifteen when they lock up—the minimum."

"I need more time than that before school."

"I'm sure you do." She made a droll smile. "The *key* to your problem, pun intended, is that I am almost always here right at seven. Why don't you just meet me near the guard shack a little before seven tomorrow?"

"Okay, that will help a lot."

"I'll be glad to have the escort, which reminds me that I have another favor to ask."

"Sure."

She was securing lids on the jars. "When we have student assemblies or activities, would you mind if we take our classes down together?"

"I don't mind at all."

"*Merci*. As they say, strength in numbers." She put the jars in the cupboards, then turned to him and began to wash up. "So how are you feeling about Sandra's inquisition?"

He vaulted back onto the counter, dangling his legs. "Thirteen votes—pretty lousy."

Drying her hands, she sat down—you could barely see her desk for all of the student art projects on display. "Try not to be too discouraged."

"I just hope Sandra isn't."

"Charmane doesn't think so." She sighed. "You have a few enemies now, but that was inevitable. You did the right thing."

"Yeah, so did you and Mrs. Berg. I liked what you said about your daughters. Are they in L.A.?"

"No, one in San Francisco, and one farther up the coast. Anyway, it's easier for Sharon and me to rock the boat a little—we're too old for anyone to bother." She smiled. "You give us some hope, *chéri*."

"C'mon, I'm just trying to make it through the week."

She chuckled a little, straightening some student papers at a small side table. "Oh, I think you'll pull that off."

"I appreciate the encouragement. I met Frank Williamson after the meeting—he gets along with Ishimoto about like I do."

An uncharacteristic frown showed some age lines around her mouth. "Frank's heart is always in the right place. Mrs. Ishimoto keeps waiting and hoping for him to slip up."

"Does she really have a shot at being the principal?"

"Worse than that, she has the inside track."

"Good God." He sighed. "I suppose Nash supports her."

"Oh, yes. The two of them tried to institute *voluntary* morning prayer after the Pledge. With Greg's help, the ecumenical Christians and some others among us put a stop to it."

"But Nash still likes you, even though you disagree."

She smiled and sighed at the same time. "Which has given me all the more leverage to get what I need around here."

Allen laughed a little. "I see—very practical." He raised a brow. "How does Nash get along with students?"

"He's quite proud that he rarely has confrontations of the sort you had yesterday."

"Are you saying they respect him?"

"No. Since he transferred here from Manual Trades, most of the older students stay away from him as if he's crazy."

"I'll second that."

"They mean crazy as in dangerous."

"Him? Why?"

She leaned over to pick up some papers. "It's not anything to worry about with your seventh-graders, but eventually you'll deal with older kids. Settle in a few more days, then Frank or I will fill you in more on Simon the Zealot."

"What?"

"Of the biblical Simons, that fits him best."

"Great." He hopped down from the counter and started for the door.

"Allen, we do have some good people here. Focus on them and your students, and stay away from the others."

"Yeah, I'm trying."

On Thursday morning, the guys in the black Olds were there, parked on Harding under a tree as Allen made his turn before seven o'clock. He tried to dismiss them to his paranoia and pulled into the lot to wait for Monique, hoping she might clue him in on Miss Watson. *Like she'd go out with a chubby white boy.* He parked and shut off the motor but kept the radio on.

The news was reporting on grievances by black sanitation workers who wanted Martin Luther King to come to Memphis on their behalf. Though not active himself in civil rights or politics, Allen had read about King's connections to Thoreau and Gandhi, guessing that he was probably into Zen as well. He considered Doctor King to be unique in the West, merging a benevolent Jesus with Eastern thought and *Civil Disobedience*.

A ten-year-old red Pontiac with the unmistakable fiery-haired woman behind the wheel pulled into the nearly empty lot and headed for the Volvo. Unlike Allen, Monique didn't close her windows or lock the doors until after she parked.

They both got out. "*Bon jour*, Allen!"

He smiled. "Good morning."

"Yes, a nice quiet one." They started toward the school, Allen carrying his fruit box, she lugging the enormous colorful purse over her shoulder.

"Anyone in there yet, Monique?"

"Yes, Linda and Jean start at seven."

"Linda and Jean?"

"Miss Watson, and Mrs. Eichler, the counselors' secretary."

*So it's Linda—***tan linda***.

"You're smiling, *chéri*."

Blood moved up his face into a full flush as they passed the locked security hut. "Uh, do you happen to know if Miss Watson . . . ." He sighed; they stepped into the crosswalk.

"My, my." She made a teasing smile. "Yes, isn't she a lovely young woman?"

"How long has she been here?"

"Just this year, and I don't think she's in a serious commitment, but I'm not completely sure."

"Oh?"

"Are you much of a religionist, Allen?"

"Uh, Christmas is about it—why?"

"I'm *not* trying to discourage you, believe me, but Linda does belong to a charismatic church."

"Like speaking in tongues, that sort of thing?"

"Maybe not, I don't really know."

"Thanks for telling me." The black car was gone from down the street; she unlocked the door, and he held it for her.

Inside, Monique smiled toward the secretaries. "I'm going straight up. Have a good morning, *amour*."

"Okay, you too." He walked into the office.

Mrs. Eichler, a thin, drab-looking white lady in her forties, was typing at Venable's desk as Miss Watson collated papers at the counter and looked up at him with a sociable but business-like smile. "Good morning, Mister Greene."

"Morning, Miss Watson." He put his box on the counter, removing the lid as if he had to find something.

"Mister Greene, in case you wondered, the homeroom mix-up happened because downtown listed you as *Ellen* Greene." She grinned slightly. "So you and Miss Latham are to switch today—your new list is in your box. They want you to take the girls to her after the tardy bell—359, at the end of your floor."

"Any chance they'd let it stay like it is?" He closed the box, leaving his hands on the lid.

"I doubt it, but you can ask."

"Thanks." Allen started to turn away.

"Mister Greene?"

"Yes?"

Allen had turned so eagerly that she furrowed her brows slightly before smiling. "You and some other new teachers have a meeting at seven-thirty with Mister Schultz."

He could barely look at her. *Bozo*. "Okay, thanks."

"You're welcome." She nodded behind. "You can come back or wait in his office."

Allen left with his box and entered the well-lit lounge, no staff in sight, so he decided to wait there for his meeting. The converted classroom had sofas and plush chairs all around, and one wall with cheap cheery posters where the windows had once been. Behind a long conference table, a door in a partition led to the other half of the room, the teachers' work area.

A white sheet cake on the table had Welcome New Teachers! in cursive scarlet frosting around a red apple, MARSHALL EDUCATION ALLIANCE printed below in green. Sitting far from the cake, he studied and reworked his plans until some jabbering teachers came in at 7:20. Allen put his materials in the box and went out for his mail.

He found the new homeroom list and put it on top of his pile as he returned to Schultz's open door. Looking in before entering, the vacant office was barely large enough for two tall bookcases, shelves, and a modest desk.

He took a wooden chair from a stack by the door, unfolded it and sat down. Before he could check his mail, a young woman his age walked in, smiled slightly, and then turned away for a chair. She was a gawky five-ten or so with dark-brown hair that almost filled the white square on the back of her crisply ironed sailor outfit. She faced him, her gaunt angular features and pocked complexion somewhat mitigated by heavy makeup and her lustrous hair. She made a nervous giggle and sat, properly smoothing the sides of her navy-blue skirt.

"Hi, I'm Allen Greene." He reached down for his mail.

"Sydney Latham. Isn't it hilarious?" Her full smile revealed a small retainer on her upper front teeth. "They took me for a male and you for a female."

"Yes. Hilarious."

"You've heard we're switching? Well, of course you have. Wait until you see what they did for us in the lounge."

God, it's Olive Oyl. Allen attempted a friendly nod as she kept talking. He looked at the principal's books, diplomas, trophies, and family photos, then heard the end of her question.

"... decided what you'll take for extracurricular?"

"I didn't know I had to."

"I have Good Grooming—I'm very pleased," she hardly took a breath, "and everyone's so nice here, and so helpful. Oh, we're in the same department too."

"Are we?" He picked up a stapled note that he hadn't noticed.

"Yes, I have two Home Ec. classes and four eighth-grade Language Arts—so I'm with the English department most of the time. I didn't think you were the one who quit."

Allen looked up. "What do you mean?"

She was checking her clear-polished nails. "There's a rumor that a new

English teacher quit. After you spoke up at the meeting, they were sure it was you."

They? He opened the paper.

"So where did you do your fifth year and student teaching?" she asked.

"I didn't." Peripherally, he saw her stand to peek through the curtain into the outer office.

"Oh. I'm working on my Master's at UCLA."

"When the smog lifts."

"What?"

He didn't face her. "You see—L.A."

"Oh," she said again, then sat down quietly.

Allen's note was from Godina. Michael had been caught with a weapon and expelled, Rupert suspended for the previous day plus detention. He picked up the new homeroom list and spotted *Marlon Brown* and *Darrel Hayes* as the door opened. The young black teacher who was so chummy with Van Burton walked in ahead of Schultz. His natural hair trimmed to a quarter-inch, the new coach was a bit shorter than Allen but obviously muscular, even in sweats.

The principal made hasty introductions, then he said that the new math teacher was absent; the other two new hires were veteran substitutes who already knew the ropes. He explained some procedures, then handed out more paperwork, mentioning the homeroom switch.

Allen cleared his throat. "Wouldn't it be easier if we didn't change?" He saw Latham's jaw drop.

Schultz shook his head. "No, we can't do that. You're supposed to have them for three years—that's the concept anyway." He then "volunteered" the PE teacher and Allen for small stipends to be two of the four sponsors for boys' intramural sports. Allen told him he didn't have much experience, but Schultz smiled and said, "Welcome aboard." The jock smirked, no doubt looking forward to creaming Allen's teams.

Latham clapped once, making a sappy smile. "My Good Grooming girls could do some cheers for *all* the teams." The PE teacher grinned; Allen checked his homeroom list again—his eyes went right to *Rupert Washington* at the bottom.

"...have plenty to do, Miss Latham," Schultz was saying, then he frowned.

"We've probably lost that math teacher, which makes three already, but don't let that be discouraging. I expect that you three and the other two will hang in there and do a good job."

Sure. He walked out a few feet behind Latham, who was nattering into the PE teacher's ear. Schultz had given them all a time and station for assigned duty; a guard would be there for the first one. Allen leaned his box on the counter, away from Venable. "Miss Watson, may I leave this behind here? I'm on duty right now."

"That's fine, Mister Greene."

"Thanks." After putting the box down, he hurried out to the courtyard. The non-uniformed guard was standing in the sun near the south archway. Without his coat, tie, and short blond hair, the guy could have passed for Allen's brother. Just over six feet tall with a slight beer-belly, he had a puffy ordinary face and trimmed mutton chops. Perhaps five years Allen's senior, the guard had two small black leather cases attached to his belt.

"Mister Greene?" His *mister* sounded like *mistuh.*

"Yes, it's Allen."

"I'm Cecil Walls, pleasure t' meet ya'."

They shook hands. "Hi, Cecil."

"So this here's pretty calm before school—be glad you're not here at noon." His twang was so loud that anyone within fifteen feet could probably hear him. In the shade of the archway, throngs of students and a few staff members filed back and forth between the two buildings, some of the kids heading for the benches under the eucalyptus.

Cecil buffed one of his black steel-toed shoes on the back of a pant leg, then he turned toward the scores of kids in the three lines up to the cafeteria, where the other guard watched over them; Cecil pointed that way. "That there's Nick Deniker."

Deniker likely heard his name but didn't respond. He wasn't as young or tall as Cecil; it was hard to tell if he was brawny or just heavy in his loose grey khaki uniform, a security patch on one arm. Deniker wore a tan cap, its flat bill down over sunglasses; his pink chin was all you could see of his face. He had more paraphernalia attached to his belt than Cecil did.

"I'm reg'lar at this school—Deniker's in charge here an' at Grant." He finally lowered his voice. "He don't say much but knows what he's about when

71

it comes to kickin' butts." A group of kids milled around the kiva; a boy tossed his gum, bouncing it off a girl who sat on the short wall, drinking juice. She loudly cussed the boy out; Deniker approached them.

Cecil turned from the little spat. "Yup, quiet this time a' day, but most staff call this here the coliseum."

"What?"

"You know, like in biblical days, folks gettin' slaughtered an' all."

"Isn't that a bit much?"

Cecil laughed a little. "Ask me that after a week 'r two." He raised an arm to point again. "Down that end's where the other teacher's at. Even better duty than what you got—that door there to the cafeteria's usually locked."

The faraway teacher's back was visible in the shade of the other arch; the few kids down there avoided him as if he had foul body odor. The man turned slightly, showing his telltale chain and briefcase.

"Anyway, this here's also your emergency station—you an' the boys' counselor. He's here at noon, when he shows."

"Emergency station?"

Cecil grinned at what he seemed to think was a naïve question. "We shut down sometimes for emergencies, an' they ask ya' to be here. Let's see, since I come this year, it's four times. Had us a outsider shoot out some windows, an' we shut down for a high-school fight that—" He stopped because a girl ran right up behind him, shielding herself from a boy who was chasing her.

"Y'all move on now." Cecil turned from the kids, smiling. "Most of 'em ain't bad. Them ninth-graders got more schoolin' than me—got my certificate in the army." He made a self-deprecating laugh. "Anyway, we had two a' our own big fights an' kept 'em from turnin' bigger." He squared his shoulders proudly. Deniker came back within twenty feet or so, but he stayed away, aloof and suspicious.

"We got all the latest crowd control devices." Cecil pronounced it, *DEE-vices*, pausing to affectionately pat a case on his belt. "This here handles most problems, an' it—"

"So what do *I* do?"

Cecil frowned a bit at Allen's change of subject. "Jus' remind 'em of the rules. It gets serious, call us or go to the office." He touched a bulge at the other side of his coat, likely a radio. "Y'r here 'til the warnin' bell from the gym."

"Okay, got it. I take it you're not from L.A., Cecil."

He smiled. "My Razorback accent stands out here, don't it? You from L.A.?"

"Born and bred."

"Dodger fan?"

"No, Pirates—the Hollywood Stars were their farm team."

"I get ya'. That Clemente's a great player, but the Cards'll do it again this year . . . ."

They talked baseball right up to the warning bell. Allen went in, took his time getting the box from near Miss Watson's desk, then hurried upstairs. *Got your smile, cad.* Back on his floor, the passing bell had rung and most of the girls were waiting by the door, not even fooling around. At the north end of the hall, the boys boiled out of Latham's room, some of them yelling and slamming lockers.

He came to his door. "Morning, girls, today's the day. I'm taking you down to Miss Latham."

One girl feigned a pout. "You don't like us, huh?"

"You know this is the way they do it. I'll see a lot of you in English or Creative Writing."

Denise scowled at a friend. "Least we ain't got him three times no more." The girls started some nervous banter about the sudden change.

"Okay, keep the same locks—clear out your space and then we'll go quietly."

They were ready when the tardy bell rang. Allen led them down the hall; Latham was helplessly shushing the boys as Denise came up to them. "Fools, get outta our way." Many of the boys just waited, some seething; the girls laughed at the ones who cringed by the walls.

Allen stopped and signaled with a hand. "All right, let's go, guys." They walked slowly ahead, a lot of them moping. About half of the boys looked like elementary-school kids; three of the others were in gold, and five in black, including Marlon, who dutifully followed Rupert.

The scar on Rupert's chin mimicked his downturned mouth as he faced Allen. "Michael said he's gonna see you, Greene."

"Is that supposed to be a threat?"

"Jus' passin' on what he said."

Acting unconcerned, he told the boys to keep moving. Behind, some girls squabbled over their lockers; Latham whined at them. Round little Darrel clutched his padlock and waddled down the hall, staying near Allen.

Cecil came to the top of the middle stairway and walked quickly toward them. From several feet away, the guard called out. "What's alla this?"

Marlon laughed, then mumbled, "Cracker." Some of the other boys snickered.

"Just switching homerooms, Mister Walls."

Cecil looked past him at the commotion down at Latham's room. "Best see if she needs help."

As soon as Cecil went by, some of the boys ran off to get first dibs on a locker; Allen walked faster. "All right, take it easy; they're all the same."

A small fair-skinned boy already staked claim to one of the lockers by the room. Half his body inside, he looked up and out at Rupert. "I was here first—can't have it, big ugly nigger!" Allen race-walked toward them.

"You dead, T.R." Rupert reached down to grab him, but a tall kid in gold jumped on his back, and they started landing blows; the other boys in gang colors began shoving each other around—arms, padlocks and books flying.

Allen pushed through the spectators. "Knock it off, now!" The scuffling stopped as soon as he shouted, probably because Cecil had returned. The boy in gold had a swollen eye and was staggering; both he and Rupert kept their fists cocked. Darrel and some small boys cowered in Monique's doorway.

Holding a canister, Cecil had situated himself right between the two rivals. "Okay, who wants some a' this?" They lowered their arms; the guard frisked them both at the wall, finding a knife on Rupert.

As Cecil led them away, the small thin boy was still inside the locker. In a Mister Magoo T-shirt, he had a freckled dun-brown face and very long auburn hair, which Marlon was clutching as if he were about to take a scalp. Allen glared at him. "Let go of him right now."

Marlon stood up straight, releasing the boy's hair; he wiped his hand on his jeans as if he had contracted cooties. "You hippie punk, T.R. I'll get you later."

T.R. launched himself from the locker toward Marlon, but Allen easily caught the slight boy by the shoulders. Monique peeked out of her door and saw Allen holding back a dervish of flailing limbs that kept yelling, "Lemme go!"

"When you calm down." The boy squirmed again, then went half-limp. "All right, everybody in—let's go." He released T.R., who grumbled and walked to the door; Allen turned to the others. "Marlon, you're going to leave him alone, got that?"

"You can't do nothin' after school."

T.R. sniggered. "You'll never catch me, elephant butt."

Allen walked in, ordering everyone to sit down and be quiet. About half of the boys were new to him, so as soon as they settled, he started on his discipline speech. When he came to the part about the rule chart, Marlon interrupted.

"Ain't no golden rules, jus' black rules." Behind Marlon, the other three remaining boys in black laughed.

He pointed at them. "In here, you follow the *Greene* rules . . . ." Allen finished his speech and made everyone stay seated. He kept an eye on those four boys; maybe Marlon would talk to him about Michael when the others weren't around.

9

Homeroom turned out to be the roughest part of that day. Allen had two bonuses after school, the last-minute cancellation of the regular staff meeting, and the news that a PE teacher would take his intramural teams.

He got out of there before four-thirty, walked to the lot and finally met the parking guard, who looked his part in a light-blue uniform, though he had no security devices. Tall and heavy-set with wizened dark-brown skin, greying hair, and a steady wide smile, the man had just closed the door of the hut as Allen walked up the driveway.

"Afternoon, Mister. New teacher?"

"Hi. Yes, Allen Greene."

"Name's Marv." They shook hands. "I guess that little ol' grey job over there'd be you." He pointed to the nearby Volvo among six or seven cars remaining in the lot.

"Yeah, how did you know?"

Marv chuckled. "Well, you're young—that usually fits a primered car with no chrome. Gonna paint it?"

"Someday, I guess—stopped the rust, anyway."

"Yes sir, ya' did." Marv laughed. "Yup, it's always between here an' the street, an' still there when I get off. Means ya' come early and go late." He reached for a padlock.

"You're quite the detective, Marv."

The guard grinned. "Part a' my job, Mister." He bolted and locked the door.

Allen waved. "Okay, see you later."

He made it out of the neighborhood well before dark but didn't go home. Allen had left Trudy another note; he stopped for fast food again, then did his schoolwork at the library.

On Friday morning, he had cereal with Trudy—Rick was already gone to the beach. Allen watched for the black Olds on the last blocks to school, but he didn't see it. After Monique came, they walked off in some rare steady rain; she asked from under her scarlet parasol why he parked near the back.

"To walk in the rain, I guess." He pulled the windbreaker's flimsy hood over his hastily brushed mop of hair.

"Yes, the air is wonderful, and tomorrow we'll have one more day to breathe all the way in."

"Yeah, I hope my brother-in-law's enjoying it." On the way inside, he told her a little about Trudy and Rick.

Unlike Monique, the other adults he encountered during the day grizzled over the wet weather as if it were a regular event. His homeroom boys were resigned to their new situation, and most of the Language Arts students did their work without much bellyaching. Allen attributed the calm day to the rain and the expulsion or suspension of about half of his twenty or so kids he considered to be aggressively or passively hostile, including Rupert and his adversary in gold, Aaron.

Sitting behind piles of student papers after school, Allen was making some calculations. Besides homeroom, he had a hundred and seventy-nine students, including ten repeats in last period. Attendance hadn't improved, but he did have at least one writing sample from every kid, except for the five no-shows.

Allen waded into the two piles he still had to check. He wrote a brief comment on each paper and made a tally before going on. He finished in an hour and a half and came up with a preliminary estimate—almost a third of his students, more than fifty, demonstrated little or no ability to write.

Suspicious of the tracking system, he dug out the levels for Creative Writing, since those kids were from all three tracks. Already knowing that Ronnie, Charmane, and several more track-one kids could write well, he discovered the complete opposite for three high-level students who, thus far, had showed very low ability. *Tracking system, my ass.* He glanced at the clock— it was almost five and probably too late to talk to Monique.

Allen had left a window open to hear the rain; he leaned back, stared outside at the clouds, then closed his eyes. *Steady drips on metal—tires on the streets—sirens faraway—bickering ravens—a radio—Aretha—r-e-s-p-e-c-t.* The song brought him back—he sat up, trying to focus on the papers in front of him.

There was a soft knock on his door before Monique entered in a dark-crimson suit with costume jewelry, not the usual handcrafted necklace. "Allen, am I bothering you?"

"You can't bother me—I thought you'd be gone."

"I'm just burning some late-afternoon oil like you are—looked in and saw you waking up from your catnap."

"I wasn't exactly napping."

"What do you mean?"

He gestured toward the folding chair by his desk. "I was sort of meditating."

"Oh?" She sat down. "How did you get interested in that?"

"Well, like the kids say, *would you believe* I started reading some Zen Buddhism in a jungle?"

"My, my." She grinned, interested, but not pushy.

Allen looked out; the clouds seemed to be bringing on an early dusk. Below, he didn't see anyone at all.

"Enjoying your bird's eye view of the coliseum?"

"What? Yeah, you really want to hear this?"

"Certainly."

He sighed. "Okay, I'm pretty good at quitting things—dropped out of college a few times before I finally made it. After that, I fooled around in Oregon, then went into the Peace Corps for something to do. They stuck some married couples and a few more of us in a Puerto Rican rainforest for training and Spanish."

"Really? How well do you speak it?"

"I get by. We heard more propaganda than Spanish from our Cuban teachers—I learned more in L.A." He paused. "They also sent us down there to get used to isolation. After two months, I *didn't* get used to it."

"Were you ill?"

Allen's sigh finished as a scoff. "Their damn shrink said I wasn't coping—*reclusive and depressed.* But they had this little library where I found a few

78

books by Zen masters. I came up with my own version of meditation and was actually feeling better before I left. It gives me a way to gather myself."

"Even here?"

"Yes, after things calm down. I figured out down there that when I'm around a lot of noise, I hear everything but listen to nothing. When it's quiet, I hear it all—my big epiphany."

She reflected for a few moments. "Fascinating. Maybe you can recommend some reading to me."

"Sure, but you didn't come to hear my sad little story."

"You shouldn't minimize what you accomplished, Allen." She lowered her eyes, making a rare frown. "Okay, I have a bit of a problem and wanted to ask another favor."

"Ask away."

"My squash-blossom necklace was stolen. I—"

"At school?"

"Yes. I put it in my purse during homeroom yesterday when I was mixing paint and didn't notice it was gone until prep. It was my grandmother's—a century old and one of a kind, so the police say they might have a chance to find it."

"Sorry, Monique, I hope they do."

"After all these years, it hadn't crossed my mind to stop wearing it." She looped a bangle with her forefinger. "It was foolish, and I'm just not as quick on the uptake anymore."

"C'mon, I think you're doing great for—"

"For such an old bat?" She laughed. "I'm sixty-eight, Allen. I'm finally going to retire."

"Oh. What I meant was I see how hard you work and, well, the kids will miss you."

"Thank you, I'll miss most of them." Her smile faded. "Anyway, my homeroom is the problem. I told Greg last year I'd rather not start a new group of seventh-graders, but he talked me into it. After all these months, I still have three or four rough girls I don't know very well. I've never had that many—I usually work things out with anyone who sticks around."

"How can I help?"

"I might need your support if things get crazy and no one happens to be downstairs. I hear the girls talking—some of them think ol' codgers like me just tune them out." She made a self-effacing chuckle. "You have about half of my girls, Allen. What I hear is they already respect your authority."

"I sound tougher than I am, believe me. It bothers me to act like that."

"Most of them understand that it's what you have to do. I think they relate to your youth, and they like that you level with them. Anyway, if there's trouble ahead I can't handle, I might have to call on you—probably won't even happen."

"Whatever I can do." He glanced at all the papers in front of him. "Will you miss teaching, Monique?"

"I still plan to teach art, maybe at night school."

"That's great."

"Yes, my passion, though I feel pretty good about my other work here." She sighed. "But the timing is right for me to go, especially if Mrs. Ishimoto is the new principal."

"Do most of the kids despise her like Charmane does?"

"She sponsors the Honor Society—a few of those kids patronize her, just enough that she thinks she gets along with the *right kind* of students. Mrs. Ishimoto is also my evaluator."

"Man, how do you deal with that?"

"Quite easily. She breezes through my room twice a year and writes the same blithering nonsense every time."

"Oh." *Wait.* "Is that how it works for Nash and Anders?"

"Yes, once the door closes, veterans are avoided like the plague. Allen, like any good teacher, you hold *yourself* accountable. You can't control the rest of it."

"You really think I can do this."

"Yes, *amour.*"

"We'll see. Got a minute for a couple questions?"

"Of course." She glanced at his file boxes. "How are the journals working out?"

"Fine for some, not so hot for others. I finished their first two papers, and I'm trying to decide what to do about . . ." As he shared some of his observations, she mostly nodded, or added examples to back him up. ". . . and haven't the kids been drilled for years on letter sounds and grammar?"

"Yes, and penmanship—some have lovely handwriting but can't read it, and there are others who can read aloud with no idea what they're saying."

"Shouldn't I try something different?"

"Yes, it's never one way fits all, though that's what our curriculum provides. I have a method that should help with some of your struggling kids. We can go look at my materials."

"That'd be great. You use this method with track-three students?"

"I usually have a few in each class who somehow tested up, the opposite of Charmane. You're right about the system—it drives some of us crazy, including your mentor, bless her heart. As she always says—"

"We can't give up on any of them."

She chuckled again. "That's right."

"Miss Dorsey is kind of a mystery to me."

"She grew up four blocks from here, a preacher's daughter. I've seen her practically eviscerate new teachers who laugh or brag about using street words like *hip* or *booty* with kids."

"Because it's a bad example?"

"That, and because it's usually condescending."

"I've made my mistakes already, but not that one."

She smirked. "Yes, and you made it to Friday, and you don't sound like someone who's about to quit."

"Yeah, four whole days." He sighed again. "What do you do about the street English?"

"Not much—most of mine can switch at will in and out of the vernacular, like a bilingual skill, and it doesn't show up much in their writing. Some of yours will be able to do the same, but the low literacy kids . . . ."

As they crossed the hall, Monique began to explain a technique she called "recitation."

In her room, she showed him catalogued stories, prompts, fables, music, and even some comic strips she used to motivate low readers to recite. She recorded their responses, then typed them up at home to use as "relevant reading material." She said it often gave reluctant readers more incentive to try.

Adapting her method on a larger scale would be his challenge. "What does the school say about it, Monique?"

She made an impish grin, accentuated by her small stature. "On the rare days I am evaluated, my students just happen to be using the textbook."

"So you play that game in order to teach something useful to all the kids."

"Yes, what our supervisors don't know won't hurt them. It's a game I've always had to play, except in art."

He gazed out at the deepening dusk and the abandoned street. "I guess it's time for white folks to hit the road."

She nodded. "Remember, a lot of people who live here are just as scared as we are."

"Yeah, good point, but since when are you scared?"

"Well, you're not the only one who can act a little."

"Then do you mind if I ask why you've stayed here so long?"

She pondered, grinning slightly. "Let's see, Helen, Milton, Ava, Charmane—"

"Okay." He smiled. "Can we talk more over the weekend about your reading approach?"

"Of course." They exchanged phone numbers, gathered their things, and walked out together to the parking lot.

He drove away with Monique's comments still on his mind. Other than fear, the damn Dodgers, and a new L.A. Zip Code, what else did Los Feliz and Watts have in common? After he left the freeway, Allen stopped to call Trudy, then got a burger before spending his Friday evening at the Glendale library.

A history book exposed a similarity between South-Central and Los Feliz right away—Watts had also been part of a Mexican land grant, *Rancho La Tajauta*. Named for its railroad station, Watts was annexed by L.A. in 1926. In the twenty-plus years since World War II, South-Central became predominantly black as people of all races migrated to the West for opportunity.

After reading that the Watts Towers were built on a whim by an Italian ironworker, Allen switched to some reports on the '65 riots. The statistics shocked him. After the National Guard restored order, more than thirty people had died, a thousand-plus injured, and about four thousand arrested. Hundreds of mostly absentee-owned buildings were burned or looted. The casualties included rioters, cops, firefighters, and whites driving by, but most were local bystanders. Allen discovered that nobody was killed until the third day, after a top L.A. official publicly compared the rioters from the first days to monkeys in a zoo.

Several reports concluded that the destruction was carried out mostly by male youth, triggered by smoldering rancor over unfair and brutal behavior by some LAPD officers, and by sub-standard schools and public hospitals. A federal commission blamed white racism for rioting in the U.S., saying the country was moving toward two separate but unequal societies, one black and one white. *Man—Selma, California.*

He didn't leave the library until they started to flick the lights. Allen stopped for a couple of beers, hoping to get home after Trudy and Rick were asleep. He pulled up to the curb after ten, but there was a light on in the dining room.

He went in and found his files, typewriter and books pushed to one side of the dining table. McMANUS FULL SERVICE income tax forms and receipts occupied most of the space. Allen put his box by the typewriter; Pedro saw him, then perked right up and started on "Reveille," getting the first part right before breaking into extemporaneous shrill whistling.

"Shut that fuckin' bird up." Rick's tired old complaint came from the kitchen, then he staggered in, drinking a tallboy. He was in a white T-shirt, red Bermudas and flip-flops.

"Is Trudy in bed?"

Rick put the beer by his papers and sat down. "All she ever does is sleep. Have big fun at the library, professor?"

Allen walked over to Pedro, now waiting quietly with his feet on the bars. He stroked the bird's head with a forefinger.

His eyes glazed over, Rick pointed to the tax papers. "You know anything about this shit?"

"Not for a business."

"My ol' man always did it." Rick tried to focus on Allen. "My brother says he hasn't seen you at the station."

"I don't go that way in the mornings anymore."

"You get your gas down there?"

"No, Atwater."

"Thanks a lot for your goddamn business—you can't drive a couple extra blocks?" He took a long slug of beer.

Allen draped the night veil over Pedro's cage. "I'm going to bed." He picked up his box.

"So you're goin' back there next week?"

"Yeah, don't forget Trudy's ten bucks."

"Fuck you. What do you think you're trying to prove?"

"Nothing. I'm working full time, isn't that what you wanted?"

"She said you might move—that's what I want."

"As soon as I get paid."

"The spear chuckers'll run you off before that."

"Maybe so—you're more scared of them than I am."

"So now you're some sorta tough guy?" Rick laughed, then stood up, pointing with his wobbly arm. "Look, I know the crap you're always puttin' in Trudy's head—"

"What are you babbling about?" His voice was getting as loud as Rick's. Allen rested the corner of the box on the table.

"It's so goddamn sweet, tellin' her what *you're* doin' is the kinda shit she should do."

"That's not what I said."

"Close enough. You butt the hell outta my marriage, or I'll kick your ass outta here."

"Yeah? You lay another hand on Trudy, I'll have you thrown in jail, friggin' Cro-Magnon." He picked up his box again.

"What're you callin' me?"

Trudy came in, squinting from the doorway in her long nightgown. "What's all the yelling?"

"Nothing, I'm going to bed." Allen walked right by her and down into the basement. While he was brushing his teeth and changing clothes, he heard them shouting, but only an occasional word was intelligible. He turned off the light and lay on the foldout bed, wide-awake, listening for a scream or something breaking, but they finally shut up.

10

After thinking over "Monique's method" at the library on Saturday, he phoned her from there to brainstorm. They came up with the idea to partner non-readers with readers, the latter writing down recitations for the former. His first step would be to hear each student read, and then figure out the matchups. Monique offered to share all of her writing prompts.

Rick went to the beach on Sunday, and Trudy felt well enough to do her volunteer time at Glenfeliz Geriatric, so Allen did his schoolwork by Pedro. Late that afternoon, he took a hike up to "The Beacon," a local name for a hill in Griffith Park tall enough for an aircraft warning light. Spellbound by city's cacophony mixed with the wild sounds from the dense chaparral, Allen stayed at the base of the tower until its huge lamp began to rotate and flash in the dark.

At school on Monday, he sensed a transformation in the students right away. Starting with homeroom, a lot of them were lethargic and so were some of the teachers he ran into. The lassitude was similar to what he first noticed among the staff and students at Adams High, then in college, and also at his delivery jobs—*the Monday-Friday BS*—Monday always the big gloomy downer and Friday the day of happy possibilities, regardless of actual circumstances.

With attendance up a bit and the unanticipated calm working in his favor, Allen jumped right into his project after homeroom. When fluency time was over, he started his first-period class on vocabulary assignments, and then heard seven students read before he ran out of time. He dismissed the class after the bell and saw Charmane dallying near her desk; Ronnie was waiting at the door again.

As the room emptied, Allen walked over to her; he held up a hand to let Ronnie know to wait. "Did you want to talk to me about something, Charmane?"

"Sandra's keeping up with her work, Mister Greene, even in math. I see her every day after school to explain some of it—just wanted you to know."

"Thanks for telling me, but I'm not surprised she's keeping up. Tell her we'll be glad when she gets back." He saw that Ronnie was still waiting.

"I will, Mister Greene—see you last period." She smiled but didn't hurry off.

"See you." He started for Ronnie at the back door. The closest thing to gold he had on was a yellow T-shirt under his thin green and grey flannel. The lights reflected off of his slick, dark scalp. "Do you have a question, Ronnie?"

"I, um, the writing we do in here is okay, but there's something else I want to ask about."

"Sure, what is it?" Charmane was hanging out nearby in the hallway.

"Poems." The word sounded like *pomz*.

"A lot of your writing is already like poetry. Have you been reading some?"

"I check books out of the library and copy the way they do it, but with my words."

"You've been *writing* poetry? Good for you."

Ronnie looked at the floor. "I try, but I need some help."

"Well, maybe we—"

Charmane came closer, then all the way in. "I want to learn how too."

Ronnie's eyes daggered right at her, then he started to leave. Allen moved toward him. "Ronnie, if both of you want to come in to work on poetry, we could do it mostly one-on-one."

The boy stopped, his brow creasing. "How?"

"I could show you some things together, but then you'd write on your own. Let's see, Tuesday won't work for me, Thursday either. Do either of you have a commitment on Fridays after school?" They both shook their heads. "After Creative Writing on Fridays then?"

"I can." Charmane spoke eagerly, not looking at Ronnie, who barely nodded to Allen.

"Okay, I'll give you a note last period to take home today—maybe we can start up this Friday." Both kids took a step or two away. "Wait, you're tardy, I'll write you a pass."

Taking different routes across the room, Ronnie and Charmane met Allen at his desk. He scribbled the passes, handed them over and watched his two students leave from separate doors, not looking at each other.

Before first period the next morning, Ronnie came to Allen's desk, his head downcast. "My mom won't sign the note."

"Why not, Ronnie?"

"She just won't."

"Maybe I could call her or visit."

"I wouldn't do that. My brother's always around in the day." Ronnie walked away to get his fluency notebook.

When period one finished, Allen went down during prep to Mrs. Berg's office—she had a spot where staff and students could sometimes make a semi-private school-related call. Mrs. Eichler found Ronnie's number and led Allen to the phone. A "no longer in service" recording came on, so he copied the address before returning to his room.

After school, he finished plans for the next day, then went out to the car and drove down Harding Place. He made a right turn and pulled up in front of a faded-blue, flat-roofed duplex with chipped stucco, surrounded by six-foot iron poles and wire. Other than the sturdy fence, the place had no improvements; the yard had a concrete path in the middle with hard dirt on both sides, a small acacia to the left. An untied German shepherd, its eyes riveted on Allen, sat by the bush in some poor shade.

He reached over the gate for the latch, watching the large dog. It didn't stir, so Allen entered slowly but acted confident, although he could hear himself breathing. The grey and black canine snarled once, glaring as Allen stepped over a turd on the path. He walked up the two steps, exhaled, then knocked on the door of the place at the left.

A guy about Allen's height opened the front door but stayed behind the dark screen; his bright green jacket was about all that was visible. "Whaddya want?"

"I'm Ronnie's English teacher."

"So, I'm his brother. Is he in trouble?"

"No, may I speak to Mrs. Crawford?"

"What about?"

"A permission slip for a poetry class."

Ronnie's brother stood there for a few seconds. "Hold on."

He left, then a deep male voice came from the middle of the house. "Who the fuck is it?"

Arguing began, but Allen couldn't pick up many more words, mostly the bellicose tone of the lower voice, the other one trying to reason with him. Ronnie's brother came back to the screen. "You better get outta here now—he's pissed."

Allen immediately started to back away; his lunch seemed to turn over in his gut.

"Hey, teach." The guy rattled the door a little. "I'll have her sign it."

"What? Uh, okay, thanks." He turned from the small porch, one foot on the dirt, the other on the path. The German shepherd was behind him, now making a steady growl.

"Fritz!" After Ronnie's brother shouted, the dog cringed but didn't back off much.

Allen walked straight but steadily to the gate, knowing from Los Feliz dogs not to flee too fast. He went through, latched it, and headed for the Volvo—a pungent odor made him stop and look down. *Shit!* He pulled off the low-cut leather hiking shoe by its heel and slammed the front sole sideways on the curb; most of the orange-brown dog crap plopped onto the ground. Allen retched, expelling the contents of his stomach into the gutter. He hobbled to the trunk, threw in the stinking boot, then got in the car and shed the clean one.

Driving through the neighborhood in his socks, he rolled down the windows to help his stomach settle. He came to the dilapidated grocery; the Olds was parked there again, this time in the shadows on the store's east side. He rolled his windows back up and accelerated past the black car to the freeway.

Without comment, Ronnie brought the signed note back on Wednesday. It took Allen until Thursday to finish the oral reading in all of his classes. The number of very low or non-readers was close to the estimate he made from the writing, almost sixty kids. Their attendance was generally worse than the rest, so he expected to have plenty of volunteers in each class to tutor them. He decided to wait until the following Monday to start the new program.

At the end of Creative Writing that Friday, Charmane stayed in her seat, grinning contentedly. Ronnie left right away but came back as soon as the room cleared; he sat four rows away from her.

"Okay, you two, before we get started, I want you to know that we might end up with a few more kids in here. Apparently, the word got out." Allen grinned at Charmane; Ronnie glared at her. "A couple of girls came to me and said they wanted to write poetry. If we keep it to five or six kids total, will you two be okay with that?"

Charmane smiled. "Sure, Mister Greene."

"Ronnie?"

"All girls? If I don't like it, I can just go."

"I hope not. Okay, let's get started. Before we work individually, I want to show both of you something about how free verse works . . . ." After his explanation, he had Charmane take one of her more creative essays and begin editing the extraneous words to convert the prose into verse. Ronnie had brought some of his poems; Allen tried to explain tactfully that his phrases were interesting and vivid, but sometimes it didn't work to force everything into rhyme.

The small sturdy boy raised a brow. "I think I get what you mean, but how—"

He was interrupted by Miss Dorsey walking into the room. She looked at Charmane, then at Allen, her heels clacking on the way to the desk where Allen and Ronnie were working. "An extra class, Mister Greene?"

"Hi, Miss Dorsey. Yes, poetry."

"So I heard." Although her dour face was again compressed, Allen sensed that she was pleased that Ronnie was there at all. "Are the parents aware of this?"

"Yes, I have written permission for both students."

"That's a relief. One small problem, Mister Greene, you have to clear something like this with the principal."

"I didn't think he'd mind."

"We cannot keep discussing this with students present."

"Oh." Charmane and Ronnie were both watching them. "Would it be okay to talk about it on Monday?"

"No, I am sorry—Mister Nash is on his way here. He heard about this, and he also has a related issue."

Crap. "All right, just let me give them some follow-up to do at home."

"That will be fine." Dorsey moved a few yards away, watching him work with Ronnie. The boy left after a minute or two, carrying a poetry anthology that Allen let him borrow.

He finished with Charmane, and then she went out, her nose in a book of poetry as Nash entered. The portly department chairman went right to Allen's mentor, his face in a scold. "So, is it true, Miss Dorsey?"

"Yes, poetry."

"Was he alone with that girl?" He sounded half-hopeful.

"No, he was not . . . ." As Dorsey explained the situation, Allen walked closer to them.

Nash rested the briefcase on a desk but didn't let it go, precisely adjusting the slack in the chain. "He didn't even notify the school?"

"No, but he *will* be asking Mister Schultz for permission to continue." Dorsey raised one brow. "Right, Mister Greene?"

"What? Yeah, sure. I don't have an extra-curricular assignment anymore—maybe it can be the poetry group."

Nash scoffed. "You might indeed convince the principal of that, Mister Greene, but word has also reached me that your students are writing poetry in Language Arts."

"A little, but we haven't really started yet."

"Yet? Are you aware that poetry is not part of the seventh-grade curriculum, except as reading material?"

"You must mean a few poems by dead Englishmen in our text. Some of my smaller students have found a use for that old book—they sit on it." Allen saw his mentor unsuccessfully cover a slight grin with her fist.

Nash scowled. "I don't find that humorous, Miss Dorsey."

Allen took a step closer. "If some students can express themselves better by writing poetry, why not encourage it?"

"Because your job is to teach the curriculum." He turned away. "And Miss Dorsey, I expect you to see that he does. Who is his official evaluator?"

"Mister Godina."

"Oh." He rolled his eyes and picked up the briefcase. "I will discuss this with him soon. Good afternoon."

Nash walked away in a huff; Dorsey went to the door, peeked out, then turned to Allen. "Mister Greene, I recommend that you try to be a little more careful about what you say and do."

"So I have to drop the poetry in my classes?"

"I did not say that. I said to be more careful—don't put it in your lesson plans."

"Oh." Allen grinned slightly. "Thank you, Miss Dorsey."

"See you on Monday, Mister Greene." She walked away, shaking her head, betraying a hint of a smile.

11

Allen spent most of that weekend preparing for his new reading/writing approach and staying away from Rick as much as he could.

On Monday before school, he was down in the coliseum at his duty station near the south arch. With his list of possible reading matchups in hand, he made some adjustments for his first-period class while also keeping an eye on the kids.

In his first two weeks of duty, Allen had dealt with a few arguments and scuffles, but nothing major, as Cecil predicted. Now there was some uneasiness, especially among the girls as they walked by or waited in the lines. It was more than the usual banter; he heard parts of dares and accusations, peppered with profanity. They seemed to be taking sides, but nothing actually happened, so there wasn't much he could do but tell a few of them to "Knock off the cussing."

He looked up from his lists, noticing that the lines had thinned out earlier than usual. A roar of voices broke out far behind him, almost like cheers after a homerun in Dodger Stadium. Stuffing the lists in a back pocket, he ran for the end of the cafeteria, came around the corner and couldn't even see the benches below the old eucalyptus. Well more than a hundred kids yelled encouragement toward a small circular arena formed by the spectators. The warning bell rang.

He put his open hands by his mouth as he moved forward. "Outta the way, go to class, now!"

Some kids shouted "Teacher!" to those closer to the fracas. Allen waded and pushed through the outskirts of the crowd, where it was nearly all boys, some of them standing on the benches and laughing. A lot of kids took off, but scores remained, mainly girls, pressed toward the circle; he still couldn't see the fight.

"Cop!" a girl yelled, and most of the kids began to leave. Deniker was up ahead, approaching two combatants, both of them tall girls, slender but physically mature—probably ninth graders. Oblivious to everyone else, they had their hands embedded in each other's long hair, one girl snarling epithets, the other fiercely quiet as she tugged back. Twirling in an unintended dance to avoid being yanked to the ground, neither girl appeared to be badly damaged, save for torn clothes and rumpled hair.

About a dozen kids remained nearby. "Outta here, all of you!" Allen sent them around the building, then turned to see the guard's large hands clamped in a vise-like grip around two thin wrists. The girls had let go of each other, but Deniker gave both arms a rough twist.

The quieter one yelped, limply submitting to the husky man's strength, but the other girl flailed, screaming, "Leggo a' me!" Deniker bent her arm to a radical angle; her face contorted and she cried out in pain, but he didn't ease off.

Damn, he'll crack it.

Deniker finally saw Allen and eased the tension on the struggling girl's arm. "If I let go, you two are going to shut up and walk right next to me, or I haul you in like this. Run away, and you're done here for good."

The more defiant one was crying now, and she said, "Okay, jus' leggo." Deniker released them, pointing at the asphalt by his khaki pant legs; the girls fell in obediently at each side, rubbing their arms and moaning as the passing bell rang. They walked by with the guard, who didn't give Allen a second look.

He hurried in and skipped stairs on the way up; a kid jokingly admonished him for breaking the rules, but Allen had Deniker on his mind. If the guard had been alone, he could have injured the girl's arm and blamed her.

As he came to his door just before the tardy bell, the boys were laughing in the hall about the "chick fight." Allen opened up and made them settle down for morning rituals, then he buzzed the office to ask if Schultz would be available second hour, but the principal was at a meeting downtown.

In first period, Allen had the kids hold off on fluency writing. Attendance was low, but he went ahead and explained the new program to eighteen students, doing his best to reduce the stigma for those who were going to be tutored. After a few gripes and questions, he read the list of nine kids who had to recite. Six were present—Charmane volunteered to be a tutor, then three more; Ronnie was the last. Allen gave the other kids a word puzzle, made the five matchups and took the sixth student himself. All six cooperated, reciting the storyline of a favorite cartoon. Then Allen had the tutors and other readers write their own papers while he worked on skills with the rest.

Typing more than fifty pages at the end of the day was out of the question, so Allen had asked the tutors to write as legibly as possible. During second-period prep, he saw that most of them had printed; he was amazed by the clarity of the transcribed material. It went nearly that well in every class, not many kids refusing to recite. The transcriptions didn't need as much correction as he expected, and there were only a few non-readable papers he would have to decipher at home.

It wasn't until Wednesday that Allen was able to tell Schultz about Monday's fight. He came out to Allen's duty area in the morning and listened to his concerns about the guard. Schultz said there had not been a complaint from the girls, but he would talk to Deniker without mentioning names. "He'll probably figure it out, though."

"Yeah, probably." On his way upstairs, Allen was more worried about Rupert, who was eligible to return that day. His foe in the homeroom fight, Aaron, was already back from a shorter suspension. On the positive side, Sandra's two weeks were finally over as well.

When Rupert didn't show for homeroom, Allen self-confessed his relief. Ronnie, Charmane and two other girls arrived before the first-period tardy bell to begin writing along with Marlon and three more homeroom boys, but Sandra didn't come early on her first day back.

It was another warm day; Ronnie hung his gold long-sleeve shirt on the back of his seat before starting on his journal. Allen smiled to himself when Charmane said "E-I" back to Ronnie after he leaned over rows of desks to whisper a question.

After the bell, Allen only had to hassle two kids to begin writing. Just four of the twenty-five were absent, including Sandra. She came in late at the end of fluency time, her eyes red and swollen.

He walked up to her and took the excused tardy slip signed by Miss Watson. "Are you okay, Sandra?"

Downcast, she spoke very quietly. "Hi, Mister Greene. I'll be all right."

He answered in a whisper. "We're glad you're back—maybe we'll talk later." He returned to his desk to mark Sandra's name and saw her quietly telling something to Charmane. "All right, everybody, let's get started." Allen read aloud an old graphic version of the Aesop's fable about a cat who teaches a bragging fox a reliable way to escape his enemies.

"Okay, retell *The Fox and the Cat* in your own words—no profanity." Most of the kids laughed because their first project, the one about cartoons, produced two recitations with profane dialogue between Bugs Bunny and Yosemite Sam.

"Storytellers get with your same scribes, the rest of you get started on your own." He was answered by a few moans. "If you finish, read or write while you wait for us. After that, we'll all be doing a *fun* exercise with adjectives. Okay, those who need a partner, come on up."

Some kids groaned as they readjusted their desks to get as much privacy as possible before starting to work. Those who didn't tutor started writing; Sandra and three boys came to the front of the room, including Ronnie, Del, and the usually wisecracking Marlon. He and Del, both new readers, were inches taller but not as robust as the wiry-strong Ronnie, whose previous partner was absent.

Sandra had settled down; he asked her to observe Charmane and see if she might want to be a tutor next time. It seemed to be an easy fix to the other matchups, with the extra boy reciting to Allen. Since Marlon was a minion of the faction in black, Allen couldn't partner him with Ronnie. Del, in a white T-shirt, was a sulky near-adolescent who preferred to sit and do nothing—at least Ronnie could work with him without any extraneous "gang" tension.

He made the matches, but Ronnie and Del glared at each other as they walked away. Keeping an eye on those two, Allen sat at his desk to hear Marlon, who was wearing a faded blue Dodgers T-shirt, not his usual black. "Good shirt, Marlon, but the Pirates are best in the league this year."

"That jacket you had on the other day sure was ugly."

Allen checked to be sure everyone was starting, especially Del and Ronnie at the back wall. "You don't like my Pirates?"

"That black an' gold jacket."

Ah, sacrilege. "Okay, let's get going."

Marlon looked around to make sure nobody could hear him. "Mister

Greene," he whispered, "Michael's still pissed—you better watch for him." Before Allen could react, Marlon raised his voice and began telling a detailed version of how "That cat was so smart . . . ." Allen printed quickly, trying not to fret about Michael, glancing when he could at the class.

Not five minutes into the exercise, there was commotion from the desks at back, where Del snatched the recitation from Ronnie and crumpled the paper into a wad. "Fuck this!"

Ronnie shrugged. "Man, all you gotta do is talk."

"All *you* gotta do is shut up, ball-headed little shit." Del got up, tossing the paper at Ronnie's face, but he missed.

Ronnie stood. "Nice shot, big baby." He began to walk away, but Del sucker-punched him in the side of the head.

Allen had started across the room, but he stumbled over some kids yelling, "Fight!" He got by them in time to see several things happen ahead, seemingly in seconds: Ronnie tackled Del, who pulled a switchblade as he fell to the floor. The blade flicked open; he pointed it right at Ronnie, who feinted one way, then pushed him over and stomped his wrist. Del cried out in pain; the knife slid under the heater. Ronnie grabbed the taller boy by the scruff and pulled him halfway up.

Allen was a few feet from them. "Enough, let him go!" Ronnie did let go, shoving him away by the shoulders, but Del tripped over a desk and toppled hard onto the heat registers, his head making a sickening *thunk* as it struck steel. Allen took Ronnie's arm; he didn't resist, staring wide-eyed at Del, who lay motionless on the floor.

"Damn it to hell." Allen got in Ronnie's face and ordered him to stay put, then turned to the front of the room. "Hit the intercom button, Charmane!" She pushed a folding chair over to the PA.

First-aid priorities from a class in Puerto Rico jumbled through his mind. Del was unconscious but breathing; blood from the injury dotted his white shirt and the floor. Allen grabbed a boy's coat from nearby and put it over Del. He pressured one hand to the wound and turned around, asking Sandra to go for some wet paper towels.

Charmane climbed down from the chair; the intercom garbled to life with Venable's voice. "What is it, Mister Greene?"

"I have a bleeding unconscious boy—get us some help now!"

"An ambulance?"

"Yes!" Some kids were crowding around Del; Allen told them to back off and sit down. A minute or so later, Sandra returned with the towels; he cleaned away some blood and applied the damp compress firmly to Del's injury.

Cecil hurried into the room with a red first-aid kit and took over with the wound. He replaced the saturated paper towels with thick white gauze and kept up the pressure. Allen turned to the class—Charmane, Sandra, Marlon and some others intently watched Del and Cecil; several more were talking excitedly. Allen scowled at two boys who were laughing.

Holding the wound, Cecil turned to him. "Which one done this?"

Allen checked the kids again, making a frustrated sigh. "He's gone. It was Ronnie Crawford, but Del hit him first and pulled that knife." He pointed to it under the heater; there was a smear of blood on the tan registers.

"Get it for me, will ya'?"

Allen picked up the switchblade and put it by Cecil's kit. With one palm pressuring Del's wound, the guard used his other hand to remove the walkie-talkie from his belt. The kids had calmed down, most just talking quietly. Cecil made a call to Deniker to report Ronnie, then faced Allen again. "Nick says the ambulance is gettin' close."

"Good." He had one of the boys go over to open the door. By the time they heard the gurney rattling in the hallway, Del still had his eyes closed. The bell rang; Allen told the kids to leave for next period by the rear exit.

At the front door, a tall middle-aged man in a plain white uniform guided a gurney into the room; some kids watched from the hall near a second ambulance attendant and a young blonde in a short skirt who Monique had pointed out previously as the school nurse.

The attendant with the gurney came to Allen and Cecil. He had unblemished fawn-colored skin. Allen read his nametag: CENTRAL AMBULANCE— SINGH, JAHAN. Moving quickly, Singh removed the coat and pulled a light blanket up to Del's waist, then he took a briefcase-sized white kit from the gurney. He put a pillow under the boy's head and took over from the guard.

Cecil stood, turning to Allen. "Won't even need no stitches, but he's out like a light—an' look at his wrist." It was limp, discolored a reddish purple. Cecil started to walk away. "You got kids comin' in here now?"

"No, this is my prep."

Cecil began shooing away gawking students from the door. Singh finished checking Del, then he hand-signaled to the other attendant with a you-can-stay-back motion. Someone laughed in the hall—it was the school nurse, not one of the kids. The guard returned to Allen.

"What's going on out there, Cecil?"

"Ol' Ernie's jus' hittin' on her again."

As Cecil walked off, calling on his radio, Allen watched Singh tape a fresh dressing to Del's head and start a temporary splint to stabilize the wrist. "How's he doing?"

The attendant responded while securing the boy's arm. "I am strictly first-aid, sir." His precise English had a melodious accent.

"Can't you just tell me what you think?"

Singh stood, signaling to the other attendant again, then he turned to Allen. "Well, the cut is minor, but the wrist is not good. He is starting to chatter, but his eyes are not reacting much. The main concern will likely be concussion."

"Is he ready to go?"

"Yes." Singh glanced at his partner, who was still schmoozing with the nurse.

Allen pointed at the door. "Does that guy know?"

Singh nodded, closing his eyes momentarily. "Mister Shaw is my supervisor, sir."

Allen hurried right for the door; as he got there, he took a good look at Shaw, about five-nine, stocky, clean-cut, and pushing forty. He had fancy insignias on his uniform and two nametags. The ambulance badge had: SHAW, ERNIE, and the other one: PO2 E. SHAW, MEDIC, U.S. COAST GUARD RESERVE.

"The boy's ready," Allen said. It sounded like an order.

Shaw leered at the nurse's cocooned rear end, swaying as she walked off in low heels. "That right, teach? Don't get your pencils in a tizzy." The nurse giggled from down the hall. "See you later, babe." Shaw smirked and walked right by Allen into the room. His beginning-to-recede brown butch was thick enough in back to show the remains of a greasy '50s ducktail.

Cecil returned to the doorway. "Nick says they already caught the Crawford kid at Grant lookin' for his brother. I need the particulars of the fight."

While the attendants lifted Del onto the gurney, Allen tried to be succinct with his account. He stopped talking to watch them wheel his semi-conscious student out into the hall. He and Cecil followed them at a distance.

"When Ronnie stepped on him, did Del let go a' the knife?"

"Yes." Allen watched Schultz come to the top of the stairs. They retracted the gurney's legs, and the principal went downstairs ahead of the attendants.

"So Ronnie didn't need to shove 'im down the second time?"

"No, but . . . ." Allen explained again.

"Between all that and runnin' off, he's in big trouble."

Damn—my fault.

Allen went down to the office at noon to find out about Del and Ronnie, but there wasn't anyone around with new information. He was also hoping to talk to Sandra before period seven, but she didn't show up. After class, he spoke to Charmane in the hall. "Do you know what happened to Sandra last period?"

"I didn't want to tell you in front of the kids—she had to go see Melissa at lunch time."

"Is the baby okay?"

"I think so. I'm going to see them now."

"Do you think Sandra would mind if you told me what the problem is?"

"Maybe she should tell you, Mister Greene."

"Okay, we'll see you tomorrow." He locked the door, then hurried downstairs; Deniker was coming up. It was the first time Allen had been near him since Monday's fight. "Mister Deniker." The guard walked right by, his eyes straight ahead.

Miss Watson was handling all of the end-of-day turmoil alone. She told Allen that Mister Schultz had just called his room. He walked past the principal's open window and knocked on his doorjamb.

"Mister Greene, we meet again." Schultz was standing by his exterior window. He turned from Allen to look through the thick wire at something going on outside. "Come in please," he said, facing him again. Schultz's jowls sagged more than before, his eyes darker in their sockets, and his frame was so slouched that he didn't seem as tall.

"I was on my way down when you called. How's Del doing?"

"He has a broken wrist and a slight concussion, but he'll be released from the hospital soon." He looked out again.

Allen sighed. "Jesus."

Schultz turned to him, frowning. "It could've been worse. So, you told Cecil that Ronnie Crawford's part in all this started out as self-defense."

"That's right."

The principal took yet another peek outside, then sat at his desk. "Okay, let's hear the whole thing."

Allen sat down and told him about fouling up the matchups, then the details of the fight. ". . . and I could tell that Ronnie was upset about what happened to Del."

Schultz nodded. "Okay, here's the deal. With his history, Del will be expelled for starting all this and pulling that knife. Ronnie's going to be suspended for ten school days."

"What, why so long?" The question came out louder and more forceful than Allen expected.

"You need to calm down, Mister Greene."

"Yeah, sorry."

"It didn't help that when they caught him at Grant, Ronnie had two live twenty-two shells in his pocket." Schultz pursed his lips. "You seem to have a lot of interest in the boy."

"He's basically a good kid, one of my best writers."

"Well, if he does all his make-up work and stays out of trouble after he comes back, he should be okay for next year. Sounds like he has some potential."

Allen nodded, sighing from deep in his chest.

"By the way," the principal said, "I finally spoke to Deniker."

"Yeah, I could tell."

"Mister Godina and I will have our eyes on him." Schultz glanced outside, then faced Allen again. "This is the third or fourth time you've ended up in the middle of things, Mister Greene. Why do you suppose that is?"

"I don't know. I screwed up this time."

"Perhaps." He took a glimpse of Allen's slightly mussed long black hair, then his colorful madras shirt. "Tell me something. Did you come to this school motivated by some sort of, shall we say, idealism?"

"What do you mean?"

"We sometimes get young crusaders who ride in here on a white stallion to save the world."

"No, I needed a job. I didn't think I'd last *this* long."

"I see. So how do you feel about it now?"

"To be honest, I'm not sure. I like working with most of the kids, but there are a few who still scare the crap—uh, I try not to show it."

Schultz made one of his deeply rutted smiles. "Well, I'll be honest too. You surprised me, Mister Greene—first by gravitating to Mrs. Morgan for some guidance."

"That wasn't hard to figure out."

"Yes, and I also think you're already starting to find a good balance between caring and practicality—something a lot of teachers never learn."

"I don't know what to say to that."

"That's fine." Schultz nodded, smiling again. "Just keep it up."

What? "Uh, thanks." He left, making a cursory wave to Miss Watson before entering the hall. Regardless of Schultz's compliment, only the students, Monique, and maybe Miss Dorsey had any idea of what took place in his room after the doors were shut. The stairway made him flash back to a recent popular movie where Sidney Poitier led all of his tough kids to the Promised Land of education. *Yeah, not in the real world.*

12

Schultz briefly reported Del's expulsion and Ronnie's suspension during the regular faculty meeting on Thursday afternoon. The meeting lasted until a few minutes after their contracted time; most teachers hurried out as soon as it finished. Monique went over to Mrs. Berg, so Allen walked out of the north exit alone. Frank Williamson caught up to him; they had spoken briefly just twice in the two weeks since the meeting about Sandra.

He looked at Allen seriously. "Greene, I need to talk to you about Ronnie."

Allen stopped. "Yeah, I have him twice."

"I know, would you get his first week's work to Mrs. Berg or me as soon as you can?" He wore the same button on his pocket; Allen had figured out it was a photo of Rosa Parks.

"First thing tomorrow morning."

"Good. So how did Ronnie's fight come down?"

"Wish I had it to do again." Allen filled him in on the main details. They stopped at the barren kiva as he finished, staring at the lone struggling arbor-vitae in the hard ground. Allen kicked a pebble halfway across the coliseum.

Williamson raised a brow. "You look pretty low."

The pot calling the kettle black—geez, Allen. "He's a good kid, and can he ever write."

"Too bad he didn't back off after he stopped the knife."

"Yeah, something was brewing before it started—should've followed my damn hunch."

"Did Del say anything about Ronnie's baldness?"

"Yes, before the fight. Why?"

"There's something about Ronnie that nobody knows." He squinted slightly, his face turning even more intense. "I'll tell you, but you've got to keep it to yourself."

"Of course."

Williamson put his orange and black notebook on the wall. "How much do you know about his family?"

"Not much. I've been to the house once."

"You're kidding."

"Why would I kid about that?"

"Can you tell me why you were there?" After Allen told him the circumstances of the home visit, Williamson raised both brows. "I'll be."

"What?"

"Nothing. It's good you got your butt outta there."

"Yeah, then I stepped in it—literally." Williamson gave him a curious look, so Allen explained, then watched him laugh at the dog poop story. "Glad to provide some entertainment," he said, but it was good to see a smile on the man's face.

"Somebody probably took pictures." Williamson laughed one more time. "Sorry, you win the gold medal just for goin' to that house." He exhaled, then lost his smile as quickly as pulling down a shade. "Ronnie's the last of four boys. You met the one who goes to Grant—he's in one of the big new gangs. The other guy you heard is the oldest—in and out of jail, mostly in. Anyway, their dad went here, and he was all-city football at Grant—a hero to us when we were kids. He was a drill sergeant, died years ago in a boot camp accident. Mrs. Crawford moved back here to her mother's—the good thing is they have government health insurance for Ronnie."

"What? There's something wrong with him?"

"Yeah, that's the secret. Leukemia—over a year now."

"My God, that's why he's bald?"

Williamson nodded. "He pretends to keep his hair like that on purpose. He thinks it's less conspicuous than wearing a hat or something—doesn't want any pity."

"What's his prognosis?"

"This is secondhand from his brother, Rob, an eighth-grader. They told the family that Ronnie would've had no chance five years ago. Now there's a new chemotherapy that uses multiple drugs—some kids are surviving, so he has a shot."

Allen stared at the asphalt. "Is the school aware of it?"

"No, Ronnie told his mom the kids would find out, said he'd stop coming. Rob isn't a tough kid—he's worried about Ronnie and let me in on it last fall."

"Man, one minute they're just kids, then you find out—"

"No, they're still just kids." He paused. "Your neighborhood has all the same things we do—drunks to VD to domestic violence. Maybe you don't have as much, but we don't hide it so effectively, and you don't have poverty as an excuse."

Allen let that sink in a few seconds, thinking of Rick.

Williamson lifted his binder. "The point is, there's no sense blaming yourself for the fight. It was probably inevitable."

"Yeah, maybe." They started off toward the south archway. "I wish there was some way for Ronnie to keep up his poetry."

"Then do it."

"How?"

"Send some extra assignments with Rob, I'll arrange it."

"All right, I'll put it with his homework. Thanks."

"Forget it."

As they entered the building, he felt like talking more to Williamson but just watched him walk off to his room. Allen went in the hall entrance to the office, removed a thick pile of mail from his box, and then started for the staff lounge, hesitating at the door. The week before, he overheard two teachers at the coffee pot, gossiping viciously about Monique and Mrs. Berg. Passing by the next day to make copies, Allen heard Van Burton speaking half under his breath to some appreciative laughter: "I never had so damn many dumb jungle bunnies."

Most teachers were likely gone now, so Allen went in. Two women chatted quietly at the sink as he sat on one of the plush sofas for only the third or fourth time. He began to sort through his boring mail; the two teachers left, but three more walked in moments later—Nash, Anders, and Mister Jackson, a short thin man who was the Social Studies chairman.

About Monique's age, Jackson always wore a brown suit, tie, belt, and shoes; his complexion was very dark, but his receding hair, tuft of moustache and brows were white. In one faculty meeting, Jackson had made a snobbish comment about some of his "fellow Negroes," but Williamson interrupted, saying "And some of my *fellow* blacks are the dupes of Jim Crow mentality."

Like imprinted goslings, Anders and Jackson followed Nash to a far couch, oblivious of Allen. Nash put his ever-present briefcase on a side table as he sat down. Anders turned, speaking just low enough to keep her voice in the room. ". . . and with both of them as finalists, we have to be more certain."

"That's right." Jackson was quieter than the librarian. "I'd take the guy from Verdugo Hills over *him*."

Godina. Allen started to sort faster as Anders responded.

". . . and he doesn't know our old hoodlums or any of the family traits—he probably doesn't *want* to know."

Nash spoke to his lackeys with a condescending grin. "The margin is still close, but I'm not very concerned. Just to be sure, I'll bring around one more vote, God willing."

Anders gnashed her perfect white teeth. "Can you imagine having someone in charge who would be even easier on the troublemakers?"

Jackson nodded. "If *he* was in charge today, it would've been detention for the Crawford boy—as it is, he should've been expelled."

Goddamn it. "Excuse me, do you always hold private conversations in public?"

Nash eyed him with one brow raised as if Allen were an armchair that didn't belong in the room. "Mister Greene, you don't need to listen, and we're not saying anything that isn't common knowledge to *most* members of this faculty, be they temporary or not."

"Is that right?" Allen stood and pointed at them. "You don't know a damn thing about Ronnie Crawford." *Easy.* He exhaled, picking up his mail.

Scoffing, Anders looked at him over the rims of her black glasses. "And *you* do? Who do you think you are?"

"Just somebody passing through, I guess." Walking out, Allen saw Nash sneer at him; the other two were sniggering. Instead of going upstairs, he turned right and walked off slowly, trying to calm down. He stopped at a fountain for a drink, then splashed water on his face and took a couple of deep breaths before he continued down the hall. Williamson's light was on; Allen saw him through the portal, reading at his desk.

He knocked, and then heard, "Yeah, come in." Allen entered his room for the first time. The walls were a gallery of civil rights and Black History posters—each with a caption covered by a flap. He spotted Rosa Parks, Doctor King, Malcom X, and a frenzied John Brown—the others weren't as familiar.

Williamson pushed his open book an inch or two away. "What's up?"

"Hi." Approaching him, Allen recognized Harriet Tubman on another poster. "So this way, they learn the faces first?"

"That's about it." The poster nearest his desk was of an older black man, studying something through the wire spectacles on his large pointed nose; he wore some sort of apron. Williamson placed a marker and closed his book. "Know him?"

"No, but he looks a lot like Gandhi."

"Hm, I guess he does. Take a look."

Allen lifted the flap and skimmed the biography of the agricultural scientist. "Yeah, he was in our history book, but Carver obviously did more than peanuts."

Williamson nodded.

"And now I know. Can I talk to you a minute, Frank?"

"Go ahead."

"I just ran into to Nash, Jackson, and Anders."

"Man, you stepped in it again." A crease of a grin crossed his face.

"Yeah." Allen told him about the confrontation.

"Welcome to Warren J. Harding. Jackson fought against the Black History class until the district supported it, then he wanted to teach it, but Schultz came through." He paused, glancing at George Washington Carver. "Next year, Moto will give it to Jackson."

"Are you that sure she's in?"

He turned to Allen. "Sharon Berg is on the interview panel. From what she told me, Nash can back up his boast. The final interviews are next Tuesday."

Allen sighed. "So if she gets it, Nash will have even more say around here."

"Maybe, but we have cut into their majority this year."

"Who exactly is *we*?"

"There are two teachers' organizations, the Alliance and our local. They're ashamed of words like *union*, and their so-called action is usually about salaries, hardly a word about education or the kids."

"So Nash just transferred in and took it over?"

"Yup, two and a half years ago—elected three-to-one over Miss Dorsey. They got just what they wanted."

"I suppose his reputation for discipline adds to his credibility with some teachers."

Frank scoffed. "That's about right, but he doesn't even deal with tough kids in class. When he does get one, Nash just moves the kid down from level three."

"How can he get away with that?"

"The demotion and promotion committee is Moto, Mister Lee, both counselors, and Nash—three votes against two."

"God, poor Mrs. Berg. What's this business about the older kids thinking Nash is dangerous?"

He glowered out of his window at the quiet street. "That's been part of the school's culture ever since he came here."

"I've seen how some kids avoid him—why do they believe it?"

His face still cross, Frank turned. "All right, most of what I'm going to tell you is common knowledge to anyone who's been here for a while—but I still don't want any of it passed on with my name."

"Monique's the only one I really talk to."

"She knows all of this. Okay, what you've seen and heard about the *dangerous* Mister Nash comes from the myth that he carries a gun in that damn briefcase of his."

"What? You're joking."

"Nope. He started the rumor himself when he came here, but I can't prove it."

"Nobody on staff believes there's actually a gun, right?"

"No, but it doesn't matter what we believe, the rumor just goes on. A few parents have come in, but it always blows over."

"How do you know Nash intentionally started it?"

"Secondhand." He turned toward John Brown and his frizzled hair, then back to Allen. "Okay, this is the part that *isn't* common knowledge: Nash's first year, two boys came and told me in confidence that he joked around with them, saying it might not be a bad idea to carry a Luger around in his briefcase."

"That's it?"

"Yeah, doesn't sound like much. I told them it was ridiculous, but the rumor just spread and keeps getting passed down that he's crazy and packs a gun. Schultz told me it would be Nash's word against mine unless I gave up the names of those boys, which I didn't."

"Did Schultz do anything?"

"Watched him for a while, all Nash did was add his thing with the silver chain. Takes his briefcase outside with him to the coliseum—the sly bastard just shakes the chain and grins—the kids get the point."

"I heard some teachers joking about the briefcase."

"Yeah, a lot of them think it's real funny—a running sick joke to the rest of us. Nash laughs at it too, then he'll turn serious and say that all he carries in there is 'the power of the Lord, the Holy Bible.' When the kids asked me about it back then, I made the mistake of talking about myth and rumor, using historical examples—ended up making it worse. Now when they ask, I just say the gun thing is baloney, and then move on."

"So Ishimoto didn't know about those two boys coming to you?"

"Schultz kept his word, never told her. She would've twisted it into something against me."

"Why did you let me in on it?"

"You asked, and you're already on her shit-list anyway."

After the homeroom tardy bell the next morning, Allen felt guilty again for his relief when he marked Rupert absent. He also missed Ronnie already, but not just because of the tutoring and his good writing. The boy had a salutary effect on first and last period—the kids seemed to respect Ronnie because he could pull off being both a tough kid and a good student.

Although dreary Mondays were the norm at Marshall, it turned out that Fridays were not about gleeful anticipation for the weekend; instead, it was the day that both the staff and students expected trouble. Allen finished homeroom attendance, then checked the coliseum. An older boy had jogged by him during duty, pointing back at Nash while yelling ahead to some others, "Not yet, it's too close to that ol' fucker." Allen stopped the boy, but Cecil showed up on rounds and took over as the bell rang.

Announcements finished, and Allen turned away from the window. His peripheral vision picked up some movement, so he turned back and looked below again. Two tall male teens sprinted by and hurdled the iron rails, stopping at an old wooden shed where the student clubs sold popcorn and candy at noon. Spotting a flame in one boy's hand, Allen hurried over to the intercom and pushed the button. Static came on right away, and then Venable. "Office."

"Two big guys with lighters are at the popcorn stand!" Before she answered, most of his boys rushed to the windows.

"Yes, the cooks just reported it—security's on the way." The PA sputtered off; Allen returned to the window and saw the two teens fleeing past the eucalyptus in the eating area. A pyrotechnic fountain of sparks burst from the booth's counter; the homeroom boys *oohed* and *aahed* as if it were the Fourth of July. The dry plywood caught fire right away.

He slid the window all the way up. A heavy cook in a powder-blue uniform shuffled out of the cafeteria with a small red extinguisher that she couldn't get to work, but Cecil was arriving with a larger one. Allen started to shout down to ask if he should call for more help, but they wouldn't hear him over the *FLOOOOOF* that spouted from the nozzle in Cecil's hands.

The booth, now a mass of flames, sent thick dark-grey smoke drifting above the school for the second time since Allen came to Marshall, though the first fire was from a trashcan. His boys jabbered excitedly as Cecil took the precaution to douse some cypress trees by the cafeteria. Godina and two cooks stood with a few kids near the kiva and watched the fire begin to burn itself out as a siren approached.

The firemen hurried through the south archway, but not with hoses; they soaked the embers using extinguishers, then poked around gingerly in the debris. After a delayed passing bell sounded, the homeroom boys left reluctantly. Those who would have first period with Allen remained at the windows as Charmane and some other girls entered from Monique's room.

While most kids rushed over to the windows, Charmane came to Allen, frowning. "Sandra's out today." She paused and lowered her voice. "She said I could tell you why."

"Okay, hang on." When the bell rang, he faced all the kids at the windows. "All right, everybody has something exciting to write about. You can stay over there *if* you're writing." All of them except two boys hurried to retrieve their folders. Allen warned those two about isolation; they went over to the file boxes.

He met Charmane near the front door, far from all the kids, but she still spoke quietly. "Sandra wanted to come bad today, Mister Greene, but she had to watch the baby."

Allen kept his voice just as low. "What about her mother?"

"That's the problem, she was drunk again yesterday morning. She told Sandra to stay home, and they got in a big fight. That's when Sandra usually takes Melissa to her aunt's, but she's visiting family in Atlanta. Sandra called at noon, and there was no answer, so she ran all the way home and found her mom passed out. The baby was asleep, all dirty, and—"

"What, Charmane?"

She started to tear up a little. "Melissa had bruises. I guess she got knocked around when she wouldn't stop crying. Mrs. Small was drinking again today, so Sandra stayed home."

"God, who could blame her? Charmane, I have to tell Mrs. Berg what happened."

"What if they take Melissa away from Sandra?"

"I hope not, but the baby is defenseless when Sandra's not there. She gets along with Mrs. Berg, right?"

"Yeah, Sandra likes her."

"Good. I'll go see her next period and explain everything. Mrs. Berg might want to talk to you."

"Okay, Mister Greene. I hope this is the right thing to do."

"I think it is, Charmane."

13

Mrs. Berg was meeting with some parents; Allen didn't get to talk to her until halfway through period two. She was already very aware of Sandra's situation but mildly surprised about the alleged abuse of the baby. Mrs. Berg thanked Allen for getting involved and said she would report the incident and visit Sandra's house right away.

The fire was followed by a hectic, unruly day in Allen's classes with more than the usual number of kids not ready to settle down. He expected that the fire marshal or a cop would talk to him, but he heard later that a cook had identified two former students, now sought for arson.

After school, Allen drove to his bank in Atwater and moved most of his meager savings into the checking account. He stopped at Bill's to grab a bite and call Trudy to tell her he was eating out again. Sipping a beer, Allen considered where he could afford to live that wasn't too close to Rick or too far from his sister, maybe the somewhat crummy neighborhoods south of his high-school's district.

He drove from Atwater up into the hills on the old bridge they used as background for so many movies. A few miles past Adams, he searched blocks of semi-rundown apartments and duplexes for an hour or so, then found a FOR RENT sign for an unfurnished third-floor studio in a brick building with a cracked, red-tile roof. It took another hour and a half to find the owner and see the place; it had one good-sized room, a bath, and two big closets. He paid the deposit and a month's rent using almost every dollar to his name, then drove back down to Bill's to call Dan about helping him move.

After eleven, he tried to tiptoe past Pedro to go down to his bed, but Trudy had forgotten to put on the cage cover. The parakeet woke up with a screech, then he squawked more and said, "Pedro boy, Pedro boy, Pedro . . . ."

"I fuckin' just got to sleep." Rick stood at the door in his briefs. "I'm throwin' that goddamn bird out."

Allen faced him from in front of the cage. "You aren't going to touch him."

"You gonna stop me, fat-ass?"

Trudy shuffled into the dining room toward Rick in her blue terry-cloth bathrobe. "Just shut up and go back to bed."

"You're not talkin' to me like that," Rick said with a snarl.

Allen detached the cage from the stand. "Stop, I'm taking him for good, right now."

Trudy came closer. "In the middle of the night? Where?"

"I rented an apartment."

Rick walked away. "Bitchin'—sooner the better," he said, leaving the dining room.

Allen put Pedro's cage down and faced Trudy. "Dan's helping me move tomorrow—a place near City College."

"Why so soon, Allen?"

He scowled toward their bedroom. "Why do you think?"

"He's extra cranky because I disgust him and he's not getting any."

"Jesus, Trudy, I don't want to hear about that. I wouldn't be so sure he wasn't . . . ."

"You know something I don't?"

He picked up the cage. "No."

"Then maybe you need to shut up, too."

"Yeah, maybe so." He walked away with the bird, then stopped. "I'm staying downstairs tonight after I take him." He sighed. "I'll only be twenty minutes away after I move. I want you to call me if, um, you ever need anything."

"Get on with your life, Allen. Don't worry about me."

"See you in the morning." He went outside and had to wipe away a couple of tears before he drove away.

With the help of Dan's station wagon and a half-case of beer, by the next afternoon they finished moving his larger possessions—books, records, a portable stereo, some brick-and-plank shelves, an old dinette set Trudy didn't want, his hide-a-bed, and a small TV. Allen moved his clothes and the rest in the Volvo, then on Sunday spent a few hours on lesson plans and student papers before he began to unpack, talking to Pedro.

Defying the old adage about the lion, the approach of March in L.A. was more like a warm grey lamb, causing early spring fever among Marshall's students and adding to the leftover buzz about the demise of the popcorn stand. Absenteeism was on the rise, and the usual Monday gloom lost out to excitement over an apparently brutal fight before school behind the gym.

In his classes, more readers had volunteered to be tutors, making the matchups go even better, regardless of so many antsy kids. After school, Allen sat down to evaluate the new program, but he also needed to see Mrs. Berg—Sandra was absent again, and Charmane didn't know why. He went down to the office; the counselor was out, so he looked up Sandra's phone number but decided not to call until he spoke to Mrs. Berg.

Back in the room, he took out his lists and estimated that for almost a third of the tutored kids the approach was working like finding a lost key—something clicked, and they were reading. About another third struggled but slowly progressed, some eagerly. Allen tried not to be discouraged by the rest, more than twenty who weren't getting anywhere. About half of those kids were making an effort—the others, his most aggressive or sullen students, usually refused to recite. As for the tutors, most of them seemed to show improved skills with their own work.

Allen went out to Monique's door, knocked and entered. She greeted him from her desk, where she was sorting papers. Pinned to a clothesline from door to door, there were about twenty-five watercolor washes of orange or red sunsets—a few had blue skies made somber with grey streaks. Every horizon had objects etched in black silhouette—rooftops, telephone poles, aerials, billboards, water tanks; one had the Watts Towers and a tree.

"Those are amazing, Monique."

"Didn't they do well? They really got the idea of mixing colors to create a mood."

They chatted more about the silhouettes, then he sighed and told her about the first results of his literacy efforts.

"Allen, don't be so down. Progress by that many kids is wonderful, and I have another suggestion for your new readers." She said they could illustrate each page, make a book, and read the new entries to an adult at home. "After all, they're mostly twelve and thirteen-year-olds, and many of them love to draw—another incentive to read."

"Good idea."

"What else is bothering you, *chéri?*"

He made a slight grin. "Is this intuition in action?"

"No, you're pretty easy to read."

"That's what Trudy says." He sighed again. "Yeah, one thing is I haven't been able to get in touch with Mrs. Berg to find out about Sandra."

"Sharon has been swamped, but I think she went over there again today on her way downtown. You do realize she probably can't tell you everything that's going on?"

"That's fine, I just want something to get resolved so Sandra doesn't get behind again."

"Sharon's going to be out until Thursday, but I'm sure she'll tell you what she can when she gets back. My guess is that you'll see Sandra tomorrow."

"I hope you're right."

"So what else is going on, Allen?"

He told her about his move to the small apartment.

"Sounds like a *lofty* new place."

He smiled at her pun. "Yeah, it's good to be out of that damn basement."

Her face turned more serious. "Allen, is being on your own going to be a difficult adjustment for you?"

"Are you thinking about my jungle story?"

"In a way, I guess. What motivated the sudden move?"

"That would be Rick the Prick." He tried not to bore her with too many details. ". . . so that's the deal—Dan helped me take my stuff over."

"You and Trudy seem pretty close, regardless of him."

"Yeah, it would help us both if I figured out what I want to do with myself."

"For what it's worth, I'm excited about your teaching, Allen, and you're dealing pretty well some of our, uh, more challenging staff members."

"You and Dan helped a lot with that. He thinks I'm too much of a loner, especially with females my age."

"I hope I didn't discourage you with Linda."

"You didn't. I don't think she's into the kooky religious stuff, but getting to know her probably isn't in the cards."

"I don't see why not, but that's none of my business."

He and Monique talked a little more "shop," then left together before dark. That night, Pedro seemed especially excited, chattering crazily and mixing up his wolf whistle with "Reveille" again. Allen carried the cage and stand to the studio's only large window; he slid it open so Pedro could enjoy some air. A nearby tall jacaranda was already in lavender bloom, its sweet perfume wafting through the screen.

"Nice, huh, boy? But no birds for you to talk to yet." Pedro hopped right over to his owner's lips at the side of the cage. Allen repeated the *puddy tat* refrain several times before he stopped. "Sorry, ol' bird, that's it." Pedro danced, then went into his *I'm a chicken* routine as Allen began to arrange the small apartment.

As Monique predicted, Sandra was back on Tuesday, preoccupied with making up the work in all of her classes. She had a new look—jeans, a flowery blouse, and a wide red ribbon like a hippie headband around her new short Afro. She didn't say anything to Allen that day or the next about the situation with her mother and the baby.

On Thursday, the last day of leap-year February, they let school out one period early for a two-hour teachers' in-service. On the way to the meeting, Allen and Monique were starting into the coliseum from the north archway. It was so hot that the black macadam stuck a little to the soles of his hiking shoes.

Adjusting the purse on her shoulder, Monique led him toward the afternoon shade by the kiva. "So, did you see Sharon about Sandra?"

"No, but Sandra seems okay. I'd still like to talk to Sharon—maybe after this meeting."

"She'll be there. We still have a couple of minutes." She rested her purse on the kiva wall; some teachers crossed the south archway to the cafeteria. "How's the new place?"

"Still a mess. My bird seems to like it."

"Pedro, right? Tell me another one of his lines."

Allen smiled. "Okay, he does Chester, cowboy twang and all—*Howdy, Mister Dillon.*"

"Priceless, I've got to meet him."

"We'll have to take care of that."

"Allen, remember the other day when you were talking about being a loner? Well, in some ways, so am I. Sharon and Greg are my only real friends here in the over-fifty crowd. As you know, I'm not above a self-serving acquaintance or two, but I don't get along very well with my generation." She made a rare sigh. "We get a lot of credit because of World War II, some of it deserved, but now a lot of us are just part of the problem."

He smiled and put one foot up on the short wall.

"What, *chéri?*"

"You're young at heart, but not like that corny old song."

"Well, thank you." Her fair face blushed a bit. "Allen, you said Dan is the only childhood friend you've stuck with. Do you want to tell me about that?"

He exhaled, just audibly, and leaned an elbow on his raised knee. "Trudy's the only one I ever explained this to."

"If you don't feel like—"

"No, it's okay." He waited for a teacher to hurry by, then told her about his parents dying in a freeway crash. ". . . and after that, it was pretty simple—my other so-called buddies vanished, and my girlfriend dropped me cold. Not Dan, he was there for all of it—the funeral, everything, although I was pretty messed up. I'll always be grateful to him." He felt pressure around his eyes. She picked up her purse, and they ambled toward the archway.

"Between Dan and your sister, I think you probably have more quality relationships than most people do."

Locking his jaw, he managed not to tear up before smiling back at her. "Yeah, maybe so, but I think I have another good friend now."

"I feel the same way, *amour.*"

They approached the entrance behind a few other teachers. She squeezed his elbow, and he patted Monique's hand before she let go. Allen reached for the cafeteria door and pulled the handle. "It's back to the fun and games. Do you have any idea what they have planned for us?"

"Yes, get ready for some fireworks."

Just inside the door, Ishimoto stood at attention in a Burgundy suit. The vice-principal turned to Allen, her seething black eyes saying, *You're late.* She ask-ordered him to sit with his department, then made a fleeting smile to Monique.

Eight or nine tables were interspersed throughout the long room this time, each one at least fifteen feet from the next. The window sliders were all pushed up several inches for some air. Monique and Allen approached Godina, who was sitting at a center table with Nash, Dorsey, Latham, and a pale thin elderly man in very thick glasses—Mister Rawlings, a recently hired long-term sub, like Allen. Frank, in his usual denim, was also sitting with them for some reason, grading papers. Nearly all of the other men nearby were in shirtsleeves, but Nash was wearing his coat, the enigmatic briefcase at his side.

Dorsey spoke with Godina while Nash held court for Rawlings and Latham, who had a powder-blue notebook with gold UCLA script. Monique was drawn unwillingly into Nash's diatribe, so Allen sat across from Frank. Two elderly English teachers—Allen met them once at another meeting—sat together nearby, whispering. Mrs. York and Miss Jorgensen both wore puffy-shouldered granny gowns, seemingly pleased that the style was in vogue again.

His face blank and drawn, Schultz stood alone in a light-grey summer suit at a microphone near the kitchen. "All right folks, let's get started." He didn't look up; it was difficult to tell if he was serious, angry, or both.

Several more teachers hurried in; Cecil entered from the narrow hall by the kitchen and began speaking quietly to Schultz. Ishimoto, now sitting with the PE department, sneered at some tardy teachers.

"Thanks, Cecil." Schultz's voice was picked up by the microphone before he faced the faculty. "Marv is out today, so Cecil checked the cars and found his own windows broken." A wave of grumbling passed through the cafeteria. Two men stood, reaching for their keys. Schultz raised an arm. "Let's just relax—Cecil's watching the lot until we're finished here."

Unlike previous meetings, he spoke right over some carping. "Here's the plan for the two hours today. Miss Dorsey, Mister Lee, Mrs. Berg, and I have put together four questions about racial tension at Marshall for you to respond to, discuss, and—"

Amidst some grumbling, Nash had jumped to his feet, not waiting to be recognized. "Mister Schultz, the Alliance was not consulted about scheduling this now. Perhaps we should work in our curriculum groups instead, and save a long-term issue such as this for the new principal." Nash bowed slightly toward Ishimoto and the PE teachers.

Frank, chin on chest, shook his head. Schultz's face had reddened during

Nash's interruption, then the principal bristled toward the mike. "Mister Nash, I've already made it clear what we *will* be discussing today. You are welcome to comment again if it relates to the topic at hand." The audience hushed while Nash muttered and sat down like Elmer Fudd with a squiggly black line over his head.

"The four of us plus the vice-principals and Mister Fogle will serve as moderators to assist with the discussion and your reports. The last question concerns recommendations—we hope to address those in our next meeting."

Some teachers groaned again as Schultz checked his watch. "Let's begin. No scheduled breaks—if you need the facilities, just go. Okay, moderators get with your groups please."

Schultz headed for the Social Studies table; Godina shed his dark-blue suit coat and began passing out dittoed pages that smelled of purple mimeo ink, tangy and cool. Dorsey had already gone; she approached the coliseum windows to work with the math department, which made it one black teacher in each of the seven groups. Allen looked around for Mrs. Berg and saw her sitting a couple of tables away, leading the science teachers.

While Godina passed out the last papers, Allen spoke softly to Frank. "So, are you here to replace Dorsey?"

"Yeah, I'm your token—she really got the short straw with that bunch." He looked across the room at Dorsey, then turned back. "At least I got away from Jackson. Hold on to your hat, it's time to raise a little hell."

14

The vice-principal faced the group, extra handouts in hand. "So two absent—let's all read this please." A minute or so later he said, "Okay, you have room to take notes on there. I'll be reporting on what we come up with for the first topic—our definition of prejudice in general."

Nash's left elbow brushed the table, rattling his chain. "We are not sociologists, what is the purpose of teachers—"

"Mister Nash, you are welcome to sit this question out if you like." Godina turned to the others. "Who has some ideas to get us going?"

As Nash pouted, York and Jorgenson huddled. Frank was the first to speak, glancing over at Dorsey's group. "I think Miss Dorsey's workshop from last fall gave us a way to define prejudice." He turned to Godina. "How about unfounded or unwarranted negative *expectations* about another group of people?"

Monique looked at Frank. "Yes, expectations based on race or economic class, also gender, um . . . ."

Thinking of Charmane and Ronnie, Allen brought up disability, then all but Nash, Rawlings, and Latham came up with more additions to the list: culture, education, religion, old age, intelligence. Latham's thin plain face flushed a little. "I'm not sure, but, uh, what about physical appearance?"

The group, awkwardly silent, turned to Godina. "Yes, very true. Okay, here's what we have." He summarized the definition and examples. "Are we all okay with this for now?"

Godina glanced at the brooding Nash, then at Rawlings, whose eyelids sagged heavily. "All right, second question—list specific examples of racial bias between general groups of people here at the school. Mister Williamson agreed to report on this one." The vice-principal turned to him.

"How about you, Mister *Godina?*" Frank said his surname in Spanish. "Have you experienced racial bias from students here?"

Nash's globular face contorted into a snarl. "Mister Williamson, it is apparent why you are with our group—maybe you could confine your comments to racial issues at *this* school."

"Is this discussion exclusively about Negroes and Caucasians?" Facing Godina, Frank pronounced the words, *KNEE-grows* and *COCK-kasians.*

Godina winced slightly at the sarcasm. "No, it isn't, but I haven't experienced a whole lot of racial animosity from the students here." He made a faint benevolent smile.

Frank stared at him. "C'mon, Ricardo, an example."

"Mister Godina," Nash said *guh-DYE-nuh*, "you don't have to tell us—"

"No, he's right. We need to identify all the examples we can." Godina paused. "Yes, a few students have referred to me with racial slurs, but they usually don't say them directly."

"Which still didn't feel so great," Frank said.

"Of course not." Godina almost sounded brusque.

Frank was still looking right at the vice-principal. "If you don't mind, what slur did they use—*spick?*"

Godina wrinkled his nose slightly, as if he were a boy hearing his mother cuss for the first time. "That's one of them, but if they don't say it to my face, I usually ignore it."

Frank sighed. "If a kid slurs you behind your back, isn't that like a teacher slurring students? I think we need to confront that behavior from both kids and staff."

Nash began to interrupt, but Godina held a hand up to him. "I agree, though sometimes other things are more immediate. I'll jot that below for later when we discuss recommendations."

He wrote quickly, then Nash, as if beginning a lecture to a group of inferior fools, raised his chin, adjusted his tie and flicked a speck from his coat. "First, I hardly think Mister Godina needs a lesson, Mister Williamson, on how to deal with name-calling. And when have you *ever* heard a teacher here utter racial slurs?"

Frank finally looked at Nash, his expression cold. "Let's see, the last time . . . maybe a week ago, and you can be damned sure that teacher heard about it from me."

"I don't appreciate your profanity. Are you telling me that he used the, uh, *n-word* in this school?"

"Sure, I've overheard it, but this was a *she*, referring to a fifty-year-old janitor as *boy*—slavery talk."

"Ah, I see." Nash smirked. "If I stopped every time I overheard students say *whitey* or *honky* in my room, I'd never have time to teach. Perhaps you're a bit too sensitive about some of these milder common terms, Mister Williamson."

"Maybe if you stopped to discuss those *common terms*, you'd be teaching something worthwhile." The rising tones made Rawlings sit up, his magnified eyes all the way open.

Nash jeered at Frank. "You have the gall to criti—"

"Okay, enough." Godina patted his forehead with a napkin.

Monique stopped fiddling with a red paper flower on her purse. "I think racial animosity by staff is often subtle, not so overt." Everyone had turned to her. "Frank reminded us how eloquently Miss Dorsey has taught us to *expect* students to succeed. I'll just say that it took much of my career to grow away from my racial bias and at least begin with an expectation that each student will learn."

A scowl and a condescending grin somehow shared Nash's face. He took another glimpse at Monique's chest. "That's all well and good, Mrs. Morgan, but we do have our adopted standards, which you and I have quibbled over at times. The policy states that the curriculum cannot be compromised for the sake of remediation. Our high standards form our expectations."

Frank glared at the table. "As usual, you're not listening. The curriculum is for kids who read and write well. Miss Dorsey and Monique expect *all* students to learn."

Nash loured at Frank as Godina responded. "We can come back for more on racial animosity between staff and students, but let's go on now to other conflicts."

"Yeah, let's." Frank turned to Nash with a menacing glare. "Between teachers."

Nash raised one brow disdainfully. "I suggest you speak for yourself, Mister Williamson."

"Fine, I'll admit my racial animosity, but I'd also say that those who deny it the loudest are usually the most racist of all." His tone was bland. Allen and Monique stifled grins.

Nash clenched his teeth, his face turning red. "I don't have to sit here and be subjected to these insults."

Mrs. York turned to him gravely. "Mister Nash, your blood pressure." Latham made a slight giggle, drawing frowns from York and her spinster friend.

Godina sighed, dabbing his postage-stamp moustache. "Yes, maybe you two could calm down a little. Okay, what other kinds of racial tension?"

Frank tapped his pencil on the papers he had been correcting. "Between students." Nash groaned; the others waited for an explanation. "Skin color, darker kids making fun of light-skinned kids, and the opposite, which was more common when I was in school."

Godina kept writing. "Yes, I see that in my culture as well." He glanced at the clock in the kitchen. "Okay, another one is racial tension between staff and community. Maybe we can discuss examples of that before we make our report. Let's go on for now to the third question—identifying our own racial prejudices, those of us who think we have them."

Avoiding eye contact with Nash, Godina wrote for a moment. Rawlings walked off to the steady ant line of teachers going to and from the restrooms. Allen watched Ishimoto pretend to disapprove of some raucous laughter from Van Burton and the other male PE teachers.

Godina took a deep breath. "Mrs. Morgan has agreed to report on this question—I told her I'd start with a story she's heard before." He sighed. "I visited my grandmother in Mexico City, the summer of '59 . . . ." Godina said she had a going-away party for her boarders, some U.S. college boys. One of them danced with an indigenous girl, a maid, and his grandmother told him not to socialize with *them*. ". . . and the boy angrily left the house. I thought he was wrong, even disrespectful." Godina sighed again. "After my *abuela* passed away, I came to grips with the idea that she, no, *we* were the ones who were wrong."

Nearly everyone at the table watched him intently, as if they wanted more of the story. Nash cleared his throat in a high tone intended to announce something important was to follow. "Mister Godina, is it your expectation that each of us must come up with some similar true confession?"

Godina, who never glared, turned to him, his irises glistening like tiny black bombs. "No, Mister Nash, I don't think there's anything else you need to say at all."

Impervious to the conflict, Latham smiled. "I'll go next. My parents have always had the same Oriental gardener, and I always thought he was poor and uneducated until my mom told me he graduated from college in Korea. My dad said that Mister Hah—that's his name, H-A-H." She giggled. "He said Mister Hah will probably have his own business someday with ten men working for him. It's good that I learned about how industrious and smart they are before I went to UCLA, where we have a lot of Orientals."

Jesus. "Yeah, many of the Asian kids I grew up with were also top students," Allen said, and he watched her nod confidently. "But not *all* of them. To be honest, we sometimes spoke of them as *chinks*, *gooks*, and *japs*." Latham, York and Jorgenson squirmed; Nash shook his head. Allen faced Latham again. "Maybe I've gotten over most of that, I don't know. What I did learn was that their individual cultures are as much different as alike."

Latham was nonplussed, her thin mouth partly open. Godina broke the silence. "Finished, Mister Greene?"

"No. The girls of Japanese descent in my high school had a reputation with us—we said they were snotty and acted superior." He glanced at Ishimoto; Frank and Monique made slight smiles. "When I run into someone now who fits our old stereotype, I still have to remind myself that she's an individual, and no one else deserves to be labeled by her snobbish attitude."

Nash scowled as if Allen were a sub-species. "Pure double-talk from our secular, so-called *open* generation. It is so typical that you would mock the attitudes of others, and then turn around and bare your own prejudice."

"Well, Mister Nash, something I've been reminded of in my one month here is that prejudice is part of me and my L.A. neighborhood—I'm trying to be aware of it and deal with it, instead of denying it or being on a big guilt trip. If my generation is the first to admit its racial prejudice, then maybe we're getting somewhere."

Nash's jaw tightened more; his eyes narrowed. "Nonsense, and I resent your implication that prejudice is common all over the city. I can't even remember the last time I heard racial epithets in my neighborhood."

"Well, I hear them every day in mine—the store, gas station, any damn bar." Allen looked right at him. "Maybe you don't hear them because they don't bother you."

Nash sputtered. "D-don't you lecture *me*." He got up, fuming to Godina. "How many more of these testimonials must we endure?" He walked off with his briefcase to the line.

Godina began a review and expansion of their responses to the questions. Nash returned a few minutes later and sulked near Rawlings at the far end of the table.

After Schultz halted the seven groups, he began his report for the Social Studies table. They finished, there was a brief discussion, then Godina volunteered to go next. He took less than a minute to read and explain their definition—Allen saw a rare smile from Dorsey across the room. Frank and Monique summed up the group's work on the second and third questions.

Schultz praised them for "sincerely addressing the issues." After discussion, Fogle began to present for the specialists. When they finished, the principal told them they did not take the task seriously enough and had to begin again later. Schultz then lauded Dorsey's, Lee's, and Berg's groups before the final department began—Mrs. Ishimoto and the PE teachers.

They finished quickly, then Schultz censured them like he did Fogle's group. Ishimoto's jaw dropped. It was 3:25; the principal said he owed the faculty ten minutes. He dismissed everyone, but Ishimoto was already up, flitting around her table to gather the papers. She began to speak covertly with all of the PE teachers.

Monique and Frank stayed on to chat with Godina. Allen hurried off to catch Mrs. Berg, who had just finished speaking with the science department's one black teacher. The counselor was in dark slacks and a white, short-sleeve men's dress shirt. Allen had only been near Mrs. Berg before when she was seated, and he was surprised that she was almost his height.

Her short dark hair was straight and she didn't use makeup, but a full smile lit up her angular features. "I'm glad you came, Allen. Am I being too familiar? I feel like I know you."

"Of course not, Mrs. Berg."

Her narrow face feigned a frown. "It's Sharon, please. So, about Sandra—shall we walk as we talk?" He nodded; they headed for the south exit, Sharon facing him. "Sandra hasn't missed school since Monday, right?"

"Right, but she hasn't said much."

"That's not surprising, but she told me she doesn't mind if I explain her situation to you."

There were teachers hanging around by the door, inside and out. Sharon led him back toward the north exit. "Sandra cares about her mother, but she thinks of her as two separate people, the sober mom and the alcoholic—no middle ground. As far as I know, this is the first time Mrs. Small has been violent, but Sandra, naturally, no longer trusts her with the baby."

"Man, that's a lot to handle for a fourteen-year-old."

She nodded. "We do have a temporary solution. Protective services is worried about both the baby and Sandra. They're both staying with the aunt now, and her mother is starting treatment. If she sticks with it, she'll be able to take Sandra back."

They walked out under the north arch. "How soon?"

"If it goes well, as early as mid-April. Sandra has some stability for now, and I think she'll open up and be her usual self. I'd like you to keep me advised about how she's doing with you."

"I will. Thanks for everything you did."

"Thank you, Allen."

Across the coliseum, Frank and Monique were chatting in the other archway. "Sharon, I'd like to ask you something. I guess it might be considered unprofessional."

They stood still in the shade, and she smiled again. "Oh my. Go ahead."

"A lot of the boys in my classes aren't very shy about saying they'd never go to Mister Fogle to talk about anything."

Sharon frowned. "I can't comment on that."

"I know, but a couple of them talk to me a little, and I usually don't know what to say. Do you ever work with boys?"

"Unofficially." Her face brightened. "If there's a sister at the school, I can sometimes stick my nose in, but I believe you might be thinking about Ronnie Crawford."

"Did Frank mention something?"

"Yes. Is Ronnie already back?"

"No, another week."

"He only has a brother here. Frank is your best bet—he's getting some resources from me to work with the Crawfords. Did you have any other boys in mind?"

"Yes, Marlon Brown. The good news is he's a kid who had the proverbial light come on with his reading and writing."

She smiled, looking across the coliseum. "Monique told me about your program."

"Yeah, *our* program. Anyway, Marlon's doing great in class, but he's all mixed up because of this gold and black thing—he has some rough friends."

"Well, it so happens that Diane Brown is a ninth-grader. I haven't needed to talk to her for a long time, but I've been meaning to follow up with Diane and her mom."

"Have you?" Allen grinned. "Thanks, Sharon."

"We'll see what we can do." They started out into the quiet coliseum. "Monique's waiting to go out for a little nip. Care to join us?"

"Thanks, but I have to finish settling into my new place."

They walked past his duty area. Frank stood under the arch like a soldier at ease, hands behind his back. Monique was sitting nearby on a concrete bench, the big purse by her legs.

Sharon walked up to them first. "So, Frank, what did you think of all that?" She nodded back to the cafeteria.

"Nash and Ishimoto are pissed, so something went right." Frank relaxed his arms, leaning on a pillar. "But Moto and Fogle will just go through the motions to satisfy Schultz—those teachers won't get anything out of it."

Monique stood up with her purse. "You never know who's paying attention, *chéri.*"

He grimaced slightly. "Yeah, I'll try to hold that thought."

Sharon flicked back her very short bangs, then smiled at Frank. "Well, enough for one day, care to join us for a cocktail?"

"Pat's expecting me—some other time."

They walked inside and split up, the women entering the office and the men staying in the corridor. Standing near the door with his binder, Frank turned to Allen. "I need to go easier on Godina—he surprised me today."

"He surprised Nash too. Do you know where Nash's idyllic neighborhood is?"

"Somewhere near Palos Verdes."

"Man, how does he afford that?"

Frank waited, returning a nod to a young male math teacher who was hurrying by to leave the building. "Inherited it, he's a widower. Nash actually grew up in Compton—still fighting all the darkies who moved in."

"He acts like they already announced Ishimoto has the job. I should've asked Mrs. Berg. Have you heard anything about it?"

"I don't know what the delay is, but it doesn't matter."

"Maybe it means Godina has a chance." He raised his brows.

"Shit, Allen." After saying his given name for the first time, Frank started down the hall.

15

Monique was at a doctor's appointment Friday morning, so Allen waited in the lot for Frank, who usually arrived a few minutes after she did. The inscrutable shiny black Olds was again parked over on the next block of Harding Place, three or four shadowy figures moving around inside. Godina arrived just before seven, then Frank pulled in a couple of minutes later in his blue '62 Ford.

It was an even warmer day, so Allen left his Pirate jacket on the seat, got his teaching box and walked over to Frank's car. He saw bright baby toys and stuffed animals strewn across the Ford's back seat. Instead of his denim, Frank got out wearing an off-white dashiki, zigged and zagged in horizontal earth tones—rich brown, forest green, and burnt orange.

Allen rested the heavy box on his hip. "Morning, Frank, can I get in there with you?"

He nodded, glum as usual, shouldering a loaded rucksack, WILLIAMSON stenciled in black on its drab green material.

"I saw the baby toys in your car. I didn't know you had a kid—boy or girl?"

Frank's face tempered into a slight smile. "Both—twins."

"No kidding? How old are they?"

The question made him smile a bit. "Eleven months, starting to walk."

They had to wait for a couple of cars, so Allen put down his box, removed the lid, and took out Ronnie's envelope. "This is probably the last one—he's back on Wednesday. Thanks again for your help."

"Sure." Frank took the envelope. "Rob thinks this is a big subterfuge—he likes helping his brother with something."

Allen picked up his box, and they entered the crosswalk. "That's good. Ronnie's doing great, though his topics are kind of surprising."

"How's that?"

"He's never very serious, writes mostly about nature. I thought he might want to get some things off his chest."

Frank stopped at the front steps to let his pack down to insert the envelope. "Sounds serious to me. Most kids take nature for granted, like we do."

"Yeah, good point."

"After he comes back, maybe he'll join Rob in the march."

"What march is that?" They started up the steps.

"You probably heard about the East LA kids protesting their crappy schools. Well, some of ours are planning a demonstration after Doctor King visits here in a couple of weeks. They'll march at noon around the block, technically off campus. Want to join us?"

"You'll be with them?"

At the door, Frank reached into his pocket. "Schultz is unofficially allowing some of us to be sponsors. If it plays out non-violent and the kids stay off the grounds, they won't be hassled by the school, which is what we're telling them."

"Is Monique going?"

"In spirit." Frank held onto his keys, turning away from the door as if he wanted to talk. "It's a bit too much for her in a lunch period. Come to think of it, this deal could be a problem for a non-contracted teacher with Moto on his case."

"Yeah, maybe so." *Off the hook.* An old airline tag fluttered on the side of Frank's rucksack. "I noticed your pack, do you mind telling me if you were in the war?"

"Cartographer on an army base—my little brother was there." He stared at his keys for a moment. "Killed by our own damn napalm."

Jesus. "Sorry to hear that."

He looked up. "Don't be. Everybody from around here has somebody dead or maimed from Vietnam."

The black Olds drove off; Allen flinched at an explosion that followed it.

Blasé, Frank glanced at the car. "Just a firecracker."

"You know him? I've seen that car a lot."

"Yeah, that guy's trouble—didn't even make it into here." Frank sighed, then faced him. "Allen, my wife likes to remind me that I'm sometimes too negative, like last night when you and I were talking—it makes sense that you'd think they had to wise up about Moto." He paused. "I wish I was wrong, but I heard that they'll announce today that she got the job."

Allen groaned a little. "Man, it's so completely nuts."

Frank opened the door. They entered, stopping by the office. "It's the 'Peter Principle'—for principals."

"Peter Principle?"

"From an article that's going to be a book. It means promoting people to their level of incompetence."

Allen made a loud one-syllable scoff. "She's *already* incompetent." After Linda and Mrs. Eichler raised their heads in the office, he spoke more quietly. "Are you going to work for her?"

"No, against her—Jackson, Nash, Fogle and the rest aren't going anywhere. What about you?"

"What do you mean?"

"After our annual September resignations, even Moto will be out looking for you."

"I doubt it." Allen sighed. "Hell, I don't even know yet if I'm a teach—"

"Later." Frank was already walking into the main hallway.

Crap, I'm supposed to be Mister Chips? He hurried upstairs and got ready for his classes.

During duty, some students were already talking about Ishimoto. The leaked news seemed to sap the energy from a lot of kids; the day played out like a dismal Monday before Schultz made his politically expedient announcement about the new principal just before the final bell.

After most of his Creative Writing kids walked out lethargically, Allen went down for his mail with the idea of eventually leaving on time to get home and start fixing up the apartment. He found his first check in the box and was astonished to have enough money to pay all of his bills and have about a hundred and fifty dollars left over.

There was also a note from Mrs. Berg. He went in to confer with her. She said that Marlon's family, unaware of his gang involvement, would meet with her the following week. Allen returned to his room, puttered there for a while, and ended up leaving after four.

He walked past Marv's locked door and out to his latest spot near the back of the lot. He put his apple box on the passenger seat, then held still when he saw Nash approaching a silver-grey Continental parked several spaces to the left of Marv's shack. Nash opened the door, detached himself from the briefcase, got in, then seemed to be organizing his things.

Allen inserted his ignition key but stopped when a young man in a blue poplin Dodger's jacket walked casually up the driveway. He circled the hut and leaned on its back wall, out of sight from the school but almost facing Allen, who scooted down to watch through his steering wheel. He heard Nash start the Lincoln and idle the motor. A couple of kids left the school with Cecil. The guard started his rounds, pacing steadily down the sidewalk and looking out to the parking lot twice before he walked around the building.

The Lincoln glided over to the shack. The enormous vehicle blocked Allen's view; all he could make out was the young guy resting his forearms on Nash's open window for what appeared to be a brief but agreeable conversation before he walked off. *Strange, but why should I give a crap?*

Heading for the freeway, he forgot school for a while, turning on his eight-track and keeping time to "The Lonely Bull" and "Red River Rock" by the Ventures. When he got to the apartment, he spoke to Pedro for a few minutes, then started on the dishes at the kitchen end of the studio. As he worked, his mind wandered to Nash, Van Burton and the rest of their cabal, and how they were likely gloating over their victory.

The bird chattered away, reminding Allen of his promise to Monique. Since he had money for once, maybe he could have a small housewarming. He would invite Monique, Sharon, and Frank; then Dan, Jen, and Trudy—if she could dump Rick.

He started unpacking some books and heard Pedro saying something different. The bird stopped, squawked, then said it again. "Sorry, sorry ol' bird, that's it. Sorry."

I'll be damned.

On Monday in the parking lot, Allen didn't see the familiar red Pontiac. He turned toward the squealing tires of a new candy-apple Mustang turning the corner; the red sports car entered the driveway, Monique behind the wheel. He walked over to the Ford, put down his box and opened the door, feeling a draft of escaping cool air.

She looked up at him, smiling, then cut the motor. "*Merci*, such service. What, you don't like my new car?"

He was gaping at the fancy gadgets on her dashboard. "No, of course I like it—just a little startled. I should've guessed you'd get something like this."

"Never too old to have a little fun." She tossed aside the cushion she was using as a booster, then lugged out her gaudy purse. They started for the street, Monique telling him a little about her new purchase.

Frank's car approached the lot as she and Allen passed Marv's hut. He put down his box. "Let's wait for him, I want to see if he's pissed at me." While Allen explained the conversation about coming back next year, Frank parked his car.

"I doubt he's angry, Allen. He'd just like to have you here on his side. Like me, he thinks you're a good teacher."

He scoffed. "Well, glad you think so."

"Your doubt is understandable, it's only been a few weeks."

"Five, to be exact." He watched Frank get out, looking for something in his rucksack. "Monique, I'm going to have a little housewarming, probably a week from this Saturday—just drinks and snacks in the evening. Is that a good time for you?"

"Well, our board meeting for the local is that night. Were you going to invite Frank?"

"I was hoping to, and Sharon."

"Good, I have an idea. Would you mind a few extra guests?"

"No, that's fine."

Frank came up to them, and they exchanged greetings and walked toward the school. Monique turned to Frank as they stepped off the curb into the crosswalk. "I think Pat needs a break from us, Frank. Allen has a new place and has graciously offered . . . ." She finished explaining as they stopped at the sidewalk before the front steps.

Frank let his pack down between his plain black loafers. "You really want to host our bunch of rabble-rousers, Allen?"

He rested the box on his hip and smiled. "I think I can handle it."

Frank took out his keys and unlocked the door. "Okay, it's almost two weeks—we'll talk later." They entered, and Frank hurried off for his room. Allen and Monique started upstairs.

She touched his arm. "See, he wasn't angry."

"I know. He's hard to figure sometimes. Is Frank your president?"

"No, Sharon. Frank is vice-president and runs most of our activities. You'll have time to investigate all of this—you don't need to join anything now."

"Sounds fair. Thanks."

They began to climb the last flight. "Allen, at your junior high, was spring fever much of an event?"

"I guess—water balloons and pranks, that sort of thing, maybe a fight or two. Why?"

"We've gone way beyond that in recent years." They stopped in the hall, outside of her room.

"You mean riots?"

"Not like big crowds destroying everything in sight, more like constant turmoil—guards and cops chasing after troublemakers. Most of it is minor, but the cherry bombs and vandalism have cost us plenty. The fights are the worst—it's awful when anyone gets hurt, but especially when it's some kid who wants no part of it." She let out a sigh. "Actually, it wasn't as bad last year as the year before, but I'm afraid this spring feels more like three years ago, before the big summer riots."

"What makes you say that?"

"The tough kids are a given, but I see a lot of anger building in others who don't usually make trouble. I'm hoping they'll vent their frustrations at the march and won't get involved in any violence. One thing we can do is stress Doctor King's message during the next weeks."

He reached into his pocket for his keys. "Do you really think the kids will listen to my two cents worth on that?"

"A lot of them will, Allen. By the way, my homeroom chatter tells me you're easing off on the discipline a bit. I don't blame you, it gets tiresome, but now is probably not a good time. It's another irony—we want things to change, but the kids also need that stability. It's up to you, of course."

"I think I'll trust your experience." He thanked her, they wished each other a good day, and Allen went into the room to finish his preparations. During duty, he watched the students closely for a while, but the crowd was Monday-sluggish again.

He reinstated strict adherence to his rules over the next couple of days in all of his classes. Some kids looked at him as if he had suddenly gone nuts. On Wednesday in homeroom, a few boys started their journals for later in the day, and T.R. was fiddling under his desk—the others dozed or stared out at another smoggy March sky. Six boys were absent, including Rupert, who, it turned out, was able to read a little and could learn if he ever showed up to try. His absence did make it a good day for Ronnie's return. The bell rang. "See you tomorrow," he told the homeroom boys, and most of them stood up to go.

"Nah, Mister Greene—later." Darrel, who was also with Allen in third period and Creative Writing, was always amused when his teacher said *tomorrow* early in the day.

Ronnie came to period one wearing a dyed goldenrod T-shirt, his smooth head still uncovered. Without looking at Allen, he sat down to work on his journal as if he hadn't been gone for two weeks.

The tardy bell rang. Allen walked around the room and made sure everyone was writing while he checked attendance with the seating chart. Missing almost a fourth of the class, he stopped at Ronnie's desk to sign his re-admit slip. "Morning, Ronnie." The boy glanced at him ambivalently.

After fluency, Allen started them on a new reading project, then did likewise with his other four regular classes during the day. Last period in Creative Writing, they were finishing up the beginning prompt as he walked up to Ronnie's desk and initialed the last line of his absence slip. Allen whispered to him. "Ronnie, I'd like to read aloud one of the papers you wrote to convert to poetry. I won't use your name."

Ronnie just shrugged, then Allen went back up front and asked the kids to put everything down, sit back, and crank up their imaginations. Rupert sauntered unexpectedly into the room, dressed in heavy black clothing for the warm day. He glared at Ronnie, then took Michael's old seat by the window, which Rupert had "earned" by staying out of trouble the last couple of times he showed up. He gazed sullenly outside.

Allen went over to him and signed his slip. "That tardy goes in, Rupert. So you got here at noon?"

"Yeah, so what?"

"The short prompt on the board is homework for you."

"Ain't doin' that shit."

"Okay, first warning." Allen walked back to the front of the room. Only four of the seven very low readers in the small class were present; Allen would transcribe for Rupert if he decided to try, Charmane and Sandra would tutor the two girls, and Darrel had his regular level-three kid.

He explained the longer prompt on the board, asking them to think of a place, real or imagined, where they would like to travel. They were to use their five senses to describe the journey and the place itself, then tell what they would do there, and why they chose that destination. "Before you start, I'll read two papers anonymously—not saying the authors' names." Allen's definition made Charmane roll her eyes.

"These were written in another class on a similar project. I'm reading them so you can see how they responded in very different ways, yet they both did it well. Pay close attention to how they start off their papers." Only a couple of kids groaned. Rupert, still in his reverie, hadn't turned from the window. The class hushed as Allen looked down at the first paper, Ronnie's. He allowed for a few errors as he read:

"'I heard my niece trying to say, 'she sells seashells by the seashore,' and that made me think about the ocean because I never saw the real beach before, if you don't count seeing it on TV or going to the docks. My uncle says we'll drive down there this summer. He said it doesn't even take an hour.'"

Allen checked the kids—only Rupert didn't appear to be listening.

"'My uncle says there's some palm trees at the beach. He says the sand is clean, no trash anywhere because people usually pick it up before they go. He says you can smell the ocean and feel the wet air when the wind blows. They have lifeguards like at the pool so nobody drowns in the waves. I might go swimming, but that's not what I really want to do.'"

He peeked again; they were still attentive. "'I'll walk real slow along the beach and look out at the water. I might see a seal or some birds that are different from here. I'll have a coffee can and look down at the wet sand to pick up what I find that's new to me. That's what beachcombing is, I think. My uncle says I'll find seaweed, seashells, rocks, even a crab I could take home in the can. Sometimes bottles and other things float up on the sand from far away. I'll keep walking on the beach until it's dark and I have to go home.'"

It remained quiet after he read the final words. Ronnie stared at his thumbnail. Allen waited a few more moments before he broke the silence. "At the beginning, there was an introduction between you, the reader, and what the author was planning to say—"

"Shit, it's all a bunch a' lies."

16

The only kids who laughed at Rupert's accusation were the two other boys in black.

"Second warning, Rupert." Allen faced the class. "This is about something you *want* to do, so that part will be made up. Rupert is apparently questioning the background information." Allen turned to him. "So what is it you're questioning?"

Rupert still moped toward his window. "All of it."

"All right, please give us an example."

"Ain't gonna give you nothin'."

"How do we know what you're questioning?"

Rupert finally looked at him, his blank face morphing into a sneer. "More BS, you'll say anything to get us to talk."

"Yes, I would like you to participate. But since you don't have an example, I'll just go on—"

"It sounds like a girl, but it isn't." Rupert glowered toward Ronnie's side of the room. "He's been there—he lied."

"I doubt the author had any reason to lie about not going to the beach."

"He said he was at the docks. What's the difference?"

"It was made clear there's a big difference. Maybe there are others here who haven't been to the beach—nothing to be ashamed of."

"Bullshit, we all been to the beach."

Allen sighed after Rupert's expletive. "Okay, Rupert, you're out of here, but I'm not going to mess around with it until I have time."

"Who gives a shit?" Rupert glared out at the coliseum.

Gathering himself, Allen turned to the class. "So, is it true, have you all been to the beach?"

"Not me, just to the docks." Sandra smirked toward Rupert, and two other girls muttered in agreement; Charmane reached over to "skin" Sandra's hand.

"You bitches are lyin' too." Rupert got to his feet and faced the class.

Allen had already reached up and hit the intercom button; now he pointed at Rupert. "You can keep right on going down to the office. I'll be having a talk with your parents."

Rupert laughed straight-faced. "She won't talk to you." He walked slowly toward the front of the room.

"Yes, office." It was Venable.

"Rupert Washington is on his way down there for disrupting the class. I'll be there right after school."

"He won't make it—I'll call security."

"Wait, let me talk to him." Rupert approached Allen. They were about eye-to-eye, a few feet apart—the white downturned scar on the boy's jaw twitched nervously. "Okay, Rupert, you want to deal with the guard or meet me in the office? Maybe we can work something out."

"Fuck you, Greene." He sounded more annoyed than angry. Rupert turned and walked toward Sandra and Charmane, slipping a switchblade out of his dark pants. Allen hit the call button again, then started for the two girls, stopping when he saw the knife snap open in front of Sandra's face.

"No more lies, fat bitch." Rupert growled at her. "Tell 'em you been to the beach."

Sandra looked at him dismissively as if he were a nagging housefly. "Don't matter to nobody but you, fool." She peeked at the knife. "You don't scare me."

Allen had moved within five or six feet of them. "Put it down, Rupert— you'll be in a lot less trouble." Although he was trying to sound stern, his voice faltered.

Rupert pointed the blade at Charmane. "Fuckin' little ugly white gimp, *you* tell 'em." Charmane glowered back, her slender jaw stiff. Rupert's eyes narrowed as Allen took a step closer. "Back off, Greene, or I cut her."

Allen didn't move; Rupert turned to Sandra again, his jaw set so hard that his head seemed to vibrate. In one quick motion, he slit the ribbon in Sandra's

hair; she held defiantly still as the red material fell to her blouse—either sweat or a tear rolled over one cheek. Rupert jeered at Charmane and raised the knife close to the elastic that held her ponytail.

"Leave 'em alone." Ronnie spoke evenly, standing up four seats behind Charmane.

Rupert turned to him, making a simultaneous scoff-chuckle. "Little baldy in his piss-yellow shirt." Focusing on Ronnie somehow made Rupert's face and shoulders relax a little. "I know *you* ain't her baby's daddy." He pointed the blade at Sandra. "Gotta have a dick for that."

This brought snickers from the same two boys, and *Ooos* from a couple of girls; Sandra and Charmane glared at him. "It was baldy who wrote all the ocean bullshit." Rupert grinned to the class. "Y'all know his uncle's crazy."

Ronnie looked right at him, unflinching. "You really that stupid, talkin' about my uncle like that?"

"He's jus' like you, crazy and yellow." Rupert jabbed the knife downward toward his much shorter adversary.

Ronnie reached into a pocket and pulled out a short metal tube with a taped wooden handle; he pointed the makeshift weapon at Rupert's chest. "Get your dumb ass outta here."

Allen took another step. "No, Ronnie, put it down."

"Stay outta this, Mister Greene."

Rupert laughed; the same boys joined in. "That piece a' junk won't shoot—probably ain't loaded, an' you're too chicken-shit to use it."

"That right?" His eyes and hand steady, Ronnie stepped forward to direct the zip gun at Rupert's forehead.

"Mister Greene." It was Venable again.

"Send security now!"

As if trying to see the bullet, Rupert had been squinting at the end of the barrel. He looked one more time before he spoke. "Shit." Rupert began to back off, gesturing at the other two boys in black to come along, but they stayed put.

Allen turned to Ronnie. "It's okay, he's going."

Ronnie still directed the gun at Rupert, who came to the door pointing at his two cohorts, still in their seats. "You two punks are done with us." He faced Ronnie. "An' you're dead, bald little prick." Rupert opened the door and ran off.

Ronnie put the weapon in his pocket, hurried to the door and peeked out. "No bullet, stupid nigger," he mumbled.

Allen walked quickly toward him. "Ronnie, I've got to report this. Let me have that damn thing and—"

"That's your freebie on the cussing, Mister Greene." He backed out; Allen followed and called after him, but Ronnie kept running for the north stairs. The end-of-day bell rang; Allen turned back and went in to dismiss the class. Most began to leave right away, but Sandra, Charmane, and a few others got up hesitantly, their faces grim.

Allen walked toward Sandra. "That knife didn't hurt you, right?"

"No, Mister Greene."

"Then I guess we're all okay." He forced a smile. "I'll see you tomorrow."

Charmane and Sandra left behind the others, looking back at Allen. After locking the room, he walked quickly for the stairs, and then met Cecil at the second-floor landing.

"Hey, sorry, Mister Greene. Had 'nother problem—jus' got word about you."

"It's okay, Cecil. Are there any administrators here?"

"Saw both vice-principals a minute ago."

"Maybe you can come along with me so I don't have to tell all this twice."

After making the report to Godina and Cecil, Allen walked down to Frank's room to tell him about the incident and ask if he'd go with him the next day to see Schultz about Ronnie.

Schultz was still gone Thursday morning, but Godina said that both Rupert and Ronnie had been expelled. Just after seven a.m. on Friday, Allen and Frank found the principal in his office. After Frank divulged Ronnie's illness, Schultz said it was possible that the extenuating circumstance might help the boy get into another school in the fall. Following the meeting, the two teachers walked down the quiet hallway.

"Frank, do you think there's really a chance Ronnie will get in somewhere else?"

"Not if Moto can help it. He'd have to show that he really wanted it, and his mom would need to go to the district and fight for him. She doesn't have much spunk, but who knows?"

Allen took a deep breath. "Damn it."

"I'll be talking to the family some more—I'm hoping his uncle can help." They stopped at Frank's door near the south stairwell and exchanged nods with a custodian pushing a wide broom down the hall, lifting a low cloud of chalk dust into the air. "We'll do what we can about Ronnie, but we've also got to move on. It's about to get real busy around here."

"How's it going for the march?"

"They're getting ready, making signs and all."

"I haven't heard much talk in my classes about it."

"The kids in charge are eighth and ninth-graders—they'll be talking more to the younger ones soon."

"Are they sold on the non-violence?"

"Yeah." He made a somber chuckle. "They're worried about the *immaturity* of the seventh-graders."

"Who are you most worried about?"

"Expelled kids, outsiders from gangs."

"You told me Ronnie's brother is in one of the big new gangs. What did you mean by *new*?"

"It's all changed since I was a kid. They called them *clubs* in the '40s and '50s, started up to defend against white gangs like *The Spook Hunters* and *Coon Dogs.*"

"Those are real names? My God, I had no idea."

"Those peckerwoods came around for years. After the big riots, they turned sneaky, looking for blacks and Mexicans in parking lots at stadiums and department stores."

"Good God."

"The new gangs mostly go after each other—more guns and drugs all the time."

"Some of our kids are into all that?"

"The ones who wear gold are like juniors to the biggest gang. The black shirts are still trying to affiliate—maybe they have by now, I don't know. The kids running the march aren't excluding them, just telling them no gang stuff. As long as we keep everyone together, I think we'll be okay."

"I'll start talking to my classes."

"Yeah, do that. If you bring up Doctor King, you'll have some kids who know the message—they'll help out."

"Good. Frank, can we keep the poetry going for Ronnie?"

"Sure, why not?"

"Thanks."

After the Pledge that morning, Latham came on the PA for an announcement. ". . . and here's something we can all be very excited about. My father's construction company is soon going to rebuild our snack booth! Our clubs will again be able to sell popcorn and . . . ."

Ignoring her, some of the boys were already up and moving around. When the announcements were over, Allen said, "Settle where you are for a minute and listen up. I told Mister Williamson I would talk to you about the student march in a couple of weeks."

T.R. was nervously tapping the floor and winding his long hair with a forefinger. "What march?"

Marlon sneered at him from the windows. "It ain't for little kids." Not dressed in black himself, Marlon was standing several feet away from three other boys who were.

"All right, leave him alone, Marlon." Allen faced the whole group. "The march is for any student who wants to support Doctor King and civil rights."

Darrel wrinkled his brow. "Wouldn't we get in a lot of trouble?"

"Good question. If you go, Darrel, you won't be in trouble with the school as long as you don't miss class and . . . ." He explained the behavior Frank was expecting, then asked what they knew about Doctor King's philosophy.

Marlon got up. "He says violence is wrong—he says if you're violent, you'll get hurt back worse, and then they put you in jail."

A tall boy in gold scoffed from a far window. "They *did* put him in jail."

Marlon didn't look at him. "Not for a real crime. When Doctor King goes to jail, it's part of his protest."

The bell sounded, and T.R. was immediately on his feet. "I ain't gonna miss lunch for no protest." Allen dismissed them. When he heard some boys agreeing with T.R., Allen decided it would be best to hold off talking to more kids until the march was more imminent.

That weekend, he straightened up his place, worked on some student papers, and took Trudy out Sunday afternoon for a belated birthday dinner at their parents' favorite chicken place out on San Fernando Road. Now in her eighth month, Trudy's girth touched the red gingham tablecloth as they sat down.

"This is fun, Allen—haven't been here for years."

"Yeah, still no menus." The choices at the "ol'-timey" knotty-pine restaurant were displayed on a sign behind the register: SMALL, MEDIUM OR LARGE FRIED CHICKEN DINNER & BISCUITS, CORN ON THE COB AND FIXINS—NO SUBSTITUTIONS.

A gruff but efficient waitress took their order, then Allen smiled at his sister. "You look good, Trude—huge but good."

"Thanks. Guess I can't call you *Bear* anymore—you look like you've lost a little weight."

"Maybe—probably because I'm on the go all day."

She smiled. "I'm proud of you, Allen. You're going to stick it out to the end of the year, aren't you?"

"I think so."

"Still fighting with those same people?"

"Yeah, but I want you to meet a few friends I've made." He told her about the housewarming and meeting.

"Sounds like fun. I assume you don't want Rick there."

"Would you?"

"Don't start on him. I'm just concentrating on making it through this." She patted her belly.

"Fine, as long as he's leaving you alone."

"He is, literally. When he isn't at work or the beach, he eats out a lot, then drinks in front of the TV and goes to sleep."

"You promise to call me if there's trouble?"

"Yes, Allen."

They agreed not to talk more about Rick, then had a pleasant meal, Trudy asking to hear more about the counselors and social services at his school.

After a relatively calm Monday, Allen wanted to go earlier than usual on Tuesday to catch up on his reading transcriptions, so he arranged to meet Godina at six-thirty. There were only two cars in the lot when he arrived. He drove to the rear, but the school seemed ridiculously distant, so he backtracked and parked in a space near the street.

Before he walked past Marv's hut, the black Olds inched by, the frame lowered halfway to the ground, its chrome hubcaps gleaming in the sun. Watching the silhouettes of three others besides the driver and his huge Afro, Allen walked to the curb, then hurried into the crosswalk as the Olds stopped at the far end of Main.

As he stepped up on the opposite curb, the car's back door swung open, three boys tumbling out. Although they were nearly half a football field away, he recognized the two taller ones—Rupert and his mentor, Michael Bradley, expelled on the first day of school.

Allen put his box down and walked very slowly toward them. Maybe they'd see him and jump back into the car, but they ran from the curb up to the arborvitae by the school, Michael lugging a galvanized bucket. From his window, the driver called, "Go on," pointing at the building. The boys just glanced at Allen as they reached into the pail and started chucking egg-sized stones up at the uncovered third-story windows.

He started to jog. Halfway there, a window above shattered, followed by their loud cheers. They kept throwing, but Rupert and the smaller boy couldn't break one. Michael nailed another pane, glass cascading down into the old cypress. The driver, now about twenty yards away, extended his torso from the window. He pointed a handgun at Allen, who stopped and moved back one slow step at a time, his pulse thumping in his neck.

Michael turned, grinning. "Fuck you, Greene!" He pitched a rock right at Allen, who jerked to the side and heard the projectile draft by, two or three feet from his shoulder. Michael laughed, then launched another stone through a window. The driver retracted into the car, calling the boys. They ran back nonchalantly, still chuckling.

Michael stopped, turned and fired off another rock at Allen. He ducked, but the stone parted his hair, glancing off his skull. He straightened up slowly and heard Michael and Rupert laughing as they got into the Olds with the other boy. The driver peeled out, screeching the tires, and the car vanished around the corner.

A block away in the other direction, an LAPD black-and-white raced toward the school. Allen made himself take a deep breath as the cop came closer; he pointed toward the getaway, trying to signal that the car went left. The squad car sped to the corner and turned right.

He moved slowly toward his box, looking down. Allen spotted and picked up one of Michael's rocks—grey, speckled and smooth, like a riverbed stone. Checking his head, there wasn't any blood, just a small knot. A cop car took the corner and pulled up to him. The officer in the passenger seat asked for his name.

"Allen Greene. I teach here." He quickly explained what happened, then the policeman asked if he recognized any of the boys. Allen hesitated, then told him the two names. After watching the cops drive away, he lifted the box and forced the stone through one of the air holes. His pulse finally began to slow, and he made another long exhale.

Still jittery, he walked across the yellow half-dead grass. Allen put the box down and had to turn sideways to get past the pokey cypress branches and dusty spider webs to look into Godina's empty office. "Shit." He made his way back to the lawn. Godina, in a dark suit, waved from the front steps. Allen got his box and hurried over.

"A custodian said a teacher was walking toward those boys—was that you?" Godina briefly touched Allen's shoulder.

"Yeah, until I saw a damn gun."

"Smart move. Did you know any of them?"

Allen told him the two names and explained what happened as they walked in. There wasn't a soul inside, not even a guard.

"I'll add assault to the charges, Mister Greene. The police will probably have more questions for you."

"That's fine." Allen hadn't checked his mail after school on Monday, so he followed Godina into the office. He found a sealed Thurgood Marshall envelope in his mailbox, MISTER GREENE typed on the front. He walked into the vacant faculty lounge, reading the letter:

```
Dear Mister Greene,
    Speaking for the administration of Thurgood
Marshall Junior High, we would like to thank
you for filling in as a Language Arts staff
member when we were short of credentialed
teachers. We have appreciated your commitment
to regular attendance.
```

```
    At this time, we are expecting to hire
certificated teachers for fall semester and
will not be offering emergency contracts.
We wish you the best of luck in your career
endeavors.
Sincerely,
Beatrice Ishimoto BI
Vice-Principal/Principal-elect
```

Although the letter wasn't unexpected, he tore it up and tossed the shreds into the trash. Allen smiled about the union meeting that would be at his place on Saturday, then laughed aloud at Nash and Ishimoto as if they were sitting there in the lounge. *Okay, Beatrice, my turn to raise a little hell.*

17

After his first-period class finished fluency writing, Allen brought up the subject of the protest march. Sandra raised her hand right away. "Mister Williamson fixed it so we could do this and not get in trouble. I hear some a y'all." She paused, snarling at two boys. "Sayin' it don't matter. Well, people *died* other places for *our* rights, even some kids, an' Doctor King was in jail for us too. Allayall got no reason not to march."

Many of the girls called out in support; a few boys nodded while others grumbled. Allen allowed more debate until it turned silly, then he had them work for the rest of the period. As Frank predicted, there were at least a couple of kids in each class ready to talk about Doctor King and the students' protest, though none so rousingly as Sandra. By the time she spoke up again last period, Allen was less informational and openly encouraging the kids to participate.

The talk of non-violence didn't ease the growing spring fever during that week. Firecrackers and vandalism were on the rise, as well as fights—usually two boys in front of a large rowdy crowd. Allen set aside a few minutes of each class with an open question like, "What are you hearing about the march next week?" A handful of students in each period talked about it for as long as he would let them, and more of the others seemed to be paying attention.

On Friday after school, he went to a market in Hollywood to shop for his guests on Saturday evening. When he got home to his small kitchen area, Allen discovered that he bought more provisions than he probably needed. He put things away, then double-checked to make sure that everything in the apartment was clean.

Although he wasn't much of a fan of basketball or UCLA, the Bruins and the amazing Lew Alcindor were back in the finals. He fooled with the rabbit ears on his small black-and-white TV, then settled on the sofa with some late dinner and a beer.

He woke up Saturday morning before ten o'clock to cartoons, half a bottle of warm beer, and some congealed spaghetti. Allen changed Pedro's cage, spruced up the kitchen, and then went shopping for a couple more things.

At about five, in clean jeans and his Pirate T-shirt, he was putting out some food when someone knocked. Both Dan and Monique were coming early to help out; he guessed that it was Dan. "Come in if you're able!"

His very tall but slightly built friend entered in jeans, a brown polo, and his red California Angel's cap. He dipped its brim, although Dan usually cleared doorways by an inch or two. "If I'm *able*—what's that supposed to mean?"

"Damned if I know—my dad used to say it."

Dropping two large bags of chips on the dinette table, Dan's thin but handsome face was mottled with even more freckles than usual.

Allen took carrots and celery out of the fridge. "Thanks for the chips. Where's your better half, O'Mara?"

"You got that right, wise guy. The baby has a low fever—didn't want to leave her with a sitter." He tossed his cap on a chair. A rim of thin orange hair encircled his pink and balding pate.

"Sorry to hear that. Ready for a cold brew?"

"Thought you'd never ask." Dan went over to Allen, who had piled the vegetables on an extra counter that stuck out a few feet like a wet bar, giving the kitchen a sense of separation from the rest of the large room. "What can I do?"

"Maybe push the sofa-bed to the wall and check the stereo—it's been cutting out."

Dan left the kitchen area. "Hey, your little pad's looking pretty good now."

"Yeah, it's fine."

Pedro was muttering in his sleep as Dan walked by to the brick and plank shelves that took up much of the wall space. He started to fool with the small stereo.

Allen opened two bottles of beer. "See anything wrong?"

"Yeah, your needle's shot, but the doohickey on the arm had an extra one—it's already in." He put on Bob Dylan, singing the guttural refrain in "Just Like a Woman."

"Hey, after that, put on the album with 'It Ain't Me, Babe.'" He sliced some summer sausage.

"That figures." Dan checked out some record jackets near the rows of books. He walked to Allen's poster of a steely-eyed intrepid owl diving for a kill, a full moon in the background. A Buddhist master's poem said, "Our Moments Here Are Finite, Honor Each of Them," printed in the moonlight.

"Some heavy shit there," Dan said, pushing the couch to the wall. "Man, this is all right—outta the cave and ready to line up the ladies for your fold-out."

"Right, they'll have to take numbers." He started to wash the vegetables.

Dan sat with his bottle in one of the chintzy plastic-covered chairs at the round table. Taking a slug of beer, he talked about UCLA winning the semi-finals and eyed the bowls and platters of peanuts, crackers, cheese, pretzels, sausage, and store-bought brownies. He turned to Allen, who was peeling carrots. "Who's going to eat the rabbit food—you, Chubs?"

The phone rang on the shelf near the stereo. Allen hurried over to turn down the music, then answered. Trudy told him that she would be late but was still going to drop by. Rick heckled her in the background, but Allen couldn't make out the words. "No pressure, Trude—just come if it works out."

She spoke furtively. "I'll be by. I think he's going to leave."

Allen hung up, then Dan walked over with his beer, munching some peanuts. "What's wrong?"

"Rick the Prick."

"I thought he wasn't coming."

"He isn't."

"Then take it easy—you're ready for this." They sat on the sofa. "You hear that Kennedy announced today? Waited until McCarthy gave LBJ a good run—what an opportunist."

"Aren't they all?"

Dan took a drink. "That's pretty cynical. I'm stayin' *clean with Gene*—you?"

"A lot of my kids like Bobby almost as much as Doctor King."

"That's a reason to support him?"

"He represents some hope—hard not to be for him."

"Man, a month and a half and listen to you. Does this mean you want to keep teaching?"

"All I know is I don't have a job in September. I'm just doing the best I can for now—don't know about after that."

"I get it, Gunga Din. Gotta hand it to you—our kids are jumpy too, but I sure as hell haven't had any weapons in my room."

"Just those two times."

"Same kid involved, right?"

"Yeah, but he wasn't the aggressor either time."

"You hear about the high-school march near us the other day? It got so out of hand they had to call the cops."

"I heard it was the cops who got out of hand."

"That's the rumor—I don't know."

"Our kids are having a march next week."

"You're not going with them are you?"

"I wasn't, but I changed my mind."

"Jesus, Allen, you're the same as a sub—they'll can your ass, like that." He snapped his fingers.

"I get along with the guy who's still in charge."

"If you say so." Dan shook his head and took a swig. "So all these people here from the local—that means you joined?"

"Not yet, what about you?"

"No, just the Alliance."

"From what I've seen, the majority of the Alliance teachers at Marshall either don't like teaching or don't like our kids."

"Aren't you exaggerating a little?"

"Maybe, but not much."

"The teachers here tonight won't mind us hanging around their meeting?"

"Not at all. We're playing poker with a couple of spouses." There was another knock at the door. "There's Monique. I have a feeling you two will hit it off." He hurried over to open up.

"*Bonsoir, amour!*" With her winsome smile and looking relaxed in a red summer dress that came down just above her knees, she seemed twenty years younger.

"Hi, Monique, glad you're here." He squeezed her hand with both of his. She had the big purse, but not overloaded, on her other shoulder. "Come in, come in—this is my friend, Dan."

Dan walked over and reached down for her hand after she put the purse on a dinette chair. "Nice to meet you, Monique." Like most men, his eyes paused a fleeting moment on her chest.

She was looking up at him, wide-eyed. "Well, *merci*, Dan—a pleasure to meet you. Pardon me, but for someone my size, your height is impressive, and a redhead to boot."

"It's okay." He made a broad smile. "Just so you don't have to ask—yes, I did play third-string basketball, and the weather's about the same up here."

Monique laughed. "Good attitude." She took out two slim bottles of red wine from her purse and handed them to Allen. "Northern California, not Southern France."

"Would you like the wine? I'm making frozen margaritas."

"That sounds wonderful—no salt, please. How can I help?"

"Maybe chop some vegetable sticks?"

"My specialty."

Her liveliness seemed to bring Pedro out of his stupor. The bird clicked and bowed, then he came out with, "I'm a stinker, I'm a stinker . . . ."

Monique hurried over to the cage. "My God, just like that?" Pedro clammed up immediately but jumped onto the bars near her face. Startled, she pulled back a few inches. "Oh, I made him stop. Did I scare him?"

"No, he wants you to teach him." Allen told her the *puddy tat* line. "Just say it to him over and over." He poured mixer with tequila and asked Dan to get the ice from the refrigerator.

After Monique spoke to the bird several times, she backed away a little, still watching him, mesmerized. Pedro bowed twice and said, "Sorry, ol' bird, that's it. Sorry."

"Should I be insulted?" Monique asked with a laugh.

Allen tasted the concoction with a spoon. "He's just showing off—picked that one up on his own."

"Amazing. Oh, he's eating now." She stepped toward the jacaranda outside, inhaling its fragrance. "How old is Pedro?"

He added ice to the blender. "About fifty, in human years."

"Ah, almost a fellow senior citizen." As she checked out the books, Allen raised his voice to tell her more about the bird. Monique stopped at the owl poster, staring at it and turning her head sideways as if she were in an art museum. "This is beautiful, Allen."

Dan stopped cracking ice. "Whoa, Gunga Din doesn't need any encouragement."

She smiled and walked back to the kitchen as the blender's racket began.

Monique took a knife and deftly chopped the carrots and celery while Allen finished mixing. He poured the drinks into small glasses that once contained cheese.

Monique put the vegetables in the refrigerator and picked up her glass. "They won't be here for a while. Shall we sit?"

Dan grabbed a chair and the sausage plate. "Yeah, since the bird stopped squawking."

Cocktails in hand, Allen and Monique walked to the sofa and sat down. She took a long swig of her drink. "I like your apartment, Allen—lively and cozy at the same time. This margarita's delicious." Allen turned Dylan way down so that it would be easier to talk, and Dan got up to get sausage from the plate on the bookshelf. He and Monique finished chatting about Jen and the baby as Dan sat on his chair again.

Allen took a sip of his margarita. "You two are just the ones to answer a rookie question." He turned to her. "I told Dan that the majority of our staff don't like teaching at Marshall."

"*Majority* is probably generous. What's your question?"

"Okay, so what goes on in teachers' college?"

She sighed. "Well, unless there have been some recent changes, I'd say that most teacher-training is simplistic and irrelevant."

Dan nodded. "Still the same—just jumping through hoops."

Monique turned to Allen. "All right, no more shop talk for now. Is your sister coming? I'd like to meet her."

"Maybe. Rick's being an ass again."

"Well, you still have enough for poker. Pat is home with the twins, but you'll have Connie and Linda, at the least."

"Linda Watson?" Allen looked down to inspect his clothes.

She laughed at him a little. "Yes, Mitch is on the board, and Linda usually tags along with him to our functions."

"Oh."

"Such a frown, Allen. They're childhood chums—they went to the same schools and still go to the same church."

Dan raised a brow. "Linda, huh? You've been holding out on me."

"One of our secretaries—nothing going on, O'Mara."

"Sounds like you haven't tried."

"He's right, *chéri*. If you ask her out, all you'd be doing is showing interest. Even if she declines, I'm sure she'll appreciate the gesture. She's a sweet girl."

"Yeah, out of my league."

Monique finished a long drink. "Why do you think so?"

"Because I'm *this*." He moved a hand dismissively from his face down to his spare tire. "And she's, um, beautiful."

Monique shook her head. "Oh, dear, I can't let that one go. First, you're a good-looking young man, and if you think Linda's that superficial, why would you be interested in her?"

He sighed, downing more of his drink. "I see what she does—I don't think she's superficial."

Monique raised a brow. "Perhaps you do, but in a different way. Do you think part of the reason she might not go out with you is because you're white?"

"Yeah, I guess so."

Dan had been reaching for more sausage, but he sat down without it. "Hold on—she's black?"

"Yes, O'Mara."

"Man, it's good you didn't find the nerve—you can't start up something like that when you hardly get along with, uh—"

"White people?"

Dan's freckled face contorted. "Sorry."

"Forget it, you're right." Allen raised his glass to Monique. "But my new redheaded friend here is proof I'm getting along better."

Monique smiled back. "Yes, that's true." Her face turned more serious. "But I don't agree with you two."

During their ensuing discussion, Dan maintained that most whites and blacks weren't ready for such drastic social change as interracial dating. Allen stayed out of it, retrieving the rest of the batch of margaritas.

After they started a second round of drinks, Monique was speaking even more adamantly. ". . . and an interracial relationship is similar in some ways to the one I have now. Who's going to tell *me* I can't date whomever—"

She stopped because Pedro had started to jabber, shuddering his bright feathers before blurting out, "Geev Pedro beeg kees, beeg kees . . . ."

"Oh, my God." Monique stood and walked toward the bird, downing the last of her drink.

Allen got up with his empty glass. "When you neglect him, he says that to get you over there."

Dan scoffed. "You think you could prove that?"

"Of course he can." Monique grinned. "Pedro has it all figured out. I'll just give the little doll a *kees* and some more *puddy tat* instruction." She held up her glass. "I'm dry here, *amour*, can you whip us up another recipe?"

Allen and Dan looked at each other and laughed. "Comin' right up. A little help, O'Mara?" As they went to the kitchen, someone knocked at the door. Allen answered it.

Frank was there with a large bucket of chicken and two full paper sacks, a small crowd behind him. "Hey, Allen—rounded 'em up below. Two aren't showing, but we have a quorum."

"Welcome, welcome." They started coming in, some with folding chairs, others with food, plastic plates, utensils and cups—plus beer, pop, whiskey and vodka. Mitch put his bags on the counter, but he didn't stay close to Linda.

In dark slacks and an opened-collared white dress shirt, Mitch Warner was about five-ten, thin, and nearly as fair as Linda. He had his black hair slicked back. A couple of years older than Allen, he was a genial, reserved man—a music teacher who worked non-stop with the students, but he was hassled a lot by some tough kids. Frank was still trying to change Mitch's mind about leaving Marshall to sell insurance.

After giving Sharon a hug, Monique introduced her tall friend to Dan, then shouted, "Look everyone, Mutt here!" She pointed to herself, then to Sharon and Dan. "With Jeff and Jeff!" Sharon, in a bright cowboy shirt tucked into long tapered blue jeans, smacked Monique playfully on the arm.

Monique introduced Ron Lee to Dan, then Connie Lee to both Dan and Allen. In a tropical shirt and new jeans, Connie was in her fifties and Asian like Ron, who Allen knew was of Korean descent. Wearing an outfit similar to his wife's, Ron's grey-streaked black hair almost touched his shoulders; hers was short and dark. Both of the Lees were about five-six, a bit chubby with pleasant round faces, though Ron's had more stress lines.

Connie smiled at Allen. "You'd better be a good poker player, or I'm going to take all your loot."

"Guess I better hope it's penny-ante."

Not introducing Mitch or Linda, Monique looked to Allen. Mitch was closer, so Allen shook his hand and introduced him to Dan. Mitch took it upon himself to present Linda; Allen tried not to look annoyed. She was in brown slacks, a white blouse and thin cardigan, her smile radiant as always.

Allen nodded to her. "Evening, good to see you."

Linda lifted her slender arm toward him. "Thanks for being the host."

He held her incredibly soft hand a bit too long, then pointed out the bathroom to his guests. They poured drinks, filled their plates, and sat down to eat from their laps. Frank took a few 45 RPM records from his sack and put them on the stereo. The first song, "Dance to the Music," was by a group Allen recently heard about, Sly and the Family Stone. Tapping one foot to the lively beat, he made another batch of margaritas and a plate of food for himself.

Allen grabbed a folding chair and sat by Dan, who was on the sofa, Monique and Sharon next to him. "Good people, Allen," Dan said, then he spoke under his breath. "Man, no wonder you're so gone on Linda. Except for the Afro, you can hardly tell she's black."

"Jesus, Dan."

"What? You were right—she's way out of your league."

Monique leaned in. "Don't listen to him."

Holding a chicken leg, Allen whispered back to her. "You sure there's nothing serious between Linda and Mitch?"

"No, I'm not sure."

Dan laughed. "Gonna have to be brave and find out yourself, Chubs."

"Clam it, O'Mara."

Connie danced with Ron, and Monique with Frank while the others finished eating, then Sharon had the board members pull up chairs around the sofa to start their meeting. Allen and Dan cleared everything from the dinette table, then they sat there with Connie. She took cards and poker chips out of a bag. "Okay, it's penny, nickel, dime—nickel ante, three raises. Three bucks minimum to start—I have change." Linda came back from the bathroom and sat in the chair opposite Dan. She held a five-dollar bill and a cheese glass with *crème de menthe* over ice.

As they played mostly seven-card stud, Allen furtively watched Linda and lost nearly every hand, then he heard Sharon say something in the meeting about the upcoming march. ". . . the kids will get a good boost from Doctor King being in L.A. tomorrow." Frank started talking about a teachers' wildcat strike later in the spring. "... we can't let our walkout get smeared by the press like the one in East L.A. did."

Sharon nodded. "They only interviewed Alliance teachers, for God's sake."

"Right. For our deal, everybody has to have a copy of the grievances, or know them. Tell people to remember *ODORS*." Nobody laughed at Frank's acronym; he ticked off the list on his fingers: "O—Overcrowded classes, D—Decrepit facilities, O—Out-of-date materials and equipment, R—Racist curriculum, and S—Staff development relevant to our school."

Pedro piped up with, "Howdy, Mister Dillon. Howdy ...."

When they stopped laughing, Allen called over. "You want me to move him?"

"No, he's fine." Monique was still chuckling.

By the time it sounded like the meeting was about to break up, Connie and Linda had the tallest piles of chips; Allen was getting up for another knock at the door. "They killed us, Dan." He walked over and opened up. His sister stood there, wiping away tears and forcing a smile. "What's wrong, Trude?"

She walked just inside, looking uncomfortable and unbalanced in her pup tent-sized blue smock. She smiled to the poker players, who had all stood when she came in. Trudy turned to her brother. "Can we talk just a sec?"

"Sure." He led her back out to the small porch.

"Allen, I had to bring Rick along—he's down in the car, sleeping it off. I'll just see your place, meet your friends, and then go."

"Okay, if that's what you think."

They went back in. The poker players had hauled their chairs away to socialize with the others. "My sister Trudy, everybody." Allen said each name as she shook hands, stopping for a longer chat with Sharon and Monique, who had been talking to Pedro. Then he left his sister with Linda and Connie, telling them that Trudy, like Connie, had studied social work.

While the three women struck up a conversation, he slipped away over to Dan, who was on the sofa, where Monique and Sharon had joined him again. Allen sat in a chair, facing them. Out of Dan's sight, the two women were holding hands.

Man, are they .... Except for high-school jerks bragging about *rolling queers down on Ivar*, the extent of Allen's knowledge of homosexuality came from his reading. He turned awkwardly to Dan, but someone started banging on the door.

Before Allen got all the way up, Rick stumbled in, wearing jeans and a yellow T-shirt, a coconut palm on front—his long bleached hair was unkempt and had a black streak, probably car grease. Everyone stopped talking to watch him stagger over to Trudy at the cage, where she had been showing Pedro to Connie and Linda.

"Fuckin' bird." He slurred his words in a low voice. "Less-go, Trudy."

She glared at him. "Go back down to the car—I'll be there in a few minutes." Trudy faced Connie, and the guests started to talk a little. Allen walked toward the kitchen.

Rick was focusing on the booze over on the counter. "I'll jus' have some refreshment while ya' finish yapping."

Allen got between Rick and the liquor. "How about something to eat, Rick?" Everyone was silent again.

"Outta my way, fat-ass."

"Know what? You can just get the hell outta here."

Trudy took Rick's arm from behind. "C'mon, we're leaving right now."

"Wait a minute." Rick's bleary eyes finished scanning the party. "What's this shit, niggers, chinks, and ol' dykes? This's who yr' asshole brother wants you to know?"

Everyone stood as Trudy tugged at his arm. "Damn it, Rick, that's enough."

"Fuck off!" He hooked his arm inside of Trudy's and flung her away as if she were as light as a small child; she fell with a horrible thud, rolling on her side like an oversized ten-pin. Linda and Connie got right down on the floor with her before Allen bear-hugged his brother-in-law from behind. Rick yelped, bursting from his grasp and turning to Allen with his fist cocked, but Ron Lee was there to slug Rick with a quick left jab to the upper cheek. He crumpled to the floor, semi-conscious.

18

Connie told Allen that Trudy had some spotting; they left right away for the emergency room at a nearby hospital in Hollywood. In the back seat of the Mustang, he held Trudy in a blanket as Monique sped down Vermont Avenue. Frank and the Lees stayed behind with Rick to wait for the police.

After a half-hour or so at the hospital, a nurse told Allen that Trudy was going to be okay. She said the doctor would be more specific as soon as they finished moving her upstairs to a regular room. Allen told Monique the news. She hugged him briefly, then left with Sharon to "handle a few things."

As soon as Trudy was settled on the fourth floor, Allen went in. She was half-awake but not talking. He held her hand until the doctor arrived and asked Allen to leave for a couple of minutes. When the doctor came out, he said that Trudy had not miscarried, but it was still a concern. She was in a mild state of shock; there were also some suspicious bruises unrelated to the kind of fall she had taken. Trudy wasn't concussive, so they gave her something mild to help her sleep. The doctor wanted her to stay at least two days for rest and observation.

Allen returned to the waiting area. He told Dan, Linda and Mitch what the doctor said. "When she gets out, I guess I'll take her back to the house and just keep Rick away from there."

Dan got up. "She can stay with us in our extra bedroom as long as she wants—I called Jen."

"Are you sure, Dan?"

"Jen said she'd love to have her."

"Thanks, I'll see what she says." Allen turned to Mitch and Linda. "Sorry you had to witness all that tonight."

"All that matters is your sister and the baby are okay." Linda stood up and embraced him from the side.

Detecting a scent of citrus, Allen didn't let go until she did. "Thanks for coming over—see you guys on Monday." Mitch nodded and shook Allen's hand.

Dan was still standing nearby. "I'm riding back to your place with them. I got Frank's number so I can find out about Rick. Call me later."

They shook hands, holding their grips for an extra moment. "Thanks for everything, Dan."

"Sure. Try to get some rest yourself."

"There's a big chair in there where I can crash. Call you in a while." When he walked into Trudy's room, she was snoring. Allen stood there a minute or two, his eyes getting heavy.

He settled in the comfortable chair for more than an hour, but thoughts of Trudy and Rick overcame his drowsiness. Allen went out and called Dan. He said that Rick was arrested and the cops had already spoken to the doctor about Trudy's condition.

His sister was still asleep when Allen left her early Sunday morning. Monique was in the waiting area, drinking coffee. "Morning. Were you here all night?" he asked.

"Most of it. I checked on you two—you were both sawing wood."

"I appreciate it, but you didn't have to stay."

She smiled a little. "You might want to go home to freshen up and get your car. When you're ready, I'll take you."

"Okay, thanks. So you heard they arrested Rick?"

"Yes, I called Frank."

He sat by her, and she reached over to take his hand. He squeezed back, then patted her and let go. "What a night, thank you so much."

"Of course, *amour*—you had a lot of help."

"Yeah. Tell me, where did Ron come up with that jab?"

"Lefty was a lightweight boxer in the army."

"Man, I owe him a call. If Trudy's still doing okay, maybe I'll clean up my place a little before I come back."

She *tsked*. "We handled all that, Allen. You have food for a week in your fridge."

"Oh—thanks." They sat quietly for a few moments. "Monique, I'm sorry for the way Rick spoke about you and Sharon."

"He spoke like that to everyone—no need to apologize. He's just one pathetic person. Believe me, we can handle it. I guess you were a little shocked by us."

"Yeah, but it's none of my business."

"Well, let me say this much. Sharon and I loved each other as friends for years before it became an even stronger bond. The people who were there tonight make up most of our friends we can relax around."

"I can't even imagine what you two run into."

"We're not ashamed of who we are, but life's too short for constant hassles, so we usually pass for two sweet ol' widows—the tall and the short of it."

Allen smiled, then thought for a few moments. "I heard you guys discussing a teachers' protest."

"Yes, do you really want to talk about that now?"

"Why not? I already decided to go out with Frank and the kids. What's the worst that Ishimoto can do, try to fire me?"

"Yes, but they need you for now, and being in the march isn't something she can take to Greg."

"When do the teachers walk out?"

"Two weeks after the kids' march, probably during last period. I'll be out there if it isn't too hot."

"What about the Alliance?"

"Some of their members are in both organizations—a few will join us."

"Well, we'll see if I'm still around."

Allen caught the doctor on morning rounds, coming out of Trudy's room. He said she was doing better, and they were more confident that the baby would be okay. Trudy was crying when Allen went in. He held her for a while until she slept again.

An hour or so later, she woke up, her dark eyes deep in their sockets, her hair loose and sticky. She said that she remembered most everything except the ride. A nurse came in to help her clean up, and he waited outside the door.

Her bed was raised a little when he returned. The nurse had left the TV on low to a Sunday news show. "All fresh and clean. Feel better, Trude?"

"I sure do. Did you get any sleep at all?"

"Yeah, I'm fine. Are you up to hearing about Rick?"

160

She nodded, then he told her that Rick would be in jail until the cops spoke to her. "You'll press charges this time, right?"

"A day or two in jail won't change anything, but he can damn well do it anyway." She was facing the TV, her eyes glazed over. "I'll tell them that'll be enough, and that's the last he gets from me. I don't want a nickel from him, except for one thing." She turned to her brother. "He's damn well going to pay for me to finish my Master's. Would you bring my address book from home? It's by the phone—I'm going to call my lawyer."

"Sure, do you need anything else?"

"Not yet." She made a deep sigh. "Allen, when they let me go, I don't think I'll be quite ready to stay at the house alone."

"You don't have to." He told her about Jen's offer.

"That's so nice of them—I'll just need a couple days."

"If Rick is actually gone, I'll move back in with you until after the baby comes."

"Oh, he's gone." She was crying again. "Sorry, Allen. Thank you for everything."

He wiped his own tears and hugged her, then she sniffled a while and began to stare at the TV again. He went to her sink and threw some cold water on his face. "Trudy, I'll be back in an hour or so." He walked out to Monique.

After Allen rode with her to his apartment, he spent most of that Sunday at the hospital trying to limit Trudy's visitors—the gals she grew up with had gotten word of her situation. He had his schoolwork with him and tried to read some papers after Trudy went to sleep. Allen found Michael's stone in the box and stared at it for a long time before he got back to work.

That evening, he retrieved Trudy's address book at the house, then came back to the hospital to watch some TV with her. Allen was cheered by the news that Doctor King's sermon and march in South-Central Los Angeles had come off without any major problems.

All day Monday in class, at least one student brought up Doctor King every hour, a couple of them trying the old *get-the-teacher-to-talk-so-we-don't-have-to-work* strategy. Whatever their motivation, Allen explained

Doctor King's connections to Gandhi and Thoreau, then started each class on a project about civil rights.

Early Monday evening, he went by the house to pick up some clothes for Trudy, then he drove to the hospital to get her released. He settled her in with Dan and Jen before going back to the apartment, which he would keep until he was sure that Trudy followed through with the separation. Rick had been released to his brother and was to appear in court again that Thursday.

During the week at school, some serious fights broke out, causing two kids to be taken to the hospital. High-school truants and other young adults were constantly chased from the grounds; cherry bombs exploded regularly, two more trashcans were set ablaze, and a commode was blown to pieces. An LAPD squad car patrolled the school every day.

There was an after school meeting on Wednesday in Monique's room for the eighth and ninth-grade march organizers and their faculty chaperones, including Frank, Sharon, Mitch, Ron Lee, and now Allen. With all of the recent turmoil, the importance of non-violence was again stressed by everyone.

Allen arranged for his first-ever sub on Thursday afternoon so he could take Trudy to Rick's court appearance. The judge announced that the city and the defendant had reached an agreement. He summed up the crime, then statements from witnesses and the doctor. Rick sat there, looking clownish in a dark suit and his bleached hair, just staring at the table. Trudy's lawyer spoke briefly, saying that she had already taken initial steps to sue for divorce. The judge explained Rick's probation and restraining order, then glared at him, promising immediate incarceration for violation of either decree. Allen took Trudy back to Dan and Jen's—he wouldn't have time to move her back to the house until the weekend.

Friday morning in the parking lot, Allen told Monique the latest on Trudy. She gave him a hug, and they started for the street, Monique telling him that the kids seemed ready for their march after period four. "Sorry to follow all the good news with bad, but it was crazy in your room yesterday afternoon. As soon as I saw the sub they sent, there wasn't much I could do."

When he entered his classroom, three things were normal: the desks in rows, the floor swept, and the chalkboard washed. Salvageable rubbish had been left by the janitor in two large piles in the corner by his desk. Dictionaries and texts were stacked there precariously and surrounded by pencil pieces, paper, school forms, fluency notebooks, chalk, a super ball, rubber bands, and the tiny green boxes for hole-reinforcement stickers, which had been swept up like round white confetti into a small separate pile.

His closet and desk, neither of which he ever locked, were in shambles. Walking by some pencil and ink graffiti on the yellow walls, he came to the file boxes. The morning folders had been bothered but were mostly in tact; those from period five and six were nearly all gone, notebooks strewn over the table or among the piles on the floor. Allen picked up one of the few folders that had made it back into the period-five file. It was Randall's, a kid who belonged in a higher level:

> **What were doing today is nothing its a day off because this ladys a big joke. She looks like Ant Bee but not so fat and she sounds like her and just as dum. Everybodys laughing at her and somebody just hit her big but with a spitwod. She's always warning us how Jesus watch's how we all behave. Like hes Santa Clause or something. She's in the school everyday but its not even funny no more.**

He put Randall's folder back, then glowered at the mess. The file for Creative Writing appeared to be in good shape; Sandra, Charmane and some others must have kept things fairly calm in seventh period.

During morning classes, he said little to the kids about the state of the room, since they weren't involved. Knowing exactly what had happened, most of them said nothing; a few smart-alecks laughed. After Allen spoke to each class about the march at noon, he didn't sense much new enthusiasm.

At the end of period four, he and his students entered the hall; most of them headed for lunch instead of to the march. The noon stampede was about normal; Monique came out with her ninth-grade French class. Almost half of them stayed with her in the hall—four kids held up WE HAVE A DREAM signs they had made. Monique had to shout over the racket to him. *"Bonjour, professeur!* I'm coming down to see you off."

Only six kids from Allen's period-four class were standing nearby. "I guess this is all of them." He walked with Monique toward the middle stairs, his hand touching the back of her shoulder so she wouldn't get bumped or jostled by the kids.

She spoke over the noise as they started downstairs. "Food is a tough competitor, but there should be a fair turnout. It's about eighty-five out there—I would've melted."

"Do you think it will go all right?"

"I admit to being nervous about it."

When they came down to the first floor, most kids turned right for the east doors out to the cafeteria. The marchers went straight ahead through the foyer toward the front steps. Allen and Monique followed them outside to the waiting crowd. The student leaders and teachers were asking the kids to walk up to the north corner; Cecil was waiting there to escort them in his '59 Chevy.

"Good luck, I'll watch from here." Monique backed up into the shade by the doors. Allen helped with the herding of more than a hundred mostly older kids toward the corner. Besides the staff sponsors, several parents were there and two local ministers in white collars. Three Kennedy campaign signs waved in the air, plus about twenty homemade pickets with WE HAVE A DREAM, WE SHALL OVERCOME, and FREEDOM NOW.

Allen joined Sharon, who was in dark-blue slacks and a plain summer blouse. She held up a hiking stick with a Kennedy placard secured to the top. As they assembled with the kids in front of Cecil's car, Frank came up to him. "What did the judge do with your brother-in-law?"

Taken off-guard by Frank's question in the middle of all the excitement, he quickly told him the results of the hearing. "...it's been so busy that I never did thank you for all your help on Saturday."

"Yeah, I'm glad your sister's okay." Abruptly changing subjects, he asked Allen and Sharon to be at the back of the line and not let it spread out very far. Frank hurried away, clapping to encourage the kids ahead.

The front of the procession finally moved from the corner, marching almost in unison, about six across, two older boys out front keeping time by striking their snare drums to the chant of "Freedom—now! Freedom—now! Freedom . . . ."

The kids near Allen were mostly from the very low turnout of seventh-graders, relegated to bringing up the rear, including Sandra, Charmane, Marlon and a few other homeroom boys. The end of the procession finally started to move. Cecil followed about twenty feet behind in low gear.

As the middle of the demonstration approached the front of the school, four students and Mitch struck up "We Shall Overcome" on various instruments. The marchers chimed in with a loud choral rendition of the protest song that Pete Seeger had adapted and expanded from an old Negro spiritual—information that Allen had chosen not to "teach" to anyone.

The last of the column started to pass the steps; Monique and a few other teachers applauded enthusiastically. Godina and several more adults, mostly classified staff, including Linda, just watched. They were surrounded by a small crowd of gawping kids; at least half of them, about twenty, ran out to join the end of the parade.

Allen turned to Sharon. "Too bad there aren't more kids, but it's going well." She beamed. "Yes, wonderful."

After a couple more minutes of exuberant marching, the front of the line circled the street corner. When the middle arrived there, all the noise stopped. The kids ahead held still for a moment, then they broke ranks, most of them running forward. Allen turned to Sharon. "What's going on?"

She was wincing. "Doesn't look good." Cecil drove carefully around the last third of the march, all that remained. Allen ran off with some kids to the corner and looked down the side street. The old dry palm tree down there was engulfed in flames, like some torch for a storybook giant. Allen jogged down the block; Cecil was out of his car, running with Frank toward five or six boys, who cheered for the burning tree before they fled into the neighborhood. Frank and Cecil gave up the chase and returned to where Allen joined the remaining students, who milled around by the fence, glaring at the flames as the adults began urging them back to school.

They started to move slowly away as the police and firemen showed up. Allen called to a small group of older boys walking just ahead. "Any of you guys see how it started?"

"Some punk with a California candle." The others agreed with him, sounding just as aggravated.

"How about a name?"

They didn't answer. Allen got back up to his room as the passing bell rang. A few period-five kids began to show up right away. He considered letting them watch the fire trucks for a minute, but this was one of the two classes that had trashed the room the day before. A couple of boys came in talking about how the fire was *so cool.*

Allen glared at them and some others who were at the windows. "Sit down, now!" About half of the large class was missing at the tardy bell. He asked a few kids who had started writing to stop; two girls and a boy came in late. Allen pointed out the mess in the room, throwing doors and drawers around a little and warning them that it was an automatic suspension to forge a signature on a stolen tardy slip. ". . . and you guys are going to clean up half of this mess—period six will do the rest."

Randall, the boy who wrote about the substitute, spoke up without raising his hand. "You're all mad about the fire, Mister Greene. Most of us here didn't do any of this."

Allen took a long deep breath. "Yeah, probably so." He sighed again. "All right, you guys come on up to these piles and try to find your notebooks, then go ahead with fluency time. If you can't find it, here's extra paper." While they got up, Allen took some cleaning spray he borrowed from Monique and started to scrub some graffiti off of the wall. A minute or two later, some kids to his left were sorting through the two large piles and straightening the mess in the cabinet; others worked on fixing the file boxes.

A girl took the spray bottle from his hand. "I'll do this, Mister Greene." He turned around. The kids not cleaning up were writing, and not one of them had drifted over to the window to watch the firemen. He saved some of the cleaning for sixth period—twenty-one of them showed up, and most of them were also cooperative.

Sandra, Charmane and ten more students who came for seventh period got right to work on their writing prompt, unaware of Allen grinning at them. Between the kids and Trudy, how was it possible to be so high or low so many times in one week?

19

That evening, he called the landlord, forfeited his deposit and still had to pay another month's rent. At least there would be no big hurry to get his larger things out; he could concentrate on helping Trudy move and settle in.

Allen slept in on Saturday morning, then moved his bird, school stuff, some clothes and toiletries back down to the house. He took another load on Sunday, then went over to Dan's and drove Trudy home. Though glad to see Pedro, she started talking about getting a big dog. She insisted that Allen stay in the spare bedroom, not down in the cave, because she had decided to use half of her bedroom for the baby. Trudy's next big idea was a vegetable garden in the space behind the house where their mom used to grow hollyhocks. After sharing all of her plans, she gave Allen a stern "big-sister" look and dictated some household chores for him to handle.

While he worked on his lessons that night, even his school challenges seemed to be mitigated by the return of the feisty "old" Trudy. Feeling pretty good about a lot of things, Allen made a solemn decision that he would ask Linda to go out.

His positive weekend was offset right away by a dreary Monday at school, accentuated by smoggy grey overcast and the beginning of school-wide testing during extended homeroom every morning that week. Allen looked for an opportunity to speak with Linda, but after two failed attempts, he felt like he was stalking her and let it go for later.

Between sixth and seventh period of the normal afternoon schedule, a long white dual-cab pick-up and a flatbed truck loaded with building materials rolled right onto the black macadam and parked by the cafeteria. He let the Creative Writing class go to the windows for a minute to watch the LATHAM CONSTRUCTION COMPANY crew. Three men organized tools, lumber, and roof trusses; two others began to form an eight-by-eight square on the asphalt with concrete foundation blocks. The new booth would be a bit farther from the cafeteria and have about half the area of the old one.

"What's going on?" Darrel asked no one in particular.

Charmane answered him, pointing below. "Don't you ever listen to anything? See that? It says *Latham*—that's her dad's company putting up the new popcorn stand."

Darrel looked at her helplessly. "Whose dad?"

Charmane quickly explained the Latham family's largesse, then she turned to Allen. "If they wanted to spend all that money, why don't they buy us something we need like calculators or new microscopes?"

Darrel grinned. "I like popcorn." Before Charmane could ridicule the boy again, Allen sent the kids back to their seats to start writing. He told them they could check out the new popcorn stand later.

Just before the end of the hour, everyone went over to the windows. Allen, whose carpentry never surpassed a crooked shoeshine box he made in wood shop, was impressed that the small booth was already standing on the blocks, the walls connected with beams. Monique came in after school to see the new construction and to give him the names of some reliable subs.

"Hopefully, I won't need another sub, but thanks. This testing is a joke, Monique—half my boys finished early and slept. I didn't think I'd ever see this place as dead as it was today."

"That's how it goes during testing week—just stay alert in the afternoons."

After she left, Allen checked the clock. Since Linda worked forty-five minutes later than the teachers, his plan was to go down to the office at four o'clock and maybe walk out with her. Trying to concentrate on the papers he was correcting, he kept watching the minute hand creep along toward the twelve. Before Allen left, he looked out. They were already beginning to slap a coat of white paint on the new booth.

He paused near the office with his box. Linda was there, typing with such dispatch that he couldn't hear the individual keys striking the paper. Allen walked in as if heading for his mail, although he had checked it three times that day.

She glanced up at him. "Afternoon, Mister Greene."

"Afternoon." He smiled, and she resumed her furious typing. He went into his mailbox and took out two papers—they trembled in his hand. After returning to the office, he put his box on the counter and removed the lid. Linda was packing up to go. Allen dropped the papers inside, his hand still shaking as he put on the lid. In her pastel-yellow summer pantsuit, she opened and came through the small door in the counter, holding a mid-sized brown leather purse.

"Heading out, Miss Watson?" Allen opened the office door and backed up at the same time with his box to hold it for her.

"Yes, thank you."

They exited the school's inner and outer front doors. He opened each one for her, Linda smiling at his good manners. Had he been polite to the point of playing the fool? Half expecting someone to show up and ruin his big moment, there was no one nearby as they came to the driveway together.

Before he got up his gumption, she spoke first. "How is your sister doing, Allen?"

Allen—man. "Fine, thanks. I'm moving back in with her for now."

"They're separating?"

"She's divorcing him."

"Oh."

"Do you like the ocean?"

"Excuse me?"

Smooth move. "Uh, I was wondering if Saturday you'd like to take a ride down toward Laguna—I know a good place to eat near the beach."

They stopped by the booth, and she turned to him. "That sounds very nice. What time?" she asked with a neutral smile, but he couldn't hold eye contact.

He tried to face her. "Pick you up at four?"

"Okay." Linda made a broader smile, then took a pen and small writing pad from her purse. She wrote for several moments. "Here's the address, phone, and directions—you take the Santa Monica."

"Okay, great." He took the paper but didn't look at it.

"Do you know my first name, Allen?"

"Sure."

She smiled. "Well, I think it's okay to use it out here."

"Okay, I'll see you Saturday then, Linda."

"You never know, there might be a chance to say hello between now and then." She chuckled good-naturedly.

Speak, Bozo. "Right, see you tomorrow."

"Bye." She walked to some cars parked near the booth, stopping at a new light-yellow two-door Malibu. Allen shuffled slowly away, stalling for her to drive off so she couldn't see him walk over to his old Volvo at the other side of the lot.

Wanting to click his heels, he settled for half-shouting, "Holy shit!" Then he checked Linda's paper. Her directions would take him to Baldwin Hills, an area of L.A. he didn't know other than hearing it mentioned on TV.

Still on his natural high, he drove the freeway scarcely paying attention to the bad traffic and another grim war report on the five-o'clock news. After greeting Trudy and Pedro at home, he spread out his schoolwork for later. He found two sharp pencils and a few sheets of typing paper, then took care of collecting and putting out the trash. While Trudy started dinner, Allen spent the time writing and re-writing a haiku until he was okay with it, proper syllable counts and all:

> *Nature's beauty shies*
> *From the stunning black eyes of*
> *A girl named Pretty.*

Trudy waddled into the dining room. He folded the poem and grinned sheepishly, his face completely flush.

"Dinner. My gosh, Allen, what's with you?"

"Nothing."

During the dull testing in the mornings that week, the kids laughed at his mistakes and distractedness. Trying to keep his mind off of Saturday, he immersed himself in his teaching during the afternoons.

Allen saw Linda two or three times each day. She was the same as always, except she said his first name once when it was quiet. He chided himself for his silly disappointment that her routine, unlike his, was unaffected. In the office on Wednesday, he discovered that his shirt pocket was empty and ran up to the room, mortified that someone might find his sentimental haiku. He found the paper in the fruit box and secured it in his wallet.

On Friday morning, Allen met Monique in the hallway after his duty. She had been absent on Thursday for an outpatient procedure. "Is everything okay, Monique?"

"Fine, *chéri*, just some ol' lady stuff. Could you tell how things went in my room?"

"I checked in on your sub. She seemed fine, just had a question on the testing. The only excitement all day was a fight after school, but I don't think anybody ended up in the meat wagon."

"That's good." She laughed a little. "I haven't heard *meat wagon* since the war."

"From my dad, I guess."

"Well, hopefully the lid will stay on next week."

"Yeah." He paused. "Monique?"

"Yes?"

"Um, Linda's going out with me tomorrow night."

She smiled. "How very nice, but you look worried."

"I guess. Any suggestions?"

"Sure. Have fun and be yourself."

Allen went home after school on time for once and recited the *puddy tat* line to Pedro before dinner. He and Trudy watched an old Gary Cooper movie that evening, but he lost track of the simple story line twenty minutes into the show.

Saturday morning he took the vacuum and an extension cord out to the driveway, then gathered buckets, rags, and soap to do what he could to spruce up his jalopy, wishing he'd swallowed his pride before and asked Rick to paint it. He finished the car and was putting things away in the kitchen when Trudy walked in like a misshapen gourd with legs.

"So, who's the lucky girl, Allen?"

He shrugged. "Think you're pretty smart don't you?"

"No, it's about time you went out. You could've borrowed the Ladybug."

"Yeah, that'd be perfect."

"So who is it?"

"Linda."

"Oh? Nice girl, and what a looker. At least I don't have to worry about you running off."

"What do you mean by that?"

"My, aren't we touchy? I don't mean because she's black. Sorry, I'll shut up—you'll figure it out."

"Crap, figure what out?"

"You're too damn serious—it's just a date. Relax and have a good time."

"Man, you and Monique."

That afternoon, the barber trimmed Allen's hair, moustache, and sideburns a little more than what he asked for. Then he went home and cleaned up but couldn't decide what to wear. His only "nice" outfit was a dark-blue sweater with a dress shirt, but it was too hot for that, so he ended up in a light-blue shirt tucked into black half-bells. Self-conscious about his fat roll, he walked out to the car, rehashing Trudy's cryptic remark.

He drove the Harbor Freeway to the Santa Monica, half-listening to the radio until they played Joan Baez singing a Dylan song that Allen didn't know. The traffic made it difficult to pick up the lyrics except for its melodic but strident refrain, "Love is just a four-letter word."

Whatever that means. He took the La Brea exit, drove a few blocks, then turned left and wasn't all that far from USC and the L.A. Coliseum, which he always approached from the east through a shoddy commercial area. Allen soon came to a higher income neighborhood—a realtor's office had BALDWIN HILLS on its sign. He went on a ways, found the street and turned, starting uphill past modern ramblers and two-story houses.

The few people he saw were black, starting with a boy and girl who could just as well have been Marshall kids if not for their shiny bikes and sporty new clothes. He saw a dark elderly woman with very white hair tending her manicured yard, and then a man playing catch with two boys in Little League jerseys.

He pulled over near a corner to check if he had confused an *Avenue* with a *Street*. He hadn't, and he was only a few numbers away from her address. Allen put the Volvo in neutral, set the hand brake, closed his eyes and took some deep breaths. All he could hear was the motor idling, so he looked out again.

A middle-aged man eyed him suspiciously from a Spanish-tiled veranda. Allen drove up the block. Linda's car was parked in a long driveway before a closed garage by a white two-story house. It had four columns out front and rows of neatly trimmed decorative shrubs around showy flower beds and a big lawn.

It's Ozzie and Harriet. My God—her parents' place. He parked in the street and took another long breath. Allen got out and walked slowly up to the tall ornate door. What would he say if her mother or father answered? He pushed the button, then flinched, startled a bit by the first loud chime.

Linda came to the door, smiling. "Hi, Allen—all set."

He tried to smile back around his exhale. She stepped out and turned to lock the door. Her short canary-colored skirt showed off her shapely legs, and a matching thin velour pullover looked achingly soft. Linda's light-brown Afro had been treated to make it a bit puffier, and her gold necklace's single pearl just touched the line in the sweater formed by her bra.

"Allen?" She was touching the fleecy coat on her arm.

"Yes?"

"I can't decide if I'll need this near the ocean today."

"Maybe later on." It was well over eighty outside and he hadn't even brought his windbreaker. He waited so Linda could walk first down the driveway, carrying her coat and purse.

She stopped by the Malibu and looked toward the street. "Is that your car, Allen?"

"Afraid so, but it's clean."

"I'm sure it is, but should we take mine? Just to be more comfortable, since we're taking a ride."

"Okay." Acting as if her suggestion didn't bother him, he opened the passenger door for her. As he walked behind the car, Linda slid over on the bench seat a little toward the driver's side. If she sat right by him, it would take even more guts later to reach into his pocket and read the poem to her.

Allen got in. She hadn't moved much closer, settling near the middle of the seat to hand him the keys. Putting the automatic in reverse, he backed up to the street and started off, the gas tank full.

They began a standard first-date conversation, which was fine because she knew way more about him after witnessing the fracas with Rick. Linda said she attended public elementary before going to private schools and a local Christian college. She was visiting her parents for the weekend and still lived with her college roommate, Esther, who went to some of the same schools that she and Mitch did. She interrupted herself to give directions to the Pacific Coast Highway. Not wanting to hear any more familiar talk about Mitch, Allen acted half-lost, asking about cross streets.

Linda seemed both modest and proud when she began to talk about her bi-racial parents. Her father was a celebrated doctor in the black community, her mother a top Southern California real estate broker. ". . . and she also manages the house and my little brother. Anyway, I'm going back next year for my Master's in Business. I'll probably intern with my mom, but I'm more interested in securities."

"Why the year at Marshall?"

"Allen, you just stay on Western now." She sighed. "My dad says I've been slumming it, trying to get to know *real* black people. Mitch agrees, maybe they're right . . . ."

Mitch gave Allen another pang of jealousy.

". . . I guess I've found out that I'm not really cut out to deal constantly with so much conflict and despair."

"You'd never know it, seeing how you work with people."

She smiled as they waited for a red light. "Well, thank you. I put on a good front. Don't get me wrong, I very much admire the dedication I see from some of the staff, but for me it's an accomplishment just to make it to the end of the year."

He started off from the light. "Yeah, that's about the same for me, except the front I put on is acting tough. And I don't have much choice about coming back."

"I know. Will you stay in teaching?"

"I'm not sure. One thing I do know, I've learned a lot from Monique, Frank, Sharon, and Miss Dorsey."

"Well, you found some of the best people there. Allen, do you mind if we talk about something else besides the school?"

He was going to ask what she thought of Ishimoto, but he said, "Sure, that's fine." Allen made the left turn onto the Pacific Coast Highway. "Okay, here we go." They smiled at each other, then he touched his shirt pocket and the poem inside. He asked if she had traveled much.

"Oh, I love to." She spoke for a long time about an annual family vacation to Hawaii and a regular Christmas visit they took to New York to be with her father's family. As she told him about her other trips in the U.S. and Europe, he couldn't offer much but a nod or a smile.

". . . listen to me go on. Where have you traveled, Allen?"

"Mostly Arizona and Oregon—one trip to the east coast, then Puerto Rico. I want to travel more, though."

"Why were you in Puerto Rico?"

"Peace Corps."

"Oh."

He was about to tell her that he was a dropout, but she had turned away and was looking ahead at a beach community they were approaching. He spotted a road sign outside. "Speaking of travel, we passed Huntington Beach—we're now in lovely Orange County."

"Yes, where else can they brag about two attractions like Disneyland and Knott's Berry Farm?"

"I'm okay with Donald and Goofy, but not the other place."

"Mom and I like to go there for the country-style food."

"And your dad?"

"He won't go there again."

"I doubt it's the food."

"Yes, you're right." She looked out at a hint of dusk. "This is one of my favorite little towns. Would you mind if we stopped for a minute?"

"No, not at all." He turned off and found an open spot on a bustling block of faux-quaint shops selling clothes, antiques, and art. There was also a bakery and a small false-front bookstore amidst the eucalyptus, lemon trees, flower boxes, benches, decorative wrought iron and old-fashioned streetlights.

They got out and walked by an art store. The paintings were treatments of shorelines, seagulls and nautilus shells. Linda walked right into a chic women's clothing shop. He waited for her to look at some scarves until she put on a garish yellow one with brown paisleys, tying it jauntily around her slender neck. She raised her dark brows. "Look all right?"

Since any old dishtowel would look good on her, he just nodded with a smile. She paid for it, then they went back to the car. He turned onto the beach road and glanced at her. "Are you planning to travel this summer?"

"Yes, Esther and I are going to Paris—my first time to be there for more than a day or two. I'll relax and think about things." The car came to a curve, where she checked the view of the ocean, about a quarter-mile below. "Now there's a postcard sky."

Allen kept from saying that all the crap in the air guaranteed a colorful sunset. "Do you want to stop and watch it?"

"If you'd like. There's a turnout just ahead."

"You really know this area."

"Not so well past here. My mom has some land a few miles back—half in my name, half in my brother's."

He found the wide spot on the next curve and pulled off. "There, a few more minutes left."

"Our land isn't quite this good—the view here makes it prime residential. This will be developed in the next few years."

"That's too bad."

She gave him a blank look, then stared outside. Not an hour earlier, he might have taken the subtle orange rays on her delicate face as a cue to read his poem, but now he touched his chest pocket and re-creased the paper.

"Allen, I want to tell you something." She turned to him. "So there won't be any misunderstandings."

"Okay."

She faced the sunset again. "You're very nice, and I'm enjoying this a lot, but I want you to know that Mitch has asked me to marry him. He's asked since we were kids—he, Esther and I have always laughed about it. He's serious now, but I told him I'd go out with other guys until I got back from Paris, and then we'd talk. Sorry for being so abrupt, but I just wanted you to know."

He made sure that his exhale didn't come out as a sigh. "No, I appreciate it. I like Mitch. I think it's too bad he's leaving the school."

She turned to him, her face as close to angry as he had seen. "Well, I don't. He's such a sweet man and gets so much aggravation he doesn't deserve from the, um, hoods."

"True, but a lot of kids think he's a good teacher."

"I should hope so, the time he gives them. To be honest, I'm part of the reason he's leaving, and I don't feel guilty about it. By changing careers, Mitch eliminates two things I can't stand—the abuse he takes, and the fact that he's a brilliant musician getting paid peanuts. I'll always be loyal to him as a close friend."

"Do you think he'll be happy selling insurance?"

"Are you criticizing him?"

"No, I'm in the same boat, just finding my way."

"He has his own jazz group and does the music for our church—I think he'll be happier in a new career. I don't know yet if we'll be together, but we seem to want the same things."

"Does that include *your* career?"

"Well, he's not against it."

"And he's for a big house, private schools for the kids, and the right church."

"Pretty close, you make that all sound like something bad."

"Sorry, I guess I do." They silently watched the last slit of sun melt away. "Well, now that we've talked about all this, I would still enjoy taking you to dinner."

"Thank you. Yes, I'm starved."

He drove off down the coast road. Although he doubted his chances with her even more, Allen's infatuation remained strong enough that he was silently rationalizing their differences. "Do you like Mexican food?"

She said she did, and they chatted about food preferences for several minutes until he pulled into the parking lot of a small stucco restaurant right off the highway. He hurried around the car to open her door. "This little joint doesn't look like much, but they make great burritos."

They walked below a red neon sign, MARCO'S CANTINA, then into an alcove decorated with faded *piñatas* and *sarapes*, a tall green plaster saguaro, and a spray-painted gold Aztec calendar. They stood by a PLEASE WAIT TO BE SEATED placard. No one approached them right away. The distant bar was packed, but the restaurant section wasn't half-full, some open tables nearby. Allen asked a pimple-faced busboy to let someone know they were seating themselves. The kid shrugged and pushed his cart away.

After peering into the kitchen, Linda whispered, "Never saw a Mexican restaurant without Mexicans, not even the cook."

"It's okay—the food's good." He led her to a vacant booth away from the windows, where they sat across from each other and made small talk for a couple of minutes. A middle-aged blonde waitress in a wide-skirted red, white, and green outfit walked down the aisle by the windows. He called, "Ma'am?" and raised a forefinger. He said it again, a bit louder, but she scooted away.

"Allen, let's just go."

"Must be short-handed, I'll check." He stood up before she could answer, left, then came back a minute or so later. "She gave me a dirty look and said Marco would be over. What's with this place tonight?"

Linda briefly closed her eyes, then shook her head like Charmane sometimes did for one of Darrel's naive questions.

Shit! "*That's* what's going on?"

"Keep your voice down. Let's go, please." Linda got right up. An older white couple in a nearby booth scowled at her.

Allen stood, glowering back at them. "You people have a nose problem?"

They pretended not to hear him. A fat, dark-haired guy, maybe Italian or Greek, walked up in a black suit in time to hear Allen's insult. "I'm Marco, and I want you outta here now, or she calls the cops." He nodded to the cash register, where the waitress held up a phone. Linda headed for the exit.

Allen pointed at Marco. "There are laws against this now, and I'm damn well going to report it."

Linda was gone—Marco made a dialing motion to the waitress. "Don't know what you're talking about. I'm telling the sheriff I got a hippie yelling at my staff and customers. They're on the way." A few nearby patrons applauded.

Allen started for the door. "Screw you, Mussolini."

20

Allen drove off slowly, telling Linda that the cops were coming.

"Then maybe you should get moving." She was wearing her coat now, huddled right next to the passenger door.

"I wouldn't mind talking to them, especially outside of that damn place."

"Why? They'd just laugh, or arrest you."

He glanced at her. "Yeah, we are in Orange County."

"It would probably be the same in L.A."

Instead of going up the beach road, he headed inland, driving at the speed limit.

"Allen, you shouldn't have said that to those people."

"When I left, the bastards were clapping for *Marco*."

She raised her brows at the expletive. "Telling them off didn't change anything."

"Maybe not, but they deserved it."

Linda just watched the mostly unlit countryside until Allen found a new section of interstate and drove north for a while. They decided to stop at a fast-food joint; he ordered burgers and fries while she used the bathroom, then they ate quietly in the parking lot.

She mostly watched the lights on the way back to L.A., chatting a little about landmarks they passed. Allen let go of some of his anger but couldn't think of much to say.

He got out with her at the house and escorted her to the door, apologizing for making the incident worse at Marco's.

"I just try to avoid that sort of thing. I'm sorry if I was snippy with you."

"You weren't. I owe you a decent dinner sometime."

The front door opened, and Linda looked relieved. A short pretty blonde in her late forties stood there in shorts and a blue T-shirt. "Hi, dear. I heard you talking."

"This is Allen, Mom."

He stepped up to shake hands. The Pepperdine College logo on her shirt had a tower with a holy cross. Her sulking brown eyes said, *Fat chance **you** have with my daughter.*

Barely hearing her mumbled greeting, Allen released the woman's small clammy hand. "Glad to meet you, Mrs. Watson."

She faced Linda. "Your father's waiting up for you, dear. Good night." She closed the door.

Linda thanked him. He had already dismissed the idea of a customary first-date peck on the cheek. They said good night and Allen left.

The freeways were busy but moving very fast, making for a quick but gloomy trip home. He went in and jabbered with Pedro until Trudy entered the room, asking if he had a good time.

"A good time." He scoffed and put on the cage cover. "You were right. That's how I should've looked at it. 'Night." He walked into his room, tore up the haiku, and went to bed.

Dan helped him finish moving his scant furniture back to the house on Sunday. Allen said nothing about his date. They worked quickly, then he concentrated on student papers for most of the afternoon.

When he quietly said good morning to Linda in the office before school on Monday, she was predictably courteous but distant. Allen had forgotten it was April Fools and snapped out of his funk halfway through duty when he saw the kids pulling the same old pranks from his school days. *What's that under your chin?* and *Hey, your shoe's untied!* felt strangely comforting.

After duty, his homeroom boys came in, pranking each other noisily. He had recently lost two more of them to suspension—Aaron for fighting in the coliseum, and another boy who missed his mark with a peashooter and hit a cook on the cheek. Of his twenty-six remaining boys, nineteen were present when they stood after the tardy bell—some of them mumbled the Pledge along with the kids on the intercom. Allen took roll and let the boys talk before announcements, but he had to referee a dispute over a prank and move the squabblers apart. When the PA buzzed again, he told them all to sit down and be quiet.

A male student droned away on the intercom in slow, choppy sentences. "... and the popcorn stand is selling red licorice today. During period seven on Tuesday, the ninth-grade boys will play the faculty in softball and ...." Frank had told Allen that this annual rite was a lame attempt to counteract spring fever—what it amounted to was Van Burton drubbing the boys with a team of PE teachers and non-staff ringers. "... and we think the ninth-graders are going to win this year." The boy made a stilted laugh. "So watch out, faculty."

"Who cares?" Marlon's remark started the laughter again.

Mrs. Ishimoto took over on the intercom with a lilting voice. "... and I'm sure the ninth-graders will do their best, but I have to warn them that Mister Van Burton promised to hit two homeruns tomorrow." Ishimoto paused, then nonsensically began a scold on poor attendance to the kids who showed up. Most of the boys glared at the black box as she changed subjects to explain how extended homeroom that day was for make-up tests.

When she finally stopped talking, Allen held up answer sheets and pencils. "All right guys, most of you have one test left—a few have more. Those who are finished can write, do homework, or read." He pointed to a shelf of multi-level books, mostly borrowed from libraries. "We'll start in about ten minutes—you can talk quietly, but stay in your seats while I pass out tests. Do *not* begin." A cherry bomb blasted from one of the floors below, rattling the windows. Some of the boys snickered.

Allen was halfway through the rows when there was a knock, then Frank stuck his head into the room. "Mister Greene, can we talk out here for just a second?"

Reminding his boys that he would be right at the door, Allen went out to the hall, puzzled by the uncharacteristic grin on Frank's face. His denim pocket had a BOBBY '68 button along with Rosa Parks. Kennedy's bumper stickers were now ubiquitous at Marshall, the kids slapping them on notebooks, lockers and any other surface they could get away with.

"Sharon's watching my homeroom, I just have a minute."

Allen kept one eye on the boys. "So what's up?" Impish little T.R. sneaked over to Marlon, whose head was down.

"First, this is for you." He gave him the envelope they used to exchange Ronnie's poetry.

"Thanks." T.R. flicked Marlon's ear and dashed back to his seat as Frank began talking quietly. Marlon sat up, turned to T.R., then just shook his head. Allen re-focused on Frank.

". . . election—times are a-changing, like the man says."

"Sorry, I missed the first part of that, Frank."

"Jesus, LBJ halting the bombing and quitting the election."

"Right, that was something."

His brows furrowed, Frank looked right at him. "Something? It means the protests have paid off—students, women, vets, Doctor King—all of us."

Allen tapped the envelope on the portal because T.R. was bothering somebody else. "Yeah, I know. I have all I can handle right here."

Frank chafed at his response. "It's all related, Allen. See that little guy?" He pointed emphatically at Darrel in the front row, his belly touching the desk. "He'll be in the war in a few years if it isn't stopped. As bad as LBJ is, what if he'd lost in '64?"

"I was twenty—couldn't vote."

"But old enough to go to Vietnam." He sighed. "Look, I came to talk to you about *our* walkout. Are you still with us?"

"Yes, but I have a couple of questions."

"Has anyone from the Alliance spoken to you?"

"I got a pamphlet that says to honor the contract and don't listen to agitators." Allen smiled a little.

"Yeah, the Alliance won't even invite you to join—they don't consider you to be a teacher."

"Some truth to that, right?"

"No, your lack of experience should be irrelevant as far as representation." He paused for two kids to walk by.

Allen glanced at his homeroom again. "Okay, so how's it going to work?"

"We leave after period six on Thursday. It screws up the last hour, mostly electives—the school will probably run a movie. We hope to have thirty teachers plus some parents and others. We'll take the same route the students did, rally on the front steps, then maybe go around again. We're not officially encouraging it, but some kids will go out with us."

"What do I do about Dorsey?"

"She's in both organizations, but she won't be in the walkout. It's Nash and his pals who might hassle you." Frank started walking away. "See you, fellow agitator."

All the boys finished testing by eleven. Allen took out word games and was playing anagrams with Marlon and some others when there was a loud slam from the direction of Monique's room.

He walked to the door and looked out but didn't see anything unusual until Monique's red hair bobbed past her portal, followed by a streak of yellow tempera powder. He hurried into the hall as Monique swung her door open and came out, her dark suit a maelstrom of dry orange and yellow paint. She seemed more frail than usual but spoke calmly. "I need some help, please."

He took a step toward his boys, pointed, and said, "Stay put, I'll be *right* back." Allen left his door open and crossed the hall to her. "What's going on?"

Without answering, she went in with him. The gaudy paint dusted the desks, floors, and tables; the aisles were littered with construction paper, testing sheets, and yellow pencils. About twenty girls leaned against the long counter by the windows, their bewildered eyes wide open. Charmane and some others turned to the teachers; the rest were watching three classmates at the chalkboard, two of them drawing florid, looping, undecipherable graffiti in pastel chalk. The third girl was playing teacher, directing them with Monique's pointer.

He moved forward, Monique at his side. The three girls turned around—two of them were a foot taller than their teacher. "All right, *what's* going on here?" It was his most authoritarian tone—the two big girls laughed; the small one scrambled to sit in the nearest desk.

The girl at the board kept drawing, the one who was playing teacher hiked her pink skirt slightly to sit on the corner of Monique's desk. Physically mature, she had short processed hair and a plain light-brown face with heavy makeup. She grinned, directing the wooden pointer at Allen. "Frenchy's back with bad Mister Greene." She rapped the pointer on a desk, breaking it. "Oops." The nearby small girl snickered, then got up and ran back to the chalkboard. The girls by the windows remained a quiet and rapt audience.

With half of the broken stick, the ringleader pointed at Allen again, raising her brows in a pretend flirt. "Heard 'bout you, Mister Greene." Peripherally, Allen saw she was crossing her legs; he focused on her face.

She scoffed. "Ha, you looked, ofay—jus' another white boy who likes to look at—"

"Knock that crap off!" Allen turned guiltily to Charmane and the others.

The leader gave him a smug look. "Oooo, now listen to those *lang-widge-arts*. That today's lesson, Mister Greene?" Her two followers hooted with laughter.

Allen pointed at her. "You want to go to the office now or wait for security to come get you?"

"Shit." She hopped down from the desk. "We're goin', all right—goin' out." She tossed the stick on the floor and turned to skin palms with the tall girl at the board. The smaller girl laughed again, mimicking Allen as the three of them bantered and strutted for the door. The tall quiet one who did most of the drawing turned back and said, "Bye, Frenchy." The three of them walked out, guffawing.

Monique turned to the others by the window. "Well, that was entertaining." They stood up silently. "Thank you, girls." Monique walked to the front of the room and reached up with half of her pointer to push the intercom button.

Allen faced the girls. "A little help for Mrs. Morgan here, please." He turned to Monique. "I'll get my boys—we'll be back to help out."

Monique sighed and bent over to pick up some paper. "Thank you."

Back in his room, Allen discovered that one boy had left—nobody volunteered anything about his disappearance. "All right, we're going over to go help Mrs. Morgan's class." He reported the truant boy on the PA, then they walked across the hall.

A few boys laughed at the mess in Monique's room. Some of it was already cleaned up, and two girls were sweeping. Using a whiskbroom, Charmane was trying to brush the bright powder from her teacher's suit. Marlon, Darrell and some other boys pitched in until the lunch bell.

Back to regular classes in the afternoon, Allen tried to teach patiently around more silliness and harmless pranks. After sixth period, the Creative Writing students seemed to come in more seriously than the previous two groups. They finished the writing prompt, then Darrel, unaware of a streak of chocolate on one cheek, raised his hand. "Mister Greene, I don't get what's goin' on Thursday with the teachers."

"You mean the walkout?"

"Yeah. Are you in it?"

"Yes."

"I heard it's gonna be this period. What do *we* do?"

"Just sit there and cry, Tubby," a boy named Henry muttered from Rupert's old seat by the window. His tall frame attired in black from shirt to shined shoes, he was the only cohort of Rupert's still in the class.

Allen glared at him. "First warning for you, Henry." He turned to Darrel. "The school will cover the class."

"You have permission to leave?"

"No, we don't."

Henry pointed at Allen. "I get it. When teachers want somethin', it's okay to break the rules."

A boy near Darrel raised his hand but didn't wait to be called on. "Is it true the teachers just want more money?"

"That's what I heard," a girl said.

"All right, hang on, I'll tell you what I know." Allen waited for quiet and saw Sandra scowling at the class. "The teachers are divided about the walkout, and I made my choice." He explained the two teachers' groups, trying not to make it sound like good guys versus bad. He wrote ODORS on the board. Some kids laughed at the word, then Allen explained the grievance that corresponded to each letter in the acronym.

A couple of kids raised a hand, but Henry, combing his short Afro, spoke out. "See? All they're worried about is money and tellin' us what to do." A few others grumbled in agreement.

Sandra turned to the class. "Allayall hush. Mister Williamson explained it same as Mister Greene, and same as Mister Lee. Mister Williamson said it's a non-violent protest like Doctor King's. If what they're protestin' means money for these no-good schools, then so what? You know who's all cryin' over nothin'?" Sandra paused for effect. "Van Burton and Snash." She almost spit the words in disgust.

Snash? Allen turned away to hide his amusement.

"An' that ol' fool *Nee-grow*, Jackson—oh, an' Anders." At mention of the librarian, Sandra's nostrils flared as if she smelled something rotten—she continued over the laughter. "I see 'em all talkin' to each other. You believe *them* or Mister Williamson, Mister Lee and Mister Greene?" She didn't wait for a response. "Won't see *me* goin' to no last period on Thursday."

Charmane stood halfway up. "Me either, and Mrs. Morgan said the same as Mister Greene." A few kids called out with *Yeah!* or *That's right!* Henry looked sourly outside.

Allen waited, then spoke in a matter-of-fact tone. "We are not asking you to march with us. You'd be counted truant."

Sandra faced him. "No matter—that fool startin' a fire in a palm tree don't take away *our* right to protest."

21

The next morning, just twenty boys came in sluggishly to homeroom as if the usual Monday languor had been April-fooled to Tuesday. Some of them slept through Latham's effusive patter on the intercom about a coming awards ceremony.

Ishimoto took over and explained procedures for the ballgame last period. "... students on the study hall list are to be taken by period-seven teachers to Harding Hall on the way to the field. Students assigned to detention must ...." The boys weren't listening. "... anyone who doesn't show up is truant and will serve detention on Wednesday. Have a nice day."

Marlon grinned at Allen. "Hey, Mister Greene, what position are you playing in the game?"

"I'm playing left out, rooting for the ninth-graders."

As the day progressed, attendance declined more. After the bell rang at the end of sixth period, Allen overheard some kids saying they were going home. On the way outside, he and Monique had less than thirty period-seven students between them. They dropped off eight more in the cafeteria, then started for the end of the building, where a few teachers were heading back to Main. Walking well behind their listless kids, Allen turned to her. "I assume it was quiet in your homeroom this morning."

"With those three gone, like cherubs in church."

He nodded ahead to their group and spoke quietly. "Do a lot of kids always disappear for this deal?"

"Yes, part of the game-day tradition."

"Why does the school even do it?"

"Greg wanted to cancel two years ago, but staff and the kids voted to keep it—anything for an easy day." They passed the auditorium. "Allen, did your date with Linda go okay?"

He scoffed a little. "Do you know much about her family?" She shook her head, and he explained.

"So there was, uh, an economic gap you weren't expecting."

"That, and more." He mentioned Linda's uncertain marital plans, then told her some details of the row at the restaurant. "Although we didn't hit it off, she's a good person. At least we can face each other and say hello."

"That's good. It sounds like you both learned something."

"I guess that's one way to look at it."

They came to the baseball field—not even half of the student body had ended up there. The kids sat on the old bleachers or the grass and mostly ignored the adults' easy rout of ten less-than-enthused ninth-grade boys.

By Wednesday, attendance was better but the weather turned summer-hot. Allen spoke to his classes about the teachers' walkout the next day, explaining that Mister Williamson had made an arrangement with the principal for students to sign in at the march for social studies credit. Pretty much the same kids were either interested or apathetic. He had most of them work on the final draft of an old assignment.

Allen received another anti-demonstration pamphlet on Thursday morning before duty. Skirting the faculty room with his mail, he heard Anders browbeating a substitute about the walkout.

After the first-period tardy bell, Sandra hurried down the hall while Allen was putting out the absence slip. She was nearly out of breath and uncharacteristically disheveled in a rumpled blouse and messy makeup. "Mister Greene, I'm sorry. We stayed at my mom's last night, and this morning she was, um—she wouldn't let me call my aunt to pick up Melissa." She exhaled loudly. "I had to call from the office."

"Didn't they give you a pass?"

"It was Mrs. Venable. That ol' lady hates me."

"Okay." He put out his hands, palms down, to calm her.

She looked into the room, then spoke more quietly. "Sorry, I'm bothering everybody."

"Thanks, they're working now." They went in. "That tardy is your freebie, Sandra. I have to send it in next time."

"I know." Pouting a bit, she walked over for her fluency folder, then to her seat. She started writing, making demonstrative periods at the end of sentences.

After a couple of minutes, he went over to her and whispered as she kept writing. "I think we can work something out with the phone. Today's not a good day—maybe tomorrow after school when Charmane is here. We'll see what we can do."

"Thanks." She looked up with a slight grin. "Mister Greene, my aunt's bringing Melissa for the march today." He returned a smile, then went on to help a boy who had his hand up.

During the day, many students were ambivalent about the teachers' walk-out, but there was enough tension between some supporters and skeptics that Allen had to break up a couple of arguments that got out of hand.

Before the bell at the end of period six, Venable came on the speaker. ". . . a special movie next period for students, '20,000 Leagues Under the Sea'. . . ."

"That ol' thing again," one girl said while most of the boys looked pleased.

". . . are to go to the auditorium and sign in with Mister Fogle. Those who will be with Mister Williamson can sign in outside of the office. Students who don't sign in will be truant. Please wait now for the bell."

The girl who was suspended for two days back in February for cussing at Allen raised her hand. "Yes, Pauline?"

The gangly girl pointed at him. "Y'all are walkin' out now, right?"

"Some of us, yes—we discussed this again yesterday."

"I wasn't here. No detention if we go with the teachers?"

"If you sign in and stay with the march. Your social studies teacher might ask you to tell about it." The bell rang at the end of his sentence. "Okay, that's it—see you."

Pauline stood up. "See you right now."

A boy at the door shouted, "Anybody stays is chicken-shit!"

Pauline glared at him. "Fool, you jus' cuttin'."

While the room emptied, Allen looked out at the warm spring day to gauge if it would be too hot for Monique. A normal between-class onslaught surged across the coliseum toward the auditorium. He put on his Pittsburgh Pirate cap and headed for the door.

After locking the room, Allen turned to Pauline and a few of his sixth-period kids waiting in the hall with some older students. Scores of others hurried back and forth past Frank, who had come upstairs during his last-period prep. In his bright dashiki, he held a furled sign under one arm and was telling students who weren't there for the walkout to go to the auditorium. Wrapped from head to sandals in a shimmering green Indian sari, a dark-eyed older lady was helping him. Apparently, Allen had wrongly assumed before that she was of Arabic descent.

Monique came out of her room in an embroidered white blouse, a full skirt with petticoats, and a crown of daisies trailed by a rainbow of long thin ribbons. She carried her closed red parasol under her other arm.

Allen smiled. "Very festive, Monique."

"*Jawohl*, celebrating cultures! I'm actually Bavarian, you know."

"No, I didn't." He touched his cap. "Mine's baseball."

Frank turned from the kids. "Mister Greene, you can take one end of this sign when we get started." Staff members down the hall in both directions saw the strikers and turned for the north or south stairs like most of the students. Carrying some clipboards, Ron Lee joined them in regular clothes, but his long hair was cinched by a white headband with black Chinese symbols.

Allen spoke to him under his breath. "Hey, Lefty."

He smiled, holding up a clipboard. "Yeah, let's get going."

Frank led them away with about thirty kids. Two teachers were waiting at the second floor with nine or ten students, including Charmane. Most everyone chatted nervously as they descended the last flight and found about fifty more kids, several teachers and a few classified staff waiting in the foyer as the tardy bell rang. One woman wore the colorful finery for a Mexican *folklórico*; an elderly math teacher donned his Scottish tam. There were some Kennedy campaign placards and several homemade signs with NEW FUNDS FOR OLD SCHOOLS, and 3R's = FREEDOM, plus others from the students' march.

As Ron started the clipboards around to the kids, Allen and Frank unfurled the sign. They held up a picket at each end of a four-by-eight precisely lettered banner: WE HAVE A DREAM—FREEDOM AND GOOD SCHOOLS. Allen grinned at Monique. "Good sign, Mrs. Morgan."

Though he had less than twenty teachers, Frank didn't look discouraged; he said to wait a minute for stragglers. Over half of the faculty members there were under forty, and every department was represented, including a PE teacher in her thirties, who arrived late in shorts to appreciative applause. Half of the black teachers showed up—Frank and Mitch plus two more who Allen didn't know, an older woman who taught science, and a recently hired young male math substitute.

Mrs. Berg joined them in some brown and green lederhosen, complete with feathered Tyrolean hat. Sharon's long limbs seemed only slightly thicker than her hiking stick; it had a sign at the top with ODORS and the five grievances. They gave the counselor a rousing cheer.

Sharon, Monique, Ron, and Mitch stayed with the kids as Allen and Frank dipped the sign and led the other staff into the office. Linda stopped typing to smile at them. Mrs. Ishimoto stood in a back corridor with a smoldering glare, arms folded.

Frank watched the vice-principal leave. "Mrs. Venable, our board plus these staff members are on unpaid leave for one hour."

"Yes, Mister Williamson." The heavy woman checked out Allen and some others through the top of her bifocals. "Mm, I do see a couple I wasn't aware of." She jotted names. "You have more out on the steps." Her tone betrayed an inkling of support.

"Okay, let's go." The teachers followed Frank and Allen back into the busy foyer. He and Allen dipped the banner again for the front doors. "All right, let's start with: New funds for old schools! New funds for old schools! New funds . . . ."

They took up the chant and walked out to find a crowd of at least thirty additional kids, a few more teachers, about a dozen parents, and the same two ministers—all standing around until they saw the banner emerge from the school. They launched more homemade signs and Kennedy placards skyward and chimed in loudly, "New funds for . . . ."

As the clipboards circulated among the kids on the steps, Frank held up his arms to stop the chant. "Okay, Channel Four said they'd be here, and the last thing we need is violence on the evening news. We have a police escort, but pass it on to watch for troublemakers."

Frank resumed the chant, then he and Allen stepped down to the street with the banner, followed by the elongated crowd. They moved slowly for the corner, and another twenty or thirty excited kids ran along the sidewalks on both sides, some joining the protest while others darted in and out as teachers kept telling them to sign in or go to the auditorium.

A few feet behind the large banner, Sandra had joined them, striding arm and arm with Charmane, Monique, and Sharon. Sandra had the baby, all in Sunday ruffles, balanced on one hip. Allen started to call over to Frank that those five were about the cutest thing ever, but he thought better of it.

Marlon marched on the other side of the banner with a few boys from homeroom. Two L.A. squad cars waited at the corner; one pulled ahead and stayed about twenty yards in front of the procession, now at least a hundred and fifty strong. The line narrowed to about five across before turning the corner onto the side street that intersected the PE field and mostly two-bedroom stuccos and old frame houses.

Mitch began a steady, soft rendition of *Down by the Riverside* on some sort of long woodwind. The chanting ceased; the kids picked up the lyrics, "I ain't goin' study war no more, study war no more . . . ." The quickened tempo made Mitch adjust his music. Many of the adults added their voices to the next verse, "Gonna lay down my sword and shield, down by the riverside . . . ."

They passed the charred black torso of the palm tree. Allen turned back to see the other cop car closely following the march. *Relax, guys, it's all non-violent today.*

The CHANNEL 4 station wagon, a cameraman, and reporter waited for them at the next corner. The protesters belted out, "Gonna talk with the Prince of Peace, down by the . . . ."

"Your cue, Frank, you're on." Allen pointed ahead to the TV people.

"Real funny." Frank turned to say something to two teachers, who took over the banner's poles as they reached the corner. Frank grabbed Allen's elbow. "Come on, this has to be black and white together."

"What about Sharon?"

"She wants me to do it."

The young cameraman came closer in his jeans and a T-shirt, filming the marchers. A middle-aged blond reporter approached them in suit, shirt, tie, and clashing white tennis shoes that would be off camera. He looked right at Allen. "Who's in charge?"

"That would be Mister Williamson here."

The man turned to Frank. "Okay, we'll edit later, so don't worry when you make a mistake or something." The reporter asked for Frank's name and position, then began the interview.

As Frank listed the five grievances, the middle of the march slowed down to shout the "New funds" chant for the TV crew. Frank answered questions until the rear of the march caught up. ". . . and next month at the school board meeting expect a demonstration by concerned teachers, parents and others from all over the city. Thanks, we need to get back."

The reporter started summing up his story for the camera as Allen and Frank jogged back to join the end of the line; the marchers there cheered for them. The bell rang over at the gym. "Shower bell," a girl called out.

Frank and Allen moved up gradually, then stayed about ten feet behind the banner until the marchers ahead came around the last corner, singing, "I ain't goin' study war no more . . . ."

Approaching the front of the school, they sang louder. The special ed. bus idled down the street, a line of cars waiting behind to pick up kids. The march arrived at the steps, and Frank raised a fist to proclaim, "New funds for old schools!" The crowd shouted the refrain, waving the signs as the last bell rang.

Some puzzled-looking kids left the school and stopped at the top of the stairs. Schultz and Cecil were just inside the front doors. The principal came out, causing a lull in the racket until it was obvious that he wasn't upset. Schultz called down that they needed a path through the middle of the crowd.

Frank kept chanting and made his way up the stairs in a Moses-like parting of mostly dark faces. "Make room here, please!" He came to the top step as more kids left the school. A few joined the demonstration, but most hurried away through the opening.

Frank raised his fist again. "Right on, Thurgood Marshall students!" The crowd cheered excitedly, then the noise slackened. Many of the kids looked around at each other—they had a decision to make about staying or leaving. With open hands, Frank quieted the last of the chanters. "Okay, we're proud and appreciative that so many students joined us today." He waited for more cheers and applause. "Now, if you have responsibilities of *any* kind after school, you need to go take care of them. Those who don't, you're welcome to join us as we go around one more time. Thanks again to those who need to leave. New funds for old schools!"

The chant echoed back to him from the adults and kids who stayed; those who had to leave passed on picket signs to their friends. Mitch started playing *We Shall Not be Moved*, and the remaining marchers sang as they assembled on the stairs.

Sandra and Charmane walked up to Allen with Melissa, who was fussing in her mother's arms. The baby had cherubic cheeks and large pretty eyes, moist from crying.

"She's beautiful, Sandra." Allen patted the child's head. Melissa shied away.

Sandra shouted over the noise. "She turned cranky, Mister Greene, so we gotta take her. But she's gonna grow up doin' this. I'll be takin' her to see Bobby like I did to Doctor King—then after that, an' after that. She'll remember some of this when she's big."

Allen smiled. "I'm sure she will."

"Bye, Mister Greene," the two girls said one after the other as they walked away from the marchers who stayed, about a hundred.

Monique told Allen and Sharon that she'd had enough sun. She sat on the steps, shading herself with the parasol. "I'll wait here—see you in a few minutes." The column had already started moving away. Allen and Sharon fell in with Frank at the end, half a block behind the large banner, now held by kids.

The demonstrators seemed to be in a mellower mood, some of them walking arm in arm and singing "We Shall Overcome" with Mitch's music. They came to the first corner, no squad cars this time, and started up the side street. The procession began to spread out more than it did during the first time around.

The banner passed the black stump again, then around the second corner, followed a minute or two later by Allen, Frank, and Sharon at the end. The singing began to fade when the marchers saw commotion up ahead past the middle of the block, where several students at the front took off in a panic like the day of the tree fire. The adults and kids still up there didn't seem to move. Allen turned to Frank. "What's this about?"

"No idea." He was already running off. Allen and a few of the other tailenders jogged after him. They passed some perplexed kids, asking them futilely what was going on. Frank had stopped to talk to three tall girls, probably ninth-graders. They were bawling and rambling on at once, their feet standing on the edge of a fallen WE SHALL OVERCOME sign.

Frank yelled at one of the girls. "Who? Start again."

She made a horrible sob. "S-some lady, sh-she came out t-to the street, a-an' tol' those kids up there."

"Told them what?"

"R-Reverend King. They sh-shot him."

22

Staring at the girl, Frank froze in place. Crazy jumbled color images of JFK's assassination in Dallas crossed Allen's mind like film fluttering through a faulty projector. Vaguely, he heard some screams as the news spread back through the crowd.

Frank had put his hands on the girl's shoulders, making her look at him. "Listen to me, Donelle! Did the lady say if Doctor King is still alive?"

Turning away from Frank, her moist eyes glowered at Allen, then Sharon, who had just caught up with them. "We don't know." She sobbed again into the arms of her two friends.

"Damn it." Frank turned back. A few kids were running away while the rest stood in the street like most of the adults, stunned or crying. "Teachers and parents, please escort as many kids as you can back to the front of the school! Go straight across, the back gate's open." Frank turned to Sharon and Allen. "Let's go on up to the corner for stragglers."

Amidst the confusion, the three of them spent the next few minutes shooing along the kids who were still around and picking up some of the discarded signs. They came to a grizzled old man on his porch, sobbing in his beach chair. A radio next to him blasted unintelligible noise. Frank called to him. "Is Doctor King alive?"

The man blubbered through his tears. "It's bad, real bad." Frank turned and ran ahead. Wiping their eyes, Allen and Sharon herded the remaining few kids to the last corner and onto Harding Place. About twenty kids and adults milled around aimlessly in front of the school; others ran in or out of the front door. A couple of cars waited in the bus area.

Monique was sitting on the stairs in her now ridiculous outfit, holding the small red umbrella against the sun. She had retrieved her purse and was watching a small crowd gathering across the street in the parking lot. Frank put his signs by the stairs, then went right to her.

Allen dropped off his signs as Monique turned and stood up, releasing her parasol to hug Frank. She let go of him as Allen and Sharon approached. "All we know is they took him to a Memphis hospital." A run of mascara slalomed down Monique's face. "Apparently he's still alive."

"That's all that matters now." Frank hurried inside.

From the second step, Monique embraced Sharon, mashing the feather on her hat. Still crying, Monique hugged Allen, who lingered in her comfort, holding off his tears as they let go of each other. "Did you hear how it happened?" he asked.

"They're not sure yet, maybe a sniper."

"Good God—again."

Sharon was wiping her eyes with a forearm, looking toward the small crowd of kids and adults in the parking lot. "What's going on over there?"

"The preachers are organizing a vigil, walking over to a church in a few minutes." Monique picked up her parasol and purse, making a long sniff. She turned to Allen. "I think I'll just go home and watch the news."

He sat on the steps. "Yeah, me too. See you tomorrow."

"If we have school." She gently touched his cheek, then walked glumly down to the street with Sharon, their arms locked together before they stopped to talk to a parent. In the lot, some of those in the growing crowd had found and lit candles. Allen stared at the tiny flames, barely visible in the sunshine. The enraged face of the girl not thirty minutes before came to mind, then someone tapped his shoulder. He turned around to Miss Dorsey, who held a box of long candles, her eyes swollen but undaunted. "Please join us, Mister Greene."

He stood, nodding dejectedly to her. "Thanks, Miss Dorsey." They started down the steps.

"Candle?"

"No thanks. I'll probably turn back at the church."

"It's quite a ways from here, but there will be some others walking back." They joined the crowd, and he took some of the candles to help pass them out. When the procession began to move slowly from the parking lot, Allen looked around and saw Linda, walking with her arm around an older lady's shoulders.

One large homemade WE SHALL OVERCOME sign led the new march—Marlon and another boy held it high. Frank had returned and was walking slowly with Ron Lee. In the middle of the procession, Allen found himself near a reticent Rick Godina, who had a transistor radio plugged into one ear, his face ashen and grave.

Mitch, now at the front, softly played "Amazing Grace" on a long flute. Block after quiet block, the marchers sang, including Allen, who knew some of the lyrics from a Judy Collins version. They finally arrived at a small white church with a trim lawn around it. Nobody walked in right away; the crowd turned inward, humming or singing the old hymn together.

Crying, Godina tried to clear his throat. "It's over."

Allen turned to him. "What did you say?"

"Excuse me, everyone." Godina slightly startled Allen with the unexpected strength of his call. The marchers had quieted to face the vice-principal. Tears racing down his cheeks, this time he spoke just loud enough for all to hear. "Doctor King was pronounced dead at 7:05, Memphis time." There was complete silence for a moment, followed by cries and moans.

Looking out at the silent street through his clouded vision, Allen started walking back alone. He came to a forgotten sprinkler on a waterlogged lawn, where most of the worms on the flooded sidewalk had been flattened by shoes or tires. The same image came back to him from a fifth-grade essay he wrote about L.A. rain and the wanton carnage of so many beneficial creatures. *You and Ronnie—they're worms for God's sake.*

Back at the nearly empty lot, he started to go in for his box but instead walked over and unlocked the Volvo. Driving through the still neighborhood, he turned on the radio and listened to reports of rioting in Washington, D.C., Baltimore, Detroit, and Chicago. Allen took the Hollywood Freeway to Sunset, then he headed west for Zuma Beach, turning off the radio.

The shore was practically abandoned. He left his shoes and socks by a boulder, then walked off into an inch or two of water. As the wave receded, some sand crabs burrowed down below the surface, tickling his toes and leaving bubbles behind—Ronnie's beachcombing muse right at his feet. *My God, what's **he** doing today?* Allen walked up to sit on dry sand, then let the ocean sounds lead him practically into a trance. He came out of it several minutes later, guilty for his reverie as the blood-red sun inched below the horizon.

Back home just before eight, he found a note from Trudy saying that she was watching the news at her friend Rose's place. He fed Pedro, turned on the TV in the living room and sat on the couch. Walter Cronkite looked aside glumly to someone off camera, his drooping mouth and jowls haltingly but clearly announcing the assassination of the "apostle of non-violence" as if someone had yet to hear the grim news. Cronkite explained that King was in Memphis because of a riot at his march there a couple of weeks before. He had returned to show that non-violence would prevail. Memphis Police, Cronkite said, had found a high-powered hunting rifle one block from King's hotel and were looking for a "well-dressed young white man." *There it is—now the riots start here.*

Allen picked up a red pencil he'd left on the coffee table and rubbed the wood surface so hard with his thumb that his skin began to burn. His mind's eye saw more old newsreel clips, this time of stunned black and white mourners lined up ten deep along the side of the road, watching JFK's casket roll slowly by.

Louring at some hokey Tennessee politician on TV, Allen rubbed the wood again. He broke the pencil in two, stood up and fired the pieces at the floor. "Goddamn it to hell!" One small red missile ricocheted up and hit the screen. He slammed his closed fist on a nearby end table, knocking the telephone and a drinking glass onto the hardwood floor.

He stared at the results of his deed, unsure for a moment what had caused it. *Freaking mad man.* He made himself breathe deeply a few times before starting to sweep up the mess. As he scooped up the shards with a dustpan, a tear fell below onto a piece of glass.

After he sat down again, head in hands, he looked up at the report on TV, but it had no immediacy for him until minutes later when Cronkite was back on saying that the worst of the rioting was still in Washington, D.C. A different reporter talked about how the coming dawn could bring even more violence in the cities. They showed two little girls, cowering by a store's broken window—a Pulitzer shot if it had been a photo.

Trudy came in before ten. They hugged and cried a little, then watched the reports together for a while before the phone rang. "Who'd be calling now?" Allen reached down to the floor to pick up the phone—its casing was cracked. He heard tavern or party noise on the other end. "Who's this?"

"That's how you answer my damn phone?"

"Not yours anymore. What do you want?" Allen turned to his sister. She had her eyes closed, shaking her head.

"To talk to Trudy."

"She doesn't want to talk to you."

"How the fuck do you know?"

"She just told me."

"What are you two doing?"

"Not that it's any of your damn business, but we're watching the reports on Doctor King."

"Yeah, you would be."

"Your surfing bums are waiting for you, Rick."

"An' you two are all cozy there in your own little house—that ain't natural."

"You are so full of shit. Call here drunk again and we turn you in for violating the restraining order."

"Fuck you, fat-ass."

"Have a good life, prick."

Rick slammed the phone. Allen held the receiver in the air, looking at it. He dropped it carelessly into the slot.

Trudy was sobbing a little. "Thank you, Allen."

"Yeah, he's not worth any tears."

"I know." She dried her eyes on the sleeve of her smock. "A few years ago, that wasn't him at all."

"If you say so." He sighed. "There's nothing new on TV about Doctor King. You need some rest."

"Yes, you're right." She got up and hugged him, then limped off to bed.

Allen stayed up with the news until he couldn't keep his eyes open. He didn't sleep well and was up earlier than usual the next day. Eating some cereal, he turned the TV on low, since Trudy was still asleep.

It was a local station. "As in other Western cities, it is eerily quiet here, very little of the usual early morning activity in the streets. Only a few cases of sporadic violence were reported last night in South-Central Los Angeles." A reporter asked a black preacher why Watts had remained mostly calm.

". . . our community leaders are in agreement that violence is ultimately self-destructive. 'Alive, you can fight—dead, you're dead.' One thing that *doesn't* help is some of you people on TV scolding rioters in other cities."

After switching to a national feed, a reporter said that the rioting back east was going strong—in Chicago, the mayor gave shoot-to-kill orders. Then they showed a photo of Doctor King's desperate, shocked entourage on the motel balcony, pointing off to where the shot came from, the fallen martyr at their feet. There had been no substantial progress on catching the assassin by Tennessee law enforcement or Hoover's FBI. **That** *bastard called him 'Martin Lucifer King.'*

He dropped the spoon, splashing milk and cereal onto his lap. Allen walked to the kitchen, tossed the bowl into the sink with a loud clatter, then dried himself. He walked back to the couch, picked up the phone and dialed Monique's number.

"Hello." Her answer was low and hoarse.

"Hi, Monique. Sorry for calling so early. I needed to hear a friendly voice."

"Of course, Allen. I'm glad to hear yours too." She made a loud sniffle. "This whole thing is so hard to grasp. It isn't even four years since—"

"Yeah, who the hell is next?"

"Maybe this is the end of a horrible cycle."

Sure. "At least Doctor King got to hear LBJ's announcement last week. Did you see that report from . . . ." He ranted about the investigation, finishing with, ". . . goddamn crackpots hiding with guns in half the cellars in this country."

Monique was silent for a moment. "Yes, but you sound almost violent yourself. If we do have school, it won't work for you to be so angry."

He sighed heavily.

"Allen?"

"I'm not going to listen to one damn crack from Nash or his asshole friends."

"If you confront them, they'll be delighted to get you in trouble and make this day all about you, not Doctor King."

He took another deep breath. "Yeah, you're right. I'll calm down before I get there."

"I know you will, *amour.*"

"What do you think we'll see with the kids today?"

"I doubt we'll have many at all. Hopefully, that's true for the visitors too."

"I think I'll go in now. Somebody will open up for me."

"Why so early? They still might cancel."

"I didn't even bring my teaching stuff. I just want to get there and get ready, stop stewing about it. Thanks for listening to all my crap."

"Of course. If we open, I'll be there, but late."

"Okay, bye." Allen selected the closest he had to mourning clothes, a navy-blue cotton shirt and black jeans, then went out to his car and drove down the block. It was getting warm, the portent of another hot, smoggy day. The sluggishness he knew so well in Puerto Rico descended upon his temples like a dark heavy curtain. He took some coffee, turned onto Los Feliz Boulevard and drove only a block before nearly blacking out.

He pulled into a parking area next to RAY'S, a bicycle shop. Allen shut off the engine, closed his eyes, and listened to the myriad sounds of the morning commute, but he wasn't able to isolate them. Allen opened his eyes a couple of minutes later and drank the rest of the coffee. Fighting off his dejection, he drove away.

Although it was past daybreak, many cars in the very sparse traffic were burning their headlights as they did for JFK. He turned his lights on again and crossed the L.A. River to the on-ramp. He merged without difficulty into a long gap in the freeway's funeral procession—it was like the old science-fiction movies that used a filter at three in the morning to make L.A. look dead quiet.

He maneuvered his car easily onto the Harbor Freeway, but there was a back-up forming ahead, probably from an accident. Allen came to a complete standstill near downtown L.A. and looked around at the other commuters. Those going in his direction were mostly white—it was a cosmopolitan mix on the other side. Many drivers looked tense or frightened, not mournful.

Allen turned on the radio to see if there were any school closures, but the announcer was leading up to a recording made after a service for Doctor King. A girl from Grant High told a Burbank minister to go home and talk to his own people, that he and other whites "weren't wanted down here."

Here we come anyway. He inched along by a disabled city bus until the traffic began to move again. His melancholy finally began to retreat to the back of his head.

After Allen took his exit, there was a red light at the bottom of the ramp. He pulled up behind three cars, the last one a huge old copper-brown Chrysler. He secured his windows and doors—the rearview mirror of the car ahead reflected an image of white tips on a short Afro. The man adjusted his mirror until his somber middle-aged face was visible.

Allen sighed. *See my headlights, brother?*

The eyes of *I ain't your brother, white boy,* glared back at him.

The left arrow came on, and the first two cars made their turns, but the Chrysler glided up to the line, where his motor apparently stalled. Their eyes connected again; Allen read, *You're gonna be late, honky—what you gonna do about it?*

He shifted to neutral and released the clutch. *Nothing, nothing at all.* Then, behind him, a white guy in a pick-up blasted his horn. Allen turned back. "Stupid jerk."

Ahead, the man in the Chrysler tried the motor; it caught, but he got out of his car. At least six-four and three hundred pounds, he held a crowbar and turned toward the Volvo.

His hand trembling on the gearshift, Allen double-checked his doors and slouched in the seat, but the huge man just walked by and approached the pick-up's burning headlights. With level baseball swings of his iron bar, he busted the truck's lights one at a time—the other driver wasn't in sight, likely on the floor.

The man nonchalantly walked by Allen again, got back in the Chrysler and intentionally waited for the end of a yellow light before he took off, leaving Allen, the pick-up, and a line of vehicles to wait through another red light.

He made a long exhale. *Okay, that counts as my incident for the day.*

23

After they finally made their turn, the guy in the pick-up floored his accelerator and passed right away as if he intended to carry out some sort of retaliation. Allen drove on; most stores were closed, and almost no one was on the street. Leaving the first arterial, he made the turn onto 103rd, where the deserted city blocks near the Watts Towers gave the dark steel pinnacles an air of mourning.

When he turned onto Harding Place at 6:45, there were four cars in the lot. Marv was at the booth, laughing heartily to someone on his phone. Irritated, Allen hoped to glide by.

Marv hung up, still chuckling. "Hey, Mister."

"You're early, Marv," Allen said, stopping.

"Principal called me in—believe you're the first teacher here. Got your lights on, real good idea."

"You mean for Doctor King."

Nodding, Marv sipped his coffee. "An' it might give you a little more protection goin' through the neighborhood. Sure did have mine on."

"Yeah. I'll be in my car until somebody shows."

"No outside key?"

"Not for rookies."

"Remember your lights, Mister."

As was now his habit, he pulled in far away from the booth but near the street, and left the radio on. Instead of non-stop news, they had commercials again. Even worse, a parrot was promoting an L.A. bank in a cartoon voice.

Allen turned the ignition all the way off and watched the school; it was completely still, not one kid or adult hanging around. If they did have classes, he would start with some normalcy—the journals, then let them read. *Hell, they can sleep if they want.*

A staff member finally drove into the lot in a small silver sports car—no lights. Van Burton parked near Marv, but they ignored each other. The P.E. teacher unfolded his tall muscular frame from the small cab, then race-walked to the street in sweats, holding a whistle and keys. He looked around warily, then jogged south past Main to unlock the back gate and enter the grounds. He locked up and was gone.

Godina's Chevy rolled in and parked near the driveway; its lights went off. The vice-principal got right out and walked away with his bulging briefcase, making a casual wave to Marv before hurrying into the crosswalk.

Allen got out to catch up with him. He hustled past Marv and was about to yell, but Godina was setting the doorstop for someone. Slowing down, Allen approached the far curb; he saw two big kids, maybe ninth-graders, sneaking around in the old cypress trees at the far end of Main, where Van Burton disappeared. He crossed over to the front steps, then turned again toward the end of the school. A boy stood up from behind a metal trash can and shouted to the other one. They ran off, looking back, then an explosive larger than a cherry bomb blew off, launching the garbage can a few feet into the air before it landed on its side with a clank, paper and plastic descending all around.

He walked up the steps and reached for the handle. The door was locked, the stop lifted. Peering through the thick glass, he saw Deniker walk away from the door, clipping a radio to his side. Allen grabbed the handle and rattled it. Looking bored, the guard came back to open up.

"Didn't you hear that outside?" Allen pointed south.

Besides the usual leather packs on his belt, Deniker had a new one shaped like a small covered holster. "M-80, maybe two."

"I didn't recognize the kids. They blew up a trash can and took off."

"Good." Deniker turned dismissively and walked away. Shaking his head, Allen entered the office, discomfited not to have his box with him to rest on the counter. Linda was alone, typing, her soft smile missing. Godina spoke on the phone in his office with the door closed.

Linda's hair and her clothes, a dark-grey suit, were very neat as always, but her mascara was smudged. He spoke just loud enough to be heard. "Hi, are you alone out here today?"

She glanced up from her keyboard, her eyes slightly swollen. "Not sure—one of them called in." She did a slow double take, looking right at him. "Are you okay?"

"Yeah, not enough sleep I guess."

She nodded, dismally for her. The phone rang, and Linda picked it up, frowning but determined. "Thurgood Marshall Junior High." She waited. "Yes, we're going to start on time, then a short assembly before we close . . . you're welcome."

He spoke quietly again. "That answers most of my questions. I wonder if any kids will show."

"Not many, they're saying." She returned to work, her slender fingers a blur over the vibrating keys. The phone rang; she answered and began the same kind of interchange. Walking away, Allen furtively watched Linda's demeanor, consoled by her grim resolve. He was almost to the doorway when she hung up.

"Mister Greene, today's bulletin will be in your box soon. The gist is that there'll be an announcement before homeroom, then a bell to go to the auditorium for," she briefly closed her eyes and exhaled, "the program. Students will be dismissed from there." Head down and a tissue in hand, she didn't move for a moment, staring at her desk. "Uh, teachers have a short meeting afterwards—classrooms are to be locked, except to let in the students."

"Okay." He checked for anyone within earshot. "Linda."

Dabbing a tear, she looked up. "Yes?"

"Thanks for just being here today." He turned to go.

"Wait."

He faced her; she was already more composed.

"Allen, be careful the next few days."

"Yeah, thanks." He made a slight smile, then entered the hall. Cecil had replaced Deniker inside the front door.

The guard waved at him. "Mornin', I'll be near your duty area. Won't hardly be no kids—no need to come."

"Thanks, Cecil." He climbed the middle stairway to the third floor; the dim hallway was empty. He walked down to his room and entered, keeping the door locked. He had forgotten to tell his sixth-period class the day before to realign the desks; the janitor had put them back in rows and would be pissed again. Everything else was about the same, except his box was moved from the floor to his desk, and the chalkboard had been needlessly washed again.

Allen sat, staring up at his bulletin board, where student papers were interspersed around a Xeroxed jacket of *The Pearl*, which he had read aloud ten minutes a day to the Creative Writing class, most of whom became entranced by the story. Deciding to start a new bulletin board, Allen walked toward the butcher paper he kept in a corner at the back of the room. He spotted a faded red blotch of blood on one of the heat registers. *Del's—Jesus.*

At the last window, he looked down into the coliseum; Cecil wasn't around yet and the cafeteria portals were still closed. Only one of the regular kids who always tried to be first in line was waiting there. Allen put the roll of white paper under his arm, went back up front and started to dismantle his old bulletin board.

By his usual duty time, he had finished stapling and trimming the paper. Allen looked out to see Cecil and a boy chatting near the kiva. A male loner cowered by himself near Main—a handful of students trudged around aimlessly.

After the bell rang, a quiet kid named Thomas came in first, sat right down in a far desk and rested his head on both arms. Darrel and three more boys walked in silently, then Marlon. He was in black again, but probably for Doctor King instead of his usual reason. He sat, frowning at peripatetic T.R., who entered in his faded Mister Magoo T-shirt, jabbering excitedly about a messed up trashcan he saw outside. Marlon told him flatly to shut up.

The other boys were glum, except Aaron, the only big kid so far. He wore his usual gold shirt and was gazing expectantly out of the window. Two more boys wore black shirts, both of them steady track-three kids, one who pretended to be dull, another who liked to brag about his smarts and had been beaten up after school.

T.R. sat near Aaron, who defended him weeks before during the homeroom changeover. The small boy rewound the rubber band on his ponytail, raised his fair brows and started beating his palms on a desk as if playing bongos.

No more boys arrived before the bell. The intercom buzzed to life—instead of a chorus leading the Pledge, it was just one girl. Allen's seven homeroom boys got to their feet, most of them leaning on a desk, mumbling some of the words.

The PA was quiet for a few seconds. The boys sat as the principal's familiar deep voice came on, even lower and slower than usual. "Morning. Doctor King would have appreciated that you showed up for school today. Nevertheless, out of respect for him, we will be closing early."

Schultz paused, as if waiting for some reaction. The only noise in Allen's room came from T.R., who shouted, "Yeah!" He made another bongo flurry on his desk.

"When the bell rings after a twenty-minute homeroom, move in an orderly fashion with your teacher to the auditorium for a remembrance of Doctor King. School will be dismissed right afterward—buildings and grounds will be locked ten minutes later. Please wait now for the bell—thank you." Other than the fidgeting T.R. and Aaron, who was looking out again, the rest had their heads down.

After the bell, Allen had to wake two of them. They all entered the quiet corridor, where Monique and Charmane, both all in black, plus about ten more girls began to move silently toward the north stairs, the boys several feet behind. Marlon walked close to Allen, his solemn face down, watching their footsteps.

They walked out below the arch, then into the oven-like coliseum to cross to the other side. Aaron had lagged behind, then he took off running back through the north arch. Before Allen could even shout, the boy was scaling the fence. T.R. laughed while Marlon seemed to enviously watch Aaron run down the street. "He'll end up in juvie tonight," Allen said to them. "Let's go, guys."

The boys stayed together, about twenty feet behind Monique's girls. Except for T.R.'s nervous babble, hardly a word was spoken as they crossed the coliseum's hot asphalt. Two other small groups were walking in front of Monique. They passed the cafeteria building and headed for the auditorium's main entrance. Darrel stooped to tie his shoe; Allen and the boys waited, falling even farther behind.

Up ahead, Ishimoto was standing in the propped-open doorway in a pastel-peach business suit, giving herself a quick check-up in a compact mirror. She put it away, forcing a smile for Monique, then saying something to the girls.

As the boys came to the door, the vice-principal's smile turned to a sneer.

"Last one here, Mister Greene." She pointed inside and began to pre-scold the boys while flashing her practiced grin. ". . . and fill in right behind Mrs. Morgan's girls—*no* open chairs between homerooms. All right, go ahead now." The boys moved slowly. "Well, go on."

"They're going already," Allen said in a mutter, away from her.

Ishimoto's eyes darted to him. "What was that, Mister Greene?"

"Keep going, guys."

Marlon looked at Allen curiously as they walked into the auditorium. The lights were dimmed halfway for the program, but it was stifling inside, even with all the exits open in hopes of a cross-breeze. Sharon had joined Monique and her girls, seated in the last half-full row. The boys made sure it was Darrel who had to sit by the final girl, then they filled in behind him.

Instead of sitting near their students, some of the teachers convened in small groups by the open doors. Less than a fourth of the auditorium was occupied. After waiting in the aisle for his boys to settle, Allen sat down in the first of the walnut-stained seats. Marlon was nearest, three chairs away, but he got up and moved next to his teacher—the rest of the boys followed him, leaving three unoccupied chairs in the middle of the row.

To hell with Moto's rules. Except for a spotlight on the closed curtain, the stage was dark. Allen turned back for a moment—a few parents and classified staff were making their way in past some teachers who were yapping in the foyer.

T.R. had found a girl to bother in the row ahead. The rest of the boys stared at the curtain as it began to part slowly but steadily, just as some kid on stage crew had been taught. A dozen or so members of an adult choir waited in two lines at mid-stage in glistening royal-blue robes. Mitch stood before them in a black shirt and slacks, his back to the audience.

Schultz walked slowly across stage to the microphone in the spotlight. He turned, shaded his eyes to gauge the readiness of his audience, and then lowered his head, almost like praying.

Accustomed to telling the student body two or three times to settle, Schultz looked up, his facial folds creased even more. The principal's brows lifted in mild surprise when the few noisy kids hushed right up. His voice croaked as he began speaking slowly. "I, uh, wish there was something I could say that would somehow comfort you on this most difficult of days." He paused, tearing up and barely holding it together. "All I can tell you is that my family, like yours, is deeply saddened by the tragic death of Martin Luther King."

He sighed, looking down gravely again. The audience remained silent. Schultz gradually raised his head. "The majority of your classmates have chosen to stay home this morning. You will be joining them soon—no one is absent today. I want to thank all of you for coming in and honoring, with your behavior, the non-violent legacy of Doctor King.

"Mister Warner has invited some members of his church choir. They will perform two songs, and then you are dismissed from here. We will have a full assembly on Monday to honor Doctor King. Thank you." Just a handful of kids, including T.R., applauded foolishly; Schultz turned to the choir. "Mister Warner." The principal went down the side stairs to sit with those in the first row.

Mitch walked the five or six feet to the microphone, then spoke in a soft clear voice; his face looked numb. "The first hymn is known to be a favorite of Doctor King's. Those who wish to sing with us are welcome to do so. After that, we'll sing 'We Shall Overcome,' and then you may leave. Thank you."

He backed up to the choir. The singing started, and the audience began to stand. The devout hymn wasn't one of the standards Allen had heard before. With everybody now on their feet, a few of the nearby students sang softly while others began to sob.

When the choir finished, the auditorium was again completely silent, save for some sniffles, before a fire truck rumbled by the school, its klaxon and siren blaring. Allen tuned out the routine racket like everyone else did.

As the truck noise faded, the choir began the civil rights anthem, singing wistfully and slow, as if to remind the audience of the lyrics. His eyes swelling, Allen softly sang the lines he knew and looked over at T.R., who was drumming with two pencils on the back of his seat. Monique, Sharon and all the girls were singing.

On the second time through "We Shall Overcome," more kids and adults were crying and their voices were louder, the cadence moving a bit faster. Most of the students in front began to move side to side, then Marlon took Allen's elbow and the arm of the boy on his other side; their whole row began to sway.

"Deep in my heart, I do believe . . . ." resounded even louder. T.R. fooled with his pencils, but the rest of the boys and Allen moved in unison. The choir softened for a third and final round. When the music came to a close, Marlon released his teacher's arm.

Allen could barely see and had to wipe his face with a sleeve. He stole a moment to look gratefully at Marlon, then at Mitch and the choir before he stepped back to let his small group of mostly subdued boys file out slowly.

Monique and the girls went the other way, so Allen followed the boys and some other kids up the aisle. Back at the main doors, Ishimoto hadn't budged from her post and was repeating "Good job" as she grinned to the solemn students.

To keep from saying something to her he'd regret, Allen made a hard right turn and crossed through the last row of chairs, flipping up seats and banging his shins once. He turned left up the far aisle to leave through that exit, which was manned by Cecil, wearing a brown summer sport coat with a dark tie. The usually friendly guard seemed to look suspiciously at the few kids who walked by.

Allen stayed near the wall, trying to slip past, but Cecil avoided the kids and moved into his path. "Excuse me, Cecil."

The guard tugged Allen's sleeve. "Be ready for Monday." He paused to lower his whisper even more, then spoke faster than usual. "The you-know-what's gonna hit the fan when all the cryin's done." His glare turned to a faint grin. "We'll be ready, just got us a new *dee-vice*, an' is it ever somethin'...."

"Cecil, I need to get going."

"Oh. Yeah, everybody's hightailin' it outta here."

"See you." He walked out, then around the cafeteria and into the coliseum, where a few kids were dashing between buildings. Allen started up the quiet north stairway.

In the hall by his room, two boys were at the lockers. "We're goin', Mister Greene," they both said, then took off.

"See you, Monday." He entered the room; it was completely quiet before some static came up on the intercom.

"Attention, please. The special ed. bus is here." Linda paused, then continued in monotone. "Also, any teachers still in the classrooms are reminded to lock their doors—all exits and gates are now locked. The short meeting will be at ten-thirty in the cafeteria, then staff is dismissed."

The PA crackled off. He went to the door to lock it, then returned to his desk. Leaning back in the wobbly swivel chair, he put his feet up and closed his eyes. *Okay, now you can breathe a second.*

Allen came out of his meditation minutes later when he heard someone trying his door. Not having seen Sandra since the demonstration, he was surprised to see her with Melissa through his portal.

24

Allen went out to the hall. Sandra's long black dress and the deep bags under her swollen eyes made her look much older. The baby slept soundly on her shoulder.

"Hi, Sandra. How are you doing?"

"Nobody's doin' good, Mister Greene."

"Yeah." He patted her once on the back.

"Am I disturbin' you?"

"No, just finished a little rest."

"You wanted to see me."

What? "Oh, right, I'm glad you remembered."

"I stayed home this morning, but this is real important to me too. My aunt's waiting in the car."

He craned his neck to see the hall clock. "Good, I have twenty minutes. Let's go." He locked his door, and they started down the quiet corridor. "I think we can work something out with Mrs. Berg's phone so you can check on Melissa from school."

"That'd be real good, Mister Greene."

"How did you get in here now?"

"Knocked on Mister Godina's window."

He grinned a little. "That's my trick."

They came to the middle stairway and started down. "Just remember, Sandra, you can't make calls unrelated to Melissa or you'd lose the privilege."

"I know. I promise I won't do that."

"Good enough." They passed the second floor. "Can I ask you something? I think you're an expert on the subject."

Melissa fussed a little; Sandra patted her gently. "Ask what you want, Mister Greene, but how am I a expert?"

"On the kids. They respect you, and you understand them as much or more than anybody. I think you have, um, a kind of leadership that could help you a lot someday."

"How do you mean?" They stepped off the last stairs to the first floor—no one was around in any direction.

"Well, I think you could be a lawyer, a politician, or maybe a businesswoman—something like that."

"That means college. You see what's on my shoulder?"

"I'm not saying it would be easy, but you have a lot of determination."

Sandra turned pensive for several moments before they stopped outside the office. "What did you want to ask me about the kids, Mister Greene?"

"To be honest, I'm trying to get some idea of what to expect next week."

"Are you afraid of what might happen?"

"Sure. I'm not as tough as I sound." He sighed. "I'm also worried about all the kids who aren't looking for trouble, like you and Charmane."

"In some ways, Charmane's stronger than I am." Her dark-red lipstick and smudged black eyeliner arched with a frown. "So many kids are mean to her, makin' fun of her birthmark an' callin' her worse things than *gimp* if I'm not around."

"I wish I could do more about that—not sure what."

"Charmane handles them pretty good. Don't do anything in front of the kids, Mister Greene—that'd make it worse."

"Okay, I'll remember that."

"She had a muscle disease when she was little—they can't ever fix the limp. They could take off that birthmark when she's older, but Charmane says it's part of her."

"She seems to make the best of all of it."

"That's right. She showed me how to be proud of who you are and not be a fool like some of these kids."

"You two have found quite a friendship."

"Best friend I ever had." Sandra stared past him. "You an' me are the same in one way, Mister Greene—everyone thinks I ain't afraid of nothin'. That's how I get by, but it's different now—sometimes I'm real scared." Sandra faced him, her eyes moistening. "If somethin' happens to me, Melissa's got nobody but my aunt." She hugged the baby without waking her.

"Things aren't getting better with your mom?"

She closed her eyes briefly, pursing her lips. "No."

"Sorry, none of my business."

"It's okay." She sighed and turned to him. "About next week, Mister Greene—all this with Doctor King is worse than anything before. I heard a lotta talk about trouble—it's mostly boys the school knows about an' some from Grant. Don't know when, but there's gonna be some bad days here. My aunt said the funeral's Tuesday—nobody'll come to school, hardly any on Monday either."

"Sandra, without using your name, I'd like to pass on what you said to Mister Schultz."

"All right."

"Thanks. Are you coming on Monday?"

"If they have school. I can't miss no more."

"Okay, let's see if Mrs. Berg is available."

They approached the office door. "Mister Greene?"

"Yes?"

"You're doin' okay here."

Allen stifled a scoff. "Well, thanks—you are too."

Melissa woke up in the office; Sharon gave Sandra a hug, held the baby, then listened to Allen explain the problem. She said she would arrange things on Monday with Mrs. Eichler. After Sandra said thanks, Allen went outside with her and the baby, then watched them walk all the way to her aunt's car.

He climbed the middle stairs against a flow of teachers, then walked into Monique's open room. She was at a window, staring out front before she turned to him. "Hi, Allen. Well, we made it through that day easily enough."

"Yeah, but I'm scolding you for not locking your door."

"Hard to break old habits." She leaned on the counter.

"We have a meeting."

"Oh, that's right."

After she locked up, they went down the hall to the north stairs, well behind another teacher. Allen and Monique descended slowly; a middle-aged math teacher met them at the second-floor landing. Monique chatted with her as they all walked down, then into the coliseum.

The heat radiated off of the brick and asphalt. There were no kids around, just a dozen or so teachers walking quickly ahead in small groups. Most of them passed close to Cecil, who was talking on his radio near the south archway. The math teacher went off to join someone else.

Allen turned to Monique, who shaded her face with a hand. "Are you surprised there hasn't been more trouble so far?"

"Let's just take it as testament to a brilliant and gentle man." She flinched slightly at a cherry bomb exploding somewhere near the auditorium. Cecil ran off in that direction.

"Geez, right on cue." He reached for the cafeteria door. A few feet inside, York and Jorgenson walked ahead of them in stifling heavy black dresses. Several tables were set up near the kitchen, where most of the faculty had arrived, some of them prattling away as if it were an ordinary day. Maybe half of them were wearing dark clothing.

Jorgenson and York headed for a table to sit with Latham, who was in a dark skirt and white top. Allen followed Monique there, and they settled between Latham and Dorsey, who held her charcoal suit coat as she spoke quietly with Mitch at the end of the table.

Monique chatted with Mrs. York while Dorsey, a black armband on her blouse, stopped her conversation to face Allen. "Hello, Mister Greene."

He tried not to sound unnecessarily cheerful. "Hi, Miss Dorsey. Great job today, Mitch."

They both nodded back, then went on talking. More teachers filed in from the stairs and doors. On the side facing the auditorium, a janitor was sweeping glass by a far window, likely shattered by bullets that passed through the grating. A closer pane was already covered with plywood.

Mrs. Ishimoto, a black armband now on her light-orange sleeve, stood up front by the serving line, unrolling a large paper shopping bag. Frank was at a table by himself; Allen got up, telling Monique he'd be right back. Frank was glaring out at the coliseum, his thick arms folded, an armband on the sleeve of his denim shirt.

"How are you doing, Frank?"

"I'm here." He handed over Ronnie's envelope. "Sorry, I read this one."

"I don't think he'd mind."

"You're right about him, he has a gift."

Allen sat on the edge of the table, opened the envelope and read Ronnie's printed poem:

> The sparrow gathers twigs—it doesn't know.
> The swallowtale flutters to plants—it doesn't know.
> The yellowjacket dabs the mud—it doesn't know.
> The bumbelbee sips necter—it doesn't know.
> The mawking bird mawks us all—it seems to know—
> What we do to each other.

He closed his eyes briefly, taking a deep breath.

Frank was watching him. "Serious enough for you?"

"Yeah, and I was going to ask him to try to write about Doctor King. Thanks, I'll get it back to you on Monday."

Frank stared at the coliseum again, then Allen walked over to Monique and sat down. She spoke to him, sotto voce. "Gird yourself, here he comes."

Nash was approaching in a light-brown summer suit; Allen turned away to the other teachers. Ishimoto waited up front, filing her nails with an emery board.

"Well, Mrs. Morgan and Mister Greene, good morning." After his brash exuberance, Nash sat across from them, his chain rolling noisily along the table's glossy Formica surface.

"Mister Nash." Allen didn't look at him.

"Morning, Simon." Monique stood. "Excuse me, I have to see Mrs. Berg for a second. You two be civil while I'm gone."

Allen turned from Nash, opened the envelope and started to read the poem again.

"So, Mister Greene, I assume you would agree that it is much too perilous to have school on Monday."

Allen didn't respond.

"Well?

"Perilous for who?"

"Whom, Mister Greene."

Allen finally faced him. "What did you say?"

"Perilous for *whom*."

"Oh, right. So, for *whom* is it going to be perilous?"

"You are well aware that any of us could be in danger at a time like this."

"The kids who show up might be in danger—we've got cops and security guards."

"Good glory—*we got cops*? Do you really consider yourself to be an English teacher?"

"No, I was drafted. Anyway, I said, *we've*—look it up." Trying to tune out Nash's answer, he saw Schultz entering, now with an armband on his white sleeve.

". . . not acceptable in formal Standard English, which is what *you* are supposed to be modeling. Our students are shallow enough as it is."

Screw it. "Jesus, if that's what you think, why do you even bother to teach them?"

"Don't take the Lord's name in vain to *me*," Nash said, pointing a finger. "And you dare to question *my* motives?" He lowered his arm and his voice. "It is the permissiveness by you and your kind that is the scourge of our educational system. Fortunately, even *this* school won't require your services in the fall. I assume they have already made that clear."

"None of your damn business, but you're right about the danger—unless somebody happens to have a scary briefcase."

Nash's face contorted, then he jeered at Allen with a hiss-like noise. "What in creation do you *think* you're talking about?"

"You know, Mister *Snash*."

"How dare you call me that? I will have you reprimanded for your impudence and unprofessional—"

"Schultz is here, knock yourself out." Monique was heading back to them.

"No, I will be talking to our new principal. You have not heard the last of this." Nash picked up his briefcase and walked toward Ishimoto, who was busy with Schultz, passing out papers selectively to some teachers.

Monique sat down. "All right, what did you say to him?"

"Snash is very touchy about his nickname."

"*Snash?*" She suppressed a chuckle. "That's a new one."

The cafeteria intercom crackled loudly, then Godina came on. "Mister Schultz?"

The principal called back from a far table. "Yes?"

"Mister Schultz?"

"Yes, I hear you!"

"This damn thing never works right." Godina's aside caused some chuckles from the teachers. "What?" Dead air followed his question. "Please excuse that slip," he said to more giggles. "Mister Schultz, my radio is out, and we have a situation. If the guards aren't there, I was about to make an all-call."

"They aren't here. Do you need me?"

"Oh, there's Mister Walls. We'll be okay."

While most of the audience speculated to each other about what was going on, Ishimoto gave a handout to Latham and Allen; he quickly read the procedures for emergency closure.

Schultz and Ishimoto came back to the serving line. The principal, wan and hollow-eyed, cleared his throat. Everyone was immediately quiet this time. "Thank you, this won't take long." Ishimoto sat near the grocery bag showing her half-grin—it transformed to a scowl for a straggler who walked in.

"My thanks to Mister Warner for putting together today's assembly at the last minute—it was inspirational for us all. I also want to thank him again, plus Mrs. Ishimoto, Mister Jackson, and Mrs. York for already starting to organize our students and the community for Monday's full program to honor Doctor King. I'm sure it will be equally inspiring." He paused and exhaled.

"Also, I want to inform you that we will gradually be transitioning next week to Mrs. Ishimoto being in charge. She will take over full-time a week from Monday, although I will be around." Schultz waited for some pleased chatter and light applause before nodding to the vice-principal. "Also, for those who want one, you can pick up a black armband from Mrs. Ishimoto after we finish here in a few minutes."

After another contented murmur passed through the faculty, Schultz's face tightened. "As for what else to expect next week, we don't exactly know, of course, but word is spreading about possible trouble here. We expect lower than normal attendance on Monday, then very low on Tuesday, the day of the funeral." He paused when Deniker entered from the narrow hallway by the kitchen.

"The current plan is that Monday will be a half-day, mainly for the assembly, and Tuesday will be another half-day so students can get home in time to watch the funeral. We also expect to get clearance for staff to be dismissed at noon on both days." A few teachers, including Latham, made an audible gleeful response to that announcement. Schultz excused himself to speak quickly with Deniker.

Following her interjection, Latham had turned timidly to Miss Dorsey. "Oh, I didn't mean any disrespect. It's just that the extra time gives me a chance to finish shopping for my parents' silver anniversary."

Dorsey's face turned severe. "Miss Latham, why are you apologizing to me?"

"I thought you were mad when you looked my way."

"No, I think most of us looked at you. I have no reason to be angry with you, Miss Latham. Rest assured that I would express myself clearly if I did."

"Oh." Latham attempted to smile. "Okay."

Schultz finished with Deniker. "All right, where was I?" He checked his notes. "Okay, we are hoping that Wednesday will be a somewhat normal day." He pointed to the nearby plywood. "That incident is from last night." He nodded to the janitor and his broom. "And that happened during the assembly this morning."

Over some low grumbling, Schultz said the highest priority would be to assure the safety of the students and staff. He explained other security steps that had already been taken. Nash, now sitting with Anders, got to his feet. Schultz faced him. "Make it very brief, Mister Nash."

"I believe that the measures you have described, Mister Schultz, are inadequate to protect the staff and students. The only sensible recourse is to close school for both of those days and to have the assembly on Wednesday." Nash's comment was met with strong applause. He sat, smirking.

Schultz waited. "That's not going to happen. We will start school each day, then reassess the situation. If it turns out attendance is very low along with major disruptions, we will consider closing before noon. You new teachers and subs just received a copy of the procedures for emergency shutdown, in case it is necessary. Please read it, if you haven't already."

Nash stood again, clearing his throat pompously. "I must remind teachers that emergency duty, by contract, is voluntary, and your only requirement is to inform an administrator if you won't be there. Considering the situation next week, I advise all of you to do just that. Perhaps it will result in more security provided to the school by the authorities."

"It will result in *less* security for the kids." Frank got to his feet, facing the audience. "If we do have emergency closure, it's no skin off our noses to stand out there for ten minutes to be sure students get off okay."

Nash spoke smugly from his seat. "And if there are hoodlums, what will you do Mister Williamson, save the day by stopping them with your bare hands?" Some teachers chortled.

Frank's face contorted into a slow burn. "I'll tell you what *you* can do, Nash—"

"All right, enough." Schultz sighed. "First of all, Mister Williamson probably *would* physically defend a student if he had to, and I don't see any humor in that. However, we don't expect teachers to do anything of the kind—we ask you to be there as a deterrent and to report any suspicious activity. I need to know how many of you are willing to show up in case we do ask for emergency duty."

Monique and Allen raised a hand; he looked around and saw that those he expected had volunteered and about half of the rest were also holding up an arm.

Schultz finished a quick count. "That will help a lot—thank you. As Mister Nash said, we need to know the emergency areas that won't be covered. Please inform the secretaries—the list will be discarded later. Any questions?"

Scowling at Schultz, Nash kept his mouth shut this time.

"All right then, if you must stay in your room this afternoon, be sure it's locked. That's it. Oh, and the armbands, if you would like one." Before Schultz finished his sentence, most of the teachers were on their feet, including Nash, crowding toward the vice-principal. Some teachers grabbed at the bag like early arrivals at a Christmas sale. Ishimoto dumped them all out and moved aside from the frenzy.

Monique tugged Allen's sleeve. "Would you get me one?"

"Okay, be right back." He got up to join the crowd.

Frank was on his feet, watching the teachers. "Plenty of armbands, Allen." He walked closer to him. "Did you bring them?"

"No, Dorsey." Frank nodded toward the pile. "It's downright heartwarming that Moto and Nash care so much."

"Yeah. Well, I gotta get a couple too." He sighed and walked away from Frank toward the frantic teachers.

A few minutes later, Allen and Monique crossed the coliseum, armbands in place. Many of the teachers again scurried along near Cecil, who was talking to the only two students in sight. Allen held the door for Monique and another teacher; they entered Main and were startled for a moment by an explosion that wobbled the doors—it seemed to have come from below, near the boiler room.

On the stairs, they heard someone clamor behind them into the building and scuttle down to the basement. They climbed to the second floor landing. "If we do end up closing early, where's your emergency duty, Monique?"

"I'm in that little hall by the kitchen that goes to the nurse and guards—that's why I so bravely volunteered."

"If it does happen, I could walk you back after we dismiss out front—we'd be going the same direction."

"Yes, thank you. Allen, if it gets crazy in the coliseum, don't deal with it by yourself."

"No, I won't." They came to the top of the steps and started down the hall.

She faced him. "I apologize for leaving you with Simon."

"It's okay. As much as I hate to agree with him, why *are* we having school on Monday and Tuesday?"

"Policy. A half day counts as a whole for funding. Unless the district closes the school, the principal has to show he has sufficient reason. Simon, of course, knows that—anything to get the teachers behind him."

"I was surprised Schultz had so many volunteers."

"Yes, some just need a little push." She jangled her keys. "Simon was beet red when he walked away from you. Did you say something besides the nickname?"

"I made fun of his briefcase."

"Oh my."

"He's going to report me to Ishimoto."

"He doesn't have grounds for anything, but he won't stop goading you."

"I'll keep avoiding him, but if he comes looking for trouble, he's going to find it."

25

Allen spent much of the weekend in front of the TV with Trudy, watching the famous and the ordinary reacting to the murder of Martin Luther King. There was no progress in finding the assassin, the rioting continued back east, and the National Guard was called out in several cities. More than twenty people were already dead.

Reading student papers on and off, he stayed up with the news on Friday and Saturday night until the early morning, and then didn't sleep in very long. Sunday was declared a National Day of Mourning by LBJ. Some national black leaders said his pleas for peace in the cities were hypocritical. Black clergy and other spokesmen in L.A. called for non-violence; the city remained relatively quiet.

After Trudy left for a while on Sunday, Allen watched film of two speeches he would never forget. In Memphis, the night before the assassination, Doctor King essentially predicted his own demise in a sermon. The other speech was by Bobby Kennedy, halting a campaign rally to tell an unsuspecting crowd the shocking news about Doctor King. A close-up of four grief-stricken but somehow hopeful kids in Bobby's audience reminded Allen of Sandra, Ronnie, Charmane, and Marlon.

Watching the news alone until after two a.m., Allen slept through the alarm Monday morning. Probably late to Marshall for the first time, he let Monique know with a quick call, then got himself together, putting on his rumpled clothes from Friday—the navy shirt, armband, and black jeans.

Traffic was very light again. He turned onto Harding Place at 7:30, fifteen minutes before duty. Allen's frantic trip had kept his dejection at bay, but he parked in the first open spot and took a minute to finish off his coffee before he got out. It was already very warm, so he tossed his jacket into the Volvo, and then walked quickly from the lot, making a passing wave to Marv.

He hurried across the street but slowed down for several students who were huddled on the front steps listening disconsolately to the news on a transistor radio. Two of his boys from homeroom said, "Mister Greene." Some kids had red eyes from crying or lack of sleep.

Inside, Deniker was standing there, his face not quite as dour as usual. "Ishimoto wants you." He almost smiled.

"I'll be late for duty."

"We'll live."

Linda wasn't in the office, and he didn't see either of the vice-principals. He could hear Schultz on the phone, his door open and the curtain closed. Venable, in a dark-grey shift, was waiting on hold with the phone by her ear.

"Morning, Mrs. Venable. Miss Watson didn't make it in?"

"She's delayed. Mister Schultz wants to see you."

"Now?"

"If it's convenient."

The snideness of her remark barely registered. "What about Mrs. Ishimoto?"

"What about her?"

"Never mind. He's on the phone—I'll just get my mail."

Checking the bulletin on the way back, Allen read that the schedule was the same as Friday's. He approached Schultz's door; the principal called him in, but Venable came over and walked in first. Ron Lee and Frank were sitting by Schultz's desk, armbands on their sleeves, going over some lists. They nodded to him and went back to work.

Venable stood before her boss. "LAPD just called. They'll have one squad car here for the next few days, another one at Grant." She turned to leave.

"Starting at what time?" Without his suit coat, Schultz looked even lankier than before.

"They're not sure—by eight, they hope." She backed up to the door.

Schultz got up, sighed, and opened his curtain. "Tell them we need at least two cars, or use my name and I'll talk to them." He returned to his desk. "Mister Greene, we need your help for a minute. Sit down if you like."

"I'm okay." He took another step forward from the door as Frank and Ron concentrated on their lists.

"Like that student told you, we have more reports of high-school boys bragging about making trouble here, but still no idea when—damn it all." Schultz glanced self-consciously at the outer office, then pointed at Frank and Ron. "Anyway, we're concentrating on *our* kids, and we've already checked off the regular troublemakers. Now we're identifying marginal ones, especially if they've been in this black and gold business. We'll gather those who show up, talk to them, and hopefully convince some not to get involved in anything destructive."

"Who's going to talk to them?"

"Frank, Ron, Mrs. Berg, and Mister Fogle."

"Not to rock the boat," he lowered his voice, "but I doubt that many boys will listen to what Fogle has to say."

Frank turned from his work. "Like we said, boss."

Venable signaled to Schultz from her desk; he put a hand on his phone, sighing toward Allen. "Okay, I'll think about that. Anyway, some of the seventh-graders are already checked off on this list—please take a minute with it." He handed over the paper and took his call.

Putting his box on a chair, Allen used it as a writing surface. There were already about thirty seventh-graders singled out, mostly boys. He marked only three more, two boys and a girl. He jotted down the names of his homeroom boys who had already been checked—eight of them, but five were suspended or expelled. Frank and Mitch kept working as Allen gave them the list and started to leave.

Schultz covered the receiver with his hand. "Thank you, Mister Greene."

"I only added three, and I don't agree with some who are on there, like Marlon Brown."

"That's okay, see you at the assembly."

Allen left his box by Linda's desk, then went outside and heard a fire-cracker blow off somewhere near the gym. Only a few kids sat under the eucalyptus, and the lines at the cafeteria were not even half as long as normal. Another group of students surrounded the kiva, talking quietly and eating. Instead of the typical two or three loners, there were about ten, standing by a wall or wandering slowly in the coliseum, downcast, but Allen didn't know any of them. They avoided the kids in line, who, as always, were mostly self-segregated by age, the older ones on the first iron rail, and mostly seventh-graders using the third. Many of the girls were in their Sunday best, and a few students wore black armbands.

There was very little of the usual banter or messing around. Deniker walked through the lines of dispirited kids, glaring at them. Allen made himself take a deep breath, then took the bulletin from his shirt pocket and skimmed the rest of it for pertinent information. It was mostly daily trivia, nothing about Doctor King or the student interventions, just a command that everyone was to have a "great day." It had Moto written all over it.

As soon as Deniker left on his rounds, a small boy started goofing around with a very thin, tall girl from Allen's period-six class. They were ducking under the iron rails to avoid one another, one moment laughing and shrieking, then making exaggerated threats to each other from a few feet away.

They were mostly ignored by the others, but a big girl who could pass for an adult berated the two seventh-graders when they crossed over into her territory in the first line. Oblivious, the two younger kids went right on playing around. It was the kind of silliness he wouldn't have paid much attention to on any other day, but after the older girl warned them loudly again, Allen walked toward the commotion.

Approaching the backs of about fifty kids, he turned toward the first line, then had to circle around the rails before starting through the growing crowd. Ahead, the big girl held the twosome by their collars as if restraining two squirming cats. Some of the onlookers jeered, daring her to hurt them. Before Allen came very close, the girl shouted at her captives, "You can't be grab-assin' around here on a day like this!"

Amen. This probably wasn't going to be a volatile situation, so he tried to steady himself.

When the girl saw Allen, she pulled the two young kids closer—they were crying a little. "You gonna show some respect an' stop it?" They mumbled something, then she released them. After walking away slowly and wiping their faces, the boy and girl squealed again and took off after each other.

Some of the kids berated the husky girl for not beating them up, but she pointed back at her detractors in a way that reminded Allen of Sandra. "Ya'll are jus' like them, ignorant."

He got between the girl and the crowd. "All right, everybody get in line or move on." Several kids, mostly boys, booed or catcalled as they left.

She faced Allen. "Teacher, I didn't hurt those little babies."

"Yeah, I saw that. Your name, please?"

"Maxine Reynolds. I suppose I'm in trouble."

"No, Maxine, just promise me you won't be grabbing anyone else."

"I told 'em three times—the last time I got mad." She tightened her lips in a pout. "Yeah, I promise."

"She hardly ever gets mad like that," a nearby girl said.

Yeah, me either. He nodded. "Okay, let's all just get on with what we were doing." Allen walked away from the lines. During his last minutes of duty, the faces of the kids in the mob who had called for blood kept coming back to him.

He hurried upstairs after the warning bell. In a black skirt and blouse, Monique was just about to open her door. "You look exhausted, Allen."

"So do most of the kids, but we have a lot more here today."

"Yes, more than I expected."

"I just broke up a squabble. Do you know an older girl named Maxine Reynolds?"

"Yes, a real good kid. She was fighting?"

"No, not really." Allen explained Maxine's indignation.

"'Out of the mouths of babes.'"

"Yeah. Shakespeare?"

"Matthew, I believe."

"Some of the kids in that crowd really wanted blood."

She frowned. "Bad sign." The passing bell rang; some students were already clomping up the stairs. "Okay, see you out here in a little while."

"Right." As soon as Allen walked into the room, his middle window perfectly framed the year's second popcorn-stand fire. The new hut was half involved in flame, the cook standing uselessly nearby again with a small extinguisher. Deniker was there, spraying the blaze, then Cecil came running from the cafeteria. Sirens blared in the distance, and Venable made a bossy call on the intercom for the custodians.

About a dozen kids below stood by the kiva, staring at the fire until Cecil shooed them away. The smoke appeared to be more black and acrid than the last time. Allen stretched his neck out of the window. A dark haze had already drifted far above the school in the warm stagnant air.

Darrel walked in. Instead of coming over to the window, he squeezed his short rotund body into his usual front seat. He turned to his teacher.

"Hi, Darrel."

"Hi, Mister Greene." He arched his brows in bewilderment. "Can I come over there?"

"Sure."

Darrel stood, walked across, looked out and said, "Again?" Two more boys entered, then came right over to watch. The Davis twins, at times as squirrely as T.R., ran in, both of them out of breath and excited as they joined the others at the windows.

"Cool," Darrel said, admiring a ladder truck parked outside of the south arch. A red pick-up with panels drove right into the coliseum. As before, the firemen didn't mess with hoses—they quickly opened the side panels and lifted out extinguishers. Moving over to the open space between the booth and the cafeteria, they aimed toward the base of the flames and quickly reduced the fire to embers.

A boy drifted into the room like a sleepy cat and sat in front with his head down. Marlon and a few more entered just before the tardy bell. They walked over to look outside. The tallest of them, Sam, was a minion of the gold faction and on the list to go to the counselor's office. Allen went back to his desk to check off names—two more came in late.

Darrel gushed about being a fireman; the others paid no attention. Static began on the intercom, and Darrel turned to the front. "Mister Greene, can we watch this and listen from here?"

Allen nodded, then Venable came on again. "Your attention. Announcements will be delayed a few minutes."

He joined the boys at the windows—residual smoke clouded whatever was left of the booth. The PA crackled again. "Mister Greene?"

"You made it, Miss Watson."

"Yes, I'm doing a quick survey for Mister Schultz. How many in your homeroom, please?"

"Twelve. Is that about what the others have so far?"

"Pretty close. Also, Mister Fogle or Mister Van Burton will be by to pick up some of your homeroom boys—"

"I have my list, only two of them are here."

"Okay, someone will be there soon." She was gone.

"Marlon and Sam, I need to talk to you."

Sam turned from the window. Marlon, at his desk with his head down, sat up. "Why me? I didn't do nothin'."

"Easy, Marlon, it's not anything to—" Someone dashed across the back of the room. It was Sam, running out the far door. Allen reached up to hit the intercom button, then turned to Marlon, motioning for him to come over.

Marlon dawdled but walked to the teacher's desk in a faded Dodger's T-shirt and blue jeans. Linda answered the PA. Allen reported Sam, then he and Marlon went out to the hall.

"Okay, don't take this wrong, you're not in any trouble." Allen explained why Marlon had to go down to the office.

"I ain't runnin' with nobody now, Mister Greene."

Allen saw Fogle coming down the hall with a small group of boys, all but one taller than him. "I know, Marlon, but—"

"I won't talk to nobody but Mister Williamson."

The nearly bald counselor, apparently relegated to delivery boy, was in a white dress shirt and dark slacks. He stopped at Monique's door and knocked.

Fogle glared at Allen, who was whispering with Marlon. ". . . Mister Williamson will be there, just ask for him. We'll save you a seat at the assembly."

"I bet they keep me."

Monique came out and released one of her homeroom girls. Allen turned to Fogle. "Sam ran off. Marlon's the only one on the list who's here."

The counselor just snarled at the kids. "Let's go." After watching Marlon walk away with them, Allen went back into the room and over to the windows. Half of his boys were still looking out, the rest sitting lethargically at their desks.

Like a charred marshmallow, the bottom third of the white popcorn stand had not been consumed by the flames. The firemen were already packing up the extinguishers. Two cops stood near their squad car, chatting with Cecil and a cook—not a kid in sight. Allen started for his desk, but Darrel yanked his sleeve. "Look, Mister Greene, they're not in school."

Allen turned in time to see five or six junior-high boys and girls, laughing away as they ran around the far corner of the cafeteria past the picnic benches. The cops jumped into their black-and-white and went after them.

The intercom buzzed and Venable came on. "Your attention, the assembly is delayed. Remain in your homeroom and wait for the bell."

When Allen, Monique and their kids finally entered the auditorium twenty minutes later, about half of the student body was there along with scores of parents. Schultz started the program, then turned it over to Ishimoto. Local dignitaries made long-winded speeches interspersed with off-key musical solos by students, Mitch trying to rescue them on the piano. Then some heavily clichéd essays by Mrs. York's track-three seventh-graders made Allen judge that his so-called low students would soon be writing more germane and heart-felt responses to the tragedy. The very long assembly was topped off by Mister Jackson's rambling, passionless biography of Doctor King.

Before she dismissed the students, Ishimoto told the teachers to help clear the grounds. Apparently not realizing that most of the kids were bored or half-asleep, she looked almost disappointed by their orderly egress. Allen and Frank ended up walking together across the coliseum well behind the last of the kids.

"How much of that did you get to see, Frank?"

"About half, thank God. Promised my wife I wouldn't get too pissed today—I nearly lost it when Jackson said Doctor King won the *noble* Peace Prize."

Allen chuckled without smiling. "Jackson wasn't even the worst of it." He watched a man in a suit kick at the popcorn stand's rubble. "How did it go with the interventions?"

"Didn't take long, not many were there. A few listened."

A janitor rolled a wheelbarrow full of black debris past them. "Except for the fire, it hasn't been so bad. I wonder if it will stay like this all week."

Frank sighed. "It's going to blow eventually, but not tomorrow."

"What about the rest of South-Central?"

"The mood is mostly dejection so far, but everything's changed by the assassination."

Allen worked in his room a few more hours, wary for a visit from Ishimoto or a call from her on the intercom, but neither happened. He spent that evening with Trudy, watching the news.

As predicted, less than a hundred students showed up on Tuesday, the school and the grounds eerily tranquil. Schultz and Ishimoto were gone to a meeting, so Frank arranged with Godina to have two televisions set up in the cafeteria. Ron, Allen, Frank and a few more teachers supervised the students, many of whom had their heads down, watching or listening to the lead-up to Doctor King's funeral. Godina dismissed them from the cafeteria after period four.

At home that afternoon, Allen sat on the couch, sipping on a can of beer and watching the news. Pedro was asleep and Trudy was gone to a doctor's appointment. One of the L.A. channels was on with a man-in-the-street report, interviewing a middle-aged tourist couple from Phoenix. They stood over the sidewalk stars on Hollywood Boulevard, whining about the postponement of the Academy Awards for King's funeral.

Allen got up, glaring at the TV. "Shut the hell up." He changed the channel to CBS, settled on the sofa again, and took a swig of beer. Reverend Ralph Abernathy was already beginning to conduct the service for Doctor King. The church was full, and at least fifty thousand people were outside, listening to loudspeakers. They said the ceremony would likely be the largest funeral for a private citizen in U.S. history.

A hymn began, another one Allen hadn't heard before. The camera zoomed into the veiled Coretta King and one of their daughters, the child's eyes glazed and traumatized. The camera then panned over the celebrities in the audience, holding for a moment on Harry Belafonte, then dwelling on the Kennedy clan, especially Jackie and Bobby.

His stomach growling, Allen went to the kitchen to make a sandwich. He could hear Cronkite say that Hubert Humphrey was standing in for L.B.J. because they were worried about protesters. "In that church? Bull, even Nixon's there," he said, then came back with his food and another beer.

They started a recording of Doctor King eulogizing himself in a sermon. Moved to tears, Allen dropped his sandwich on the plate. He cried for a few minutes, then Trudy came home, and together they stared for hours at the rites on TV, followed by the procession rolling through the streets of Atlanta.

26

On Wednesday morning, Allen was running late again. He called Monique, then put on the only clean clothes he had, a medium-blue summer shirt and tan khaki bellbottoms. He slipped the armband over one short sleeve, said good-bye to Trudy, and left for school. On yet another warm smoggy morning, the heavy traffic was back, and he was caught in a jam near downtown. Allen turned onto Harding Place and parked after seven-thirty. He ran by a cop car parked near the crosswalk, then right upstairs with his box. Although he was late, he took a minute to write a prompt on the board before hurrying down for duty.

This time, the lines were almost normal at the cafeteria. A uniformed cop stood with Nash at the north arch, Deniker patrolled the coliseum, and Cecil was in Allen's duty area. The guard was talking to Monique, who had her coffee cup and two saucer-sized cinnamon rolls. Cecil was just finishing his sentence. "... make it through this day here an' we should be okay." He turned to Allen. "Mornin'."

"Hi, sorry I'm late—hit a traffic jam." He nodded to Monique. Her mouth was full.

"Right on time for me to start my rounds," Cecil said.

"Looks pretty good. How many cops?"

"Two if it stays quiet. Don't ya'll worry, we'll be okay." Cecil smiled and walked off.

"So how did you end up here, Monique?"

She swallowed, holding up napkins and the rolls, the partially eaten one separated from the other with waxed paper. "Missed breakfast, thought I'd eat here and go upstairs with you. This one's for you, if you'd like it."

"Thanks, I didn't eat either." He glanced at Deniker near the quiet lines as she gave him the bun. "Well, I guess we can try for some normalcy today."

"We can give it a shot." They ate and chatted until the warning bell, then went up to their rooms.

Twenty boys showed up for homeroom. A few were despondent, but some others seemed to be excitable and nervous, especially after a cherry bomb went off outside. Allen attached a note to the attendance list to tell Schultz that Aaron, yet to have his intervention, was there.

After the Pledge and a short reminder that they were on a regular schedule, Darrel pointed at the armband on Allen's sleeve. "Is that for Reverend King, Mister Greene?" A few boys laughed before Allen told Darrel that he was right.

His first-period class came in more subdued than the homeroom boys. Because of suspensions, the small class was now about the same size as Creative Writing, and there were also five absent. Two doleful-looking girls had their heads down. Allen left them alone.

Taking attendance during fluency time, he stopped at Sandra's desk. She was still in Sunday clothes, a pressed chartreuse dress, black armband, and faux pearls. He spoke to her softly. "Hi, Sandra. All set now with Mrs. Eichler?"

She looked up with a brief affirmative smile, then kept writing. After they put away their notebooks, Allen quickly explained the difference between an autobiography and a biography. "I want you to be Doctor King's biographer today. There are no wrong answers, just tell what you know and remember about him, and, if you want, how you feel about his death."

The fifteen students made five matches plus an extra low reader for whom Allen would transcribe. There were four readers there who never tutored, including the two girls who had their heads down. The kids did the work willingly, interrupted only by a couple of explosions somewhere near the gym. After the transcribing, Allen worked with the low readers while the tutors wrote their papers. The two downcast girls had perked up a bit and also did the work.

With about ten minutes remaining, he said, "Okay, hang on to your papers for a minute. Tutors, remember, those were private thoughts you heard today." Most of the kids looked at him seriously. There were a couple of grumbles.

"Maybe one or two of you might want to share your first draft now—we have a few minutes." He paused. "Completely voluntary—anyone?"

Sandra's hand went up, and then Charmane's. The girl who Charmane regularly tutored, Francis, hesitantly raised her hand.

"Thank you, that's plenty for now. If you'd like, more of you can read aloud tomorrow. Sandra?"

"I'm gonna stand up, Mister Greene."

"Sure."

Sandra cleared her throat and started reading without looking up. "I forget exactly where Martin Luther King was born. I know it was in the South like my mom an' my aunt. They have stories about growin' up down there, about how if you don't complain, the white man pat you on the back like a farm animal. You complain, you get beat up or worse. I think that's how it probably was for Doctor King.

"My aunt says he was smart and got to go to college. She says he cared about everybody, always comin' back to help his people—in the city too, places like here and Chicago. He's famous all over the world and won that big prize, but Doctor King used the money to help poor people—black and white." Sandra stopped for a loud explosion somewhere inside the building. Some of the kids mumbled to each other. "You want me to go on, Mister Greene?"

"Quiet, please," he told two nearby boys. "Yes, please, Sandra."

"They say a white man shot him, but I'm tryin' not to hate white people because Doctor King said that was wrong, jus' like when white people hate us. My uncle says they'll never catch that man because they don't want to. My aunt tol' him the problem is men, not jus' white men. She said it's men who do the killin' no matter where—an' he got mad. I jus' know I'm sad my baby won't see Doctor King alive again. So I'll have to tell her all about him."

The room was silent. Allen made a long exhale. "Very good, Sandra. Thank you."

"Welcome." She sat, staring down at her paper.

He turned to Charmane and Francis. "You two can read tomorrow, okay? All right, last thing. You've all heard there might be trouble this week—" The bell rang; the kids didn't move. "Well, maybe there won't be, but if there is, please be careful and stay away from it. See you later." They handed in their papers, then left, talking quietly.

At the beginning of his prep hour, he tried to read the King papers, but he went to the windows twice for explosions. The second time, he saw the backs of some boys, running off toward the gym. He hit the PA button and waited a while, but there was no answer.

Allen tried to relax and breathe for a minute, but he heard more commotion outside. He went to an open window and saw three high-school guys beating up on two Marshall boys. "Knock it off, now!" They ran away, laughing. The two younger boys writhed on the ground as Cecil and a uniformed cop came into the coliseum.

The intercom crackled. "Attention, teachers." It was Venable. "Double-check immediately to be sure your classrooms are locked." Allen went out to the hall. Monique was locking her door as about fifteen kids, mostly boys, ran away from her toward the north stairwell. "Hey!" he yelled, but none of them turned back. "Were those yours, Monique?"

"A few of them—they got up and left when the others came to the door." Another boy snuck out behind her.

"Stop right there!" The boy ignored him and sprinted away. Allen turned to Monique. "Are you okay?"

"Yes, but please come on in for a minute."

They walked into the room. Her remaining eighth-graders, mostly girls, were in their seats, looking up apprehensively at static from the intercom. Schultz came on. "Your attention, please. In a few minutes, we will ring a bell for the end of classes today. Students are to walk with your period-two teacher to the front steps, where you will be dismissed. Teachers on extra duty, then go to your locations, please. All gates will be closed after ten minutes—students may enter the office from out front if they need to make a call. Wait for the bell now, and please stay calm. We'll see you all tomorrow."

Monique turned to her class. "Okay, we'll be walking out with Mister Greene." A few kids stood right away.

Allen motioned with both arms for them to sit down. "Easy, not yet."

Her students chatted nervously until the bell rang a couple of minutes later. They followed the teachers out to the hall, where there were about a dozen more kids, including Sandra, Charmane and some other seventh-grade girls, plus Marlon, Darrel, and a few homeroom boys. They all walked up to Allen and Monique. Sandra carried a notebook, one text, and her purse. Some of the others were lugging two or three schoolbooks.

"Why aren't you kids with your second-period teacher?" Allen looked at Sandra.

"We're all in the same class, Mister Greene—she let us go."

Charmane scoffed. "Ol' Aunt Bea was afraid to go out."

"Okay, you can just come with us."

The handful of remaining boys from Monique's class joined the ones in the hallway. About twenty-five kids headed for the middle stairs with Monique and Allen.

"Mister Greene, did you check our poems?" Charmane scowled at Marlon, who was close enough to hear her question.

"Afraid I'm behind on my homework, Charmane."

"Yeah, me too." She adjusted the black armband on the sleeve of her long white dress as they started downstairs.

Sandra was on her other side. "Mister Greene, I don't have my math or science books. Can I go to my locker?"

"Where is it?"

"Third floor cafeteria, by my homeroom. I gotta get 'em—those are the classes I'm behind in."

"You can't go now, Sandra. I guess you two could walk back when we go over there for duty, but then you'll have to wait a little while and leave school with us."

"That's okay, we need to make a call anyway."

When they came down to the first floor, the office and foyer were jammed with kids and a few adults. The middle of the crowd pushed toward the front door, where Godina and Frank were trying to keep things orderly.

Allen and Monique escorted the kids gradually to the door. She tugged Frank's shirt to get his attention. "This is your duty area now?"

Frank had his arms up, trying to slow down some kids. "Yeah, they moved me here—I guess until Deniker's free."

"Lucky you," Allen said. "Maybe we'll catch you on the way out."

"Yeah, you two stay on your toes back there."

They dismissed their kids into a dispersing throng that encircled the squad car in front of the school. At the curb, Allen turned back to the crowded stairs, then to Monique, Sandra and Charmane. "Maybe we should go around, ladies." The girls grinned slightly before the four of them walked off toward the north end of the grounds. They went around the corner and into the coliseum; a janitor locked the gate behind them.

A string of dull-sounding firecrackers rattled off somewhere on the other side of the cafeteria. Fogle and the other teacher had yet to show up for emergency duty while Nash, of course, had opted out. They crossed over to Allen's area, where only two kids hurried by into Main. Allen stopped, took out a hall pass from his wallet, then hesitated, gazing out at the strange lack of activity between the two archways.

Charmane arched her brow. "What's wrong, Mister Greene?"

"Nothing. Okay, after you guys go to Sandra's locker, I want you to come straight down to Mrs. Morgan in the cafeteria, then back out here with her." He signed the paper. "Then we'll all go out front together." He handed the pass to Sandra.

"Thanks, Mister Greene."

Monique forced an upbeat smile. "*Oui, merci*, we'll see you back here in about fifteen minutes."

She and the girls started off for the nearby south entrance to the cafeteria, passing a solitary boy going the opposite direction. The kid entered Main, where Fogle waited just inside the door, although he was supposed to be outside.

Allen looked to the left at the quiet street. Moments later, somebody far behind him moved a metal trashcan. He turned to the noise—a line of mostly big boys, two of them wearing all black, moved by in a low lurching sprint under the north arch to the cafeteria doors. By now, only the south door was supposed to be unlocked.

He took tentative steps toward the boys, then a few more hurried by. He recognized one in black—Rupert. Allen started to shout, but they were gone; the door was evidently ajar or open. He ran for the nearby south entrance, cursing himself for letting the girls go into the building.

Allen went in and quickly checked the office doors for the cook, nurse, and security guards. They were all locked, but there was a light under the nurse's door, so he knocked hard—no answer. He slammed both fists on the metal—still nothing. Allen ran for the stairwell, where Monique was hurrying toward him down the narrow hall from the cafeteria.

"We need a phone, Allen! A big gang of boys just ran upstairs—some are from Grant."

"I know, but nobody back there answers. I'll go up and see if I can get to the girls before they do."

"And if you do?"

He started upstairs. "We'll hide or run—I don't know."

"I'll go to Main to get help. Be careful."

"Okay, *you* be careful." He was already halfway up to the second floor. Skipping three stairs at a time, he passed the landing and saw two Marshall boys in black standing guard up at the third floor—they took off right away.

He came to the top and stopped to look down the corridor. The gang was at the far end, surrounding somebody, yelling and laughing. Maybe they were just messing with each other, but he ran toward them, shouting, "All right, that's it, the cops are right behind me!"

An older voice above the others called out, "We're outta here, forget her!"

Her? Damn it. The gang thinned out, fleeing down the far stairs. As the bodies cleared, only two remained. One was Sandra, the back and one side of her lime-green dress splotched with blood. She was crouched, facing Rupert, who pointed a switchblade right at her, a streak of blood on his own cheek.

He was cackling. "Had enough, bitch?" He saw Allen in his peripheral vision and swung the knife his direction.

"It's over, Rupert, the cops are right behind me."

"Fuck you, Charlie." He shuffled backwards, turned, then casually skip-galloped down the stairs as if he were heading for his next class. Sandra remained stooped over in a daze, both arms straight ahead, her fingernails extended like tiny scarlet bayonets, ready for more battle.

27

Allen moved in front of her. "Easy, Sandra, take it easy. He's gone." She had a bad wound behind one ear; blood ran along her neck and beneath the collar, soaking through the fabric down her side. She finally dropped her arms and turned to him.

"Mister Greene." She started to fall.

Allen lunged but couldn't catch her head before it thumped on the linoleum, the rest of her a sickening mass of crimson and chartreuse. He kneeled, put one hand behind her neck and saw some white material in a side pocket of her dress. He took out the folded hankie and used it to apply pressure to the cut, but some blood began to soak through.

"Shit." He got down to both knees and put his arms all the way under her, then struggled to his feet with the hefty girl. Reaching with his hand that held the makeshift compress, Allen pressed it onto her neck again. He carried her back to the other end of the hall, his arms aching by the time he got there.

Navigating down the steps, he had to lean on the iron banister to keep his balance. Halfway to the bottom, his arms began to tremble from fatigue. *Think about something else—where's Charmane?* Before he made it down to the first floor, Sandra's blood had soaked through her dress and into his light summer shirt, turning sticky on his chest.

The hall below was empty; Allen could barely feel his arms, so he readjusted her body to regain his circulation. He hobbled over to the nurse's door, turned around and struck the base as hard as he could with the heel of one of his sturdy shoes. Sandra moaned, her eyes still closed. He gave the door another hard backwards blow. "C'mon lady!" Allen took a step toward the exit, then someone moved the door handle behind; he turned.

The young blonde school nurse opened the door, her eyes open wide. "What do you think you're doing?"

"What's it look like to you?" He started by her, his arms about to give out.

"There's a cot in the main office—she can wait for an ambulance there."

Allen saw her name badge as he went by. "She can wait here, Miss Swanson." Inside the white office, he was vaguely aware of a scale, eye chart, and a padded examination table; some tall grey cabinets stood by the far wall.

"You can't just come in here like this."

He laid Sandra as gently as he could on the table. "I already did." He pressed the wound, and she groaned again. "Okay, nurse, there's the cut, and she has a knot on the back of her head."

Swanson came over but only gave Sandra's injuries a cursory look. She left Allen a light blanket and hurried to her desk. "I'm calling the office right now." She reached for the phone on the wall.

Allen pulled the cover up to Sandra's neck. "Make sure an ambulance is on the way."

"I'll do more than that." She made the call and spoke to Venable, describing the situation in one long frantic sentence and complaining about "some teacher in my office." She demanded that Mrs. Ishimoto be sent immediately, then turned to him, smug and angry at once. "The ambulance is already on the way, and so is Mrs. Ishimoto."

"Fine, help me slow the bleeding and clean her up. Maybe she's cut somewhere else."

"By now you'd see if there was another bad wound—what you're doing is correct procedure. The ambulance will probably be here in less than ten minutes."

"Then why the hell can't you help?"

"We're not allowed to treat serious wounds."

"What are you *here* for, Miss Swanson?"

"Prevention and . . . I don't have to answer to you."

"Okay, so *prevent* something. Get me some towels, moisten some of them, and bring damp washrags, half of them cold."

"I'll do it, but *you* are responsible."

"I get it—move, for God's sake."

Sandra mumbled a bit while Allen watched the nurse grudgingly pull linen from a cabinet and begin to wet some of it in her sink. She brought over the towels and washcloths before returning to her desk.

"Thanks a million." He wadded a cold towel with his other hand and put it under the knot at the back of her head. The hankie still in place, Allen cleaned around the wound without touching it. Swanson was right, there was only the one bad gash.

When he let the saturated hankie drop to the floor, blood began to drip onto the table. He re-applied pressure right away with a wet towel, then took a damp cloth and draped it over Sandra's forehead; she murmured. Swanson was beneath him now in plastic gloves and a surgical mask, snatching up the fallen hankie from her immaculate floor—she minced over to the trashcan with it as if she carried pestilence. Someone tried the door, then knocked, but Swanson didn't move.

Trying not to bother Sandra, Allen kept himself from shouting. "Open the door—now."

Still in her mask, Swanson grabbed her large purse and held it to her chest. "What if it's, uh, one of—" There was another knock.

"Open up, damn it."

She walked slowly toward the door, her hand holding something inside the purse. Allen watched fresh blood seep to the center of the washrag. "C'mon, move it."

She poked the button in the handle with her free hand to release the lock, then jumped away. Monique walked in with Charmane.

Allen sighed. "Thank God you're both okay."

"Mrs. Morgan," the nurse said, flabbergasted.

Charmane went right to Sandra, reaching up to hold her shoulder. "How is she, Mister Greene?"

"She's hurt pretty badly, but she's going to be okay." Monique was already at the table, removing the bunched washrag from Sandra's forehead. She began to fold it. "Thanks, Monique. Did they call Sandra's family?"

She applied the neat cloth to Sandra's brow. "Her aunt's out of town, but Charmane had the office call her mom and the ambulance before I even got there."

"Good going, Charmane."

She was watching her friend, tears lodging in the corners of her eyes.

The school nurse *tsked*. "I can't allow all these people in here, especially that child."

Allen didn't look up to answer. "She isn't a child, and she's staying here for now."

"I am reporting *all* of this."

Monique turned to her. "You won't have long to wait, Miss Swanson. Mister Schultz isn't far behind us."

"I *asked* for Mrs. Ishimoto."

"Too bad." When Allen said that, Charmane was glaring at the nurse, so he gave Monique a peek at the wound and snatched a clean towel, tossing the bloody one out of Charmane's sight.

Monique smiled at Charmane and put her other arm around her. "They'll be here soon, sweetheart. They'll take real good care of Sandra—she'll be okay." Sobbing a little, Charmane hugged her homeroom teacher around the waist and didn't let go.

The principal opened the door without knocking and came in with Deniker and a cop. Holding a walkie-talkie, Schultz looked at Sandra, her three caretakers, and then the nurse at her desk.

Swanson got up. "Sir, I want to file a complaint."

Schultz turned from her and approached the examination table, watching Allen. "Mister Greene, what's the situation?"

He described the wounds, then pointed at Swanson. "She wouldn't treat her, so we're doing what we can. It's still bleeding, but it's starting to slow a little. It was Rupert Washington who cut her."

Schultz sent Deniker and the cop out to check the building, then he came the rest of the way to the table. "Let's have a quick look." Allen lifted the cloth, then resumed the pressure.

Schultz shook his head. "Okay, keep it up. The ambulance had a flat—they're changing it. It'll be at least ten more minutes." He pointed his radio at the nurse. "Do you know how to dress this wound, Miss Swanson?"

"Yes, but it needs stitches, sir."

"Wouldn't a firm dressing help to slow the bleeding?"

"Maybe, along with the pressure."

"Then do it."

"You know our guidelines, Mister Schultz—I can't be responsible for this." She got up again.

"The responsibility is mine. Go on, Miss Swanson."

"If you say so." She reached for a small white cart.

Allen shook his head and mumbled, "Thank you, Florence Nightingale."

Charmane looked fiercely again at the school nurse. Wheeling the cart to the cabinets, Swanson turned to Schultz. "I want him out of my way. Mrs. Morgan can help me."

"Okay, Mister Greene, please let Mrs. Morgan in there."

"Fine." He switched places with Monique; Charmane took over the washcloth on her friend's forehead. Sandra moaned with the new activity as Allen and Schultz backed up closer to the door. The principal went out in the hall to answer his radio.

Swanson finished placing gauze, pads, tape, ointments, metal implements and more linen on the cart, then pushed it over, glaring at Charmane. "That girl isn't needed here."

With her free hand, Monique squeezed Charmane's arm. "Thanks, dear, the nurse needs plenty of room. Please wait over there with Mister Greene."

Charmane closed her eyes for a moment, then let go of the cloth and patted Sandra's shoulder again. She started slowly over to Allen. He saw that her birthmark had darkened, flush with blood. "How did you get away from that gang, Charmane?"

"They let me go when you yelled at them." Her scornful eyes darted back to the nurse. Swanson began to treat the wound while Monique maintained the pressure when she could.

Schultz came back in, looked at Swanson, then turned to Allen. "I'm leaving to deal with another problem. If you don't mind, wait here for the ambulance. They'll drive it right into the coli—uh, courtyard." He reached for the door, nodding to Charmane. "Thanks for your help today, young lady."

She turned from Sandra for a moment and looked up at him miserably. "You're welcome."

Schultz left; Allen propped the doors open so he could hear the ambulance. They all watched Swanson until she finally stopped working and faced Monique. "That holds it pretty well, just keep up the pressure." She glared at Allen. "And *I'll* begin my report."

Allen put his hand on Charmane's shoulder. "We can go see her now."

After they walked over, Monique gave a dry washcloth to Charmane. "Here, *amour*, put some nice cool water on this and wring it out, please." Eager to help, Charmane smiled slightly and hurried past the frowning nurse to the sink.

Monique spoke to Allen in a low tone. "After they get here, I'll go with Charmane to call her parents. I can drive her over to County General."

"They'll take Sandra way over there?"

"That's the closest public hospital. Anyway, they won't allow Charmane in the room, but at least she can wait outside."

"I'll come over as soon as I can get out of here."

Charmane returned with the cloth. It wasn't dripping, but Monique said, "Please wring it out a little more, dear."

"Okay."

As soon as she left for the sink, Monique peeked at the wound, then whispered, "Allen."

He winced at some blood seepage in the dressing. Monique resumed the pressure before Charmane returned and looked keenly at Allen. "What's wrong, Mister Greene?"

"We're just impatient for the ambulance to come."

Swanson slammed a desk drawer. "I just heard the doors close outside. Now maybe things will get back in order."

Allen was already in the doorway, heading for the outside exit. He held the door all the way open and waited. Seconds later, a gurney rolled around the corner, pushed by an attendant, another one lagging several feet behind— the same two who came for Ronnie and Del's incident.

Jahan Singh's white uniform was smudged with dirt and grease, presumably from changing the tire. He hurried the gurney by Allen and through the door, thanking him. Ernie Shaw walked up, grinning, his uniform spotless, its short sleeves rolled all the way up, Elvis-style, to show off his muscular arms. His receding blond hair was combed over; he had a pack of Luckies folded into one sleeve, the brand's red circle showing through the thin white material.

The attendant paused a moment to take in Allen's appearance, especially his facial hair, then his chest. "I remember you, teach." He pointed. "Who shot you?"

Allen lowered his chin for a glimpse of his shirt. Like one of Monique's color-blending art lessons, the blood had soaked into the blue fabric to make a large purplish stain shaped like a lopsided continent on a map.

Shaw smirked and walked casually by, making a condescending salute, as he might to a hotel doorman. "Ol' John there acts like he's going to a fire."

Literally biting his lip, Allen followed him into the office; Singh was already with Sandra, putting on gloves. The nurse stood behind her desk. "Thank God you're here, Ernie."

"Hey, Swanny-babe what's wrong?" He went over to her.

Charmane was a few feet from Singh, watching him inspect the patient and check vital signs. Allen scowled at the lovebirds; she was explaining what happened in a long whine. Her almost middle-aged suitor put his arm around her.

"Mister Shaw, I need you to check this." Singh was holding the dressing with the plastic gloves, Monique at his side.

"Okay, be there in a sec."

I'll be goddamned. "Right now, Romeo."

Shaw sneered at Allen. "What did you say?"

"You heard me."

"Yeah, who put you in charge?" He grinned to Swanson.

"Nobody, but I'll get somebody here right now." He started for the wall phone.

"Relax, teach, everything's under control." Shaw and Swanson walked over to Sandra, everyone glowering at them. "All you people are too serious, including you, John."

Singh moved back a step, and Monique joined Charmane. Shaw began his inspection, Swanson standing right by, the top button of her blouse open suggestively. Her arm grazed the anchor tattoo on her boyfriend's left biceps as he worked.

Shaw turned to her. "Skin and blood under her nails—the girl got in some licks. This is a nice job, babe, but it's starting to come through a little—the blade must've nicked an artery. Okay, let's get her going."

Allen went back by the door to Monique and Charmane, who were talking quietly to each other and watching Sandra being prepared for the move. Swanson minded the wound while the attendants lifted Sandra from the table. She grumbled unconsciously as they transferred her to the gurney.

Charmane and Monique went to the nurse's door to hold it for Singh, while Allen ran to open the one outside. Pushing the gurney and holding Sandra's wound with his other hand, Singh went through the doorway but kept turning to look for his partner.

Allen ran back in as Monique and Charmane came out. He opened the nurse's door to find Shaw with his arm around her. "Jesus, are you going to do your goddamn job or not?"

Shaw scoffed at Allen, then touched her cheek. "See you tonight, Swanny."

Allen stayed at the door to make sure the medic was leaving, then waited for him in the hall.

"Okay, here we go, teach, and I got some advice for you."

"Yeah? Save it for posterity." They went out. Allen walked ahead of him toward the corner of the building.

"Posterity, huh?" Shaw sniggered, looking around to be sure they were alone as he caught up. "Don't know if you're some kinda hippie or what, man. I do know this—the niggers don't want white boys down here teaching 'em how things are supposed to be. Hell, they throw rocks at *us* when we come to scrape up uncle or junior." Shaw pointed at him. "You're gonna lose more 'n that pretty hair if you don't leave 'em alone—that's what they want, for you to leave 'em alone."

Allen shook his head. "Like I said, do your damn job."

"That's all you got for me, teach?"

Singh was waiting with Sandra behind the ambulance, and Cecil was also there, applying pressure to her wound. Monique and Charmane watched from outside the entrance to Main. Another explosion echoed through the coliseum. Two high-school boys ran to the locked north gate and scrambled over the chain-link.

"Those were M-80's." Shaw laughed. "Yup, they're gonna get you teach, one way or the other." They came closer to Singh, who was straightening his tall frame after ducking from the blast. Cecil had the radio to his ear.

Shaw went to the back doors of the ambulance as Allen walked up to the gurney. Sandra had her eyes open and was talking to Singh and Cecil. She turned her head. "Mister Greene, he says I'm going to be okay. Is that right?"

"You bet, Sandra. Your mom and Charmane will be waiting at the hospital. I'll see you there in a little while."

Monique and Charmane went into Main as Allen and Cecil jogged through the empty coliseum behind the slowly departing ambulance. At the same gate the boys had scaled minutes before, Cecil started grumbling because someone had locked it since the ambulance arrived.

As the guard sorted through his wad of keys, Allen knocked lightly on the side window of the ambulance. Sandra tried to smile back. The medic had one hand on her neck, the other held a copy of *National Inquirer*. Shaw looked up at Allen, rolling his eyes. Cecil opened the gate, then the long vehicle rolled into the street, Sandra looking around helplessly while Shaw read his periodical.

Meat wagon—now I get it.

28

As the ambulance left quickly, no siren, Cecil closed the gate. He unlocked the north entrance to the school and they entered, but Cecil stayed by the stairwell for some reason. Allen walked down the first-floor corridor toward the office, hoping to catch Monique and Charmane.

Not only was the hall quiet, someone had turned off the main lights. The first two rooms were dark and the third had the outside shades drawn, but the lights were on. His back arched over a pile of mid-semester report cards, Nash worked on his grades with a sinister grin—a lugubrious opera throbbed from inside the room.

Allen went on. A small firecracker blew off ahead and some glass shattered, the noise reverberating down the corridor. He moved cautiously toward a shout and a slamming door from near the office. He walked faster and came around the corner into the foyer.

Glass shards by his feet, Deniker was searching outside through the front door's thick window. He had a radio in his hand. A pane of the trophy case was gone, but the display of ribbons, plaques and group photos seemed undisturbed, save for a dusting of glass splinters. Linda stood just inside the office in a grey suit, an armband on her sleeve. She stared at the destruction, her arms folded as if she were cold.

"A goddamn ladyfinger." Deniker was swearing to himself over the smallest kind of firecracker they made. He turned halfway around, clipping the radio to his belt without looking directly at Allen. Deniker craned his neck toward the door again, grumbling. "You're all supposed to be out of here."

"Fine, I'm going in a minute." Allen reached for the doorknob and entered the office. Linda was the only one there, staring glumly now at some papers on her desk. "They left you to hold down the fort?"

She looked up, her face blank. "Hi."

"Did you see—" He stopped because she was pointing at his chest.

"Allen, is that what I think it is?"

The gory shirt had slipped his mind again. "Afraid so." She bowed her head reverently. He waited several moments for her to look up. "Did you see Mrs. Morgan and Charmane leave?"

Her dark eyes moist, she nodded. "They left for the hospital before that firecracker. How is Sandra doing?"

"She woke up and was talking. I think she'll be okay."

"Thank God." She paused, making a long sigh. "Did you hear the announcement that the buildings are to be vacated?"

"Deniker told me. Shouldn't you be going too?"

"In twenty minutes—he'll be out there until then." She glowered at the guard in the foyer, then faced Allen. "You must have had quite a morning."

"Yeah." He glanced at the back offices. "What have they said about tomorrow?"

"They're going to try again for a regular day."

"Then I have to run a ditto—can I ask a favor?"

"Of course."

"Could you find the address for County General? I know it's near Boyle Heights, just not sure exactly where."

"I'll get it for you right now."

"Thanks."

"You're very welcome."

A bit puzzled by her emphatic answer, he went into the lounge, where a teacher's aide and a custodian were talking. Allen just nodded, then went to his box in the hall and found the assignment page he had left there. He needed to burn a master in a contraption that didn't always work, then hope for the ditto machine to behave.

He went back to the office. She was still alone, finishing a call. "Linda, any chance I could use the photocopy machine?"

"Sure. Here's the address you wanted and the nearest main intersection."

She handed over the note along with a grey cartridge about the size of a thick candy bar.

He read the paper. "Good, I know about where that is. Don't I need to sign for the key?"

"I'll put down my name, the office is way under limit."

"Okay, thanks."

She made a slight, lackluster smile. He left and passed by the now vacant lounge into the back workroom. The copier resembled a grey coffin over a long cabinet of the same color. Allen inserted the key into the slot at its side, lifted the rubber flap on top and placed the page carefully on the convex glass at the spot for 8.5 X 11 masters. He selected the correct tray, twisted the dials for the number of copies, then hit the start button.

The massive machine thumped, thought for a moment, and then rattled before it began to *ka-chunk, ka-chunk, ka-chunk*; the copies started to spit out, each one making a satisfying *click*, moments apart, against the edge of a distant metal tray.

The steady rhythm of the copier made him a bit drowsy. He had a couple of minutes, so Allen returned to the lounge, leaned back in an arm chair and rested his eyes, listening to the distant *ka-chunk, ka-chunk* for several moments.

He heard a door shut behind, sat up, then got to his feet. *Man, gotta take a leak.*

"Well, look who's here, hiding from the huddled masses."

He turned around to see Nash standing with his briefcase by a table. *Easy, Allen.*

"They want everyone out of the building."

"I know." He headed into the workroom and heard Nash following him. Allen removed his papers from the tray.

"A hundred and forty-five copies?" Nash was facing the display at the front of the machine, his briefcase in tow. "Do you realize you have already exceeded your share of the department's allotment?"

Allen held the pile to his chest.

"Well, Mister Greene?"

"You can bill me."

"I might very well do that." Nash leaned over, opened the flap and removed the master. "Let's just have a look at this." He read for a few moments. Holding the sheet by one corner as if it were flypaper, he handed it over. "Poetry again? Langston Hughes and Archibald MacLeish?"

"That's right." Allen turned away and put his pile down; there was blood on the page that had been on his chest. He put the soiled paper and the master on the bottom, yanked the copier key and put it in his pocket, then began to straighten the pile.

Nash was still standing there. "Beyond the fact that your propaganda is extraneous to the curriculum, why does every student need to have one?"

Allen picked up the copies and held them at his side, debating with himself whether to answer or go straight to the bathroom. He faced Nash. "Because some kids will *like* the poetry and might even want to read it again."

"Good glory, look at you." He pointed at Allen's shirt. "Were you in class like that? What is it, juice?"

"Yeah, spilled it in my car." He started for the door. Nash followed, scolding him with non-stop patter.

". . . in school like that? Do you have *any* concept of our standards of professional conduct and—"

"Don't you ever stop running your goddamn mouth?" Allen entered the lounge, Nash right behind.

"And for *that*, Mister Greene, you can expect an official reprimand, and it's possible that your termination could very well begin a few weeks early."

Allen faced him again. "You don't have the clout—Schultz won't buy it."

"We'll see about that." Nash walked out the side door with his briefcase and a supercilious smirk.

Allen went into the office and gave Linda the cartridge. "I should sign for these copies—Nash knows I made them."

"Don't worry. I'll handle him."

Her acerbic tone gave him pause. "Okay, thanks again." He went out, but Nash was pontificating to Deniker at the middle stairway, so Allen turned right to take the longer route up the south stairs. He passed Frank's dark room, then listened to his own footfalls in the corridor and on the steps, echoing through the school.

At the second floor, his full bladder ached; he couldn't put it off any longer. Allen walked into the wing of mostly math classrooms and took a right turn immediately into the boys' lavatory. The lights were off, but a small opaque

251

window allowed him to make out the urinals ahead. He put his copies on the edge of a sink, moved over and reached for his zipper, but the lights came on. He turned around to at least ten high-school boys, mostly masked, standing back by the stalls. Allen took a step for the door, but a chubby guy moved over there right away. About half of them were at least six feet tall, one as huge as a pro-football lineman. Some wore slacks and good shirts, others jeans and tees; several had thin nylon stockings pulled over their heads, altering their faces. Most of the rest wore bandanas like outlaws in a cowboy movie, but the few who weren't masked looked nervous.

A short guy at the front sent the chubby one out to stand guard, then two tall slim kids replaced him at the door. The apparent leader was only about five-six, but not small in any other way. His square waist and thick legs filled his blue jeans; a white sleeveless T-shirt showed off brawny cocoa-brown arms. He had cut a slit in the nylon fabric for his mouth, but the mask didn't hide a large misshapen nose.

He finally spoke to Allen. "So whatta we got here?" The others were obediently silent. "I think it's a teacher, a big one." A few in the gang made low snickers.

A dark thin guy about six-two in a faded green poplin jacket stood at the leader's side. He had a shiny conk job and spoke in a subdued voice through his red bandana. "Naw, man, check the hair and threads. He's, what they call it, a flower child." Most of the gang seemed ready to laugh out loud, but they stifled themselves with chuckles and muffled wisecracks. The one in the green jacket motioned for them to keep it down.

Behind the leader, a guy about six feet tall squinted fiercely over his bandana. He had an enormous Afro that wouldn't have fit under a nylon stocking; a white scar stitched from his forehead up into his scalp. He kept pounding his fist into the other palm.

The gibes from the hippie joke faded. Sullen eyes glared from those wearing bandanas while two unmasked younger boys at the back shared a joint. His mouth dry and his neck pulsing, Allen wished they were all high. His best shot was to act confident and stall for a guard or cop to come by.

The leader stepped forward but was still several feet away. "You *are* a teacher, right?"

"Sort of." *Gotta piss so bad it hurts.*

The guy tilted his head slightly to one side. "What's that supposed to mean?"

Allen moistened his chalky lips. "I'm temporary."

"You got *that* right, teach."

From over by the stalls, four or five younger boys, some in gold shirts, joined the back of the gang, hiding their faces behind the older ones, but Allen saw Sam among them.

The leader turned back. "Keep those little punks away, he might know some of 'em." He faced Allen again. "Okay, straight answers. Who's out there besides Schultz, the lady Jap, an' the fat spick?"

"Uh, two guards and some cops."

"How many is *some?*"

"I don't know, maybe two—"

"Then *say* that, goddamn it." He walked over and picked up the copies. "Poems, how nice." He dropped the pile into the sink and twisted the spring-loaded faucet for a couple of seconds. "So you come all the way across L.A. every day to *improve our inferior English?*" His pronunciation of the last few words was mockingly perfect. "That about right?"

"Not exactly. Look, they probably have more cops now. You guys probably haven't done anything they can arrest you for. Maybe you should think about—"

"*You* should think about shuttin' the fuck up."

The leader's lieutenant in the green jacket scoffed. "They arrest us for breathin', dumb-ass teacher."

Allen knew him from somewhere but turned back to the one in charge. "Okay, I know you don't have anything to lose here—"

"Nothin' to lose, huh?" Drooling, the leader drew an arm across his mouth as he moved forward. His white but uneven teeth and bizarrely distorted features came closer; Allen flashed to an old Halloween cartoon of a bloodthirsty mouth, cackling in the dark.

Green jacket right behind, the leader had to look up to speak directly to his captive. "Teach says we got nothin' to lose, thinks we jus' ignorant niggers got nothin' to live for."

"No, I—"

"Nobody asked you nothin'. Shut—the—fuck—up." Each word was angrier but not much louder than the last. He turned to his lieutenant again.

"Maybe we jus' don't understand him, maybe he's *concerned about our general welfare*." His precise, sarcastic pronunciation again made the gang chuckle, some obligingly, perhaps not sure of what he meant.

Allen's legs trembled. He hid his jittery fingers in a pocket. *It'd be real good, teach, if you don't piss your pants.*

The leader reached ahead and flicked the second button on his shirt. "What's all this, you bleedin'?"

"No."

"Then where'd all the blood come from?" Some of the others moved a little closer to get a look at the stain.

"Does it matter?"

"Man, you don't get the rules here—*I* ask the questions. Now what'd you do, knife somebody?" His voice was deadpan, but the others laughed, and green jacket quieted them, palms down.

"Of course not."

"Of course not—shit." He turned to the gang. "See? He thinks knifin' somebody is just for *hoodlums* like us." He faced Allen. "Right, teach?"

"I hope not." He removed his hand from the pocket.

"He thinks we're too violent." He pointed, almost touching Allen's nose. "*You* fuckers are the violent ones, draftin' us into the army to do your killing."

"Hey man," green jacket said, "you want the cops to hear?"

"Yeah, let's keep it down for a little lesson. Hold 'im."

The taller boy went behind Allen and grabbed his arms, crossing them roughly, making his chest stick out. He removed Allen's wallet and opened it. "Jus' seven bucks." He told a small guy to hold the money and drop the wallet in a toilet.

"C'mon, my driver's license."

"Tough shit, teach." The leader's face came within inches of Allen's again. "Now, the blood—" He stopped for an explosion from the direction of Main. "Good, the cops can chase those punks all day. So where's the blood from?"

"A student."

"How'd it get on you?"

"I carried a girl after some big *brave* boy cut her."

"Listen to that shit." The leader turned. "That's what we call *sarcasm*, class."

He pointed to a guy in a nylon mask who was about the leader's height, cleaning his nails with a stiletto. "He's sayin' only cowards use a knife, man."

"Yeah? Don't need no knife to mess 'im up." He put the dagger away, stepping forward.

"You'll get your chance." The leader faced Allen. "My man must've been absent for the lesson on sarcasm."

"Obviously, you weren't."

"You hear me ask a question?"

"No."

"Then shut up." He turned to the others. "This teacher ain't jus' the man, he's fuckin' *Super*man, down here savin' all us poor black folk. An' Superman thinks he's a big hero." Several in the gang mimicked his words, taunting and jeering in low tones. The leader stood on his toes, almost nose to nose with Allen, the brown stocking damp around his mouth. "Carryin' that girl makes you a big hero, am I right, teach?"

"No." He sighed. "She was."

"Damn, you did it again. The rule in *this* class is you answer once, then you shut up unless we ask another question."

"All right, I'll do that." The leader threw an uppercut to Allen's gut. "Ohh—" *Son of a bitch.* He tried to catch his breath as the guy behind let him double over and the gang tried to restrain their laughter. A trickle of warm urine touched his groin, but he kept from releasing more.

The leader *tsked*, shaking his head. "Ya' see, teach, that wasn't a question, an' *right* after I told you my rule."

He straightened up slowly. Behind him, green jacket crossed Allen's arms again, not quite as tight.

"Good, you kept your mouth shut that time." The leader was a foot or two away. "Now you know my rule by heart?"

Allen took a long exhale. "The gist of it."

"Ooo, *gist*, a vocabulary word, class. Okay, I'll make it real simple for you, since you're such a slow student. The rule is, 'I keep my mouth shut after I answer the question.'"

"I keep my mouth—" Allen took another fist to the solar plexus, crumpling almost to his knees, but the guy behind kept him up again. He felt warm pee, this time all the way down to his upper thigh, but he stopped the stinging flow again. After he was pulled back up, he didn't lift his head.

The leader pushed up Allen's chin and got back in his face. "Since you're so dumb, now I'm tellin' you ahead a time that I'm askin' a question." He paused. "You teach your class what a interrogative is?"

Exhaling again, Allen eyed his tormentor. "Yes."

"When I said my rule, was that a interrogative?"

"No."

"See there? It was all your fault. Now, you think you can repeat the rule?"

"Yes."

"Then do it."

Not this time, sucker punching little shit.

"You know it or not?"

"I think so."

"Why don't you say it?"

"'Do it' isn't an interrogative."

"Damn, you finally passed."

Green jacket was holding Allen with one hand. "Enough a' this shit, let's mess 'im up and get—" He stopped and snickered. "Look, man, he pissed his self."

"Say, teach, your bellbottoms are wet—you hold any back?" The gang laughed louder than before at the leader's joke.

Green jacket stopped chuckling. "Okay, cool it."

The leader looked at Allen, whose chin was down again. "Still gotta go, teach?"

He lifted his head. "Yes."

"Why you wearin' that?" He pointed at Allen's armband.

"For Doctor King."

"That's *your* goddamn violence again. I know why you wear it—so people think you liked him—to protect your white ass." The gang grumbled in agreement. "Is that right, teach?"

"Yes, that's probably right."

"Probably. Man, you'll jus' say any ol' shit to keep your ass from gettin' kicked."

"Yeah, maybe so."

"You messed up again, that wasn't a question."

Allen cringed, readying himself for another blow.

"No, man, not this time, my brothers here are fixin' to mess you up good. Let 'im go." Green jacket released his grip. "Okay, teach, take off the armband."

What? He slowly pulled off the black elastic.

"You're so stupid in my class, this'll be your *remedial* lesson. How far from here to the pissers, teach?"

He turned to the two urinals. "Uh, four or five feet."

"Okay, throw that thing into one of 'em."

He tossed the armband; it hit the porcelain and fell below onto a pink sanitary cake.

"Well, you still gotta piss or not?"

Jesus. "Yes." Allen walked up to a urinal, the one that didn't have the armband.

"No, that one's outta order."

He moved over and unzipped his jeans.

"Okay, piss on it."

He finished, zipped up and turned around. The gang was several feet away, most of them chortling.

The leader pointed. "You just pissed on the reverend's memory. You shouldn't a' done that."

Screw you.

"Answer me, Superman."

Most of the gang laughed again—Allen shook his head, refusing. The leader took a step closer. "Answer me, damn it."

He didn't budge, but green jacket spoke up from behind. "You didn't ask him a question."

The leader's mouth stayed open briefly. After slobbering on the mask again, he wiped his mouth. "You're really a smart-ass, teach, but you're gonna leave here with some bad marks. You get it—bad marks?"

"Very funny." His heart thumped in his chest and neck.

The leader turned to the gang. "Who wants to finish our lesson?" The guy who pocketed the stiletto moved forward, then two others, the football lineman and the surly hood with the huge Afro, fitting himself with brass knuckles. They came closer—two amorphous faces under nylon, and one pair of malevolent dark eyes.

Allen leaped for the galvanized trashcan that was between the urinals and the sinks. He latched onto it, slamming the can intentionally into the porcelain tiles. The racket echoed in the bathroom walls; the three hoods stopped briefly, then moved ahead. Allen lifted the can to defend himself.

"That's it—leave 'im alone!" The shout came from behind the gang.

Everyone turned to see who yelled—a small boy pushed his way through the crowd in sunglasses and a grey sweatshirt with the hood pulled over. The guys nearby backed off a step, and Allen lowered the impromptu shield down to his waist. *My God, Ronnie?*

The leader faced the boy. "What you think you're doin'?"

Ronnie walked right up to Allen, turned around, bristling at the three thugs. "I said leave 'im alone."

The leader made a humorless, scornful laugh. "You punks ain't here to tell us nothin'—get the fuck outta the way." After Ronnie backed up closer to Allen and folded his arms, the leader growled. "Move 'im."

The three guys took another step, but Ronnie pulled a zip gun from his front pocket and pointed it at them. They laughed at the weapon but stopped.

"Ronnie, I don't think that's a good—"

"Quiet, Mister Greene."

"*Mister Greene*—shit." The leader chuckled coldly. "You crazy, little man. You think that popgun gonna stop us?"

Ronnie defiantly aimed at the three guys in front. "Who wants it, then?" They retreated a step. Allen put the can down, wiped his sweaty palms, then held onto the rim.

The leader faced green jacket. "Talk some sense into him."

From behind, a guy in a nylon mask spoke up. "Yeah, he's *your* goddamn little brother."

The leader turned back. "Shut the fuck up."

The three guys out front had almost retreated back to the gang. Ronnie still pointed the gun at them, but he turned to his brother. "He's the teacher who says my poems are good."

The leader scoffed. "An' you believe that bullshit?"

"You sayin' my poems are no good?"

"I ain't sayin' nothin'—you better not be pointin' that piece a' crap at me."

"Pointin' it at them."

Green jacket pulled down his bandana. "Everybody take it easy. I know who this teacher is—he came to our house," he said, then Ronnie lowered the gun a little.

The leader snarled at his lieutenant. "Who gives a shit? You gonna' take the popgun or not?"

Ronnie's brother grumbled. "I say we let the teacher go."

"You tryin' to take over?"

"Ain't takin' over nothin'. I'm *askin'* you to let him go. Ronnie's got his reasons."

The leader was silent. His masked features didn't move under the thin material. He came out of his daze and walked by the three would-be enforcers. Ronnie tracked him with the zip gun, but it was directed at his feet. The leader removed a small revolver from his pocket and passed Ronnie as if he weren't there. He pointed the gun at Allen's chin. "Put the goddamn trash can down, and do it quiet."

He laid it down gently, but the can rolled almost 360 degrees and rumbled back to his leg. Looking into the gun barrel, Allen's neck trembled. "I didn't try to do that."

The leader scoffed, then lowered the revolver and snarled at Ronnie. "Now drop that thing."

Ronnie had already let the gun down to his side. "No bullet anyway." He defiantly released the small weapon. It landed on its masking-tape handle, hardly making a sound.

"I'll say this, little man, you got some balls." He wiped his mask, picked up the zip gun, then smirked at Allen. "Lucky for you, teach." He turned away. "Let's get outta here."

The leader led the lot of them out to the hall. Joining his brother, Ronnie still didn't look at Allen, who took a couple of steps back to the wall and slid all the way down the tiles to the floor. He exhaled and drew in some long breaths. *It's cool down here.*

29

Eyes half-closed and his back against the tiles, Allen listened to a siren outside, another firecracker, then Linda's indistinct but cross words on the PA, searching for someone.

"Clear, ma'am," someone said, echoing in the bathroom walls. The voice sniggered. "Except you got a teacher lying down in here."

Allen turned. Deniker stood near the door. Ishimoto walked in past him, heels clicking on the linoleum, no sign of her condescending smile. "Well, if it isn't Mister Greene."

He stayed put, grinning wryly. "Just call me *Teach*."

"Not if I have anything to say about it."

"Oh, that isn't nice. Too bad you didn't arrive a little sooner, madam principal-elect, there were some former students here who would've loved to say hello to you."

"What do you mean?"

Deniker stepped ahead of her. "That other gang was here?"

Allen chuckled. "Yup, but long gone now, off to some new fun and games."

An imperial sneer crossed Ishimoto's face. "Get up from there, Mister Greene, and pull yourself together."

He grinned, getting slowly to his feet. "Yes, ma'am, I'm together."

She pointed at his chest. "Is that blood?" She looked down at his damp trousers. "My God, did you—"

"Just a minute." Deniker approached Allen, pointing to his shirt. "Is all this blood from before with that girl, or did they cut you?"

"No, just a fist to the gut." Allen puffed out his cheeks, pulling in his chest as if he'd just been slugged.

Ishimoto shook her head. "I don't find this funny."

"Really? You smile at everything else, expulsions, assassinations—"

"Enough!" Startled at first by her own shrill voice ricocheting through the bathroom, she tried to compose herself.

Deniker was still facing him. "How many were there—did you know any of them?"

"About ten, they wore masks," he said more seriously.

Ishimoto backed off toward the exit while Deniker continued his questions. "Any from here?"

"A couple maybe—couldn't tell who they were."

"You didn't recognize any voices?"

"Only the big kids spoke. Were they in some other trouble?"

"Far as I know, just with you. How did you get away?"

"Talked them out of it, more or less. They could've really wasted me, but they didn't, so we're even as far as I'm concerned. If they're caught, I won't file charges."

From the doorway, Ishimoto raised an eyebrow. "Are you protecting someone?"

"Yeah, myself."

"We're not getting anywhere, Mister Deniker." She glared at Allen again. "I'll see you in my office with Mister Nash first thing in the morning—maybe your *last* morning."

"Maybe, but I won't come unless Greg is there."

"Oh, *Greg* is it? He can't bail you out this time." She was already walking away, Deniker following her.

Allen went to the sink and fished out the soggy copies. He dropped them a few feet away, then took a wad of paper towels and tried to dry his pants. He got his wallet from the toilet, wiped it off best he could, then wetted more towels and began to rub at the blood in his shirt. His lower chest and stomach were tender from the two blows, so he stopped.

He tossed the towels and picked up his copies; some of them looked salvageable. Allen walked slowly out to the hall and upstairs to his room, where he spread the papers around to dry, enough for at least two classes.

After carrying his box out to the hall, he locked the door. Two custodians were talking at the top of the middle stairs, so Allen went the other way to the north exit. He walked down and found Cecil by the first-floor stairwell, talking quietly with a tall young towheaded cop in full black uniform, including a side arm and nightstick.

He held the box to his chest against his soiled clothes and turned sideways as he walked by them making a casual wave. They just nodded back. Allen came to Nash's portal. He was back in his room, speaking seriously from his desk to someone out of view, probably one of his cronies.

Almost to the foyer, Allen turned to the noise of someone behind entering the hall. A high-school boy left Nash's door open and walked rapidly for the north exit. Cecil and the cop came out from under the stairs and escorted him outside.

*What was **that** guy doing with Nash?* He turned and saw Schultz in the office. Linda was still there with a family, embracing the mom. She released the woman, then nodded to the principal. *Tell Schultz about Nash? Crap, tell him what?*

Watching the family leave, Allen took a step or two to follow them out, then he stopped and glared at Nash's door. *What the hell.* He left his box on the floor, then hurried down the hall and walked into the room, closing the door behind.

Startled, Nash slammed his briefcase shut, but it caught on some papers; he yanked at them. "What are *you* still doing here?" He fooled unsuccessfully with the jammed briefcase.

Allen was just a few feet inside the room. "I could ask you the same thing."

"Whatever it is you want, make it quick, I'm leaving now."

"That boy who just left here, was he bothering you?"

"That is certainly none of your business. But since you have already invaded my privacy, I was having a pleasant chat with a former student—something you wouldn't know about, not having any former students." He stood up to put on his tan summer coat, an armband on its sleeve. Nash attached himself to the briefcase, though it was still ajar. He turned toward the other door, the chain clamoring over his desk.

Allen moved forward a couple more steps. Nash spotted the wet pants and wrinkled his nose. "Glory, and I suppose you have some bizarre explanation for that."

Feeling an adrenaline rush, Allen exhaled and unclenched his teeth. "Nothing more bizarre than why you're chained to that stupid briefcase."

Nash made a cold laugh from near his desk. "You and Williamson make a good pair. Our homegrown Negro agitator thinks he undermines my authority by reassuring the rabble that I am harmless, which is, in fact, true. He does a fine job of spreading those ridiculous old rumors."

"I saw you the other day in the parking lot with a high-school kid. I think Schultz would be interested in your little meetings."

"I doubt that. He's busy cleaning out his desk and reading travel brochures, for which we can all be thankful."

"You're lying about your little *chats* with former students."

Nash smirked, shaking his head. "Your incorrigible attitude is exceeded only by your lack of professionalism. I'll just add this little incident to Mrs. Ishimoto's list for tomorrow. Now leave my room."

"I'm going, but first I need something from you."

"I won't listen to any more of your nonsense." Nash completely enveloped his jammed briefcase with one arm as if he were a halfback clinging to an oversized football. He scooted toward the other exit.

Allen moved right over and easily intercepted him in front of the closed door. "What's your big hurry?"

Nash stayed several feet back from him. "I am not in a hurry. Are you forcibly preventing me from leaving my room?"

"No, I wouldn't say that. I just have a simple request before you go. I don't think you want that armband anymore—mine got ruined."

"What?"

He pointed to Nash's sleeve. "You heard me, I'm just asking for your armband."

"Ah, yes, you certainly wouldn't want to be without a symbol of your remorse for the dearly departed reverend. Well, you're right, I don't need it anymore. If it satisfies your pathetic devotion, please take it." He put the briefcase on the floor between his legs, removed the armband and dismissively tossed it like so much refuse onto the floor by Allen's feet. "Happy now? Step aside." Nash picked up his briefcase.

Allen squatted for the armband, then stood. "One last thing." He touched his stained shirt with the black elastic. "I think you should know what this *juice* is."

"What are you prattling about now? Move, this instant."

263

"This is blood, Mister Nash. Not movie blood or TV blood, the real thing—blood from a kid in this school."

Nash's doughy clump of a nose flared. "So what am I supposed to do?"

"Maybe you could wonder why, or give a shit. If you had been out there just *standing* in your duty area, it might have kept a girl from being cut up and sent to the hospital."

"Ridiculous." Nash scoffed and took another step. "Move aside or I will report you for personal assault."

"Oh?" Allen laughed. "Then maybe I should get my money's worth." He held up the armband, then began to rub it repeatedly into his bloody shirt.

Nash shuddered a bit. "What are you doing?"

"Mister S. Nash, a.k.a. Snash, English grammarian extraordinaire and despot of our non-union of teachers—since you cared so much about Doctor King, you shouldn't be without an armband." He rubbed it again into the blood.

"You are clearly unbalanced. Move!"

"Not until you get your memento. Catch." He tossed it; Nash squealed slightly and tried to jump back, but the armband bounced squarely off his paunch. His tethered briefcase had whipped around and hit a desk, bursting open an inch or two. Nash immediately surrounded the luggage with both arms and pulled it to his chest protectively.

"What are you hiding, Snash?"

"You enjoy saying that, don't you?" As he spoke, Nash was stuffing the jammed papers into the briefcase. He locked it with a key from the line to his belt, then faced Allen. "If you think I'm hiding something, then why don't you report me? Oh, that's right, there are several witnesses who will attest to your open and constant hostility toward me. Any suspicions from you will sound preposterous."

"Maybe to Ishimoto."

"I'll take my chances, even with Schultz." He made a smug grin. "And after what you just did, I will definitely include personal assault in my complaint."

*Grab the briefcase? Shit, that **would** take an assault.*

"What's wrong, Mister Greene? Ha!"

The door opened from the outside. Cecil and the same young cop were waiting there in the hall with Schultz.

Nash beamed. "Excellent, you gentlemen are right on time. I wish to file personal assault charges against this man."

Allen shook his head. "I didn't touch him. The creep is hiding something—"

"Hold on," the cop told Allen, "I'll talk to you if I need to." He stepped in, holding out a document with his long arm. "Simon Matthias Nash?"

"I just told you, officer, this man assaulted me." Nash took the paper. "What's the meaning of this?"

"It's a search warrant for you, your residence, and this classroom, including that briefcase."

"What? That is preposterous—I refuse. Mister Schultz, you can't stand by and allow him to come in here and do this. I have my rights."

Schultz grinned. "Indeed you do, Mister Nash, and the officer has his duty."

"I have a right to call my lawyer."

The cop nodded. "Yes, after I arrest you. I have enough to do that now, but I'll do my search first. Unlock that briefcase."

"I certainly will not."

The policeman eyed the nest of keys attached to Nash's belt. "I have the authority to break it open."

"And destroy my personal property? We will see what my lawyer has to say about that."

"Over here." The officer took the briefcase and pulled Nash by the chain a few feet away.

"What do you think you are doing?"

"You're not cooperating, sir." The cop yanked him another foot or two and put the case flat on the ground, bracing it against the wall before he turned to Cecil. "Would you give that lock a good kick with your steel toe?"

"Sure, glad ta' help out." Cecil smiled at Nash, then moved his leg back as if he were kicking an extra point. His shoe struck the lock, but the case held. He wound up again and kicked much harder; it cracked open a little.

The tall officer leaned down and pried the lid halfway with his nightstick and searched inside. He put papers, report cards and a pocket Bible on the floor. Using his pen, he lifted out a small handgun by its trigger guard. "Is this registered to you?"

Nash just looked at him defiantly. After the cop had Cecil help him bust the chain to the briefcase, he frisked Nash at the wall before handcuffing him. "Simon Nash, you are under arrest for reckless endangerment, possession of a firearm in a public building, and as an accessory to trafficking firearms to minors. You have the right to . . . ."

After the cop finished the arrest, Nash sneered at Allen, then Schultz. "You two will rot in hell." His voice was subdued but cocky as the policeman held his arm and the ruined briefcase. "My parents prayed for the day that these heathens would be put back in their place, and now they're killing each other." His tone was still muted, but almost euphoric. "Martin Lucifer King was only the beginning—I'll be back to help reclaim this city and country for God Almighty." The cop escorted him away.

At the classroom door, Allen turned to Schultz. "Jesus, Simon the Zealot."

Schultz frowned. "Yes, and he's not alone. One thing he is right about— he'll be out before you know it, and after that, he could show up in some desperate school somewhere."

"How is that even possible?"

"Oh, I could tell you way too many stories of reprobates hired to teach, but not right now." They started down the hall.

"Who finally tipped you off to Nash?"

"Cecil. He took the briefcase thing seriously when he came here last fall— they laughed at him in security meetings. Cecil overheard something weeks ago and began tailing him. Nash was a middleman, setting up meetings, not having to touch the money or the weapons. I guess the guns didn't show up in the news enough for him to get his thrills—started getting careless."

"Didn't you need something more concrete to get a warrant?"

Schultz nodded, sighing deeply. "It's hard to imagine anything positive coming from Doctor King's death, but a very sad little boy told Frank he knew about a gun deal—that was all we needed. That high-school boy also just gave him up."

"I'll be."

"Yeah, justice wins out once in a while." Schultz sighed again; they walked on, then stopped in the foyer. "Mister Greene, even if you still have doubts about teaching, I'll make you an offer. How would you like to finish out the year in ninth grade with our top students?"

"Take Nash's classes?"

"That's right."

"I appreciate it, but I'll stay with my kids."

30

After Schultz noticed the damp trousers, Allen told him an understated version of the gang incident. The principal said he should go home and take it easy, but Allen went out to the car, trying to think of what he could do to make himself more presentable at the hospital. He rifled through his crap in the Volvo's trunk and changed into an old white T-shirt he had thrown in there to use as a rag. Allen drove off with the windows down to let his pants dry in the warm air. He was glad to have the travel time to think about everything that had happened.

Although he didn't recall ever going to County General, he had no trouble finding it. It wasn't very far from his old junior high, about two-thirds of the way from Los Feliz to East L.A. He recognized the multi-story white towers at the front of the building—they must have used the old hospital repeatedly for cop shows and medical dramas.

Allen started to put on his Pirate windbreaker over the T-shirt, but it was too warm. Inside the main lobby, he found a cross-section of L.A. residents. Amidst the scores of blacks, Latinos and whites—most of them in work clothes—he saw two men in turbans, a lady in a sari, and an old couple wearing traditional dress he didn't recognize.

There was almost no chatter. A nearby man with detritus in the whiskers of his very long beard was curled up on a couch and seemed to be the only one who was not gloomily paying attention to the boxy TV on top of a tall steel cart. The news was reporting on the search for Doctor King's assassin.

Half listening to the TV, Allen walked over to a lady at the information desk, who looked askance at his holey T-shirt and rumpled khakis before she agreed to find Sandra's room number for him. He heard the news report change to a commercial, then took the elevator up a few floors.

Allen got out and walked ahead toward an open-ended Plexiglas room, about twenty feet down the corridor, where several people waited, including Charmane. She was bouncing Melissa on her lap and talking to a gaunt woman in her late thirties. He saw Monique at the back of the area, chatting seriously with a young man in a white shift who was at least six-eight.

Before Allen was very close, Charmane handed off the baby to the woman, and then ran-limped up to her teacher. With both hands, she embraced one of his arms. "Mister Greene, you were right, Sandra's going to be okay."

He patted her clumsily on the back. "That's terrific, Charmane. What did they say?"

She squeezed his arm again, her dark brows hopping excitedly. Charmane took a breath, and her words came out rapid-fire: "At first they said she probably had to have an operation on an artery, but she didn't need it after all, just a lot of stitches. Her head is okay—a mild concussion, they said. She's sleeping right now and might get to go home in two days." She exhaled with a wide smile, let go of him, and hurried back to the baby. After handing Melissa over to Charmane, the woman walked away before Allen got there.

He softly tweaked Melissa's cheek; she reacted to him this time with a smile. Grinning back at the infant, Allen told Charmane that he was going to talk to Mrs. Morgan for a little while. He walked past a few disconsolate people, excusing himself as he went by. Allen approached the tall young man and Monique. They stood, her red hair well below his chin. "Mister Greene, this handsome gentleman is Charmane's brother."

She was exactly right about his appearance. He was in his late twenties with a slender chiseled look, and not as fair as his sister. The young man offered a hand and said, "Mister Greene," averting his eyes from Allen's unkempt wardrobe.

"A pleasure, I'm Allen." He unintentionally squeezed his hand too hard. "And your name?"

Monique cleared her throat. "My fault. I was trying *not* to say Miles. Let's see now, Faisal Muhammad. Right?"

"Correct, Mrs. Morgan."

She faced Allen. "Well, it looks like Charmane gave you all the latest on Sandra."

"Yes, great news." He turned back to Faisal, lowering his voice so as not to embarrass Charmane. "Your sister's a remarkable girl. She's an enthusiastic learner, and Sandra couldn't have a more loyal friend."

Faisal gave him a bland look. "We are very proud of her."

After a brief awkward silence, Monique grinned at Allen. "Mister Greene, maybe you can spring for a cup of coffee for a tired old teacher." She lifted the big purse over her shoulder.

"No, but I'll buy *you* one." Faisal ignored Allen's joke and sat down. "Can we bring you something, Mister Muhammad?"

"No thank you." He turned toward his sister, who was sharing a sip of soda from a can with Melissa.

"We'll just be down by the vending machines at the end of the hall," Monique told Faisal, who nodded, then respectfully stood up again as she and Allen left.

They walked slowly down the long spic-and-span corridor, not speaking until out of earshot from the waiting area. "Monique, was that Sandra's mom? It seemed like she avoided me, but I'm not sure."

"I think she's hung over and desperate for a bracer. You're not the first person she's avoided. Charmane is upset because Mrs. Small waited so long to call Sandra's aunt—she's on her way back from San Diego." They walked on. "What did you think of Charmane's brother?"

"He seems, uh, pretty formal."

"He was very serious even when he was with me—now he's serious and angry, but still a fine young man."

They came to a nursing station where a blonde nurse in a winged white hat was listening to a loud joke from a male staff member in plain blue scrubs. The short fair man paused to size up Allen and Monique, then continued his story, not as loud.

Allen heard *coon* in the punch line, stopped and scowled at their muffled horselaughs. "Jesus, what's wrong with you pe—" Monique tugged Allen away like a child coaxing a reluctant parent. He heard them laugh again. "Assholes."

"Yes, just forget them." She shook her head dismally. They passed a stairway door and entered the last section of the corridor. She patted his arm and let go. "This morning I was listening to something on the radio about Doctor King that might perk you up a little."

"Good, let's hear it."

"You know that Buddhist master's material you gave me?"

"Thich Nhat Hanh."

"Yes, I still can't pronounce it."

Allen sighed, glancing back at the nursing station. "He'd be impressed with how I let those jerks get to me."

"That's not what I meant. Did you know that Doctor King nominated him last year for the Nobel Peace Prize?"

"What? Thich Nhat Hanh? I didn't know *anybody* nominated him. I don't even remember who won."

"There was no award the last two years."

"Figures, but it's great that Doctor King supported him. I'll check that out—thanks for telling me."

"You're welcome."

They neared the end of the hall. She grinned at his clothes. "Allen, how did you end up, um, so disheveled?"

He looked at her wryly. "There was more fun after you left." Allen heaved a long sigh.

"Tell me about it. I don't really want coffee."

They came to four unoccupied black leatherette chairs beneath a tall and wide picture window. Allen turned two of the chairs around so they could sit and face the glass. There hadn't been wind or rain in L.A. for many days; the unrelenting smog had settled below the inversion in a stubborn thick yellowish-grey layer.

It took him a few minutes to relate the main details of what happened at school, Monique breaking in for explanations. While he spoke quietly, Allen gazed down from their high vantage point at some tall old eucalyptus trees. The grove was similar to one at his junior high, only a few blocks away, where they would sit in the shade at lunch hour, tossing seedpods at each other. ". . . then after Ishimoto and Deniker left, I . . . ."

While telling her about Nash's arrest, he stared up at a very small island of clear blue at the center of the sky. Then he looked down at a man and woman greeting each other in a parking lot. He guessed they were saying, *At least it's another beautiful day.*

". . . so that's about it. Cecil was quite the hero." He told her that he declined Schultz's offer to take Nash's classes.

"Of course you did. My God, I knew Simon was a little off, but think of the damage he's done, and in so many ways. Maybe Miss Dorsey will run again for Alliance president."

"They should be so lucky."

"Yes, a ray of hope for the old place. Allen, what did you take away from Ronnie's willingness to stand up for you?"

"I'm grateful, of course. I just hope Frank and Sharon can help him get into school somewhere." Allen shook his head a little, breathing deeply again. "Ronnie said something I won't forget for a while."

"Go on."

"After he told them to leave me alone, he said, 'He's the teacher who says my poems are good.'"

"Well, there you have it, *chéri.*" She smiled. "I take it you've made a career decision."

He nodded slightly. "Yeah, I'm going to give teaching a shot if Ishimoto doesn't get in my way."

"She can't do anything except stop you from coming back to Marshall. You have Greg, Miss Dorsey, Sharon and me for references—and Frank."

"Yeah, I think we're actually becoming friends." In the distant waiting area, Sandra's mom was handing the baby to Charmane. "Monique, I have a gift for you, if you want it."

"A gift? Allen, you don't realize how much you have given me already."

He smiled. "I want you to have Pedro."

"What? You can't just give him up."

"I'll have to, and you'll love him just like my mom did. After Trudy's baby comes, she won't have time for him. I hope to travel some after that, then I'll probably go for my credential somewhere in the boonies. Pedro needs a stable home and some attention in his last years."

"Yes, don't we all." She paused. "Are you sure, *amour?*"

"I am, but I also have an ulterior motive. Wherever you guys are, I'd like to visit—you, Sharon, and Pedro."

She smiled through her tears. "Do you promise to do that, Allen?"

"Absolutely."

She hooked her arm around his elbow, and they started down the hall together toward Charmane and Melissa.

REFERENCES

BIBLIOGRAPHY

A Call to Conscience: The Landmark Speeches of Dr. Martin Luther King, Jr., 2002, Grand Central Publishing.

At Canaan's Edge, America in the King Years, 1965-l968, Branch, Taylor, 2007, Simon and Schuster.

Autobiography: The Story of My Experiments with Truth, Gandhi, Mohandas, Renaissance Classics.

Black Boy, Wright, Richard, 1945, Harper and Brothers.

I Have a Dream, Davidson, Margaret, 1986, Scholastic, Inc.

Civil Disobedience, Thoreau, Henry David, Empire Books.

The Last Days of the Late, Great State of California, Gentry, Curt, 1968, G.P. Putnam's Sons.

The Martian Chronicles, Bradbury, Ray, 1950, Doubleday.

The Miracle of Mindfulness, A Manual on Meditation, Hanh, Thich Nhat, 1975, Beacon Press.

Notes of a Native Son, Baldwin, James A., Copyright 1955, renewed 1983, Beacon Press.

The Pearl, Steinbeck, John, Viking Press, 1947; Penguin Books, 1976.

The Peter Principle: Why Things Always Go Wrong, Peter, Laurence; Hull, Raymond, William Morrow and Company, N.Y., 1969.

The World Book Encyclopedia, 1970 Edition, World Book, Inc.

Walden, Thoreau, Henry David, Empire Books.

WEB

About.com (N.Y. Times), "Martin Luther King Jr. Assassinated,"
http://history1900s.about.com/cs/martinlutherking/a/mlkassass

About.com (N.Y. Times), "Martin Luther King Jr. Assassinated, (Part 2)"
http://history1900s.about.com/cs/martinlutherking/a/mlkassass 2

American Radio Works, "King's Last March."
http://americanradioworks.publicradio.org/features/king/

History Matters, "Excerpts from the Kerner Report."
http://history matters.gmu.edu/d/6545/

The Los Angeles Times, Archives, 1968.
http://www.latimes.com

The Martin Luther King Jr. Center for Non-Violent Social Change.
http://thekingcenter.org/archive

Museum of Television, *"The Martin Luther King Jr., Assassination."*
http://www.museum.tv/eotvsection.php?entrycode=kingmartin

New World Encyclopedia.
http://www.newworldencyclopedia.org/entry/Martin_Luther_King,_Jr.

Political Cortex, "When America Burned . . ."
http://www.politicalcortex.com/story/2009/1/18/181150/879

Project 1968. http://www.project1968.com/in-the-news-april-7april

Robert F. Kennedy Center for Justice and Human Rights
http://rfkcenter.org

University of Colorado American Studies, "Time Magazine—
The Generation Gap" http://www.colorado.edu/AmStudies/lewis/film/gap

Wikipedia, "Watts Towers" http://.wikipedia.org/wiki/Watts Towers

DOCUMENTARIES

Martin Luther King Jr.: More Than a Dream, February, 2013, Audience Network, Direct TV.

Smithsonian: MLK: The Assassination Tapes, 2012, The Smithsonian Channel, Smithsonian Institution.

About the Author

T. Lloyd Winetsky was born and raised in Los Angeles and has been an educator for more than four decades.

After serving in the Peace Corps, his first teaching post was in South-Central L.A.–six classes of low-income seventh-graders. It was the spring of 1968, when Martin Luther King was assassinated. That event, the violence that followed, and then Robert Kennedy's assassination, had a great impact on Winetsky's life. They validated his life's mission, and he devoted his work to those who lack access to quality education. Those first teaching experiences were germane to both the setting and conflicts of his new historical novel, *Los Angeles, 1968: Happy Ranch To Watts.*

Later, Winetsky returned to college, then taught English and Spanish in the Southwest and Northwest, including four years in Alaska.

Winetsky faithfully writes every day. His rich stories are woven with real-life experiences. In 2008, he published *Grey Pine*, a psychological novel set during the devastating ash fall after the eruption of Mount St. Helens. Initially published in 2010, *María Juana's Gift,* is a fictional account of a tragic, preventable human medical error. The novel is inspired by the struggle that the author and his wife had in trying to save their infant daughter.

Winetsky is currently at work on his fourth novel, *Belaganna*, which takes place in the Navajo Nation, where he taught for five years. He lives near Yakima with his wife of 44 years, Kathleen, a Special Education teacher. They have four grown children.

For more information, please visit:

www.tlwinetsky.com or www.happyranchwatts.com.

Acknowledgments

Novelists' lament: "They say that editors in publishing houses used to welcome a novel that had literary potential but wasn't quite ready, and many editors enjoyed collaborating with authors in those days." Congratulations and many thanks to Duke Pennell, the publisher and final editor of this work, for being one of the few to keep that concept alive.

My appreciation also goes to the first readers who contributed much to the revisions of *Los Angeles, 1968: Happy Ranch To Watts*—Carl Kleinschmitt, Ona Maria Winet, and Dr. William T. Cox, who reviewed the medical material. Finally, my thanks to Peter Gelfan (*Found Objects,* Nortia Press), the original editor, whose collaboration was instrumental in refining the focus of this story.

Made in the USA
San Bernardino, CA
20 March 2014